Eiriksdottir

A Tale of Dreams and Luck

Edwina C. Borghed

"His designs for you predated time.
'Hear Me'? He spoke again, as you
look through your telescope, the scene
blurred, left wrong focus (a focus in TIME)
you are looking at your life as if TIME
said it all, but, I am preparing you for
the endless reaches of eternity

In this world you had no choice
over many lines in your pattern.
You did not choose
Your era of birth
Your country, family, social status.
You did not choose
Your forms, abilities, limitations.
These, I chose.
But, you are choosing your heavenly
pattern.
You will be rewarded or suffer loss
as you invest the gifts — the talents — I
have given you!"

with love
Nada Price

Eiriksdottir

A Tale of Dreams and Luck

A Novel by Joan Clark

Macmillan Canada
Toronto

Canadian Cataloguing in Publication Data

Clark, Joan, date.
  Eiriksdottir

ISBN 0-7715-9009-1

1. Freydis Eiriksdottir, fl. 1014 – Fiction.
I. Title.

PS8555.L37E5 1994   C813'.54   C93-094292-2
PR9199.3.C53E5 1994

1 2 3 4 5 FP 98 97 96 95 94

Cover design by David Vereschagin
Cover illustration by Sara Tyson
Author photo by Ned Pratt
Typography & Illustrations by Joe Lobo

Macmillan Canada wishes to thank the Canada Council and the
Ontario Ministry of Culture and Communications for supporting its
publishing program.

Macmillan Canada
A Division of Canada Publishing Corporation
Toronto, Ontario, Canada

Printed in Canada

For Jack

Freydis walked to the door of the brothers' house.
Someone had just gone outside, leaving the door ajar.
She opened it and stood in the doorway for a while
without a word. Finnbogi was lying in the bed away
from the doorway; he was awake, and now he said,
"What do you want here, Freydis?"

Greenlanders Saga

✠ ✠ ✠

Branches they bore of that enchanted stem,
Laden with flower and fruit, whereof they gave
To each, but who so did receive of them
And taste, to him the gushing of the wave
Far, far away did seem to mourn and rave
On alien shores; and if his fellow spake,
His voice was thin, as voices from the grave;
And deep asleep he seemed, yet all awake,
And music in his ears his beating heart did make.

The Lotos Eaters
Alfred Lord Tennyson

✠ ✠ ✠

They came out and over the wide expanses and
needing cloth to dry themselves on and food, away
towards Wineland, up into the ice and uninhabited
country...Evil can take away luck so that one dies
early.

Runic inscription, Ringerike, Norway

GREENLAND CREW

From Einarsfjord:

Freydis Eiriksdottir
Thorvard Einarsson
Balki and Gisli, the Gardar twins
Bodvar
Bragi
Falgeir
Hogni
Oddmar

From Eiriksfjord:

Avang
Flosi
Lodholt

From Vatnahverfi:

Evyind
Ivar
Ozur
Teit
Thrand
Uni

From other farms:

Alf
Asmund
Bodman
Bofi
Bolli
Erp
Glam
Holti
Hrollaug
Hundi
Koll
Lopt
Nagli
Sleita

Thralls:

Groa
Kalf
Louse-Oddi
Orn
Ulfar

ICELAND CREW

Helgi and Finnbogi Egilsson
Aesrod
Aevar
Atli
Bersi
Bjolf
Blund
Eystein
Gnup
Grimkel
Gudlaug
Halldor
Hauk Ljome, *Norwegian ship
builder*
Hrapp
Hrut
Ingald
Jokul
Karl
Ketil
Olaf
Olver
Skum
Solvi
Thrasi
Ulf Broad Beard
Vemund

Thralls:

Mani
Svart and Surt, dwarf twins

Ambatts (concubines):

Alof
Finna
Grelod
Mairi
Olina

Freydis's Paternal Forebears

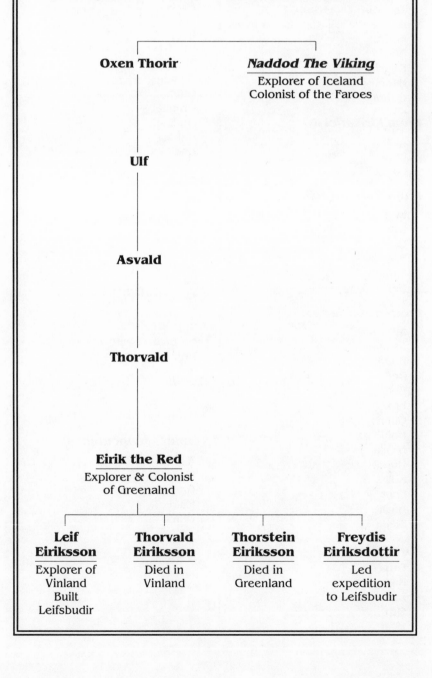

Oxen Thorir   ***Naddod The Viking***
                        Explorer of Iceland
                        Colonist of the Faroes

Ulf

Asvald

Thorvald

Eirik the Red
Explorer & Colonist
of Greenalnd

Leif Eiriksson	**Thorvald Eiriksson**	**Thorstein Eiriksson**	**Freydis Eiriksdottir**
Explorer of Vinland Built Leifsbudir	Died in Vinland	Died in Greenland	Led expedition to Leifsbudir

Acknowledgements

I would like to thank Birgitta Linderoth Wallace, Archaeology Director of L'Anse aux Meadows, Environment Canada, and Anne Hart, Head, Centre for Newfoundland Studies, Memorial University, for helping me research this novel. Both were unstinting in their efforts to provide me with information vital to this story. I am immensely grateful for this help as well as their encouragement and suggestions about the manuscript.

I also want to thank the people in Iceland, Norway, Denmark and Britain as well as in Canada who, one way and another, provided me with assistance:

Gwyn Jones, Jon Gaudal, Einar Borgfjord, Alex Becker, Jenny Hougen, Jorgen Melgaard, Aslaug Sverrisdottir, Ragnar Thorseth, Suzanne Lacasse, Kristjana Gunnars, Torill Hauger, the late Anne Brimer, Roy Decker, Bill Milne, David Pelteret, Alan McPherson, Morag MacLeod, Mora Oxley, Don Shields, Barbara Reiti, I.H. Ni, Bruce Roberts, Bill Meade, Tony Dickenson, Merna Summers, Ingeborg Marshall, Betty Jane Wylie, Captain Alan Rowsell, Lloyd Decker, Bruce Bradbury, Dale Wells, Gail Crawford, Carol Shields, Anne Holloway and my intrepid editor, Susan Girvan.

As well, I would like to acknowledge the usefulness of Helge Ingstad's book *The Norse Discovery of America*, Volume Two, to my research.

Lastly, I would like to express my appreciation to the Canada Council, the Newfoundland and Labrador Arts Council and the Scottish Arts Council for assisting me financially in the research and writing of this novel.

Joan Clark
St. John's, Newfoundland

IT IS ANNO DOMINI, ONE THOUSAND AND FIFTEEN.
Today twenty-nine men and I leave Greenland
to embark on a voyage across the Western
Sea. We are going toward the Outer Ocean where
the land of honey and grapes—Leif's Vinland—is
said to lie. In my youth when I worked among the
Culdees on Iona, Brother Ambrose showed me a
drawing of the world made by the learned
Spaniard, Solinus of Seville. The drawing was a
circle divided into parts and surrounded by Mare
Oceanum. The two lower parts were Europe and
Africa. The upper part was Asia and Paradise.
Whether Vinland lies in Paradise or Asia is not
known, for Leif Eiriksson never saw the drawing
and made his entire voyage without a written
map. Though we will be using Leif's ship for our
journey, he will not be aboard. Instead his half-
sister Freydis and her husband Thorvard will be
in command. I consider it bad luck to be undertaking an expedition with a woman at its head,
particularly a woman as arrogant as Freydis
Eiriksdottir. Whatever happens, I will remain
faithful to Christ, as I have in the past. I pray Our
Lord will remember my piety and devotion and
that if I should perish on this voyage, He will
receive me into His Heavenly Abode.

—from the Ulfar Vellums

DREAMS

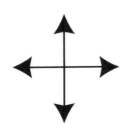

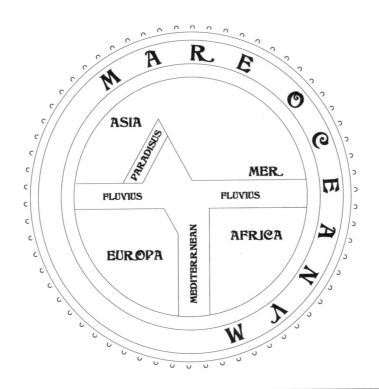

THERE WERE NO TREES IN GREENLAND. When Eirik the Red came to the island in 986, a few stands of birch were growing here and there but these had quickly been used up to provide posts and beams for set- tlers' houses. An attempt had been made to plant birch in a sheltered area across the fjord from the settle- ment at Gardar, but the seedlings were so spindly and slight they could scarcely be counted as trees. There were some osier and alder thickets and juniper shrubs, but these were neither large nor sturdy enough to be used as timber. Occasionally driftwood came ashore, arms and legs of uprooted trees, sometimes the tree itself, usually a waterlogged pine which remained brittle and stiff even after months of fire drying. Benches and stools could be made from this flotsam as well as pails and bowls and other household items.

Two or three logs might, with careful handling, make a small boat, but sea timber was unsuitable for building what the Greenlanders wanted most and what folk in southern countries took for granted, namely ships and houses of wood. Though they had more ice than they wanted, the Greenlanders would not live in ice houses. In any case this far South ice houses would melt during the short Greenland Summer. Skraelings, ugly, dwarfish crea- tures who wore furs next to their skins, lived in ice houses far to the North, but they were seldom seen even by the Greenlanders who went to the hunting grounds of

Northsetur each year. The Greenlanders were Norsemen whose forebears came mainly from Iceland and Norway. They were Europeans at least by pretension, and preferred to build themselves houses of stone and turf rather than live like skraelings.

Because they lived on the edge of the Western Sea far from Norway, the Greenlanders were not regularly tithed by the Norwegian king. Though he was greedy for riches, King Olaf was unwilling to dispatch a ship each year to cross the treacherous Greenland Sea to collect nose scat from a few thousand poor farmers scattered up and down the west side of an island all too often locked in ice. Every two or three years one of the king's ships might be spared for the Greenland trade, but that was as far as it went. The ship would come down Eiriksfjord to the main settlement of Brattahlid in high Summer. Aboard would be a vat of honey, a barrel of salt, three sacks of barley, six bars of iron, scraps of wood, eight or nine planks pitted by termites, a few bits of silver: a dented cup, four spoons, a handful of arm bracelets, a goblet perhaps or a bowl. Once a gold ring was among the king's trade goods but was quickly snatched up by Gudlag Herjolfsson who was better off than most. For these goods the king expected to be paid a hundredfold with furs and falcons, walrus hide rope and ivory as well as bolts of coarse wadmal used for making awnings and tents.

The king's ship seldom stayed longer than the time it took to unload the meagre trade goods which the Greenlanders treasured far beyond their market value, not because the goods came from a royal ship, but because it took so little to put gloss on their lives. Just as water magnified a pebble on a clear stream bed, so too a spoon of dullest silver brightened the darkest room. Barley and salt were dipped out with a bone cup until the sacks and barrels were bare. Afterwards the containers themselves were traded. Similarly honey was sold by the cup. The better-off farmers ended up with most of the iron and wood.

*   *   *

The Summer before Freydis Eiriksdottir crossed the Western Sea, she heard that one the king's ships had recently arrived in Brattahlid. She lost no time leaving her home in Gardar, which was a short distance southwest of Brattahlid, on Einarsfjord, less than half a day's journey from Gardar in good weather. After walking overland from Einarsfjord, Freydis was rowed across Eiriksfjord to Brattahlid by her thralls, in this case Kalf and Orn. Freydis took along six rolls of wadmal she had woven herself. Freydis was a shrewd bargainer and managed the Norwegians so cleverly that she gave up only four rolls of cloth, returning with two of the six as well as two bars of iron.

The next day she took one of the bars to an iron worker who lived a full day's journey from Gardar: across Einarsfjord, then a long walk Southeast. Freydis could have used the services of Nagli Asgrimsson, the itinerant iron worker who often came to Gardar, but she knew from Nagli's tale telling that he was idle tongued and she didn't want the reason for her journey known all over Greenland. She preferred a stranger to make the harness which she had designed herself. This was a thin iron pad that fit snugly between her legs and was held in place by a chain that came between her buttocks from a belt, up over her belly to lock at the waist. Now that her third child, Asny, had been weaned, Freydis planned to wear the iron harness whenever her husband was near.

To improve her Luck Freydis intended to go to Vinland where her brother Leif had built some houses and named them Leifsbudir. So strong was Freydis's determination to make the Western journey that she resolved to overcome any obstacle blocking her path, including the arrival of another child. Once, Freydis had gone high into the fells to seek out the witch Hordis Boldolfsdottir who was said to know which plants growing close to the glaciers would, when brewed with water, prevent conception. When Freydis told her why she had come, Hordis railed at her and beat her off with a stick. By then Hordis had become infected by the Christian priest who preached that in the matter of child bearing, women must follow the will of his church. Freydis scorned the priest and his church. Why should she follow the dictates of a stranger who knew nothing of farming or hunting and relied on the goodwill of others to put food in his mouth? How could such a man advise folk about improving their Luck? It was far better to keep the old gods on your side and rely on yourself to better your fate.

After Freydis had been rowed across the fjord, she bade Kalf and Orn wait for her in the pram. Then she set off for Hafgrim Sigurdsson's steading. By the time she had climbed the hill to Hafgrim's hut, the iron worker was already outside.

The old man's eyes had been leached of colour but he could see well enough. His hearing was also good and having so few visitors, he heard them long before they came over the ridge that obstructed his view. As soon as he heard a foot fall on the rocky path, Hafgrim went outside and waited to see who was coming. He was pleasantly surprised to see that the visitor striding down the path was a young woman and that she was alone. He didn't recognize her, which was to be expected since most folk he knew had long since died. She was a pleasingly built woman of middle size with crooked red hair and a proud haughty face flushed from the exertion of climbing uphill. In one hand was a sack that seemed to be heavy; in the other hand was a snood she had taken from her head. The snood told him she was a married woman. Her loosened hair and reddened cheeks excited Hafgrim; he put his hand into the slit of his breeches and began stroking himself.

The woman appeared not to notice his rising penis, but asked if he was Hafgrim Sigurdsson.

"I am, and who are you?" He went on stroking.

She wouldn't say. Instead she took a large iron bar from the sack and handed it to him, forcing him to remove his hand.

"I want you to make me this." She drew forth a woman's garment made from scraps of cloth and held it up so that he could see its shape and size. Clearly the garment was intended to fit between a woman's legs. Hafgrim's wife had been dead ten years, but he well remembered the harness of scraps she wore long after her monthly flow had stopped to dissuade him—or so he'd thought—from putting his penis between her legs. By the time his wife was dying, her rags had become so foul smelling and putrid they had to be changed twice daily along with the rest of her clothes. Fortunately this woman looked healthy. She asked if he could make a harness the same size and design as the cloth.

"It will be heavy for the wearer," he said to find out if it was for herself.

"That's the least of my worries. I only want to know if it can be made."

"I think so."

"How long will it take?"

"A month. I'm too old to work quickly." Since the harness was for her, Hafgrim would find it exciting to prolong the work.

"Then I'll come back in a month." Before she turned to go she told him to be sure to make the waist loops large enough to hold a lock.

"One more question." He wanted to detain her. She had peculiar eyes, alternately round and questioning, then narrow and flat.

Because of her linen shift, Hafgrim knew she was well born, but it excited him to think all women were whores.

"Where is an old man like myself who's not yet feeble enough to go without satisfaction," his plaintive voice wheedled and burrowed, "to put his risen penis after his wife has passed on?"

She looked at him with her flattened eyes.

"Why don't you stick it between the rocks?" She put on her snood and looked at the stony hills. "There are enough small holes and cracks hereabouts."

As he thought, the woman was a slut; no well-born woman would speak so coarsely.

She had disappeared over the ridge before Hafgrim remembered that he had forgotten to settle payment between them. He weighed the bar in his hands to see if there would be enough iron for the task. His ore bog was empty. The only iron he had left were a few lumps of ore and two knives. He would have to make the chainwork small and close fitting, the pad between her legs thin, though not so thin that it would cut her legs and make her bleed. Was her cunt hair as red and crooked as the hair on her head? Who was she to go about bare headed? What kind of woman would lock out her husband, denying him what was rightfully his?

* * *

Leif Eiriksson, Founder of Leifsbudir, Explorer of Vinland, was the son of Eirik the Red, Explorer and Colonist of Greenland. Eirik was the son of Thorvald, who was the son of Ulf, who was the son of Oxen Thorir, who was kin to Naddod the Viking, Explorer of Iceland and Colonist of the Faroes. Eirik the Red married Thjodhild, daughter of Jorund Ullfsson and Thorbjorg Ship-Breast. Eirik the Red had three sons by Thjodhild: Leif, Thorvald and Thorstein. Eirik had a daughter, Freydis, by Bribrau Reistsdottir.

Leif Eiriksson left Greenland and sailed West toward the Outer Ocean looking for the lands Bjarny Grimolfsson found some years earlier when blown off course during a storm. Leif found an island of the blessed called Vinland, from which he brought back honey and grapes as well as fruits and timber of various kinds.

Leif's younger brother Thorvald also crossed the Outer Ocean but died on an expedition from Leifsbudir when a skraeling arrow pierced his neck. A third brother, Thorstein, attempted to cross the Outer Ocean but became storm tossed near Lysufjord and died of the plague.

* * *

Leif Eiriksson could not read or write. Nor could anyone else in Greenland except Geirmund Gunnfard, the priest sent from Thingeyvar, Iceland, for the purpose of converting the Greenlanders to Christ, and the thrall Ulfar, who had been a scribe on Iona before being abducted by the Viking Harek Eel Swallower and later traded to Leif Eiriksson.

Leif owned several vellums and from time to time dictated words he wanted Ulfar to inscribe with his goose-feather quill. Leif could trace his forebears back several generations and wanted his family recorded as to who they were and what they had achieved. Leif held the written word in high regard and seemed to think his family grew in stature by having their comings and goings written down.

Ulfar also believed words gained value when written. That was why since boyhood he had wanted to become a scribe like Brother Ambrose, who had glorified Christ's words by writing them on vellum. But the scriptures on which Brother Ambrose had toiled in Iona had been embellished with pictures of Christ and the Evangelists. There were drawings of birds and beasts, angels and dragons interwoven with spirals and lacings that coiled and twisted into fabulous shapes. Luminous colours emblazoned each page: yellow, green, carmine, purple, blue. Occasionally when Ulfar finished copying scripture, he was allowed to paint a leaf, an eye, sometimes a wing. At such times Ulfar felt he had entered Paradise itself. So glorious were the colours, so richly textured the paintings of animals and plants that Ulfar was able to transport himself from the daub and wattle hut that served as the scriptorium on Iona to the Lord's sacred garden.

Leif's vellums had no such colours. In Greenland there was little that could be used for paint. There were mosses and lichens women used for dying cloth but these were unsuitable for colouring vellum. Ulfar used a greyish ink made from a lump of lead Leif had obtained from an Icelandic trader who had bought it from a Swede. Because no one in Greenland except the priest and Leif showed any interest in what he did, Ulfar found some satisfaction in writing about himself, if only to convince himself that his enslavement wasn't some terrible dream from which he would never waken, but was the result of bad Luck he hoped to change one day if it was willed by Heaven's Lord. Sometimes Ulfar didn't record events at all but made assessments of various kinds. As a young man on Iona, Ulfar had spent many hours with scholars and scribes from countries to the East who knew nothing of Greenland. Because Greenland was an empty space in the minds of civilized men, Ulfar regarded it as his duty to record his thoughts and opinions about what he saw and heard on the island, in the event they might come to the attention of learned men one day. It didn't occur to him that his judgements were harsh and one sided; fairness was a luxury even lucky men could seldom afford.

* * *

Greenlanders have many qualities I dislike but the one most abhorrent to me is the overpraising of Eirik the Red. They brag about Eirik being descended from Naddod the Viking, disregarding the fact that Naddod drove away and doubtless murdered the Irish Anchorites who were living in Iceland before he arrived. As for Eirik's forebear Oxen Thorir, he can only be regarded as a man of distinction by folk willing to ignore the ways by which he achieved his ends. To hear Greenlanders talk you would have thought Eirik the Red had been honoured by King Olaf himself. Though Eirik has been dead some thirteen years, his reputation among these folk continues to grow. Greenlanders find it convenient to overlook the fact that Eirik and his father were murderers outlawed from Norway and Iceland. I am told Eirik referred to the Icelanders who accompanied him as colonists, as if they were brave and courageous folk rather than renegades who refused to live within the laws of the land. More than once I have thought that the best of these settlers must have perished at sea. Of the twenty-five ships which sailed from Iceland with Eirik the Red, only fourteen made it safely here.

*It may be that folk who live far from the civilizing
influences of abbeys and courts are driven to making
heroes of their kind. Greenlanders are fond of telling
stories about themselves, relating them with such
gusto and swagger that anyone listening would find it
hard to know the truth.*

*Greenlanders have a crude system of justice taint-
ed with treachery of various kinds. Every Summer folk
from outlying steadings assemble in Leif's home field
to hold what they call the Althing in order to judge
petty disputes of various kinds. Usually this is the
slaughter of someone's cow or pig, the laming of a
horse or the wounding of an arm or leg when a dis-
agreement gets out of hand. Armed with the pretence
of fairness, Greenlanders puff themselves up at others' expense. They put forth their cases in the mistak-
en belief that they are capable of establishing the
truth, when as far as I can see, it is a matter of who
can tell the better lie.*

*   *   *

Before her husband returned—he was away fishing for sea
trout—Freydis went to Brattahlid again, this time to visit
her half-brother Leif Eiriksson, with whom she was on
good terms. Leif lived in the house built by their father. It
was the finest house in Brattahlid, having a luxuriously furnished great hall and numerous rooms. Freydis had once
lived in the house, but after her father's death she had
been forced out because of a falling out with her step-
mother, Thjodhild.

When she had been rowed across Eiriksfjord, Freydis
sent Kalf to tell her half-brother she was waiting for him at
the water's edge. Though Thjodhild was often bedridden
with joint ill, Freydis wouldn't go near the house in case
the old woman might suddenly appear while she was con-
versing with Leif. Freydis couldn't risk having her step-
mother interfere with important arrangements she intended to make with Leif.

Though he had never inflamed her passion like her half-brother Thorstein, Freydis felt a certain fondness for Leif. Of her three half-brothers, he had always been the most generous and helpful. She knew he was unlikely to deny her whatever she asked, as long as it was a reasonable request. Freydis knew she would never get to Vinland without Leif's help. Though she had been little more than a maid when Leif's ship, the *Vinland*, returned from the Western voyage laden with wine grapes and wood, she had resolved to make the same journey one day. Even as a child it had been clear to her that a journey to Vinland was the only way open to any Greenlander wanting to better her Luck.

Leif Eiriksson favoured his mother in looks, which meant he was tall and had once been fair skinned. Now like most Greenlanders his hands and face were leathered from sun and wind. His hair had also darkened to the colour of pond water on a rainy day. Freydis never weighed Leif for his handsomeness or ugliness; she never gave his appearance a second thought. This was because Leif's disposition overshadowed his looks. In this, as in most ways, he was unlike his half-sister, who could be ugly or beautiful by turns and was widely distrusted for her sudden shifts of temper. At the moment Freydis was smiling and humming, plucking shore grasses and tossing them into the fjord which shone calm and blue at her side. This demeanour, which she fancied was offhand and mild, was intended to quell her impatience, which seldom fell short of being expressed.

When Leif came to where Freydis was sitting, he leaned over and kissed her lightly on the cheek. Then he sat beside her and hunched forward toward the water, elbows on his knees. Freydis left off tossing grass and said she wished to speak about the situation in which she found herself.

"Then speak."

"Since my marriage I've been somewhat poor. My husband is no farmer and never will be. But as a hunter he is second to none."

"We all have our strong points," Leif said, "as well as our weak ones."

"My husband is no builder either, which is why we lack a suitable house." Freydis paused, not for Leif's assent but to change course. She didn't want to overplay her hand as the poor half-sister; she couldn't abide self-pity. Nor was it in her nature to admit defeat. She couldn't bring herself to say that her marriage to Thorvard Einarsson had worsened her Luck. She had noticed before that complainers were often blamed for their grievances. Instead she spoke of how she intended to gather riches and improve her fortune.

"So far in my marriage, I've been busy bearing and rearing three children as well as running the farm. From now on I intend to take better care of my fate. It's my wish to go to Vinland before I'm too old or overburdened to make the journey."

Leif of course knew what Freydis had been leading up to. Considering his half-sister's wilfulness and ambition, he was surprised the request hadn't been made before this. "So you want the use of my ship and my houses in Leifsbudir."

"Yes." As Eirik the Red's daughter, Freydis thought she was owed this much.

"Have you thought of someone who could serve as helmsman?"

Leif was an experienced helmsman but Freydis knew he was unlikely to return to Vinland himself; he had said so many times. As gödi he couldn't easily leave Greenland, especially since his eldest son, Thorkel, was too young to be chief in his place.

"I haven't given any thought to a helmsman since I needed your permission first."

"Evyind Hromundsson would be a good choice for helmsman though like me, he's getting on in years. He was helmsman for Rodrek Hognisson before Rodrek died. Evyind has never been to Vinland, but any helmsman who has crossed the Greenland Sea can manage the westward crossing. Evyind's taken my ship twice to Northsetur. I'm sure he could take the *Vinland* safely across the water. If he can't go, try Ivar Sorlisson. He's a good helmsman. So is Uni Magnusson." Leif glanced at the shed further down the fjord where the *Vinland* was dry hauled; it had been three years since the old ship had been put to sea.

Leif asked what Thorvard thought about the voyage.

"As you know, my husband is no more sailor than he is farmer or builder. But he'll do what I ask, especially when he considers the advantages of the proposition."

Folk commented on how Freydis managed her husband, and on how often he escaped her overbearing ways. Freydis was quick to deny these charges; not only did they reflect badly on herself, but the remarks as reported to her by her husband's sister were only part of the truth.

"If you can persuade your husband to go and Evyind will serve as helmsman, I'll lend you my ship. I won't give you my houses in Leifsbudir but I'll lend them to you while you're there. I also know several men who would be eager to crew. I can approach Evyind and Ivar if you like. One way or another I'll help you out." Leif paused. "But there is a complication. As you know, the Icelander Thorfinn Karlsefni took two ships and sixty-five people to Leifsbudir two years ago, which means he's making use of both my houses as well as the other buildings. There'll be no room for you over there until he returns."

"When do you expect him back?"

"Who can say? My guess is next year, but if he's run into bad Luck over there, he could have decided to return this year."

"I've waited so long for the chance to go to Leifsbudir," Freydis said. "My hope is that he returns this year."

"Then it will have to be soon, while the ice is out."

* * *

When Freydis's husband, Thorvard Einarsson, returned from fishing, he told her that when he had taken shelter on shore one night, he had met up with two brothers, Finnbogi and Helgi Egilsson, who had come from Iceland aboard a ship named *Sigurd's Steed*. The brothers told him they would be overwintering in Greenland, and intended to go to Brattahlid to see Leif.

"They have a Norwegian shipbuilder aboard and want to use Leifsbudir for the purpose of building ships." Thorvard spoke matter-of-factly as if he was relating the number of sea trout he had caught. Thorvard had a nasal voice that seldom varied but relayed both the unusual and mundane as if they were of equal import. Nor did his expression help. His dark brows never arched to show surprise or dismay. In eight years of marriage Freydis had yet to see him frown. Thorvard's features were so unremarkable that he was barely out of her sight than she forgot his looks.

Though he had been absent for nearly a month, Thorvard made no attempt to embrace Freydis. Except for coupling they seldom touched. Nor did she offer an embrace. She was inside the dairy hut when he entered, and continued pouring out milk as if he had been standing there all along. Thorvard sat on the milking stool while he told her about the Egilssons.

When she had finished scrubbing the milk pails, Freydis turned them upside down on the stone floor.

"It's interesting that you should be telling me about these Icelanders," she said, sitting on one of the iron pails, "for I've recently arranged with Leif for us to go to Leifsbudir."

Thorvard had told the Egilsson brothers that his wife hankered for Vinland, that she never lost an opportunity to harass him about making the voyage for he had no wish to go himself. He was a hunter, he had told them, primarily of large sea animals and white bears of which there were plenty in Northsetur. Why should he go to a place far away when he didn't even know where it was or what he was likely to find when he got there? Yes, he had told the brother named Helgi, he had heard the tales of Vinland. There was no shortage of such tales around Winter fires. But the tales contradicted each other too much for his liking. Thorvard told the Egilssons that he sometimes humoured his wife by listening to her plan a voyage to

Vinland but he had never taken the matter seriously himself. Thorvard had not mentioned his wife's tirades and
beratings. How many times had he heard her complain
about having to sleep on furs and skins piled on the floor?
Was it too much, she would say, to expect their daughters
to sleep on a bench? Didn't Thorvard know children got
worms and abcesses from sleeping on the ground? It was
Thorvard's opinion that his wife had been badly spoiled
during the years she lived in her father's house where she
had been given a sleeping compartment of her own and
other luxuries besides. Most folk in Greenland slept on
twigs and rags. He often slept on stones himself and
thought he had done well to have provided Freydis with
furs. Freydis also complained that she and her children
had no tables, that they had to eat from their laps while
sitting on the floor. How much longer did she have to
endure a marriage with no furniture? Thorvard had heard
all this and more. So he said nothing inside the dairy hut
in response to Freydis's announcement that she intended
they should go to Vinland.

As for Freydis she was weary of trying to persuade
Thorvard about the rewards of making a voyage to
Vinland. "If you refuse to go to Leifsbudir, I'll make the
journey myself with Evyind Hromundsson as helmsman,"
she said. She drew the butter pail closer. Before she
began to churn she had one last thing to say. "Listen
closely, Thorvard Einarsson, for I intend to say this only
once. I refuse to lie with you as wife to husband until we
find ourselves in Leifsbudir." Freydis was well aware that
Thorvard would react strongly against this ultimatum. He
seldom said much when thwarted; instead he punished
her in various ways.

To slight her this time Thorvard moved to his sister
Inga's farm, which was next to his, and helped her husband, Guttorm, cut turfs. The turfs, which were at the bottom of Thorvard's home field, had long been coveted by
Inga and Guttorm who wanted them to insulate their
house. Now Thorvard was giving them turfs he cut himself, something he had never done for Freydis. It didn't

concern him that he and Freydis might run short of turfs for their own house when it came time to be built. Thorvard also brought some of Guttorm's cattle into his home field knowing it would irk Freydis, who had an ongoing feud with Inga and Guttorm over cattle grazing. Soon after Thorvard went off reindeer hunting with Guttorm on Hreinsey, Freydis put the cattle back in Guttorm's field where they belonged.

When a month had passed, Freydis returned to Hafgrim Sigurdsson with the second bar of iron, which she handed over in exchange for the harness. Hafgrim had been forced to melt down an iron knife in order to complete the chain work, but he was pleased with the result. He was loath to part with the harness once it was finished since he had become accustomed to stroking its parts. On the other hand he was greedy to own the new bar of iron, and after fondling the cunt lock—which was what he called it—he handed it over to its owner without a word. When Freydis reached her hut in Gardar, she locked the belt inside her marriage chest against the day when Thorvard returned.

Three days later two strangers came up Einarsfjord to Gardar. These were Icelanders who had been with Thorfinn Karlsefni in Leifsbudir and had brought back various trade goods. Freydis bought nothing from these men. They had already given her what she wanted, which was the welcome news that Thorfinn and his men had returned. Unable to get through the ice in Eiriksfjord, the Icelanders had decided to spend the Winter farther South. The expedition to Leifsbudir, they said, had been successful, except for skraelings which they had encountered more than once. Freydis asked if these encounters had been in Leifsbudir.

"No, in a place further South," one of them replied, "a place named Hop where Thorfinn tried to settle. It seemed the further South we travelled in Vinland, the more skraelings there were."

The presence of skraelings did not thwart Freydis's enthusiasm for crossing the Western Sea since she had no

interest in travelling further South in Vinland than
Leifsbudir. It was a stroke of good fortune that Thorfinn
Karlsefni had returned this year; now she could begin
making preparations for a journey next Summer.

* * *

*The same Summer Thorfinn Karlsefni returned from
Vinland, a ship commanded by two brothers, Helgi
and Finnbogi Egilsson, arrived in Greenland. The
brothers were Icelanders by birth and had come from
the Eastfirths.*

*One day Freydis Eiriksdottir travelled from her
home in Gardar to visit the brothers. She asked them
if they would join her with their ship on an expedition
to Vinland the following Summer, sharing equally with
her all the profits that might be made. They agreed to
this. They also agreed that each party should have
thirty able-bodied men aboard besides women.*

* * *

The Egilssons were staying at a farm whose owner had
gone to Norway for a time. The farm was on the south side
of Eiriksfjord which meant Freydis did not have to cross
water to visit the brothers. All she had to do was walk
overland from Gardar. She wanted to have plans for the
voyage so far under way that by the time her husband
returned from Hreinsey, he would have difficulty stopping
them.

The Egilssons did not seem like brothers. They did not
look at all alike and appeared to have opposite dispositions. Helgi was red faced and big nosed enough to be
ugly but he had a friendly outgoing way. Finnbogi was dark
haired and strongly built. Unfortunately his handsomeness
was marred by a sourness in his face. He showed no pleasure in seeing Freydis, though she introduced herself as
Leif Eiriksson's sister. In fact he seemed to regard her as
an intruder when she appeared at the door. It was Helgi
who invited her inside and offered her a drink of warm
water sweetened with honey.

When she accepted, Helgi told a woman to fetch a horn cup. There were four or five female thralls inside the room which was twice the size of Freydis's hut, and several men as well. Except for the size of the room and the hearth, the room had no more to recommend it than Freydis's, there being no sleeping benches or tables and next to nothing in the way of decoration. Helgi indicated a stool and Freydis loosened her cloak and sat.

"Does your crew bed down here at night or have you other quarters?" Freydis said in an effort to find out how many men the Egilssons had brought.

"There are thirty of us altogether, not counting women," Helgi said obligingly, "too many for this house. We've spread ourselves between here and the overseer's house which is further down the fjord."

The woman who brought the honeyed drink was too well dressed to be a thrall. She was wearing a brown linen robe with a silver key hanging from a silver brooch. Her brown hair was dressed with red ribbons.

"Is this your wife?"

Helgi laughed. "There are no wives here, only thralls."

Freydis was wearing a robe of plain blue wool herself. She didn't let her envy show until later, when she was telling Thorvard about the visit. She asked if Helgi had been speaking to her brother.

"Not yet," he said. "We've dry hauled our ship and covered it with its Winter shed. We've been advised to wait until Eiriksfjord freezes over before making the crossing on foot to talk to Leif."

Freydis thought the Icelanders had been overcautious in covering their ship so soon. On the other hand, they had been lucky to make it up Eiriksfjord to the end for once again the nights were cold enough to freeze water. The fjord had begun to freeze along the shore and there were chunks of ice floating here and there, which made crossing Eiriksfjord unwise.

"I've come to see you now so that we might reach an agreement regarding the use of Leifsbudir," Freydis said. "As you know from talking to my husband, I intend to make the journey to Vinland next Summer as soon as it can be arranged. Now that Thorfinn Karlsefni has returned and Leif's houses are empty, I'll be using Leif's ship to make the crossing. If we can reach an agreement that suits me, I'd be willing to share one of Leif's houses with you."

Finnbogi made a sound at last, something halfway between a snort and a bark which Freydis took to mean he didn't like the idea of sharing Leif's houses. Perhaps he expected to have them to himself. But Helgi continued to be congenial and asked what sort of agreement she had in mind.

"I understand you have a shipbuilder," Freydis said. She looked around the room, expecting one of the men to declare himself to be the Norwegian. When none of them did, her eyes settled on a black-haired thrall who seemed to be more girl than woman. Perhaps she was older than she looked. It was hard to tell. The girl sat with her head bent, her hair in her face.

"In Greenland, yes," Helgi said, "but not in this room."

A woman sitting far back in the shadows behind the men laughed in a coarse bold manner that was surprising in a thrall.

"He's at the overseer's farm."

"I'd like to see him," Freydis said.

"He's too ill to see visitors." The laugh came again. "Perhaps later on."

"The agreement concerns him," Freydis said. "I would like him to build me a ship."

"That may be possible," Helgi replied, "especially if we can reach an arrangement with you that will provide us with the things we need. I'm having a ship built for myself, since *Sigurd's Steed* belongs to my older brother."

"We should be able to settle something between us," Freydis said. She was dismayed to learn that the unpleasant brother owned the ship.

More honeyed water was fetched while Freydis and Helgi discussed how they might share trade goods and how many men should be taken as crew. They made arrangements to supply sailcloth and rigging for the ships they would build. Freydis said she would weave enough wadmal for two sails; her husband would supply the rope for the ships' rigging. Finnbogi made no attempt to join the discussion but sat silently throughout. It was only when Freydis was preparing to leave that he spoke.

"It seems you'll be making the journey without your husband. He told us he had no wish to go to Vinland."

"I'm sure he'll change his mind once he considers our proposition," Freydis said and drew on her cloak.

"I wouldn't be too sure of that."

"May I ask if you spent one or two nights in conversation with my husband?" Freydis kept her voice pleasant yet firm. She had no wish to get on the wrong side of the shipowner, but Leifsbudir had been put at her disposal first. If Finnbogi expected to make use of it at the same time as she, he would have to regard her as being on an equal footing with him. Unfortunately the older brother showed the kind of scorn some people reserved for folk they regarded as less worthy than themselves.

"One night." Finnbogi looked at the floor.

"Then surely I, who have spent countless nights with him, am better able than you to know his mind." Freydis immediately went outside followed by Helgi, who was courteous enough to walk some distance with her before turning back.

* * *

Thorvard, Guttorm and four other hunters returned from the island of Hreinsey a month before Yule. Between them they had sixty reindeer which was all they could load onto their prams. With a ship they would have been able to return with twice that number, since the herd was plentiful on Hreinsey and a ship could have borne more weight. As it was the prams were so low in the water they were difficult to manoeuvre, especially since their passage was slowed by ice. Unlike Eiriksfjord, Einarsfjord was free of ice pans during Midsummer, but now that Winter was near it too was rapidly filling with ice.

Freydis's oldest child, Thorlak, saw the men coming up the fjord well before they came ashore. A boy of seven Winters, Thorlak in no way resembled his father, being pale of hair and narrowly built. He was a nervous child who sometimes woke screaming and clutching himself. Freydis thought her son probably resembled her dead mother but she was fond of him all the same. When Thorlak came into the hut where Freydis was weaving and told her his father was home, she told her oldest thrall, Groa, to bundle her daughters in their cloaks and take them outside.

"They need airing," Freydis said, "too much smoke is bad for their eyes."

In fact the room was hardly smoky. Both the door and the second roof hole were open. Freydis had positioned her loom beneath this second hole to make the most of fresh air and light. This time of year she kept a small turf fire burning, which was enough to take off the chill. When the snow flew outside and a bitter wind wailed through the darkness, they used whale oil lamps for light and extra heat. Seal oil was cleaner but seals had been scarce the past two years. The whale oil lamps filled the room with so much greasy smoke that Freydis would sometimes be forced to leave off weaving altogether. Despite this she had made two rolls of wadmal for the voyage the previous Winter. Now she was weaving cloth for her children's clothes: tunic and breeches for the boy, shifts and robes for the girls.

Signy had seen five Winters so far and Asny two. Asny could walk, though poorly, which meant she had to hold Groa's hand. Groa herself walked slowly. Bent over and lame, she shuffled along as if she had one foot in her grave. Freydis watched the three figures only long enough to see Signy run ahead of Groa and her little sister down the slope toward the fjord. Then she closed the door and bolted it tight. She unlocked her marriage chest and took out the iron harness and a small iron lock. Although she was alone, Freydis went behind the woven hanging that hid the piss bucket to put on the harness. This time of

year they used the privy outside, but during the night
Thorlak often needed to piss. Freydis took some dried
moss from a sack hanging above the piss bucket and
arranged it on the iron pad. Tucking her shift and robe
beneath her chin, she stepped into the iron harness and
pulled it up until it was firmly positioned between her
legs. She fumbled with the loops, trying to fit them into
the lock, swearing at Freyja and Freyr, two gods she alternately praised and defied, until finally the lock slipped into
place and she turned the key. The lock and chain were
rough and needed oiling, but otherwise the harness fit
well. The pad was narrower than she liked but was wide
enough to serve the purpose she had in mind. With the
fullness of her shift, no one would suspect what she was
wearing underneath.

Before locking the marriage chest, Freydis removed the
hangings she had woven with her step-mother's help,
shook them out, then refolded them and put them back.
The hangings were coloured with stripes of red, yellow and
purple wool which Thjodhild had taught her to dye. There
was also a linen tablecloth edged in lace, a roll of grey
cloth intended to cover sleeping benches, as well as various small cloths embroidered with fine tablet weaving.
There was a set of linen underclothes and a shift edged in
ribbon intended for her bridal bed. Freydis had never
worn this clothing for directly after her marriage she had
seen the mean hut in which she was expected to live.
Thorvard's father, Einar, had given them this hut—which
had once housed his thralls—as a marriage gift. He could
have provided something better, but like many folk who
are wealthy he was reluctant to part with his goods.

Using the bottom of her shift, Freydis wiped a large
brass bowl edged with beaten gold that was inside the
chest. Leif had given her this bowl on her marriage day, in
addition to a dowry of posts and beams that had been
used for firewood before Thorvard got around to using
them to build a house. Freydis refused to use the bowl or
the hangings until she had a house built with posts and
beams.

For eight years Freydis had been living in this miserable hut. On the earth floor, against the walls were piles of alder wood twigs over which furs and skins had been spread for sleeping. Freydis had Groa move the twigs daily and sweep beneath. The furs and skins were shaken outside as well to get rid of vermin and dirt tracked inside. Down the centre of the hut was a long hearth above which various utensils hung from hooks tied to the alder wood roof. Pails and pots were stored in a stone box beside the hearth. Against one wall Freydis had built an open cupboard, using flat stones hauled from the fells by Kalf and Orn. It had taken her months while she was pregnant with Thorlak to do this, but she had been determined to have a place off the ground where she could store small bowls and cups, trenchers and spoons as well as combs and other household items. Apart from this stone shelving and her marriage chest, the only other furniture in the room was a narrow sloping bench made from uneven pieces of driftwood, and a stool. Clothing and bedding also hung from iron hooks tied to the roof along with bundles of twigs, angelica and bags of moss. Anything that wouldn't fit in the stone shelving was hung above, where it absorbed the smoke from the hearth below. When moving around the room, Freydis had to shove aside clothing that got in her way. She often remarked to Thorvard that the roof had so much weight hanging beneath, sooner or later it was bound to collapse.

Food was stored in the outbuildings nearby which were locked to keep thralls and light-fingered children, mainly Inga's, from stealing it. Milk and cheese were kept in the dairy, the sea trout Thorvard had caught earlier in another hut. Most of the trout had been smoked and dried for Winter as had salmon and cod. From now on Freydis intended to cache a portion of their food in the hut used for farm tools. This was a place Thorvard seldom looked. Some of the food would be used for the voyage, the rest would be kept for their children. Freydis wouldn't be taking her children to Leifsbudir. Instead she intended to ask her foster mother, Halla Eldgrimsdottir, to mind them here. Halla had a small steading in the fells above Brattahlid, but with enough planning, she could likely find a tenant to look after it. Not once did Freydis seriously consider taking her children on the voyage since her purpose wasn't to settle new land but to make herself rich. Her children were too young to be useful and would be better off staying on their father's home field where their presence would remind folk that Thorvard and she would be coming back.

Freydis closed the lid of her marriage chest and locked it. Then she took a butchering garment from a hook. It was made of rags sewn into an apron of sorts. Despite washings the apron was heavily soiled with blood and grease. She went out to the tool shed for three knives and a skinner which she brought back and sharpened on the whetstone. Only after the tools were sharp enough to skin reindeer did she walk down the hill toward the fjord.

That evening, when their children were sleeping and Groa was snoring on a pile of twigs, Freydis and Thorvard sat near the fire, one on the bench, the other on the stool. Thorvard was only half awake. Freydis was only half awake herself but she was seldom too sleepy to speak.

"I'm pleased you've brought back so much venison," she told her husband. "It means a quantity can be spared for next Summer's voyage."

Thorvard's eyes were closed and his head slumped over. He didn't speak or lift his head.

"I've spoken to Evyind Hromundsson. He agrees to make the voyage if his son Teit can come. Evyind assures me there will be no shortage of men wanting to go, including Ivar Sorlisson and Uni Magnusson, who are both good with ships. Nagli Asgrimsson has also agreed to come. We'll need an iron worker over there for making ship nails and the like. Leif tells me there's a bed of iron ore in Leifsbudir near his houses. It's not a large supply but it should be enough for us. I've arranged for Nagli to make some tools for us this Winter since we'll need a large supply of axes for felling and working wood."

Thorvard said nothing; it was like talking to the stool.

"I've also struck an agreement with the Icelanders. I've agreed to share the profits and Leif's houses with them if their stemsmith will build us a ship. Ivar and Uni will sail it back."

Still Thorvard was silent.

"We agreed to take thirty men each, over and above the women. The Egilssons have several female thralls with them as I suppose you know. Expensively attired they are for slaves. The Egilssons must have a low opinion of well-born women to allow their thralls to be overdressed. One of them was a dark-haired girl who looked more child than woman." Freydis couldn't have said why she added this last remark. Perhaps she wanted to know if Thorvard was awake or asleep. Later she would question this remark, wondering if it had been foolish or wise.

Thorvard lifted his head and looked into the fire.

"I didn't know the Egilssons had female thralls with them, since they came to my camp fire alone," he said. "I didn't get a chance to board their ship."

"The one named Finnbogi seems to think he knows your mind," Freydis said.

"Why is that?"

"You'd better ask him yourself, though I can tell you one thing: he wants my brother's houses all to himself."

"Perhaps I'll ask him," Thorvard said, "tomorrow."

He yawned and reached for the tongs. He stirred the fire, took out the largest embers, placed them inside the stone ember box and put on the lid. This was a task he did only when he expected to lie with Freydis as husband to wife.

Freydis took off her robe and lay beside Thorvard beneath the bearskin in a coarse woven shift. Her husband put an arm around her waist.

"What's this you're wearing?"

"Something to stanch my monthly blood."

This would soon be true.

Thorvard felt the chainwork on her belly until he reached the iron pad between her legs.

"Where did you get this?"

"I had it made, by someone far from here."

"Then you intend to go on bleeding."

"For a while at least."

Thorvard said no more and pretended to sleep. Freydis knew by his breathing that he lay awake. She was awake herself. The chain work made it difficult for her to lie on her back as she was used to. Instead she was forced to lie on her side.

When she woke in the morning, Thorvard was gone. He stayed away the next day and the next, which meant Freydis had to finish the skinning and cutting with only two thralls, Kalf and Orn, to help; Thorvard had taken Louse Oddi with him; Gorm was up in the fells minding sheep. The work was tedious and slow; it could not be rushed without fatal results. The thralls used the knives for cutting. Freydis used a tool with a curved blade and a wide iron handle for skinning. The width of the handle and its distance from the blade made it safer to work with than knives.

The butchering, done in the open space between the outbuildings, lasted two days. Once it was finished a fire was lit inside and the meat hung above it to dry. Freydis also had a fire lit inside one of stone outbuildings and smoked the rest of the meat in there. She was well pleased with the results. Not only had none of them cut themselves but there was a large supply of meat for Winter and enough for the voyage and her children besides.

Three days after the butchering was finished, Thorvard reappeared at midday and announced that he had been visiting the Egilssons and had decided to make the voyage after all. He had taken a liking to the Icelanders, Helgi especially. Though he hadn't been able to board the Egilssons' ship, he had been able to gauge its dimensions by looking at the Winter shed.

"It's as large as Leif's ship. If we could have one that size made for ourselves, there would be no need for me to depend on Atli Loftsson to go to Northsetur."

Freydis, who was working at the loom, didn't speak in case she said something that might change her husband's mind. She kept her back to him and continued to weave.

"We could become traders and take our goods to Norway ourselves. We live near hunting grounds rich in furs and ivory, goods that are valued by the Norwegians and the Danes as well as the Saxons and, I'm told, the Frisians. Traders come here in their ships and take away our goods to resell at a price far beyond what they pay us. Why should we be pawns of the Icelanders and the Norwegians?"

Freydis kept her head averted to conceal the smile that had taken hold of her lips; she knew her smugness would annoy her husband.

"I said to myself, why should strangers come here and beat us down so that we end up trading away more than we should in order to get our hands on iron and linen and honey and barley, goods I'm told are common elsewhere but luxuries here. We've been taken advantage of long enough. With a ship of our own those profits will be ours."

Thorvard waited for Freydis to reply. When she remained silent, he asked, "Isn't that right?"

Freydis was canny enough not to remind Thorvard that he had just returned a piece of her mind she had given him more than once, almost word for word. She rearranged her features to get rid of the smugness. Then she turned and said, "I agree with every word you say."

"Well then, that's settled," Thorvard said. "We had better get on with our plans."

* * *

Later, after Yule, when the ice in Eiriksfjord was safe enough to walk on, Freydis and Thorvard made the journey to Brattahlid to discuss arrangements with Leif. During this visit, Leif offered them the use of Ulfar for a year, saying the thrall was as skilled a woodworker as he was a scribe. Leif reminded Freydis and Thorvard that because of the lack of trees in Greenland, they would be hard put to find enough woodworkers to suit their needs. Leif

regarded the loan of Ulfar as a way to make up for the dis-
appearance of Freydis's dowry, but he was prudent
enough not to mention this since he knew the burning of
the posts and beams still rankled Freydis.

"The Egilssons have woodworkers," Thorvard said, "we
can make use of theirs. They have few hunters and will be
glad to use ours in exchange."

"I'm pleased to hear you have been able to work matters out with the Icelanders," Leif said. "They came to me
two days ago to ask if they could use my houses in
Leifsbudir. I told them I had promised to lend them to my
half-sister, and that whether or not they could use them
would depend on what could be arranged with you."

Freydis then discussed the matter of Halla
Eldgrimsdottir with Leif. Since the steading where Halla
lived once belonged to their father Eirik the Red, Freydis
thought it prudent to engage Leif's help in finding someone to work Halla's farm. As gödi he knew which folk
would make good tenants. Halla had already agreed to live
in Gardar for a year. She was fond of children and had
always found it difficult to refuse Freydis; Freydis had
always been more like kin to her than a foster child.

After their arrangements with Leif had been complet-
ed, Freydis and Thorvard returned to their farm which was
now frozen in ice. There were no animals in the fields,
only a few sheep which had long since been brought down
from the fells and now moved through the half-dark like
wraiths; most of Freydis's flock were huddled against the
stone walls of the pen near the house. Since Yule the cattle had been walled up in the byre against the cold.
Beyond being given a meagre ration of dried grass and
leaves, they required little tending, since they had ceased
giving milk. Freydis's thralls were sent out daily to chop
whatever twigs and bits of turf could be found under the
ice. The stream feeding the crag pool which supplied
Gardar with fresh water was frozen over so that folk were
now drinking melted snow.

To pass the time Freydis sat beside a whale oil lamp
and spun the last of the wool that had been shorn and

cleaned the previous Summer as well as the wool she had bought from other farmers. Together with the wool she would shear next Summer she would have enough for the two sails she intended to weave in Vinland. She also made shoes and leggings from deerskin. She sewed wadmal mitts and head coverings for her children. She clapped hands with Asny and taught Signy to spin. She played guessing games with the older children, but there was so little to surprise them inside the hut that the children soon became as bored with the game as their mother. If the wind was down at midday when the sky was lightest, Freydis and Thorvard took their children outside with their pails and shovels to frolic in the snow. The daylight was grey, but they could see well enough to play. Thorvard and Freydis pulled the children around on sleds which Thorvard had made with sealskin and walrus rope. Freydis was enjoying her children more this Winter than she had before, not because of anything her children said or did but because the prospect of better Luck lay ahead.

Thorvard passed the worst of Winter mending his hunting weapons. He had an assortment of axes, spears and knives that wanted sharpening. And he had more than enough deer antlers for making new arrows and barbs. When he had finished working with his weapons, he made a gaming set for Thorlak and new spoons for his daughters. Thorvard disliked the confinement of Winter and was often morose and out of sorts. If the weather was clear, he would sometimes visit the Egilssons on the pretence of settling some aspect of the voyage. Whenever he went to see the Icelanders, he would be gone three or four days. Freydis noticed that he never failed to return from these outings in better spirits. She thought perhaps he had made use of one of the Icelandic thralls, since he never once asked if she was wearing her iron belt.

Late Winter when enough light brightened the sky to make day distinguishable from night, Thorvard packed his hunting gear and went off on Atli Loftsson's ship, which was going to Northsetur. Thorvard was after walrus whose hides would be needed to provide rope for the ships. He would be away three months. Ahead of him was a walk of several days to reach the head of the fjord where Atli Loftsson kept his ship. Einarsfjord was still frozen hard. By the time the hunters returned from Northsetur, the fjord would have opened up enough for Atli to bring Thorvard back to Gardar.

While Thorvard was away, Nagli Asgrimsson came to Gardar and stayed at Freydis's steading for several days, making tools in one of the outbuildings and sleeping by her fire. About this time Freydis made a second journey to visit the Egilsson brothers, in order to meet the Norwegian stemsmith, Hauk Ljome. For this visit she put on her blue robe with the bronze clasps, her red kirtle and the glass beads which her half-brother Thorstein had given her. She knew she would make a better impression if she was dressed as a woman of means. Though the Norwegian was confined to his bed, he didn't appear ill to Freydis. In fact she found him a vigorous quick-witted man and was much taken with him in all respects. She didn't resist toying with him since he obviously enjoyed her company and showed it in a way Thorvard never did. Hauk Ljome spoke about the different kinds of ships he had built in Norway and described the one he would build for her. What she need-ed, he said, was a skútur, which was a high-sided, sturdy ship, better suited to the merchant trade than the long ship. He could build her a skútur that could have as few as eight oarsmen on each side or as many as twelve. Such a ship was well suited for ocean travel. Freydis left Hauk Ljome feeling very well pleased, for he had promised to build her an ocean-going ship that would be second to none. When she sailed into Bergen on the ship, he had told her, she would be the envy of the Norwegians. Since this was a scene Freydis had often imagined, she thought the handsome shipbuilder had somehow read her mind.

*   *   *

There was a man named Reist Gunnarsson who came to Greenland from Breidafjord, Iceland, shortly after the Settlement. Reist married Vigdis Hallvardsdottir by

*whom he had a daughter, Bribrau. Reist was a friend
of Eirik the Red's and settled across from Eiriksey in
Dyrnes on land which Eirik had given him. Bribrau
married first Grettir Gormsson and afterwards, Illugi
Arnkelsson.*

   She had a daughter, Freydis, by Eirik the Red.

* * *

When she was younger, Freydis used to imagine her conception took place when a he-goat with rusty horns and
stars for eyes came down from the heavens and mated
with a beautiful maiden as she lay in a field. The maiden,
who wore a blue robe and a crown of white flowers, lay on
her back and slept all the while. When she awoke it was
night-time and the goat was gone from her side. Looking
up, the maiden saw the goat far above, two reddish stars
winking at her. In time the woman gave birth to a daughter. One day the woman looked up and said to the goat,
"Take me up with you." The goat leaned down so that the
she could grasp his horns. She reached up but could only
get hold of one of his horns. When the goat swung her up
into the heavens, the woman lost her grip and fell into the
sea, leaving her daughter to be fostered by someone else.

   This was the story Freydis began to tell herself after her
mother Bribrau died. When Freydis was about six or
seven, she would walk uphill in Dyrnes behind the hut
where she lived with Halla Eldgrimsdottir, the woman who
became her foster mother. Freydis would choose a flat
stone to sit on and look out across the water to Eiriksey.
She was trying to find the place where her mother had disappeared into the sea. Freydis didn't know why this was
important to her. Perhaps she thought if she could locate
the place, her mother would reappear. Possibly she was
looking for a sign, a slight stirring of water, an emerging
head, or a hand. Whatever it was, it never appeared. All
she saw was a sea that constantly shifted and swallowed
itself. Nor did she see her mother at night when she stud-
ied the stars, but she sometimes saw the goat clearly
enough. Eventually Freydis gave up looking for her mother

though she continued to sit on the hillside and look at the sea.

After Freydis went to Gardar and married Thorvard, she would climb the hill behind their steading and sit with her back to the fells. She liked looking down on the scattering of huts and steadings. Unlike Brattahlid, Gardar was built on a wide open plain that sloped down to the water. The settlement was at the end of Einarsfjord which gave it a measure of completion, for it seemed the mountains surrounding it provided a natural wall; the mountains were low and sloped in such a way that in Summer they opened themselves to receive the light. In late Winter when the sun returned and the opening began, Freydis would free herself from her chores and her children and climb the hill above Gardar until she found a place where she could sit and look at the farms and the water. She would remove her linen snood, uncoil her hair and shake it loose. If the wind was down, she would take off her robe and sit in her shift. After the confinement of the dark hut with its low, cluttered ceiling and its acrid, oily smoke, she welcomed the light and space that followed a hard Winter. Being surrounded by so much openness made her feel expansive and huge. She felt her body enter the land: her lap became a smooth hollow, her knees and elbows rounded stones, her fingers alder twigs. The longer she sat above Gardar—and sometimes she sat for an afternoon—the more Freydis felt herself transformed, becoming as silent and undemanding as stone. Had Thorvard's sister Inga looked up at the fells as she was walking between her outbuildings, she wouldn't have seen Freydis, who blended with the landscape in a way that made woman and fells appear as one. When she was a stone, Freydis neither wanted nor lacked anything. Eventually the echo of a sheep herder's whistle or the ring of a cowbell would pierce the air with such clarity that Freydis would be reminded that she was neither stone nor wood and some dissatisfaction would come to mind.

She might think of the two cows she had lost to the cold. After the worst of Winter had passed and the cows were carried out of the byre, two had refused to stand and graze in places where the sun had melted the snow and had starved instead. Or she might review the grudges she bore Inga.

Sometimes on the hillside Freydis let her mind drift toward desire and the dreams of Vinland. Freydis had been fourteen when Leif arrived in Brattahlid bringing his tales of Vinland which warmed folk long after his cargo of honey and wine were gone. Freydis had stored up the tales, hoarding them in the same way she saved the goods inside her marriage chest. From time to time she took out the tales to savour their richness. She admired the intricacy of their weft, the vividness of their colour, the smoothness of their weave, then folded them away until the day she could make use of them. Vinland and Leifsbudir might have been better named riches, since that was what they meant to Freydis.

Some of Leif's crew insisted both places were one and the same while others said they were not, that Leifsbudir was only one of many places within Vinland. Leif himself claimed the places were, and were not, the same. "How can that be?" a Greenlander would say. "They are either the same or they are not." "That depends," Leif would reply. "If you have never been anywhere except Brattahlid, then for you Brattahlid is Greenland. If you never go anywhere except Leifsbudir, then for you Leifsbudir is Vinland. Vinland is much larger than one man's comings and goings."

As the days lengthened and the sun continued opening the mountains and the water, Freydis sat on the hillside less and less. With so many preparations to make for the voyage, she could seldom free herself for a full afternoon. But one day in mid-afternoon after Freydis had sat for a short while on the hillside and was putting on her robe in preparation to leave, the witch Hordis Boldolfsdottir came upon her, whether by accident or intent, Freydis never knew.

Hordis lived by herself in the fells to the East. She had a hut up there where she kept a few sheep. She was thickly bundled in rags all year round. All folk saw of her was her shaggy mane and her scummy teeth. She seldom washed and muttered strange oaths. Whenever Gardar folk saw Hordis coming to trade her wool for a bowl of milk or scraps of food, they went inside and shut the door for none of them wanted to be cursed or given the evil eye. Three years earlier Thorvard's father, Einar, had used Hordis to curse a neighbour after he saw the neighbour's thralls dig holes in Einar's upper pasture to lame his horses. Einar's horses had strayed into the wrong field by mistake. Hordis's curse was powerful enough to lame one of the neighbour's thralls, making him useless for farm work ever since.

Hordis hobbled up to where Freydis was standing and leaned on the stick she used as a cane. Hordis had once been a tall woman, but now she was bent nearly double and had to peer upwards to give Freydis the evil eye. Hordis began muttering a spell intended, Freydis was sure, to prevent her from looking away. Freydis tried to move but the old woman blocked her way with the stick.

"You are an unlucky woman, Freydis Eiriksdottir," Hordis said clearly; there was no muttering now. "If you abandon your children and sail across the Western Sea, you will bring nothing but harm to yourself and your kin."

Again Freydis tried to get away and again the stick held her fast.

"Mark well my words," Hordis screeched, "take your children with you on the voyage or your family will suffer the wrath of the Christian god!" She swung the stick over Freydis's head so she would know this was a powerful curse. Abruptly the old woman stopped caterwauling and hobbled away.

Freydis knew that curses most affected those who lacked the strength to fight them off. Despite the stones blocking her path, Freydis descended the hill with speed. She did not turn to see if Hordis was watching. She moved swiftly, determined to protect her children and herself. The best way to do this was to make a more powerful spell than the one that had been meant to do her family harm.

Freydis immediately sent Gorm to spy on Hordis's flock until he could safely shear one of her sheep without Hordis casting the evil eye. Later that day Gorm returned with the wool and Freydis got to work. The sooner she repelled the old woman's curse, the less chance there was for it to take hold. Freydis used the wool to make five sheep dolls, one for every member of her family. First she cut their shapes out of wadmal and stuffed them. After sewing them up, she covered them with wool. She used twigs for legs and charcoal from the hearth for eyes and noses. When the sheep were finished, she poked a bone needle through the heart of each one and locked them away in the tool shed against the day when she could hang them in Hordis's doorway. Again she used Gorm to help her, bidding him tell her when he saw Hordis leave the fells and come down to Gardar.

Three days went by before Gorm came to Freydis with the news that he had sighted Hordis hobbling down the slope to Gardar. Freydis lost no time in fetching the sheep dolls and a ball of yarn and going up to the fells. She knew Hordis's hut by sight from a distance. Close up Freydis saw the hut was little more than a pile of rocks with a skin flap over an opening. It looked more like a fox burrow than a house. This was not the place for Freydis to hang her dolls. She noticed Hordis's sheep, twenty-five in all, inside the stone pen. Across the opening was an alder wood gate. Freydis tied the sheep dolls to the inside of the gate where they would escape notice at least for a time. Then she left as quickly as she had come.

Thorvard returned from Northsetur. Once again sealing had gone poorly, but he had brought back a large quantity of whale oil. Walrus hunting had not gone well either, the large herds having moved somewhere else, but he had managed to bring back the skins of twenty walrus, which would be cut and braided into rope. The ivory was set aside for trade. Freydis thought the poor hunting worked in her favour, since it further convinced Thorvard of the

importance of the Vinland voyage. Thorvard seemed to
think this himself, for he set to work straight away making
ship rope. When this was done, he went to see the
Egilssons and stayed for several days.

Summer came. There were long shining days when the
sun opened the mountains so completely that there were
no shadows to speak of except those cast by passing
clouds. As far back as folk could remember Summer had
brought them this vast open light. The air was warm and
clear. The fields had never seemed greener, the water
more blue. Sometimes the gentle breeze subsided and a
northeast wind swept down from the glaciers bringing
snow and sleet, but these squalls were short lived and
blew over quickly, leaving the Gardar plain shining more
brightly than it had been before. Once again, folk came
outside and their voices could be heard echoing across
the valley.

Now that they had enough to eat, the cows were producing milk. Freydis began making cheeses both for her
children next Winter and for the Greenlanders in
Leifsbudir. Already she had several cheeses set aside for
the voyage, as well as a vat of butter. Half the milk went
into butter and cheese to take to Leifsbudir, the rest was
being used by her family now.

One day Thorvard's sister Inga came up to Freydis
when she was inspecting the stone walls of Thorvard's
home field, looking for places that needed mending. This
was a task Thorvard should have seen to long ago, but he
always had something else he preferred to do. Today he
was hunting hares and birds. In some ways Inga looked
like a shorter, rounder version of Thorvard, being dark
haired and seven months gone with child. She had heavy
eyelids and a droopy mouth that made her appear swollen
and backward. This was misleading for Inga was clever
and cunning in all she did. Inga waited until Freydis came
to that part of the wall that divided Thorvard's field from
Guttorm's. Then she said, "It seems you have caused
Hordis Boldolfsdottir some mischief."

Freydis feigned indifference to this news by reaching down and filling two holes with stones.

"I'm told five of her sheep have fallen on misfortune," Inga continued.

"Sheep are always falling on misfortune," Freydis said. She bent over again to hide her smile. The spell had worked; she had weakened the power of Hordis's curse.

"One of them fell into the crag pool and drowned. A fox got one. Three wandered off and ate something that bloated them and they died."

"It's no surprise to me that Hordis's sheep have stumbled on bad Luck," Freydis said, "since the old witch is continually heaping bad Luck on other folk."

"That may be," Inga said. "But I think the loss of her sheep means there's another witch hereabouts." She looked across the fields at a flock of crows as if one of them might be a witch. "*It takes a witch to curse a witch*," she chanted and walked away.

Freydis knew that Inga couldn't care less about Hordis or her sheep. What she cared about was getting hold of as much of her brother's field as she could, especially the turf bed and ore bog at the bottom end. It suited Inga that Freydis and Thorvard were going to Vinland for a year, since their absence cleared the way for her to grab Thorvard's land. It was more than likely that Inga had put Hordis up to the curse, hoping Freydis and Thorvard and their children would fall on misfortune in Vinland, clearing the way for Inga and Guttorm to take over Thorvard's home field. Freydis was convinced that the reason Inga knew about Hordis's sheep was because she had bribed the witch to curse her. Otherwise she would have been ignorant of the outcome of Freydis's curse since like other folk she had little to do with Hordis. Inga lacked the power to curse others herself, which was why she used someone like Hordis to get her way. The curse doubled the importance of Freydis's children remaining in Gardar. Freydis had already arranged with Leif that if she and Thorvard failed to return, their home field would be farmed by a tenant of Leif's choice until Thorlak was old enough to take it over.

Freydis finished inspecting the stone wall and set Kalf and Orn to work mending the holes. Then she poured herself a bowl of sour milk, and taking the milking stool outside, she sat and watched two of her children. Asny was sleeping inside the hut but Thorlak and Signy were playing tag among the cattle. Summer was treating Freydis's children kindly, rounding their cheeks and bellies, ripening their skin a reddish brown. The sheep and cattle were fattening up.

Fat, too, were the sacks and bags of whale blubber inside the storage hut. Freydis's voyage provisions were increasing daily as Thorvard brought in more game, adding to the supply of deer meat, sea trout, cod and salmon already in store. Freydis drank her milk and regarded the steading with satisfaction. Then she looked up the sloping hillside, at the campion and speedwell growing there. When she was sitting outside like this, looking at the wide plain of Gardar with its green fields sloping down to the calm blue fjord, Freydis told herself she had no wish to see Vinland since Greenland was so well endowed in Summer. This contentment was short lived. Freydis would turn and see the small hut where she lived and be reminded that she deserved something better. She would see Einar's long house behind hers, four rooms built with posts and beams, and remember the first Winter of her marriage when Thorvard had burnt the dowry intended to make a house. Freydis had only to remember this and her resolve to leave Gardar and go to Vinland would harden. As Eirik the Red's daughter, she was entitled to live in a house. Freydis knew she was more determined and ambitious than was considered seemly for a farmer's wife. Thorvard's kin often told her she was arrogant and greedy.

It was her father who taught Freydis to be ambitious, to expect more than what was at hand. He taught her to insist on what was rightfully hers. He also said she should keep close watch on those who would go out of their way to cheat her then turn on her when she demanded recompense, insisting they had been cheated themselves. "People will always begrudge you having more than they do," her father had said, "which is why ambitious folk are often disliked and others look for ways to bring them down."

* * *

Eirik was banished from Haukadale in Iceland after killing Eyjolf Saur and Hrafn the Dueller after they killed Eirik's thralls. Eirik went to Breidafjord and settled on Oxen Island at Eirikstead. He lent his bench boards to Thorgest of Breidabolstead, but when he asked for them back, they were not returned, which gave rise to quarrelling and fights between them.

Eirik was sentenced to outlawry at the Thorness Assembly. He prepared his ship for a sea voyage. When he was ready, his friends accompanied him out beyond the islands. Eirik told them he was going to search for the land that Gunnbjorn, the son of Ulf Crow, had sighted when he was driven off course during a storm.

* * *

Freydis knew her father had come to Greenland as a result of stolen bench boards; he had told her the story himself. The bench boards had been part of the high seat which had belonged to Eirik's father, Thorvald, and before that to Ulf, son of Oxen Thorir. Freydis's father never did get them back. After Eirik was settled in Brattahlid for some years, he traded into some Norwegian oak which he had shaped into new bench boards. Up until then he had been using crude panels cut from flotsam. It was these he had thrown into Eiriksfjord when he first came to Greenland, following their passage through the water, knowing they would beach themselves in a place favoured with driftwood. Brattahlid had been chosen for that reason, and because it had its back to the fells.

When Freydis lived in the big house in Brattahlid she had often polished the bench boards. Eirik's face was carved on one, Thjodhild's on the other, as a way of marking their high seats. Now Leif owned them. One day Freydis intended to have bench boards and high seats when she had a proper house and wood brought from Vinland. Thorvard did not care for such things, but Freydis thought Thorlak might like to sit on a high seat one day and lord it over others.

When Freydis thought of the riches she would bring back from Vinland, Hordis's curse became nothing more than a minor irritation, an insect bite, perhaps, or a rash. The curse had shown Inga's malice more than anything else. Inga disliked having her brother married to the daughter of Eirik the Red and looked for ways to keep Freydis down. Eirik had a far greater reputation than Einar, which Inga resented; she was used to arranging matters in Gardar to suit herself. As Eirik the Red's daughter and half-sister to Leif, Freydis did not have to bend to Inga's will. Soon she would be going to Vinland, that country of dreams and Luck. It was true she had come down in the world since marrying Thorvard, but her fate was about to change.

When Nagli Asgrimsson was making various tools for the voyage, Freydis had bid him forge her an iron amulet to wear around her neck. The amulet in the shape of Thor's hammer was intended to replace the one her father had given her which had become mislaid. Freydis thought her Luck had worsened as a result. Now that the loss had been righted, her Luck would turn. As she sat on the stool watching her children, Freydis lifted the hammer from her neck and held it in her hand. Inside her head she urged Thor to be useful. She challenged him to bring her Luck. She told Thor about the goods she expected to bring back from Vinland. The old gods didn't make unreasonable demands of folk like the tame god called Christ who urged his followers to set aside their worldly goods and follow him. The old gods were far too clever to ask folk to give up their goods, such as they were. They knew their own Luck improved if they helped folk who had the wit to help themselves.

T HE NAME OF THE ICELANDERS' SHIP WAS *SIGURD'S STEED*.
When the Egilssons came to Greenland, folk
assumed the brothers were co-owners of the ship.
Only Leif, Freydis and Thorvard and a few others
knew Finnbogi was the owner. Once *Sigurd's Steed*
was put to water, however, and preparations for the voyage were under way, it became clear to all the Greenlanders watching that only one of the brothers owned the
ship: it was Finnbogi who sat at the steering oar and told
the Icelanders what to do. While Helgi helped with preparations and loading, Finnbogi remained on his bench in
the bow and watched to make sure nothing scraped or
gouged the strakes. The ship was a storfembøring, an
ocean-going vessel, swift under sail but when required,
able to manoeuvre in ice.

The previous Summer the Egilssons had brought a
quantity of goods to Greenland from Norway; salt, barley,
iron and honey, but these had been traded away to provide themselves with food through Winter and later to provision the ship. *Sigurd's Steed* was now loaded for the voyage. Aboard were bundles of dried fish and meat as well
as berries and cheese and barrels of fresh water. There
were weapons, woodworking tools and chests. With rela-
tively few goods, the ship had more than the usual number of ballast stones below deck. Finnbogi preferred to
travel to Vinland with a half-empty hold, since it meant he
would have more cargo space on his return. Finnbogi's

crew were well used to loading *Sigurd's Steed* from having traded in so many ports. As a result their ship was easily readied. It was now anchored in Einarsfjord, waiting until the Greenlanders had finished loading and were ready to sail.

The *Vinland* was far from ready. Freydis had managed the arrangements ashore but there was nothing she could do to speed up the loading and stowing. She was relying on Evyind Hromundsson to handle those tasks. Freydis sat on the shore while Evyind oversaw the placement of goods aboard the *Vinland*. Her husband Thorvard was in charge of transferring the goods from shore to ship in prams. Bundles of food and clothing, sleeping bags and bales of wool were piled on the beach.

The night before, ballast stones had been put in the hold along with iron goods and hunting gear to give it weight. This storage space, which was fore and aft, had been covered with planking. The hold in midship was left open for storing water barrels and animal pens. Freydis was taking a cow, four goats, two pigs and eight yearling sheep to Leifsbudir.

Standing at the helm beside his brother Helgi, watching the cow being loaded onto the *Vinland*, Finnbogi remarked that he hoped the Greenlanders were better at sailing than they were at getting under way. "They're working against each other," he said. "Each man is going in a different direction at once."

Helgi was amused by the loading of the cow. The cow, suspended in a leather sling, bawling from one end and pissing from the other, was being lifted aboard the ship from a pram. The sling was too small for the cow which meant that when the men pulled the ropes in front tighter than those in the back, the cow was in danger of sliding out the end. When the back ropes were tightened, the cow jerked so far forward that she had to be supported by long rowing oars to prevent her from falling into the water.

Helgi laughed. "If that cow manages to give any milk, it will already be churned into butter."

Finnbogi was far from amused. "At this rate we'll still be here tomorrow. They have yet to load the sheep and goats, not to mention the pigs."

The Egilssons had no livestock with them. Once they had worked on their father's farm in the Eastfirths but that had been long ago. Now that they were traders, farming was beneath them. In any event they had never been in a situation where livestock farming was required, since they always kept enough trade goods to obtain whatever food they needed. Moreover they were at sea so much there was no shortage of fish.

"We should never have agreed to make the crossing with the Greenlanders," Finnbogi complained.

"You were there when we made the arrangements," Helgi said. "As I recall, you didn't open your mouth."

"It must have been Freydis Eiriksdottir's idea."

"It was. She was making sure the arrangements between us were fair: she suggested we take thirty able-bodied men aboard each ship, split the profits evenly, trade rope and sailcloth in exchange for a ship. The request that we sail together was made in the same way."

"By someone ignorant of the sea."

"At the time, granting her request seemed an easy way to please the woman who will be playing our host."

"I don't regard Freydis as my host," Finnbogi said. "I'm not going to Leifsbudir to be at the beck and call of Freydis Eiriksdottir. If I wanted to be under the thumb of a woman, I would be at home with my wife."

Helgi's attention was taken by the cow. Bawling with terror the animal slid backward again. In adjusting the sling the Greenlanders let out too much rope. The sling jerked lower. The cow's back hooves touched the water.

This was too much for Finnbogi. It was late Summer. They had already missed several days of good sailing weather because of the Greenlanders' delays. Soon the season of late Summer storms would be here.

"We're leaving," he said. "The winds couldn't be better than they are right now. If we wait any longer they may turn against us." He ordered two rowers into the pram and went over the side.

Helgi watched his brother being rowed ashore to where Freydis was sitting with the Norwegian while her children played on the bundles and bales piled on shore. Now that the shipbuilder had recovered from his malaise, he couldn't get enough of women. He sat on the grass beside Freydis. They were watching the cow and laughing. Apparently Freydis was as amused as Hauk by the way her husband was managing the cow, for she kept showing her teeth and shaking her head. This was a different woman from the one Helgi remembered coming to see Finnbogi and him just before Winter. That woman had been serious, almost grim. Tough minded, he had thought at the time. Helgi was encouraged to see a lighter side of Freydis: he thought it might prove useful one day.

Helgi saw Finnbogi get out of the pram and come up to Freydis. Freydis stood up to face his brother. She and Finnbogi exchanged a few words. They didn't talk long. Helgi saw Freydis point to the pens ashore where other livestock waited. He saw his brother nod his head up and down. Finnbogi spoke to Hauk who got up, reluctantly, it seemed. The three spoke together. Then Hauk leaned forward and put his lips on Freydis's mouth. Helgi glanced at Freydis's husband but he was too busy with the cow to notice. Finnbogi and Hauk got in the pram and were rowed toward *Sigurd's Steed*.

"How did it go?" Helgi said, though he already knew the answer, or Hauk wouldn't be coming alongside.

Finnbogi grinned, showing a blackened tooth, the result of a rake hitting him on the chin when he was a boy.

"Tell the men to haul anchor," he said.

After he climbed aboard, Finnbogi told his brother that from here on in, he should make the arrangements with Freydis.

"Did she give you any trouble?"

"On the contrary, she said she was about to suggest we go ahead, that there was no point in us waiting."

Finnbogi squeezed the buttocks of a concubine who had come to his side. "You can always count on a woman to change her mind." His ambatt, a small round-faced woman named Olina, smiled and pushed against him so her breast touched his arm. Finnbogi shook her off and took his place at the steering oar. The rowers found their seats. On an ocean-going vessel like *Sigurd's Steed*, rowers sat not on benches but on sea chests to make better use of space.

The ship travelled the length of Einarsfjord before passing anything more than an occasional drifting pan. But when they entered the archipelago, the water became thick with ice.

It was a warm day in Greenland. The sun's heat melted the glaciers calving at the head of the fjords. Although the glaciers were far away, Helgi heard the ice roar through the thin Greenland air as it sheared off and thundered into the fjord. The sun had been shining strongly for several days. As a result, so much ice had entered the water that the ship had to be rowed past bergs larger than itself.

Though Finnbogi never admitted his brother was the better navigator, he always used Helgi as ice pilot on the grounds that he himself couldn't be in two places at once. Helgi was a natural sailor; had his fate been different, he might have gained the same reputation as Leif. Helgi stood in the prow and watched for ice that could damage the keel. Working together as pilot and helmsman, the Egilsson brothers guided the rowers through the worst of the ice. Only when the water opened up and the bergs were spaced far enough apart for safe passage did Helgi relax his vigilance and enjoy the splendour and beauty of the fjord. The sun shone through the clear Greenland air and onto the glistening ice and the flat shining water. Without wind the water was exceptionally still, reflecting everything above. Clouds were as white on the water as they were overhead. The ice dazzled so brilliantly it hurt Helgi's eyes. Well travelled though he was, Helgi could still be struck with wonder. He began to see all kinds of things in the ice: peaked mountains girded with high cliffs, hollow caves and swooping valleys, sleek ships with blue-green keels. These were the larger bergs. In smaller bergs he saw animals of various kinds: a winged horse, a swan, a fish. Some of these bergs were as clear and blue as sapphire, others as green as Roman glass.

"We are surrounded by floating jewels," Helgi told his ambatt. As was her way, Finna stood quietly at his side while he was watching the ice. This was the first Helgi had spoken to her, though Finna had been beside him for some time.

When *Sigurd's Steed* was rowed free of most of the ice, the sail was raised and Finnbogi manoeuvred the ship so that it would ride before the wind. They had reached the current that would take them North then West. They sailed well out from land to avoid the ice crowding the shore. The larger bergs were travelling the same current as the ship, but in clear weather they were easy to avoid. By now it was well into evening, but still so light that the Icelanders continued on, sailing through the night. By morning they were well out to sea.

It was lucky for them that they left before the Greenlanders finished loading. By leaving when they did, the Icelanders took advantage of the winds that would assure them of a lucky crossing. If they were as fortunate as Leif, they might even make the journey in fourteen days. The Greenlanders were in for a far different fate.

*   *   *

Now that I am undertaking a momentous voyage, I
find myself contemplating the nature of Luck. The
priest Geirmund bids me banish all thought of Chance
and Luck and put my fate in the Lord's hands instead.
But I have done that all my life and am no luckier for
it. On Iona Brother Ambrose used to admonish me to
work hard with my quill if I wanted to better my fate.
He claimed Luck required skill, that it could be
wrought by a man's hand much in the way a letter
takes shape. He used to say that just as the skins of
sheep could be transformed into the Holy Book, so

*too could a man's life be changed through diligence
and skill. I cannot hold this view, since I have always
worked hard and my Luck has not prospered as a
result.*

*Brother Ambrose rejected all arguments that Luck
was a birthright, that a man was either born with Luck
or not as the case may be, but I cannot help thinking
that my Luck would have been improved if I had been
sired by a different man and birthed by a different
woman. I was conceived while my mother was married to another and have been paying for her sin ever
since. Later my mother married my father and bore
him more sons. Because they were born from a sanctified union my brothers are likely enjoying better Luck
than I.*

*I have often observed how the Luck of brothers
varies. Consider Leif Eiriksson and his brothers. Leif
was lucky in every aspect of his life whereas his brothers met with unfortunate fates. It has been difficult for
me to understand how Leif came by his Luck since he
had a scoundrel for a father. It is certain that he did
not come by his fortunate qualities through Eirik the
Red.*

*Folk will sometimes say that the good character of
a man can be attributed to the influence of a woman.
I have always questioned the truth of this, for it seems
to me the character of a man is better served being
influenced by other men, unless they are men like
Eirik the Red. But in Leif's case and Leif's case only I
am forced to concede that his fine qualities came to
him through his mother. Thjodhild is a woman of high
moral standards, a woman who follows the Righteous
Path. Geirmund told me that after she had been converted, Thjodhild refused to welcome Eirik into her
bed until he renounced his pagan ways and accepted
Christ. By showing piety and devotion Thjodhild was
able to offset her husband's heathen ways. It was
through her good example that Leif Eiriksson came by
his outstanding qualities of manliness and Luck.*

*As for my own Luck, if I survive this voyage it
should have a chance to improve. Leif has told me
that if I satisfy the demands made by Freydis and her
husband in Leifsbudir, I shall return to Greenland a
free man. Since Heaven's Lord has already interceded
with Leif on my behalf, it is now up to me to improve
my Luck further by working hard.*

* * *

Ulfar wrapped his writing materials in oiled sheepskin and
placed them carefully inside his sleeping bag on top of his
woodworking tools. He waited until the last of the animals
were loaded onto the *Vinland* and the bundles and bales
were stowed aboard. While the crew were rounding up
their gear, Ulfar picked up his belongings which included
extra rolls of vellum, and put them into a pram being
rowed to the ship by Kalf and Orn. The pram contained
several bales of wool, but there was enough space for
Ulfar and his gear. As soon as the pram reached the
Vinland, Ulfar went aboard with his bag and stowed it in
the prow of the ship, hard against the bow. He knew from
observing the Greenland crew that he would probably be
the smallest man aboard which meant he could fit into the
bow stem, the smallest area aboard the ship. His years as
a galley slave with Harek Eel Swallower had taught him
that the forefoot offered the best chance aboard for sleeping undisturbed. It also provided a place between the
strakes and planking where he could stow his vellums and
tools. With the number of people aboard, it would be easy
for his few possessions to fall into careless hands.

For the first time in fourteen years Ulfar could look forward to having a life of his own. The proposition Leif had
put to Ulfar was this: if Ulfar served Freydis and Thorvard
in Leifsbudir for a year, upon his return he would be freed.
As Leif explained it, to make the expedition to Vinland
more successful, his half-sister needed a man with Ulfar's
skills, someone who knew how to turn wood into valuable
trade goods. The Greenlanders also needed someone in
their crew who knew how to repair a ship.

At first Ulfar had been reluctant to accept Leif's offer. Leif Eiriksson was a benevolent and fair-minded master. To Ulfar's knowledge none of Leif's thralls had ever been mistreated or tortured. They had never been roused from their beds to cut hay in moonlight or steal from a neighbour or injure his stock. Leif took no part in vengeful intrigues favoured by Norsemen. He provided well for his thralls. They slept on alder twigs covered with skins, two to a hut. When game was in good supply they never lacked meat. If the weather grew bitter and fuel was scarce, the thralls were invited to share Leif's hearth. Ulfar had never been in the position of providing for himself, except when he had fought for scraps Harek Eel Swallower had thrown his slaves. Ulfar knew better than anyone that being a free man in Greenland might be worse than being in thrall to Leif. Without land of his own, he would have no place to build himself a hut. Without timber it would be difficult for him to earn a living as a woodworker, and ignorant farmers had no use for a scribe. As long as Ulfar was trapped on a northern island, Leif's offer of manumission wasn't much use. If he survived this expedition, Ulfar would eventually have to find a way to leave Greenland.

Ulfar wasn't looking forward to working for Freydis Eiriksdottir. From what he had seen of her, Ulfar thought Freydis ambitious and overbold. Her behaviour was unseemly for a woman. On Iona men had been separated from women so they wouldn't be contaminated by women's thoughts. Ulfar's mother had lived across the water with the cows on Eilean Nam Bara. At the age of three Ulfar had been taken from the Women's Island to Iona, where he was raised by Culdean monks. Ulfar had discussed his reservations about Freydis with Geirmund Gunnfard. As a man of Christ, Geirmund could understand Ulfar's reluctance to take orders from a woman. Nevertheless he advised him to make the voyage. "By going to Leifsbudir, you have more to gain than to lose," the priest had said. "As for Freydis Eiriksdottir, you shouldn't miss the opportunity of bettering your Luck on account of her, for to do so would be to acknowledge a woman's influence over you, which would be most unwise, especially in view of her heathenness."

The rest of the crew came aboard with their belongings. Fortunately no one tried to take Ulfar's place. Freydis Eiriksdottir brought her children to the ship and showed them around. Geirmund Gunnfard and Leif Eiriksson boarded. Ulfar watched as the priest, his dark beard blowing in the breeze, unplugged the vial he was carrying and sprinkled holy water on the ship: the reefed sail and rigging, the chests and barrels, the planking and strakes. When this had been done, Geirmund spoke to the crew. He said he preferred to send Christians not heathens to Leifsbudir and asked if anyone aboard wished to be prime signed. Eight men stepped forward. As they knelt at his feet Geirmund dipped a finger into the holy water and made a sign of the cross on their foreheads. Because Ulfar had never seen these men in Thjodhild's church, he took them to be from farms where Geirmund had never been. Although Geirmund visited various steadings, Greenlanders lived so far from each other that most of them had yet receive the Holy Word.

"Heaven's Lord, bless these Christian men and their ship. Guide them over the rough waters and return them safely to us. Help them choose the path of Righteousness and avoid the meaner way. Teach them to turn their cheeks toward Gentleness and to look kindly upon one another. Lead them from the path of Heathenness and set their feet to follow Yours."

Ulfar had never heard so fine a benediction even from the Culdees. He thought the prayer showed Geirmund's restraint; more than once the priest had told him he found the Greenlanders stubborn and intractable folk. Ulfar thought Geirmund was using great patience and gentleness in leading these rough farmers to Christ. Following the prayer Geirmund asked Ulfar to come out of his corner and stand close by him. Geirmund then reminded the others that they would be without the benefit of a priest for some time and announced that he was entrusting Ulfar, a devout Christian, with the vial of holy water since

circumstances in Leifsbudir were bound to require the rituals of the Christian faith.

"Guard the vial carefully," Geirmund told Ulfar. "I'm
counting on you." Ulfar took the vial to his corner and put
it with his vellums.

After the ceremony Geirmund and Leif talked and
joked with the crew. These were large, red-faced fellows,
most of them twice Ulfar's size. Ulfar waited patiently for
Leif to speak to him, but Leif scarcely looked his way.
With so many men clamouring for Leif's attention, Ulfar
was easy to overlook. He reminded himself that he had
already enjoyed more of Leif's company than most men
aboard. And he knew how to guard his pride. None of
these farmers showed restraint. They seemed unable to
prevent themselves from reaching out to detain Leif,
plucking his shirt and leggings in an effort to get his attention.

Although the voyage was an adventure none of them
wanted to miss, the Greenlanders knew its outcome
depended largely on Luck; they would have preferred Leif,
not his half-sister, to lead the expedition, since he had
already proven his Luck by taking his crew to Vinland and
returning unscathed. Leif appeared to enjoy the crew's
admiration, for he allowed himself to be detained and
made no effort to go ashore, though by now it was early
evening.

Ulfar sat in his corner and waited. Even in repose Leif's
thrall had watchful eyes. His face was dun coloured, his
nose spotted from the sun. The narrowness of his face
was offset somewhat by the flatness of his head. He was
clean shaven and had no hair to speak of except a shag of
grey encircling his tonsure. The baldness belied his years
which were thirty-one. In this as in other respects Ulfar
was unlike most of the crew, who were bearded and hairy
and so fair their skin was burnt red rather than brown.

Ulfar watched Leif move around the ship. It was clear
the gödi was reluctant to see it leave without him. Leif
would no sooner begin talking to a member of the crew
than he would remember something he wanted to tell

Evyind. He would go back to the helmsman and engage him in another conversation. This happened several times over. In the meantime Freydis had taken her children ashore and returned. Geirmund had also left. At last Leif was ready to leave and Ulfar's patience was rewarded. Leif called out to him, wishing him Luck. The rowers sat on their chests, set their oars and the Greenlanders' journey began. As the *Vinland* moved down the fjord, the crew waved farewell to those left behind, especially the maidens and mothers standing on shore.

Freydis sat on the bales of wool and waved to her children. Even after Halla Eldgrimsdottir led them away, Freydis continued to sit where she could be plainly seen by her children should any of them turn and look. She didn't want them to see her suddenly disappear and thought if they saw her being rowed slowly away they would find it easier to believe that she would return one day. Before leaving Gardar, she had told her two oldest children to remember that when folk travelled far enough into the distance, they couldn't be seen by those on shore, but that didn't mean they had disappeared. Though Asny knew this already from having watched her father go away so many times, Freydis had never left her children and she wanted them to keep her words firmly in mind. Before her departure, Thorlak and Signy had wanted their mother to tell them what Vinland was like. The most Freydis had been able to say was that there were houses and forests. Since she had never seen forests, she was at a loss to say more. Instead she tried to interest her children in the goods she would bring back. She described the wooden toys they would have, the tables and sleeping benches. "We'll have a large house and a ship of our own," she told them. "Just you wait. One day we'll take our ship to Norway."

Neither of her daughters turned to look as Freydis moved away. Thorlak turned and waved but only once. Freydis was encouraged by the fact that her children could walk away without looking behind. She took it as a sign that they would get along very well without her and that

fact allowed her to think of enjoying herself. As long as
she knew her children would be properly cared for in her
absence, Freydis didn't expect to miss them much. She
knew there was hard work ahead, but she intended to
make the most of a new kind of freedom before she came
back.

Freydis had never been on a ship. She had been in
and out of boats all her life but she had never been to
sea. She thought it pleasant to sit on something large and
float through the smooth water of the fjord, looking at hills
on either side. The sun was still high and bright, which
made the snow gleam on the mountains. A cooling breeze
from the glaciers blew away the damp hair sticking to her
cheeks. Freydis had packed her snood; she had no intention of wearing a white linen cap during the voyage. If the
air turned cold cold she would pull a cloak up over her
head. Freydis had also packed her robe and shift and was
wearing a tunic and shapeless doeskin breeches. It was
foolish for a woman to wear a robe and shift in close quarters with so many men. By dressing like a man Freydis
liked to think the crew would forget she was a woman.
Because of the breeches there was no need to wear the
iron belt. In any case during the voyage she and Thorvard
would be sleeping apart. Freydis had arranged a sleeping
hollow for herself between bales of wool near the edge of
the bow platform; Thorvard was further back, near the
stern.

As the ship left Einarsfjord and approached the archipelago, the breeze stiffened. Freydis slipped into the hollow. The sides were well above her head, which protected
her from the wind. Thorvard was bedded down beside the
men he knew best. These were Balki and Gisli, otherwise
known as the Gardar twins; the sons of their mother's kin:
Hogni, Oddmar and Bragi were also there. The other
Einarsfjord hunters were Bodvar and Falgeir; Flosi, Lodholt
and Avang were from Eiriksfjord. Thorvard and Evyind had
assembled the crew, Thorvard choosing his fellow hunters
and Evyind selecting men from Vatnahverfi, where he
lived. Vatnahverfi was an area of lakes and farms south of

Einarsfjord. Ozur and his son Thrand were also from
Vatnahverfi, as were Ivar and Uni. These men sat on the
stern platform near Evyind, where they could confer with
each other about landfalls, currents and winds.

The men aboard were mainly second and third sons,
chosen for their skill and strength. Greenland farmers produced more sons than they had grazing land. Since the
oldest son inherited the land, younger sons had to look
further afield for their livelihood. Most of them were by
now one or two years over twenty and knew the opportunity of going to Leifsbudir was unlikely to come their way
again. Freydis's step-brother, Bolli, was also aboard, sitting
by himself near the water barrels. He had come from
Dyrnes to Gardar early in the Summer, asking to be included in the crew. Thorvard had been reluctant to bring Bolli
but Freydis had insisted. Bolli had often protected her
when they were children in Dyrnes. She thought he would
be useful to have on hand since he had always been loyal
to her no matter what she did.

"There's something about your step-brother I dislike,"
Thorvard had said when they were discussing Bolli. "I
would prefer he not come along. He's the sort of man who
goes out of his way to find trouble."

"There's much about your sister Inga I dislike. Yet I
must see her every day," Freydis had retorted, though she
knew Bolli was more inclined than most to find trouble.

"It bothers me that we would turn away a better man
in order to make a place for your step-brother," Thorvard
had said. "There are several good men I would like to take
with us if we could."

"How many do you have in mind?"

"Four or five at least."

"If you can get them aboard, why not take them?"

"I thought you made an agreement with the Egilssons
that we would take thirty able-bodied men and no more."

"Yes, but I've come to regret it since. When you consider the Icelanders have five female thralls, their total number is thirty-five."

"You're taking Groa."

"She hardly counts, not being able bodied," Freydis said. Then pressing her point she added, "It seems to me we have every right to take five extra men to counter the Icelanders' women. After all the Icelanders will be our guests in Leifsbudir, not the other way around. Considering the fact that they'll be using our buildings, why shouldn't we take extra men if we choose?"

Thorvard told her he was reluctant to break an agreement with men he liked.

"You didn't make the agreement, I did. I've decided that taking extra men would be useful when it comes to sailing two ships back. Leif took thirty-five men. As it now stands the numbers are unfairly weighted in favour of the Icelanders. If we count their women and I think we should, we have only thirty people to their thirty-five. I think we'll get along better if we're evenly matched." On this occasion Freydis found it convenient to overlook herself.

Thorvard thought they should discuss the matter with Evyind. "I'll go along with whatever Evyind decides," he said. This was something Thorvard would regret saying later on since Evyind, using the same reasons as Freydis, agreed they should take five extra men.

When Thorvard heard that Evyind had agreed to take thirty-five, he told the helmsman he wouldn't be responsible for smuggling the extra men aboard. "I wash my hands of the matter," he said.

The night before the *Vinland*'s departure when the crew were gathered with their families ashore one last time, Evyind had smuggled the extra men aboard the ship and hidden them among the weapons and tools. These men were so eager to go on the voyage they were prepared to endure the discomfort of lying, for days if need be, beneath the planking without food and with only a small pouch of water among them to drink. Nor were they inclined to cross Evyind's orders. Evyind was burly and grey bearded. Three years this side of forty, he was the oldest man aboard, which gave him authority the young farmers lacked. They were to lie there, Evyind had told the stowaways, until the ship was well out to sea, for if the Icelanders caught sight of extra men aboard the *Vinland* while they were close to land, they might demand the men be put ashore.

It was fortunate for the hidden men that *Sigurd's Steed* left before the *Vinland*, since it meant that as soon as the ship had cleared Einarsfjord and reached the archipelago, the planking was lifted and they were freed. The stowaways were sore and stiff jointed from having lain so long against the strakes and ribs. As soon as they appeared above deck, Freydis bid Groa smear dried fish with butter and give it to the men along with cheese. Shortly after this the crew settled into their sleeping bags.

* * *

I had just begun to record the nature of the Vinland's *departure for my own satisfaction, thinking to do so while the water was calm and the sky was light enough for me to write, when a distressing incident occurred. When I first observed some of the crew removing bales and bundles and sleeping bags piled on the aft platform, I paid them no mind. I became alarmed only when I saw planks being lifted, disturbing what had been carefully stowed. I soon saw the cause. One by one, five stowaways crawled from the hold where they had been concealed.*

I remember being told about the agreement between the Icelanders and Greenlanders. As I recall, each crew was to take thirty able-bodied men on each ship. I have just counted the number of folk aboard the Vinland *and there are thirty-five men, excluding Freydis Eiriksdottir and her thrall Groa. It is clear Freydis is part of this deceit, for she showed no surprise when the stowaways appeared and went so far as to offer them food. Most of the crew however seem as surprised as I.*

One of the stowaways, who is short and slightly
built for a Norseman, has noticed the advantages of
my corner and has placed his sleeping bag so near
mine that I am now forced to draw up my knees. The
crowding makes continuing this record impossible.
Twice the stowaway has pushed hard against my feet,
trying to force me backwards. As a result I have spoilt
the writing with unwanted ink. I shall therefore dry
what I have recorded, which is but a small portion of
what I intended to write.

*　*　*

The Greenlanders had only sun to guide them; the sky was too pale for starlight even halfway through the night. This far North the sun was never far away. As long as the sky was clear, sailing from East to West was a straightforward matter. Like the Icelanders the Greenlanders were following the current North, sailing well away from land to avoid the worst of the ice yet close enough to follow the shore. This part of the voyage was familiar to hunters like Thorvard who travelled this route to Northsetur every year. Once the ship was well into the archipelago and they had passed Hreinsey where Greenlanders regularly came for deer and soapstone, Evyind ordered the sail raised. This was the same square sail Leif's mother had made for his voyage fourteen years earlier. Thjodhild had woven lengths of grey and red wadmal and sewn them together to make a sail with vertical stripes. The pine mast creaked when the wind pulled the rigging taut. The strakes also creaked. Below deck the ballast stones knocked together, shifting slightly with the movement of the ship. These noises were as gentle and soothing as murmurs and soon put the crew to sleep. Sometimes the swish of water against the bow stem or the touch of sea spit flung onto a cheek brought a smile to a sleeper's face. Asleep or awake all Norsemen at some time or other dreamt of being carried over the sea in the arms of a ship. The *Vinland* sailed on. The archipelago disappeared. On the starboard ice mountains glowed in the eerie half-light. Someone began to sing.

The keel path leads us North
To the land of the white bear
And the prized unihorn.
Salt spray wipes our cheeks;
Day star brightens our eyes.
Sea deer leaps the waves,
Antlers creak in the wind.
Lucky the man who rides
A stag as noble as ours.

Lying in her hollow Freydis listened to the singing. The voice was thin and sweet for a man. Freydis didn't know who the voice belonged to, but she thought it was very likely one of the men Evyind had chosen, the man named Asmund. She remembered being told there was a skald aboard. Of course anyone who had a way with words could call himself a skald, reciting verses he had heard before or speaking whatever came into his head. The man sang the verse again, but Freydis didn't like the poem any better the second time. She preferred stories to verses. Stories were about folk as they really were, whereas verses were self-praising and depended over much on the particular view of the poet. For instance, in her mind the ship wasn't a stag. It was more like a bird, an enormous sea bird whose wings came together to make a sail. She was flying over the sea on the back of a giant bird, a bird that never went beneath the sea but stayed well above the waves, where it was safe. Monsters lived below the waves, sea serpents and underwater trolls, ugly folk who long ago had chewed her mother's bones and tossed them aside. One of her mother's teeth might be down there or a fingerbone, a sliver of white the Queen of the Underworld, Hel, used to pick her teeth. The Kingdom of the Dead was a dark slimy place where monsters tortured their victims and inflicted unspeakable wounds on their prey. According to Freydis's father, Hel was a rotting corpse, half-black, half-white who fed on the dead. Maybe Eirik had not expected her to believe pagan stories, since he had often claimed not to believe them himself. Even so, as long as he lived, he had made pagan sacrifices to Thor, usually in the fells but sometimes in the field behind the cattle byre. Thjodhild refused to allow pagan sacrifices inside her house. Nor, after her conversion to Christ, had she allowed the telling of pagan stories. Instead Eirik told them to Freydis whenever he took her to visit other folk. Eirik's favourite stories were about the god Thor.

"Thor was a huge red-headed man who, much like myself, had a large appetite for life. He carried a hammer named Mjollnir which gave him power. One day Thor disguised himself as a young man and set out to capture the sea serpent who lay curled around the depths of the Outer Ocean. Thor offered to go fishing for the sea serpent with a giant named Hymir. Not knowing Thor was a god, Hymir agreed. Like all giants Hymir was lazy and got others to do his work. He bade Thor fetch bait while he himself lolled in the pram. Thor went off and came back a while later with an ox head for bait. They set off in the pram with Thor at the oars. Thor rowed so fast that in no time they came to that part of the world where the sea serpent lived. The sea serpent took the bait as soon as Thor threw it over. When the sea serpent's terrible head rose from the waves, Thor lifted his hammer to strike. Just then, Hymir, terrified at the serpent's ugly teeth, cut the line. The sea serpent fell back into the ocean. Thor killed Hymir for his foolishness. The pram sank and Thor waded back to land."

The Thor stories were old even to Freydis's father. Eirik said they had come from a time long before the priests invented Christ, when folk respected each other for their cunning and common sense. He said the old gods were not much different from men. They didn't urge folk to love their neighbours like themselves. They knew that a man couldn't live without gathering enemies here and there. The old gods didn't claim they could cure illness. Eirik was fond of saying that Thor could get a bellyache like anyone else. Her father warned Freydis about the spitefulness of gods. "Remember," he would say, "you have to stay on their good side with sacrifices and the like."

Freydis had been named after the goddess Freyja, the daughter of Njord, King of the Sea. Njord sired Freyja and her brother on his sister, Nerthus. It was Freydis's mother, not her father, who named her. Freydis thought this meant her mother must have had some connection with the sea that went back to some other time when gods and goddesses lived with ordinary folk.

Freydis's mother was Bribrau Reistsdottir. When Reist Gunnarsson brought his wife and daughter over from Iceland, Eirik the Red, who was often open handed with allies and friends, gave him land in Dyrnes at the mouth of Eiriksfjord where hill pastures were good and seals came in great numbers to the skerries offshore. Otherwise Reist would have had to go North to the Western Settlement since by then the best land in the Eastern Settlement had been claimed. Reist's wealth had many legs to stand upon. He had numerous sheep and goats as well as cattle and thralls, not to mention the goods he had left with his son in Iceland. Reist built himself a fine house in Dyrnes overlooking the sound. Bribrau was his only daughter. Folk often spoke of Bribrau's looks for she was beautiful beyond compare with sea blue eyes and oaken hair. They said the farmer who got to marry her would be lucky indeed for when she married, Bribrau would come with a dowry that included a large grazing field.

Soon after her arrival in Dyrnes, Bribrau married a young hunter named Grettir Gormsson whom she had met aboard ship during the voyage from Iceland. Early in their marriage Grettir drowned with three other men in Northsetur when the walrus they were harpooning upset their pram. Soon after Grettir's death Bribrau gave birth to a daughter. Dyrnes folk who saw the babe named Freydis couldn't help but notice that the child bore no resemblance to the dark-haired Grettir but instead was the image of Eirik the Red, for she had hair that flamed like his. These folk remarked on how often Eirik had found

excuses to visit Dyrnes. During these visits he had frequently been seen with Bribrau, which made them wonder
if the cause of Eirik's visits wasn't Reist but his daughter.
After Freydis was born, the talk around the Dyrnes hearths
often turned to how the child's conception coincided with
one of Eirik's visits. Some folk remembered that early in
his marriage when the child would have been conceived,
Grettir had left his bride to go off hunting great auks and
other sea birds. This happened to be the same month
Eirik had visited Dyrnes. Eirik the Red was therefore widely regarded as the father of Bribrau's child. No one expected Eirik to divorce Thjodhild in order to marry Grettir's
widow. Not even Eirik the Red would divorce a woman
with an ancestry that was said to go back to Norway's
kings.

Within two years of Grettir's death, Bribrau married
Illugi Arnkelsson whose wife had died the previous year
while birthing a son named Bolli. Dyrnes folk were well
pleased with this match, the women especially, for Bribrau
was the kind of woman wives preferred to see married so
that their husbands would cease looking for ways to help
her out. Illugi was well liked and respected. Though poor,
having no land or cattle to speak of, he was hard working
and would make use of Bribrau's field in a way Grettir
never had.

One day after he and Bribrau had been three years
married, Illugi's scraper slipped when he was cleaning
sheepskin and he cut his hand. Illugi wasn't a man to fuss
about himself and after binding the cut, continued on as
before. Nor did Bribrau fuss about the wound. She wasn't
accustomed to concerning herself with others' discomfort
and was undergoing a difficult pregnancy besides. By then
Freydis was five Winters old; Bolli was four. Although
younger, Bolli was larger and stronger than Freydis. He
was easily enraged and inclined to bully others. Bolli had
fits during which trolls and other monsters attacked him.
During his hallucinations children would gather round and
jeer while he flailed the empty air with his fists. Later after
the visions had gone, Bolli would beat any child who

mocked him. At four, Bolli was so large he could overpow-
er a boy twice his age.

Because Bribrau kept so much to herself, Freydis was
allowed to run free with Bolli and three brothers from a
neighbouring farm. Like them she rode ponies, set eagle
traps and skipped stones across water. Sometimes one of
the boys, never Bolli, would drag her off a pony or push
her into a stream. Once Reidar bound her hands and feet
and tied her hair to the latch of the cattle byre so that she
couldn't follow his brothers and him to the hills where
they had gone to snare birds. This didn't happen often.
The brothers soon learned that Bolli would do anything to
avenge Freydis and none of them wanted to be bitten on
the arms and legs until they bled.

Illugi Arnkelsson was an unlucky man. Not only did his
first wife die giving birth to a berserk, but he himself eventually died from a wound others might have survived. At
first the knife wound merely became swollen and shiny.
Illugi himself applied hot cloths to draw out the poison.
There were no leeches in Greenland. A healer lived in
Petursvik but that was too far away to see what results she
might achieve through boiling her herbs. The wound fes-
tered badly and turned green, as did the arm. It took
Illugi's body three months to rot. By the time he died,
Bribrau's house was filled with her husband's stench.
Bribrau herself seemed halfway dead. She was pale and
listless and moved about the house as though she were
newly blind, bumping into stools and chests. She ignored
Freydis and Bolli. If Halla Eldgrimsdottir hadn't come to
the house every day bringing food and clean clothing, the
children might have had to fend entirely for themselves.
Halla was one of Reist's tenants who lived alone and kept
a few cattle on a small steading, not far from Bribrau's
home field. Bribrau's mother, Vigdis, never came down to
the house. She was afflicted with severe chest pains that
made walking hard. Instead Freydis and Bolli were sometimes sent up to her house. This was where they ate and
slept while Illugi was being washed and buried. Later they
stayed there while Freydis's half-sister was being born.

Freydis never saw this half-sister. When Halla, who had midwifed Bribrau at Freydis's birth, saw that the mother had no interest in her second daughter, she exposed her. The child was sickly and there were healthier babes in Dyrnes who needed wet nursing. When the neighbours heard that the babe had been set out in the cold beneath a pile of rocks, more than one of them said that it was obvious Illugi Arnkelsson had passed his ill Luck to Bribrau, for she had been born with more Luck than most and by marrying him had used it up. A wise man named Hedin Thorlofsson said ill Luck was a disease that spread more quickly among those who were weak in body and mind. He advised folk to seek only the company of those who were strong if they wanted their Luck to hold. This same man advised others to look for useful ways to pass the time. Winter nights were so long and dark that folk had to find ways of keeping themselves from being cast down. Hedin said it was the idle ones who found time long on their hands.

One morning after the babe had been set out to die, Bribrau got up from the sleeping platform where she had been since her confinement. She put on her leggings and cloak and bade Freydis and Bolli to dress. Bribrau would not let the children drink the bowl of sour milk Halla had brought in the day before. Although she had seemed not to notice the days slip by, Bribrau now insisted there was no time left. Her eyes were hollow and feverish and she moved in swoops and jerks. She told Freydis and Bolli they had to hurry before Halla returned. Bribrau took the children by the hand and led them outside. Through the half-dark Freydis could see the outline of the offshore skerries and the white expanse of ice. Her mother pulled her toward the ice. For a woman who had been lying so long in bed, her mother showed surprising strength when Freydis held back. Bribrau led the children to the frozen shore and tugged them onto the ice. Bolli did as he was told but Freydis refused. She was afraid of her mother. She pulled her hand free, ran some distance in from the shore, finally stopping to look back in case her mother might follow and drag her away. But Bribrau's own destiny, not Freydis's, was foremost in her mind. Bribrau stopped, drew in her cloak, then continued walking without letting go of Bolli. They had not gone far when Bolli broke away and ran ashore to stand beside Freydis. This time Bribrau did not stop or adjust her cloak, but kept walking straight out across the ice without a backward glance. On and on she walked. As she walked, the half-dark lightened so that the children were able to see the outline of her cape against the ice. While they watched, the distant sea gradually become a band of solid grey. Freydis never once took her eyes from her mother. She did not notice the coldness in her feet and hands. Maybe it was curiosity that made her watch: she wanted to see what would happen next, how far her mother would go.

Perhaps she was afraid that if she took her eyes off her mother, her mother would disappear. Did Freydis blink? Did she rub her eyes? Something happened; for a long time her mother was there and then suddenly, she was gone. Eventually someone came and found the children standing together, unmoving as stones. Not Halla, not the kind woman who had been bringing them food every day while their mother had been sick. Someone else. One of the thralls it must have been, took them inside and made a fire.

* * *

Freydis often thought about that morning. Sometimes it was a recurring dream, she was drowning in the icy sea and no one was around to help. More often it was the warnings she gave her children not to play too close to the water, the rebukes afterwards when they did. It was the stories she chose to tell her children though none of them referred to her mother. Freydis told herself her mother no longer existed, yet she continued to think her mother was lost among the stars or below the sea.

Despite its having swallowed her mother, now that Freydis was on the sea, she wasn't afraid. She was in fact so pliant and joint loose she might have been Signy's cloth doll lying in a soft hollow, bales of wool on either side. Part of the limpness was a weary letting down after months of hard work preparing for the voyage. All the wool she had spun, the provisions she had put together, the clothes she had made. Part of it was knowing that for the first time in eight years of marriage she had little work to do until she reached Leifsbudir. The food rations had long ago been neatly divided into portions and tied in sacks. True, the cow and goats would need milking but Groa would see to that. Freydis supposed she could spin. The bales of wool had been combed and spun except for one. Whether or not she spun the last bale hardly mattered. In fact it didn't matter if she did anything at all aboard this ship.

As long as she was on the water Freydis's fate was in Evyind's hands while his, in turn, was in the hands of the Three Norns. All of the Greenlanders were in the hands of three women who sat beneath the World Tree weaving the fate of others. The three sisters couldn't be bribed or browbeaten. All anyone could do was lie back and let them get on with their work. Freydis wondered how all that weaving affected the Sisters' hands, if they were rough or smooth. In the dim light of the hollow, she could see the skin of her own fingertips roughened by spinning coarse wool. The outer wool of Greenland sheep was heavy and thick, which made it long lasting and strong enough for sailcloth, but it gave little pleasure when being spun or woven. After she and Thorvard got a ship of their own, Freydis intended to buy threads of silk and linen in Norway. She would buy soft wool and make the kind of clothes the high-born wore, shifts and robes so finely woven you couldn't see the weft or warp. No doubt the Norns kept their fingers smooth by using the softest wool. Maybe not. Maybe they used fine wool only to weave the fate of the high-born, whereas coarse wool wove the fate of the poor.

The sail billowed, tugged at the rigging. The mast groaned. The ballast rocks shifted. The water hissed against the keel. The sea handled the ship firmly but gently. The crew slept. So did Freydis.

For the next three days the ship continued to follow the current Northward along the coast past icebergs and inlets, all the while enjoying fine weather and light clear skies. They passed skerries whose cliffs were white with guano from gulls and murres. Occasionally they saw great auks. The auks were good eating but the Greenlanders didn't waste time snaring sea birds when they had plenty of provisions aboard.

By now the rituals of sea travel had taken hold. Each morning the thralls who slept in the hold with the livestock shovelled the dung overboard and emptied the privy pails. The animals were given a small amount of hay. Groa left the place where she slept near Freydis and milked the cow and goats. She carried a bowl of milk to Freydis as well as Evyind, Thorvard, Ivar, Uni and the iron worker Nagli. Whatever milk was left over was taken by whichever farmer happened to be up and about. The crew woke slowly. Much of the morning was taken up with their wakening tasks, using the privy pails, dipping their cups into the water barrel. Though each man had his own spoon as well as a cup, he had little use for the spoon since the rations, served after they were all awake and then again in late afternoon, were small portions of dried fish or meat with a bit of cheese. After the first rations were eaten, the men occupied themselves in various ways. Some played board games. Others shaped bowls and cups from soapstone they had brought or made calendar sticks, uneven lengths of driftwood, grooved to mark each passing day. Only Lopt, one of the stowaways, knew runes. He refused to explain the signs he carved on wood. He said that to divulge their meaning would make them worthless. He reminded the others that the magical signs—which runes were—diminished in power if they were talked about.

After the meal was over, Groa would comb and plait Freydis's hair. The old thrall worked slowly, her fingers gnarled and clumsy by years of joint ill. Freydis's hair was thick and unruly. Whenever Groa tugged hard to get out a

snarl, Freydis snatched the comb from her and finished
the combing herself. Groa brought her a bowl of clean
water and a cloth so that she could wash in private. When
all this had been done, Freydis went round the ship and
visited various members of the crew. She usually sat with
Bolli, her step-brother, though after living apart for so
many years, they had little to say to one another, and as
always Bolli was poor at conversation. He was apt to be
cast down unless Freydis was nearby. Freydis took care to
nurture Bolli's attachment to her. She had never been
afraid of him even when he bullied others. She had seen
the helplessness in his body, the terror in his eyes when
he was under a spell. Not once had she mocked him for
his affliction. Bolli took this to be fondness, which it probably was.

Freydis was careful not to become over familiar with
the crew. Not so Thorvard. He was well known to the
hunters aboard and was regarded as one of them. But
Freydis was a woman and their leader and thought she
should keep herself apart, though not so far apart that she
couldn't observe what was going on. Once she had sat for
a time with Bolli, Thorvard, Evyind and one or two others,
she usually returned to the comfort of her hollow and
slept.

On the third day of the voyage Bjarney came into sight.
The island, which had massive black cliffs rising above a
beach, was where the hunting grounds of Northsetur
began. The Greenlanders didn't attempt to hunt but
anchored only long enough to take on fresh water. Then
they turned West. Now there would be no coastline or
landmarks to follow. During the next two days they would
be travelling an empty ocean, empty except for ice. Before
the land disappeared they saw whales and seals and once
a white bear on an ice pan.

After a half-day sailing, Bjarney's dark forehead
dropped away. There were no seals. Not even a whale was
seen. The Greenlanders were alone with sea and sky. They
passed several icebergs but these were easily avoided. It
was mainly Ivar's task to watch for icebergs. When Ivar

rested, Uni took over. These men also handled the steering oar while Evyind slept.

Though the weather held clear, the water became rougher. The Greenlanders now found the sea worked against them. As the swells increased, many of the crew began vomiting their rations into privy pails. Not Freydis; on Evyind's advice she had positioned her bed where the swell was least. Thirty years earlier when the ship had been built in Norway, the *Vinland*'s knees had been tied rather than riveted to its ribs using walrus rope, replaced many times since. This made the ship pliant and allowed a friendship between water and wood.

This friendship depended on the wind. If it chose, the wind could be generous and helpful, holding the sail in a firm embrace, guiding the ship across the sea as it was now. But just as easily the wind could be spiteful, turning away abruptly, dropping the sail, abandoning the ship to useless air. Or in a fit of frenzy the wind might suddenly sweep in from the Northeast bringing punishing cold, spitting out snow and sleet, pushing up mountainous seas.

Sometimes the god Njord himself was the wind. It was difficult to say when he was inside the wind or when he had abandoned the wind to itself. Njord came and went and could never be trusted to stay in one place. Sometimes when he left the wind, he went inside the sea and became it instead. Freydis remembered her father saying that Njord was untrustworthy because he had been spurned by so many women. He was often passed over by women in favour of handsomer gods. Though ugly, Njord had beautiful feet from soaking them so long in sea water. When an exquisite maiden by the name of Skadi was deciding who among the gods would become her husband, she chose Njord because of his feet, which were the only body parts she was permitted to see. When she saw Njord's ugly face after their marriage, she was bitterly disappointed. According to Freydis's father, it was this unhappy union that made Njord shift restlessly between water and wind.

This time Freydis thought Njord might not be following
the *Vinland* at all but showing his bad temper in some
other part of the world. This would explain the favourable
winds they were enjoying. After two days of empty ocean
the Greenlanders sighted the flat stone land Leif named
Helluland. They recognized this land not by its flatness
which was close by the water, but by the glaciered mountains far inland. The sight of the mountains reassured the
Greenlanders: once again they had landmarks to guide
them, which gave them an idea of where they were in relation to where they were going. This was a map drawn with
Leif Eiriksson's words which each traveller carried inside
his head. Where this map placed them in relation to the
rest of the world they didn't know. They knew only that
Helluland was North of Markland which was North of
Vinland. Leif said the southern part of Markland was only
a short distance from Leifsbudir and was thickly wooded
with spruce and fir. For most of the crew the world was
Greenland, each field a country fenced by stone. In any
case their maps were more felt than seen, the land Leif
named Helluland crouched like an untamed beast on the
periphery of their vision. It was now seven days since they
had left Einarsfjord, which by Evyind's estimation placed
them halfway to Leifsbudir. The most dangerous part of
their voyage was thought to be over. For this reason
Evyind agreed to anchor in Helluland for the night so that
the crew could spend a day ashore and fresh water could
be taken aboard.

At Helluland the ship was picked up by a current and
carried South. Once again land was on the starboard. With
the sun high above and the sky so clear, Evyind said they
couldn't expect fairer sailing weather. As they headed
South the evenings darkened in such a way that day was
more clearly divided from night. The Greenlanders
enjoyed the change, for it meant they could see the moon
and stars. The fine weather continued for four more days.

Late on the twelfth day, the wind shifted to the
Northeast. The sky became as dark as night. Thick clouds
blocked the sun. Evyind regarded the changed weather

with his usual composure, saying travellers must accept foul weather and ride it out until the winds turned again in their favour. The wind blew the ship seaward and the Greenlanders lost sight of land. The swells became so massive that all Freydis could see was the bottom of the swell they were in and halfway up the next. The Greenlanders lost all sense of time, which was to say the light. Nor could they navigate. The sunstone Leif had given Evyind was useless and there was no moon or stars. Evyind ordered the men to remain in place so that the ship would be more evenly weighted. The inactivity reminded the Greenlanders how helpless they were to change their fate.

The waves steepened until they loomed above the ship like Greenland's fells. The summits were so high and the valleys so deep that the *Vinland* could no longer shape itself to the water; the ship faltered on the peaks, groaning as if it would break in two. Now even those in midship became ill. Each time the old ship was stranded on top of a wave, a sickness rose in Freydis's throat then slowly sank to her belly as the ship was plunged into a trough. Freydis gave up eating, since nothing she ate would stay down. Like the others she had stopped using the privy pails, which had been knocked over by the motion of the ship. Freydis's clothes stank of vomit and piss. The entire ship reeked with foul odours that came from the hold where a swill of piss and animal dung slopped around the legs. The livestock were neglected since the thralls who tended them were hunkered down against the bales and bundles lashed to the deck. The swill was partly sea water that had leaked through the strakes. Leif's ship was so well caulked that in good sailing weather little bailing was required. Now that the ship was being driven to the bottom of deep sea troughs, the crests of waves curled over the ship so often that Evyind ordered the thralls and as many bailers as could fit into the hold to get to work with pails and cups.

Freydis struggled out of the hollow where she had spent most of the voyage. There was nothing nearby to hold on to except bundles and bales which kept shifting themselves. Freydis crawled across the starboard straking, reached up and held on to the rigging. An enormous wave broke over the deck. The rope that secured the water barrels snapped. One of the barrels careened across the deck, the other rolled past Freydis into the hold, knocking over bailers and smashing the pens. The ropes tethering the livestock tangled and crossed so that the animals fell over one another in bleating confusion. Two goats broke away and one of them leapt into the hollow where Freydis had been.

Evyind ordered the sail reefed. The reefing was done with difficulty since the men had to work around broken pens and animals on the loose. After the sail was reefed, some of the men tied themselves to the mast. Freydis wanted to reach the mast, but whenever she tried to crawl toward it across the slippery deck, another wave slammed against the ship and knocked her back. She saw Thorvard coming toward her on his hands and knees, a rope between his teeth. When he reached Freydis, he shouted at her to hold onto the rigging until he had the rope tied around her waist. He told her to stay where she was until he had the other end tied to the mast. When this had been done, he pulled Freydis toward the mast and tethered her beside the cow. Then he tied himself to the mast. Sometime later Freydis saw a gigantic wave wash over her sleeping hollow and carry away the goat. The next wave swept Lopt overboard.

The storm continued unabated for days. No one knew how many. It could have been four days, it could have been five, even seven. There was no sun. Grey clouds darkened into a blackness that could have been night, then into grey again. Freydis sat against the mast, her body stiff with terror, wet and cold. Clothing stuck to her like the skin of a fish; her hair hung in coils of dripping rope. She had no memories or thoughts. Fear had driven them out. Occasionally one of her children's faces floated in front of hers. She began to talk to her children, urging them to stick up for one another and for what was theirs, not to give Inga's children the advantage in a fight. She told them to help Halla and do as she said. She assured them that Leif Eiriksson would help them out of any difficulties they might have. Once this had been done, Freydis felt a peculiar thrill, a wild recklessness that came from knowing she was teetering on the edge between life and death. She heard voices around her pleading with Thor. Some pleaded with him to roll back Hafgeringar, that mightiest of waves, others begged him to save them from being swept into Ginnungagap, the hole of blackness at the bottom of the Great Abyss where the world dropped into nothingness. She ignored the voices pleading with Christ for forgiveness and salvation. She listened to a voice screaming at Thor, rising above the rest.

"What kind of a god are you, that you abandon us to a storm?"

The voice filled her ears in such a way that it seemed to be part of the wind. Surely this was Njord's voice. He had disguised his voice to sound like a woman's.

"Do you want Hymir and his kind to eat us? Have you become a corpse eater yourself? If you don't help us, you are hardly worth your name or the tales they tell about you."

Freydis heard someone nearby confessing to the one called Christ.

"I took my brother's wife. I damaged my brother's reputation. Forgive me, O Lord."

Freydis knew that this new voice was the voice of a fool, though who it came from she couldn't say; the voice came out of a jumble of bodies she could barely see in the half-dark. How could anyone respect a god that had to be constantly wheedled and coaxed? She preferred gods who bullied each other as Njord was bullying Thor.

Njord's voice once again filled her ears shrieking at Thor, "Who do you want to win? You or Christ?"

"Stop screaming!" Thorvard shouted at her. "Your shrieking can't save us."

There was a rumble of thunder behind the dark clouds. Thor was answering Njord. Freydis began to laugh, a high, crazed sound. How foolish her husband was, to mistake her voice for a god's. Didn't he know that what he heard was Njord challenging Thor? Maybe she was hearing Njord's voice so clearly because they had been blown out of the world to a place where gods used the same words as ordinary folk.

The wind finally retreated and the storm moved on. It seemed even the gods grew weary of being hectored and longed for calm. The Greenlanders untied themselves from the mast and rigging and began setting the ship to rights. The empty barrels were straightened and secured. The animal pens were repaired and the worst of the swill bailed out.

"We're lucky we lost only one man and one goat," Thorvard said.

"A lot of good Lopt's runes did him," Freydis said. "It was lucky for us that he kept their meaning to himself."

The sea became fitful in the restless way of someone who was severely disturbed and paced about until he was able to calm himself. The swells still heaved, but gradually they subsided from lack of wind.

Ulfar didn't know if it was the seventeenth or the twentieth day of the voyage, since he had given up all attempts to mark the days on the planking edge with his knife. All that could be said was that he awoke one morning to find the ship drifting past an iceberg partly obscured by fog. The fog was so thick and the air so cold that Ulfar drew his fur-lined cloak about him to keep the dampness from creeping into his joints. This cloak had been given to him by Leif's wife, Jorunn. It had belonged to an Irish thrall of Leif's who had died the previous winter of a mysterious ill. Although Jorunn had assured Ulfar that the cloak had been cleaned and aired, he had avoided putting it on lest he became infected with the same ill. During the storm he had been so wretched with cold, he had used the cloak. By then he had come around to thinking that it hardly mattered if he became ill since most likely he would go down with the ship. Ulfar had been fog-bound many times in the North Sea. Harek and his men often used mists to conceal their approach upon those folk whom they intended to rob. Because danger was easily concealed within its folds, Ulfar had come to think of fog as a man's cloak. But those raids had been made on the misty isles of the Hebrides whose waters, though dangerous with hidden rocks and contrary winds, were free of icebergs.

Evyind told everyone aboard the *Vinland* who cared to listen that the ice was a sure sign that land was ahead. He said the passing stragglers were harmless as long as the sea remained calm. Indeed most of the ice that drifted past was nothing more than chunks and bits. But Evyind wasn't entirely right about the ice for out of the fog came a berg that was much larger than the ship. This frightened the Greenlanders. They couldn't remember Leif warning them of ice in his approach to Leifsbudir. When the giant berg appeared, a hunter named Flosi expressed the opinion that the storm must have driven the ship North instead of South, for it seemed the *Vinland* had entered a sea of intolerable mist and ice. Lodholt wondered if perhaps the storm had driven the ship back to Greenland waters. If that was the situation, Lodholt said, then they ought to consider returning to their homes before their Luck grew worse.

Flosi wondered aloud about Evyind's competence and criticized Freydis for her failure to find them a better helmsman. He said that if Evyind had lengthened the sail and run before the storm, they might have spared themselves the fear and misery they had just endured. Fortunately these last comments stopped short of reaching the helmsman's ears but his patience was tried nonetheless. Evyind told Flosi and Lodholdt that their foolish talk about ice only showed the extent of their ignorance. Anyone who sailed northern waters knew that the amount of ice varied from year to year: it wasn't unusual to see this kind of ice in Summer. A helmsman such as himself who had sailed the Greenland Sea could certainly guide the ship safely through these waters. Rather than being a sign of danger, the iceberg was a strong indication that land was near. Didn't Lodholt notice the iceberg was grounded, which meant that there was land hereabouts? Evyind went on to say that if Lodholt wanted to reach shore safely, he should help with the bailing, since there was more water in the hold than he liked. Better still, Evyind said, they should stay in the pens with the live-stock, for it was clear to him that Flosi and Lodholt were as thick headed as sheep.

By nightfall the fog lifted enough so that for the first time in many days the Greenlanders saw the sky. Never had the moon and stars been more welcome. Such was the peculiarity of the night that while it was clear over-head, the ship was encircled by a mist so thick it sat on the water like a ring of wool. The air was windless. Evyind had no choice but to let the ship follow the current since it was pointless to row unless the men could see where they were going. Ulfar found it comforting to drift through calm water beneath the moonlight. Certainly after the ter-rors he and the others had endured, he didn't expect the worst to happen. Nor did anyone else.

The Greenlanders slept: even the helmsman dozed. At the moment of collision Ulfar's eyelids blinked open and he saw Evyind knocked off his bench. Some of the men awoke yelling and shouting. There was a second lurch, then a loud groaning as the ship rammed into an iceberg and was held on the starboard side. The second lurch, which was much stronger than the first, pitched men from their places. Ulfar was flung against Lodholt. Lodholt clung to him so tightly that it took all Ulfar's strength to push him away. Ulfar was hard put to know what to do next. Barrels and chests had slid against the rigging. The pens were smashed again and the animals were bleating and trampling each other.

The moonlight was bright enough for the helmsman to see what had happened. They were stuck on an ice shelf and unless they could free the ship, the iceberg would wrench the bottom of the ship from beneath their feet. Evyind ordered men to fetch the oars. Ulfar lost no time in picking up the oar that had fallen in front of him and car-rying it aft. As he stood awaiting Evyind's instructions,

Bolli Illugisson yanked the oar from his hands. Bolli then shoved him aside so forcefully that Ulfar fell into what was left of the pig pen. When he climbed out of the swill, Ulfar held on to the mast pole and watched Evyind instruct the men who had found the oars, twelve in all. There had been fourteen oars aboard; Ulfar looked around to see where the other two might be. It was later discovered that they had been knocked overboard along with a water barrel. Evyind ordered the twelve men to place their oars against the berg, then slowly try to lever the ship free. Do this gently, Evyind advised, the berg is grounded which is in our favour. Even so if we upset its balance, it might roll suddenly, sucking the ship into the water below. The men cautiously set their oars exactly where Evyind said. After several attempts the crew's efforts were rewarded. As the men pushed the oars against the ice, the bow eased slowly upward until it appeared to hang without support. For a time it seemed the ship might topple sideways, for the deck was slanted more perilously than before. Evyind ordered another placement of oars. When the pushing began, there was a shudder and the sound of splintering wood as the ship was lifted free of the ledge. As soon as the Vinland was upright, the men set the oars and rowed strenuously across the current to clear the ice.

While the ship was being rowed, Ivar and Uni inspected the damage. The men removed the bales and took up the planking. Three bow strakes were loose and badly splintered. The ice had broken through one strake. The moonlight was so bright Ivar and Uni could see water leaking into this hole as well as through several cracks. Uni cut a piece of tarred awning and handed it to Ivar who bundled it into a bung which he forced into the hole. This helped somewhat, but it was clear to everyone aboard that they would have to bail hard for the duration of the voyage since the swill was already ankle deep. Even with bailing the Greenlanders would be lucky to keep the water from reaching their knees. Evyind urged everyone aboard to bail with whatever container could be found. The Greenlanders didn't need urging. None of them wanted to reach the point where the only thing between them and drowning was a few pails of water. Ulfar used a milk pail, working beside Louse Oddi who used one of the privy pails. The other bailers used an assortment of pails and cups, working as if their lives depended on bailing which they did. Still the air didn't move and the sail stayed reefed. Each man took his turn with an oar not once but many times over.

Ulfar paid scant attention to the disappearing fog or the fading moon and stars. By the time dawn lightened the sky he had worked himself into a holy delirium. Though his arms ached and his back was sore, he felt lightheaded and joyful. He thought of the monks who had once rowed and bailed their way across the seas. With nothing beneath them save a currach of branches and skins, St. Columba and St. Brendan set forth on their voyages in the belief that Christ would guide them. Ulfar thought perhaps the Heavenly Lord had sent the storms to test his faith, and finding it wanting, had sent the fog and ice. Such was his elation that Ulfar thought a sea serpent could rise from the deep and swallow the ship and it wouldn't shake his faith in Almighty God. He imagined he was travelling not with heathen farmers but with the Lord's chosen few seeking the islands of the blessed.

It seemed to Ulfar that the moment he reaffirmed his faith, the Lord answered by sending down golden rays of sun, for as the Greenlanders toiled feverishly with their pails and cups, the water around them began to shine with glorious light. They were now able to see clearly in all directions. Soon after the sun appeared, Thrand threw down his cup and shouted, "Land!" Everyone aboard looked at once and saw a large cape rising ahead of them out of the sea.

They began to see sea birds skimming over the water. Evyind ordered fresh rowers, Ulfar among them, to sit at the oars. When they had taken their places on the chests, Evyind remarked that unless he was mistaken, what the Greenlanders saw in the distance was a large island east of Leifsbudir. If that was the case, Leif's houses were on the other side. He went on to say that if this was so, there would be places on the island as well as on various skerries where they might go ashore. It was his opinion, however, that they should continue on to Leifsbudir for once the crew reached land it would likely be some days before they felt like moving on. Freydis agreed with Evyind. "If we are close to Leifsbudir, it's far better to continue rather than take a rest," she said. "I expect the Icelanders are there already. Doubtless their Norwegian stemsmith can repair our ship. If not, then perhaps Ulfar can do the work."

By late morning the Greenlanders were moving West through a narrow passageway on the southern end of an island. The land on either side was mostly low green hills and rocky outcrops. Bent over his oar, Ulfar was unable to view the land. Eventually Evyind ordered Falgeir to replace him and Ulfar stood up and looked about.

Along the shore he saw various coves and inlets with pastures between. In some of these coves large icebergs were grounded. As in Greenland these bergs glistened with such beauty and peace they belied the danger concealed below. The passageway widened and Ulfar saw several small islands ahead, one of them much higher than the others. The passageway ended in a large bay. Entering this bay the Greenlanders came upon two large capes rising seaward. The shore between these capes opened up, allowing a view of the country. There were several low mountains on the land, but they were spread so far apart they looked like giant whales that had been stranded here and there and turned to stone. For the most part the land was low, so low as to be at one with the sea.

After the ship rounded the second cape, Evyind announced they had reached their destination, for straight ahead, beyond a low green island, on a long ridge pointing toward the sea were the two stone cairns Leif Eiriksson had built. Once they passed a spit of land, Evyind said, they would see Leifsbudir plainly. About this time Teit climbed the mast and shouted down that he could see houses and a stream that ran through a meadow from a lake shining in the distance. The Icelanders' ship, he said, was hauled ashore.

When the Greenlanders had rounded the rocky spit, they stopped bailing. They didn't have far to go and had come to a cove of shallow water. The cove was so shallow that had the tide not been in, the ship might have run aground before dropping anchor. When they looked shoreward the Greenlanders saw a green terrace rising above a narrow strip of grey beach. Leifsbudir: a broad windswept meadow stretching inland toward spruce wood forest. A small beach kneeling humbly, penitent, head bowed toward the power of the sea. The land, at a glance too bleak for human habitation, was flat and bare except for various grasses and dwarf spruce bent double by the wind.

Some of the men aboard remembered seeing Leif Eiriksson return to Brattahlid from this side of the water, his ship loaded with timber and wine. The men, who would have been eight or nine at the time, remembered their parents being drunk on wine. There had been much argument about whether the drink had been made from gooseberries as some claimed or from grapes. A grizzled old Saxon by the name of Tyrkir who had gone on the expedition with Leif insisted the drink was wine and passed around his drinking horn for the boys to taste. The men remembered the feasting and merrymaking that had accompanied the drinking as well as the results. For days cows went unmilked, fields unmanured, children neglected, as their parents lay about too heavy headed and weak kneed to work. The wine made some folk foul tempered. Quarrels broke out and more than one nose was bloodied before the drink ran out. It was during these orgies that the word "Vinland" first came to be used. Whether Leif used the name Vinland in jest, for the drink *was* sour, or Leif chose the name because of the grapes, none of the men knew. Like Freydis they had heard the arguments about Vinland and Leifsbudir. None of these arguments mattered now. What mattered was that they were approaching dry land. After being storm tossed and ice damaged the Greenlanders were grateful they hadn't fallen into the Great Abyss or been sucked into the Kingdom of Hel. What was more important than names was that the new land was no longer a dark shape hovering on the periphery of their minds but was spread solid and real in front of their eyes. There it was: three long turf houses set on a grassy terrace, large houses too, built of posts and beams. Smoke coming from the roof holes, which meant fires were burning inside. Wood poles drying outside. A large meadow and beyond that something they had never seen before, a forest of trees. This was enough. As for the disadvantages of the place, they would make themselves known in time. Even those Greenlanders who had been prime signed to Christ believed the Norns wouldn't have brought them through the perils and dangers at sea unless they were weaving them a better fate.

THE EGILSSONS WERE WORLD TRAVELLERS. They had been to Norway many times. They had been to Ireland and Britain. They had been to Normandy though only once. The Normans didn't welcome ships from the North if they were manned by Vikings; they found it convenient to forget that their progenitor Ragnar Hairy Breeks had been a Viking. The Egilssons didn't think of themselves as Vikings: they had never taken captives, plundered monasteries, stolen silver and sheep. Whatever goods and thralls they owned had been obtained through trade, which was why they were not as wealthy as they would have liked. Up to now the Egilssons had been middlemen working out of Kaupang, a market town in Norway. They rarely laid their hands on the raw materials where the highest profits were made. The Swedes controlled the metal trade that came across the Baltic; the Frisians, pottery and glass; the Moors, the silks and spices. By the time finished goods reached the Egilssons, they had changed hands three or four times and there was little profit to be made. The Egilssons decided their profits lay in the opposite direction, in the raw goods across the Outer Ocean, mainly timber, ivory and rope. In Norway the demand for these goods was so high that with careful handling the Egilssons expected to make themselves wealthy men.

Like the Greenlanders, the Icelanders had come to Leifsbudir for timber, some of which they intended to trade in Greenland in exchange for ivory and rope which they would then take to Norway. If all went well, they expected to reach the port of Bergen a year from now. Helgi also intended to build a second ship. This hadn't been part of the original plan. But one day more than a year earlier as they were preparing to leave Norway for Greenland, Hauk Ljome asked for refuge aboard their ship. He was being pursued by Erling the High, a powerful jarl with allies and spies all over Norway. After Hauk told them his story, the Egilssons agreed to hide him beneath the planking of *Sigurd's Steed* where he remained until the ship was well out to sea. When the brothers discussed the matter of what to do with their stowaway, Finnbogi said they should put him ashore in the Faroes. They already had a crew of thirty men and had decided on this number after a good deal of thought; an extra man aboard meant there would be more crowding on the ship and fewer rations. Helgi was against putting Hauk ashore. He thought having a stowaway who was a shipbuilder was a gift from the Sisters themselves. As he saw it, the Norns were providing the Icelanders, particularly himself, with an opportunity to better their fates. Helgi told his brother that a good stemsmith could pay his way by building them a ship in Vinland.

Finnbogi had argued against taking Hauk to Leifsbudir. Without planksmen to help him, the Norwegian would be of no use and might distract them from what they intended to do. He said shipbuilding required more skill than their crew possessed. Furthermore it would use time better spent dressing timber for trade wood. He reminded Helgi that ship wood couldn't be found in one place. To find the best wood for various parts of the ship, shipbuilders had to travel here and there, as was the case in Norway. Finnbogi said they wouldn't be able to put together a cargo if the crew was off looking for ship wood. Helgi argued that many of the crew were experienced timber cutters already, which meant they were used to working with wood. With Hauk's guidance they could certainly learn how to work with ship wood. As for cargo, with a second ship they would be able to return to Norway with twice the goods they could carry on one ship, thereby making themselves twice as rich. It was this last argument which persuaded Finnbogi that he and Helgi would be wise to make use of the fugitive they had hidden below deck.

Later in Greenland Finnbogi came around to agreeing with Helgi that beside themselves, Hauk was the most useful member of their crew, for he could be used to strengthen their bargaining position with the Greenlanders. Freydis Eiriksdottir and her husband would give up trade goods in order to obtain a ship. During the long Greenland winter it appeared that the brothers might lose this advantage, for more than once it seemed likely Hauk would die from a strange affliction. Here again the Egilssons' Luck held, for two Icelanders died of the illness instead; Hauk replaced one of the men and a Greenlander by the name of Gnup replaced the other, which held the crew at thirty able-bodied men.

The Egilssons had been lucky in other ways. Since their departure from Norway they had been favoured with excellent sailing weather. The Summer before, brisk winds and fair weather had allowed them safe passage to Greenland. And this Summer they had crossed from Gardar to Leifsbudir in thirteen days. Throughout the Western voyage the weather had remained so clear they had been able to avoid fog and ice. In fact they had even been lucky enough to unload their ship and settle into the houses before the storm that battered the Greenlanders reached Leifsbudir.

There had been some discussion about which of the three houses they would take. The largest house had been built by Thorfinn Karlsefni, an Icelander. One of the crew suggested that since they themselves were Icelanders, it was logical they should use that particular house.

"It seems to me Thorfinn's house should be left for Freydis Eiriksdottir," Helgi said, "for it's the house that would please a woman best, being the largest and newest of the three, and having an indoor storage room and a wall of panelled wood."

"When it comes to pleasing we should think of ourselves," Finnbogi retorted. "I myself would prefer to occupy the two smaller houses rather than the largest one, for it means we will have more space to spread ourselves about. I'll take the house by the stream and you can take the house in the middle. That way you'll be between Freydis Eiriksdottir and myself."

Helgi agreed to this. He thought Finnbogi wanted Freydis to have the largest house but wouldn't admit, especially to himself, that he was giving her the best. The middle house suited Helgi for another reason, which was that unlike his brother, he was willing to share part of it with the Greenlanders if the large house lacked enough sleeping space for them. Since the Greenlanders and the Icelanders had an even number of crew, they would need an even number of sleeping benches. By taking over two houses, the Icelanders had left the Greenlanders fewer sleeping places. Helgi thought it prudent to show a willingness to share with the Greenlanders if it was required. This had more to do with obligation than generosity; a man could hardly expect to receive favours if he kept everything to himself.

Helgi had already obligated Freydis's husband, Thorvard, by letting him use one of his ambatts, an arrangement that he was prepared to continue over here. Finnbogi had criticized Helgi for allowing Thorvard this favour, since there were few enough concubines to satisfy the Icelandic crew, but Helgi reminded his brother that the ambatt, whose name was Mairi, was his to do with as he liked. Helgi never used Mairi himself but loaned her mainly to settle debts when he lost at playing board games.

Even before the Egilssons arrived in Leifsbudir, they had regarded the buildings as a working camp. From the way Leif had described Leifsbudir's features and location, the brothers had formed a picture of a place intended chiefly for gathering and storing goods. According to Leif, he had chosen the site because it was well situated to

accommodate sailings between Greenland and Vinland. By
using Leifsbudir as a base, it was possible to explore better-favoured places further South and have enough time
left over to make the return crossing to Greenland in
Summer. Although the Egilssons talked to Leif on several
occasions, they had never heard him speak of settling
here, nor did they think he intended to. Neither of the
Egilssons saw Leifsbudir as a place of permanence or
beauty. The country round about was featureless and dull
compared to Iceland's fire and ice; there were no glaciers,
volcanos or hot springs, the land was open and flat. On
the other hand the air was heavy and moist and it was
pleasant to live at the same level as the sea. In Iceland
and Greenland the Egilssons had lived at the end of
fjords, where farms backed onto dark cliffs and fells.
There were no mountains in Leifsbudir to speak of, only
large capes slanting toward the sea, and in the distance
the rise of hills. There was nothing between them and a
spruce forest behind the houses but a sweep of rough
meadow. For some reason Leifsbudir made Helgi lightheaded, even giddy. It was the same giddiness he sometimes felt at sea. He thought it had to do with the spread
of sky, there was so much more of it here than where he
had come from. Or perhaps it was the result of being that
much closer to the place he most wanted to see, which
was Vinland.

After the Icelanders were settled in the houses, some
of them went into the spruce forest to cut timber for drying. Thorfinn Karlsefni had left some firewood, but it was
not enough to keep their hearths burning the way they
liked. After the winter in Greenland the Icelanders kept
wood fires burning less for necessity than for pleasure.

Hauk scouted around for a suitable place to build a
ship. He found a ship cove, as he called it, near a large
stand of spruce a short distance south of the meadow and
set the men he had chosen to work as shipbuilders to
making wooden clamps and supports of various kinds.
These were easy tasks intended to hone the carving and
whittling skills of the men. Hauk took Ulf Broad Beard and

explored the edge of the forest to see what sort of timber could be found. There was an endless supply of spruce as well as fir and tamarack. A ship could be built from these woods, but it would fall far short of the ship Helgi had in mind. When Hauk told Helgi he thought they would have to travel some distance to find good quality ship wood, Helgi advised him to make the Greenlanders' ship first, using the available wood. "Later on we'll look for better wood in the South," Helgi said.

"That makes good sense," Hauk agreed. "By the time we've finished the Greenlanders' ship, the men you've given me to train as planksmen will no longer be as green as new wood and will do a better job on your ship. Since the Greenlanders have no knowledge of trees, they won't mind a ship built of inferior wood."

The Icelanders didn't question the Greenlanders' delay. They preferred to have Leifsbudir to themselves since it made it easier to settle in, and given the varying sea winds, a few days' difference between their arrival and that of the Greenlanders was to be expected. Also, considering the clumsy way the Greenlanders had been loading their ship in Einarsfjord, it was likely their departure had been further delayed. The third day after the Icelanders' arrival the sky darkened earlier than it had on previous days. The wind shifted to the Northeast, which meant foul weather was on its way. The fourth day the sky was overcast but the weather wasn't bad enough to keep the Icelanders inside. Finnbogi had *Sigurd's Steed* hauled ashore and braced with posts and stays.

By the fifth day the bad weather had grown so severe they were forced to remain inside. The Icelanders sat around their fires and congratulated themselves for having settled into houses where it was warm and dry. Except for the murmuring voices it was quiet inside, the storm muffled by thick turf walls. Whenever the door was opened and someone went out to fetch water or to piss, the wind screamed at them from the Northeast. Once when Finnbogi came in from outside, he remarked that the wind was as swift and brutal as any wind in Greenland though not as cold. "If the Greenlanders are in the middle of this storm," he said, "they're in a bad way, since they'll be driven out to sea."

As the days passed and the storm continued, the Icelanders became convinced that the Greenlanders wouldn't arrive at all. They began to talk about what they would do in Leifsbudir on their own. Finnbogi's ambatt Olina said she thought the women should take over Thorfinn Karlsefni's house, that with the men making demands of one kind and another, the women needed a place where they might rest and refresh themselves. Finnbogi said he would never wish any mariner ill luck but it would be a relief to him if Freydis failed to appear. "We'll be in a bad way if the Greenlanders don't come," Helgi said, "since they agreed to supply sailcloth and rope for my ship."

When the storm abated at last, Helgi went outside and walked along the shore to see what the tide had brought in. There was driftwood on the beach but no wreckage from a ship. Several times a day he went Eastward along the shore, looking for some sign of the ship. Of all the Icelanders Helgi had the most to lose if the Greenlanders didn't appear. Without their ship he might never have the opportunity to travel South in search of Vinland. Helgi had already spoken to Finnbogi about taking *Sigurd's Steed* to look for better timber before Winter set in. Finnbogi insisted the ship would be going nowhere until it had been thoroughly scraped and caulked, a task he insisted on supervising himself. Finnbogi wouldn't even allow his ship to make the short crossing to Markland for wood until it was overhauled. Knowing Finnbogi was reluctant to let his ship go anywhere without himself at the helm, Helgi had intended to persuade the Greenlanders to let him use the *Vinland* to make expeditions further South. Without the Greenlanders, Helgi would be forced to depend on his brother more than he liked.

It was Gudlaug who first saw the Greenlanders' ship. He had been jigging cod in the bay and happened to see the *Vinland* as it rounded the cape. He shouted to the others ashore. By the time the Greenlanders were entering the cove, all the Icelanders were on the beach, except for the men working with Hauk.

As they stood on the beach watching the *Vinland*'s approach, it was obvious to the Icelanders that the Greenlanders had endured the worst kind of crossing. For one thing, the ship was dangerously low in the water; for another, several strakes were damaged.

"I wonder how their cow is faring," Helgi said, making light of his relief. "Her milk must be curdled by now."

Even Finnbogi was affected by the sight. "Those poor farmers must have been frightened out of their wits."

Soon the Icelanders were rowing their prams toward the *Vinland* to help bring the Greenlanders ashore. Though the water was cold, it wasn't as cold as the fjords at home. Most of the Greenlanders leapt into the sea and waded toward a small stream that flowed through the beach into the sea. By the time the *Vinland* was anchored in the bay, only Evyind, his son Teit, Freydis and her thrall woman and three or four others remained aboard. Helgi had difficulty picking out Freydis. Dressed in breeches and tunic she looked like a man. He recognized her mainly by the way she moved down the rope ladder to the pram, and by the fact that a woman followed her down.

"Unless I'm mistaken, the Greenlanders have brought extra men," Finnbogi said. He had been watching the movements of their crew, counting them as they came ashore.

"Are you sure?" Helgi spoke carelessly; he was far too relieved to bother counting Greenlanders.

"I'm certain."

"How can you be sure when the Greenlanders are moving around? I think you should count them again later on."

Freydis came ashore. As soon as she got out of the pram, she squatted on her haunches and splashed water on her face and hair. Then she stood up and looked about as if she was searching for someone, possibly her husband. Thorvard was with the Greenlanders who had waded ashore and were now bathing in the mouth of the stream where the water was shallow enough to be warmed by the sun. Freydis watched the men for some time but she made no effort to join them. Instead she looked beyond the beach at the turf buildings on the terrace. It was only then that she noticed Finnbogi and Helgi standing there. Helgi could hardly believe this was the same woman he had seen sitting on the grass beside Hauk in Gardar. This woman was gaunt and pale, her hair hanging in knots, her clothes stained and soiled. Freydis knew how she looked. "As you can see from the state the crew and myself are in, not to mention my brother's ship, we ran into a storm," she said when she came up to them.

"And more besides."

"An iceberg."

"We passed ice too but managed to avoid it," Finnbogi said.

He pressed Freydis for more details of the voyage, which she supplied willingly enough. Then she said she would look at the houses and decide where she wanted to live.

"We left the largest and newest house for you," Finnbogi said, "the one Thorfinn Karlsefni built for his wife."

"I doubt I'll choose that house to live in. I prefer to avoid any place where his wife, Gudrid Thorbjornsdottir, has laid her head," Freydis said. "I will see what there is and then decide."

When she had gone off to look at the houses, Helgi remarked that the Icelanders had better be prepared to move their goods. Then he said, "It appears Freydis dislikes Thorfinn Karlsefni's wife."

"That's not surprising," Finnbogi said. "From what I've heard of Thorfinn's wife, she and Freydis are like night and day."

The three houses were spread out along the terrace East to West above the beach. Woven alder boughs supported turf roofs; the roofs had openings to take out the smoke that rose from the hearths and were overgrown with grass and flowers. The outside walls were also thick with grass. The houses Leif had built were close together; the house Thorfinn Karlsefni had built was a slight distance away to the North. Freydis looked first at the most southerly house which was beside the stream. This house had two pairs of joined rooms side by side, each with a separate entrance and with wooden sleeping benches against the walls. Stone hearths ran down the middle of each room. Facing the doorways were a hut and a shed built in the same way as the houses but smaller. When Leif had described these buildings in Greenland, Freydis had decided she wanted this shed, which was one large room with a long wooden bench along one side.

Freydis entered the shed first. Though it was empty, she could tell it had been occupied by one of the Icelanders' crew and his ambatt. A shift and a robe had been thrown on a chest. The room was untidy. The sleeping bench was strewn with a man's clothing, the floor with tools and empty bowls. Freydis crossed the yard to the long house and inspected it. The rooms, more spacious than anything she had known in Gardar, were also taken up with the Icelanders' gear. Freydis moved on to the middle house, which had two large rooms and a hut beside it. The Icelanders had also moved in here, setting their goods down everywhere, on the sleeping benches in both rooms and on the floor. The earth floor was littered with fish bones, ashes and other debris. Freydis didn't look inside the house Thorfinn Karlsefni had built. She could see it was larger than either of Leif's houses and had an open shed attached, but she would never live in a house built for Gudrid. In any case, she didn't want to spend an entire year in a house with thirty-four Greenlanders if she could avoid it. Her hut in Gardar wasn't much but at least it offered privacy which was preferable to living in the same house with Thorvard's kin. Freydis was irked at the Icelanders. By taking over Leif's houses, they had shown themselves to be high handed and self-serving. They had taken what they wanted, giving no thought to what the Greenlanders might prefer. Maybe they thought the Greenlanders had perished at sea leaving Leifsbudir exclusively for their use. This was close enough to the truth to make Freydis resentful. She didn't like the idea of the Icelanders benefiting from the Greenlanders' poor Luck.

Freydis went to find the Egilssons. Finnbogi was on the beach watching the men bathe in the river mouth. She would have preferred to talk to Helgi, but he was nowhere in sight. Freydis went up to Finnbogi who ignored her as he once again counted the number of Greenland men.

"You will have to move yourselves into Thorfinn Karlsefni's house," Freydis said loudly to get his attention. "We Greenlanders will be taking over my brother's houses."

"It seems to me the first to arrive in Leifsbudir should be the first to choose," Finnbogi said to goad her. He knew as well as Helgi that the Icelanders would have to move.

"I agreed to share Leifsbudir with you," Freydis said. "That didn't give you the right to take it over."

"Why should we move our gear when the best house in Leifsbudir is empty and waiting for you?"

"Because I don't want it."

"That's hardly a reason."

"Listen to me, Finnbogi Egilsson," Freydis said. "Move your gear out of my brother's houses at once or I'll have my men throw it outside."

Finnbogi turned to look Freydis full in the face. What an ugly woman she was with her matted hair and filthy clothes, stinking of vomit and rancid fish.

"And if I refuse, what will you do?"

Before Freydis could threaten Finnbogi again, Helgi appeared. He had noticed an argument was under way and thought that Freydis and his brother had already found the worst in each other.

"What's all this about?" he said.

"Your brother refuses to leave Leif's houses," Freydis told him. "I have no wish to stand here arguing with someone who ignores a reasonable request. I want to bathe and change my clothes."

"You don't want the empty house?" Helgi said.

"I prefer more privacy than it affords."

"Not to mention space," Finnbogi put in, "for the extra men you brought along."

Freydis might have said, "For the extra men we'll need to keep you in your place," but she kept silent.

"We'll move our gear right away. As far as I'm concerned, the choice of houses has been an open matter. We settled where we did on a temporary basis, waiting until you got here. After all, this place belongs to your brother," Helgi said. Since there had already been a falling out, Helgi didn't suggest the Greenlanders and Icelanders share the middle house.

"The sooner the better," Freydis said. "I intend to use the shed behind my brother's house for myself and will have the goods inside taken out at once so that I can get out of these clothes." From now on Freydis would be in the company of well-travelled men, one of whom would be Hauk Ljome. She didn't want the Norwegian shipbuilder to see her in such an ugly state. She might live far from countries where women dressed in the finest attire, but with enough care she could make herself look as attractive as them.

Hauk and his woodworkers missed the Greenlanders' arrival, since no one sent a runner with the news. When Hauk returned from the ship cove, he found his goods had been moved from the shed where he had been sleeping into Thorfinn Karlsefni's house. This did not inconvenience him at all, since Grelod had arranged a new sleeping area for him beside the panelled wall. The Icelanders told Hauk about the Greenlanders' arrival and the damage to their ship. "They were storm tossed for days and looked the worse for wear," Finnbogi said. "You should have seen the hag Freydis. She stank like a rotting corpse and was monstrous enough to be Hel herself."

Hauk doubted Freydis would look that unsightly even after being storm tossed at sea. He assumed Finnbogi was peeved because the Icelanders had been forced to move into Thorfinn Karlsefni's house. Hauk knew Finnbogi was a man used to having his way. There had been many occasions when Hauk had noticed that Finnbogi expected others, including his brother, to step aside. He thought nothing of interrupting conversations and games, or helping himself to another man's food or his sitting place. One thing he did not take was Helgi's woman. Just as Olina was solely for Finnbogi's use, Helgi was the only one who made use of Finna. Helgi owned three of the five concubines: Finna, Grelod and Mairi. Finnbogi owned Olina and Alof. As part of the agreement he had made with Hauk to build him a ship, Helgi had given him Grelod for his use. Fortunately Grelod was a large, rollicking woman who enjoyed coupling as much as Hauk. Grelod often went to the ship cove so that Hauk could lie with her in the woods during the day. He intended to use what was left of the Summer to make up for doing without women the previous winter.

*   *   *

Hauk had only been in Greenland two months when he had come down with a strange fever that left him listless and morose. He could barely eat the food he was offered, usually whale and seal meat smeared with rancid butter. What he wanted was a piece of bread, but most Greenlanders had never seen such food much less eaten it; they lacked the crops to make bread. Even the Yule celebrations had failed to cheer Hauk. He couldn't drink the ale the Egilssons had brought from Norway without vomiting. He couldn't stand without swaying on his feet. Like an old man he had to be helped outside to piss or empty his bowels. He couldn't look at the lamp flame without hurting his eyes. All Winter long he lay in the gloom of the overseer's hut as if he had been buried alive. He had thought he was dying. He said to himself that he should have encouraged Erling the High to run him through with his sword in Norway. Anything was better than wasting away in Greenland.

It had been the worst Winter in Hauk's life. The cold was so bitter and the wind so fierce that he was never warm enough no matter how many furs were piled on his bed. Not only did he feel wretched, he had lost his taste for women. And he was uneasy being in a country where there were no forests, nothing in fact that could be called a tree. Whenever he was forced to go outside into the bare Greenland landscape, Hauk thought he had banished himself to the end of the world. The farm where he stayed had nothing to recommend it, being little more than rock and grass. This grass was coarse and rough. There were no fields of wheat or oats or barley, merely clumps of wild grasses fit only for sheep and goats. Amazingly the Greenlanders harvested this grass and called it winter hay. The poor forage explained why Greenland horses were undersized. The cows were also small.

Even if he had been well enough to move about, Hauk wouldn't have travelled around Greenland, since what he had seen of the country had discouraged him from seeing its other parts. Judging from the overseer's family, Hauk thought the Greenlanders were poor indeed, for they wore grey wadmal of the roughest kind and skins that had been crudely sewn together. There was hardly any metal in the hut. There were a few iron knives but they had been worn away from oversharpening and didn't cut much better than whittled bone. There were no metal spoons. The pot hooks, ladles and platters were made from driftwood, mostly arctic pine. As far as Hauk could see, the Greenlanders' household goods were either rock or bone. Everywhere he looked there were soapstone containers of various kinds: lamps and bowls and pots. The overseer's wife and daughters wore their robes high on their shoulders which made them look as though they were dressed in sacks. The overseer's wife had a walrus penis bone she hung from a peg close by the hearth where she hung other items of value, an iron amulet and an ivory comb. She was very proud of this bone which was an enormous size. When one of her young sons dipped his fingers into the whale oil lamp or got in the way of her cooking, she would take down the penis bone and use it to beat him.

When Hauk first saw Freydis Eiriksdottir in Greenland, he had thought that compared to the overseer's wife and daughters, Freydis was a beautiful woman. Later when he had recuperated, he changed his opinion. He decided that in her way Freydis was attractive but that compared to the women in Norway she was somewhat plain. When she came to see him that day, Freydis had been wearing a blue robe trimmed with yellow and her copper hair had been charmingly plaited. She had bold eyes which he liked and a comely though somewhat thickened shape. Hauk regretted not being well enough to impress her more. Freydis had come to ask him about building her a ship in Leifsbudir.

Hauk had known the voyage to Leifsbudir would be a risk. But he was used to risks and anything would have been better than staying in Greenland. Since he couldn't depend on being rescued from Greenland, Hauk had decided that if he survived the Winter he would continue going West with the Egilssons to the place where rich forests were said to lie. When his illness was at its worst, Hauk had dreamed of building ships in a country of virgin wood as a way of keeping himself warm. Helgi had said they would make the westward voyage in late Summer. In Greenland what passed for Summer was more like Autumn in better-favoured places. On these northern islands the weather was so unrewarding that folk recognized only two seasons, Winter and Summer.

When Freydis had offered Hauk a quantity of rope and ivory as payment for building her a ship, he had replied that while he would be willing to accept those goods, what he would welcome more were cordial relations with her. It was his understanding that there would be few women in Leifsbudir. He dreaded the thought of going a whole year without the company of a woman as delightful as herself. He was a man who enjoyed beautiful women and thought that Freydis would be well able to make up for the lack.

"Of course," he said, "I may not survive the Winter here."

"You'll survive," she had said and smiled.

Hauk remembered Freydis had teeth that were neither crooked nor worn and were exceedingly white. Freydis had said she would welcome the chance to become better acquainted with him in Leifsbudir. She was eager to learn more about Norway, especially since—she smiled again—when she had a ship, she intended to travel there. Perhaps he would tell her about what she could expect to find when she arrived. Hauk replied that he would tell her more than she wanted to hear and showed his own teeth which were somewhat yellow. Later after Freydis had left the hut, Hauk ate a large bowl of venison stew and cleaned his teeth.

*   *   *

Hauk was born in Mosvik on Trondheim Fjord in Western Norway. His father had a prosperous farm there. Hauk never cared much for farming and was apprenticed at an early age to Arnljot the Shipwright. Arnljot, who made ships for wealthy jarls and kings, had building crews in many parts of Norway, wherever a supply of ship wood could be found. When Hauk began ship work the supply of oak wood was already dwindling. Landowners intent on making way for crops and grazing thought nothing of felling oak. When Arnljot agreed to take on Hauk, he told him he couldn't expect to see much of Mosvik, since from now on he would be kept on the move. This suited Hauk; he had been born with an itchy foot. Moreover after Hauk had worked in a place for a time, he usually found it necessary to escape. Most of Hauk's scrapes—as he called them—were the result of his appetite for women. Hauk didn't consider himself greedy. Indeed he was never first to remove a haunch from a platter or to drink from a horn. Nor did he covet silver arm bracelets, silken tunics or cloth of gold. What he coveted were women, especially those who were betrothed or married to other men. Two or three betrothals had been broken off when the woman in question was found to be with child before she had been bedded by her husband-to-be. In each case when the woman's father came after Hauk to force reparations, Hauk was on his way to begin another of Arnljot's ships.

These ships were built where few people settled and allowed Hauk to hide for long periods of time.

Hauk had a wife named Sigrid by whom he had a son. They lived with Sigrid's kin in Rindal where Hauk seldom went. He had originally gone there to build a skútur. He stayed in Rindal only a few months after the ship was finished. By then he had tired of Sigrid who was a pleasant, well-spoken woman but far too mild mannered for Hauk's taste. Hauk preferred spirited, difficult women; he was inclined to be restless and easily bored.

Six months before Hauk left Norway, Arnljot sent him to the woods near Bjorkdal to build two long ships for Erling the High, a jarl who had it in mind to help Olaf Digre christianize Norway. King Olaf, a doughty, strong-minded man, had returned to Norway from England and France some years before. He was going about the countryside sacking and burning out folk who refused to give up the old gods and continued making blood sacrifices of various kinds. King Olaf had many powerful jarls like Erling to help him turn the Norwegians to Christ. Arnljot sent five planksmen to work with Hauk, who by then was a master stemsmith.

Erling the High had a young wife, a dark-eyed beauty named Gunnhild who liked to ride to the woods each day with her servant and observe the shipbuilders. Apparently it amused her to sit on her mount, dressed in fine clothes and jewels, and watch the labour of half-naked men. It was the custom for Hauk and his men to strip to the waist when they were felling and limbing trees. Hauk was a pleasure to watch for he moved swiftly with natural grace. He was a lean man, wide shouldered and narrow hipped. His face was perhaps over-long but the features were well sized and shaped. When he knew he was being watched by a woman, Hauk would turn and outstare the watcher, then feign indifference and look away. This ambivalence encouraged a woman to persevere, believing Hauk's true nature would be revealed to her. Hauk continued to ignore Gunnhild so that she might know that to hold his interest, she would have to make it worth his time. One afternoon

Gunnhild sent her servant to tell Hauk she would return the next day with provisions for a feast in the woods. Hauk's reply was that he and his men would be fully occupied for several days but that two days after tomorrow they would welcome a feast at midday. Accordingly three days later, Gunnhild's servants arrived bearing a large awning and a table which were set up in the woods. The table was laden with honey and corn cakes, cold venison and salmon as well as apples, not to mention ale. Gunnhild also brought two serving maids who, though not as beautiful as she, were comely enough to interest the other shipbuilders. The feasting went on until evening. The next day there was another feast which went on much as before, the only difference being that following the merrymaking, Hauk accompanied Gunnhild back to Erling's house. The old man was away with Olaf Digre harrying folk in the North and would be gone for an extended time. Or so Gunnhild had been told.

Some days later when Hauk was astride Gunnhild, her maidservant ran into the room with the news that the master's ship could be seen approaching. As a result of this warning Hauk was able to dismount Gunnhild and slip away before the jarl entered his house. Hauk got on a fishing boat which took him to the mouth of Sognefjord where he boarded a trading ship bound for Bergen. Soon after his return home, Erling inquired as to the whereabouts of his stemsmith and was told by Hallad Bjerk that Hauk had fled in order to save his life. For many years Hallad had worked as a planksman for Hauk without any prospect of advancement and now sought to better his situation by telling Erling what had gone on during his absence, in the hope that he could replace Hauk as stemsmith. Erling locked his wife in a room and sent out scouts to find Hauk and bring him back. He preferred to take his revenge by killing the adulterers together. When word reached Hauk that Erling's men were after him, he got aboard *Sigurd's Steed* which was soon leaving Bergen.

Hauk didn't know *Sigurd's Steed* was bound for Greenland for the eventual purpose of crossing the

Western Sea. It was only after the ship had passed the
Shetlands that the brothers told him where they were
bound. Helgi said they would make it worth Hauk's while if
he would do ship work for them in Leifsbudir. After Hauk
saw he had no choice but to go to Greenland, he told the
Egilssons the details of his narrow escape. Hauk's story
about bedding the wife of Erling the High was met with
much merriment. It wasn't often Icelanders heard about
someone who had outwitted a Norwegian jarl, one moreover who was aiding the king. Some years earlier King Olaf
had sent his jarls to christianize Iceland and in so doing
had offended folk, for once christianizing had been done
to the king's satisfaction, he had then sent men to collect
nose scat to be paid in homespun. This didn't sit well with
the Icelanders. One of the reasons the Icelanders had left
Norway in the first place was to get out from being taxed
by the king. They wanted to use the homespun they paid
in taxes to purchase goods lacking at home.

Erling the High was a powerful man with spies all over
the country. It would be years before Hauk could live safely in Norway or on any of the islands nearby. Now that he
had come as far West as Greenland, he thought he had
more to gain than to lose by continuing on with the
Icelanders. *Sigurd's Steed* was a soundly made ship well
able to handle the Western voyage. Even if Leif Eiriksson
was as big a liar as Thorolf Butter, who once claimed butter dripped from every blade of grass in Iceland,
Leifsbudir could be no worse than Greenland. There was
also the prospect of Vinland, which Helgi confided he was
determined to find despite his brother's resistance. Helgi
told Hauk that he would be well rewarded for making the
journey with them, for they expected to return with a large
quantity of timber and wooden goods which would bring a
high price in Iceland.

Hauk knew as well as anyone that a man set himself
up for disappointment if he expected more than he was
likely to get from a situation. He hadn't expected much of
Leifsbudir which was why he wasn't disappointed when he
first saw the place. In fact Leifsbudir pleased Hauk. He

found the houses larger and warmer than the few he had seen in Greenland. He liked living where there was an abundance of wood and folk lived at sea level as they did in Trondheim. The wood and the lowness of the land made it convenient for building ships. Hauk set Vemund, Bersi, Olver and Ulf Broad Beard to making a pram of spruce wood in the ship cove. The Icelanders had brought a pram with them but could use another. Hauk saw the building of the pram as another way to sharpen the skills of the men who would work as planksmen. Hauk thought Helgi was using the word planksmen loosely, since some of the men didn't know a chisel from a plane.

After the Greenlanders' arrival in Leifsbudir, Grelod was the first person to tell Hauk about the new sleeping arrangements. As soon as he entered the Icelanders' house, she came up to him and said, "That Greenland bitch has taken over our houses. She couldn't wait until I moved our goods from the shed but tossed them onto the grass."

For a thrall Grelod was careless with her tongue. Had her owner been a high-born man or woman in Norway, Grelod's tongue might have been slit by now. Slave owners were quick to punish impudence before it got out of hand. But she was safe enough among traders and seamen. Like them Hauk often prodded Grelod into saying something outrageous and crude. This time he spoke to her sharply, telling her Freydis was entitled to claim what was her brother's.

That night the Icelanders sat beside the hearth on sleeping benches that ran the length of the room on either side of Karlsefni's main hall, listening to the Egilssons quarrel about the Greenlanders. It was Helgi's contention that the Icelanders and Greenlanders should eat together the following night. The Icelanders, he said, had caught a large number of lobsters that should be eaten before they spoiled. Cod was plentiful as were berries of several kinds. Why not give the Greenlanders a feast? After their difficult crossing they would welcome a meal prepared by others.

Finnbogi was against this. "Freydis has already gotten her way with the houses," he said. "Why should we share anything with her?"

"Because we are neighbours," Helgi replied. "During the year there might be times when we need the Greenlanders' help."

"It's difficult to be neighbours with folk who ignore an agreement by bringing extra men."

"If it were easy to be good neighbours, we wouldn't have to try," Helgi said. "The fact is we may find ourselves in a situation where the Greenlanders will be of use. If we found ourselves outnumbered by skraelings, for instance, we would need the Greenlanders on our side."

Finnbogi replied that the company of skraelings would be preferred to Freydis's.

Whenever the Egilssons sparred with each other, Hauk usually turned his attention to something else. Now he heard himself say, "Judging by the number of times her name passes his lips, I think Finnbogi has the itch to get Freydis into his bed."

"Trust you to make such a remark," Finnbogi retorted. "No matter how ugly she is, there isn't a woman alive you wouldn't bed if you could get her down."

Perhaps Hauk's remark weakened Finnbogi's resistance to Helgi's suggestion. Perhaps Finnbogi thought it necessary to prove his indifference to Freydis. Whatever the case, he eventually agreed the Icelanders should hold a feast for the Greenlanders.

The feast was held late the next day on the beach nearest the houses. This was a small stretch of coarse sand around which the terrace curved. Logs, benches and plank tables had been set here and there. Platters of fried cod had been laid out on tables along with shellfish stewed in butter and bowls of mashed blueberries picked from the meadow. The thrall women had spent most of the day preparing this food. Many folk had already heaped their trenchers with food and were sitting on logs and benches, eating from their knees and laps. In most cases the trenchers were nothing more than pieces of slab wood. These were none too clean but they held food well enough. During the serving and eating the Greenlanders and Icelanders mingled freely which pleased Helgi who looked around often and smiled while he ate. Freydis carried her food to an empty place beside Helgi. Finnbogi was sitting on the same log but further along. Freydis ignored him. Freydis didn't mention the matter of the houses. She had what she wanted for now and was content to answer Helgi's questions about the voyage. Hauk was watching Freydis from his place on a bench beside Grelod. This was the first time he had laid eyes on Freydis since leaving Greenland. Freydis wore a blue robe with a red kirtle around her waist and looked much the same as he remembered. When Hauk saw Freydis get up, he slapped Grelod on the backside and told her to fetch more food. At the same time Freydis handed her utensils to Groa for washing and walked across the sand and sat where Grelod had been.

"I see you have your appetite back," Freydis said. "When I saw you in Greenland you were in bed with some ill."

"Until I met you. Then I recovered quickly."

Freydis knew she was talking to the kind of man women took pains to impress; that was why she was carefully dressed. But only a foolish woman would lose her wits over such a man, since it was obvious he was well practised at flattering women. Freydis took care to play along with Hauk not only for her own enjoyment but because she wanted him to build her a ship. She smiled at him and said, "Are you saying I helped you recover your health?"

"I am."

"I'm pleased to hear that for it means you may find it hard to refuse me something that will improve my health."

"Would your request have anything to do with the fact that you've forgotten to wear your snood?"

"I haven't forgotten. I don't intend to wear a snood in Leifsbudir."

"Does that mean you consider yourself unmarried over here?"

"It means I'm placing comfort over custom. I only wear a snood in Greenland to protect my children's reputation in case there are folk who don't know I'm Thorvard Einarsson's wife."

"But your children aren't in Leifsbudir, so going without your snood here might be interpreted by someone like myself as having another meaning."

"And what would that be?"

"It might mean a healthy man like myself can try his luck with you in bed."

"I can tell you right now that you won't get anywhere with me unless you respect my reputation." Freydis spoke sharply. She was offended that the Norwegian shipbuilder should think she was an easy woman. Just because her husband was a Greenland farmer and she went without her snood didn't mean Hauk should regard her as a concubine. She didn't for a moment doubt that Hauk made use of the concubines the Icelanders had brought along. As they were speaking, the woman Hauk had sent away was standing opposite, holding a trencher of food. Freydis moved further along the log away from Hauk and said, "My brother loaned me a thrall named Ulfar who is skilled with wood. It would suit me and my husband if Ulfar joined your shipbuilding crew. Leif assures me that Ulfar has had some experience as a planksman and would serve us well in repairing the *Vinland* and building our ship. Also if you're looking for someone to haul heavy timber and the like, Bolli Illugisson would be of use. He's large and uncommonly strong."

Freydis spoke briskly and firmly. She wanted to deal with the Norwegian in such a way that they would remain on friendly terms but without Hauk's advances getting out of hand. For the next year more than sixty men would be living in a place largely without women and she had no intention of making up for that lack. After she had spoken, Freydis moved to the logs where Thorvard and a group of his hunters were sitting. Before she could sit beside

Thorvard, he went off to talk to Helgi. Freydis sat down beside Asmund Gautsson, the scald whose verse she had heard on the ship. Apparently Asmund had made another poem about the voyage and Thorvard's men were trying to convince him to present it now. Asmund was reluctant to offer a poem in the company of Icelanders, since Icelanders were known to have the best scalds. In fact King Olaf was said to prefer scaldic verse made by Icelanders, claiming it to be far superior than anything offered by Norwegian poets.

"All the more reason to say the verse now," Freydis told him. "It seems to me Icelanders all too easily forget that Greenlanders share the same forebears as they. From time to time they need reminding that we are their equals. Your verse should show them that."

"I'll offer my poem later," Asmund said. "After I've thought about it some more."

Freydis refused to take no for an answer. Though she didn't care much for verses, she didn't want to miss an opportunity to impress the Icelanders. She stood up and clapped her hands. When folk turned to see what Freydis wanted, she shouted, "We Greenlanders have brought a scald to Leifsbudir. He has made some verses about our voyage and will give them to us now."

Asmund stood up, reluctantly; he didn't like offering his verses before they were ready. But he was a shy man who knew that the sooner he offered the poem, the sooner attention would move to someone else. Asmund half spoke, half sang in a high sweet voice:

> When seal oil burners
> Crossed Njord's weeping fields,
> They were weaponless against
> Vile sea troll breath that blew
> Hafgeringar down upon them.
>
> Ginnungagap yawned ahead.
> Then came the mists of Hel
> Her silent arms reached out

To embrace the noble steed,
While beneath her skirts
Knives and ice axes
Sliced the shuddering flank.

Brave the night riders were:
When Hel sat on her frozen throne,
They rammed their rowing trees
Hard into her glittering maw.
Hel toppled into the Underworld.
Her throne drifted away.

This poem was so well received, even by the Icelanders, that Asmund was persuaded to recite it again, as well as the verse he had made about the earlier part of the voyage. The Greenlanders were especially pleased by Asmund's poem. They wouldn't have cared to hear it during the worst of the voyage but now that they were safe, it seemed to the Greenlanders that the difficulties they had faced on the crossing had grown in size and importance and had gone far beyond themselves. Like most folk the Greenlanders welcomed verses that ennobled their lives. Nagli said Asmund's poem was bound to be repeated so often that even those who had never left dry land would know the risks that bold-spirited adventurers took upon the sea. In that respect, he said, the poem had more value than some object that could be traded for gold.

By this time night was beginning to fall as it did in Summer this far South. Folk began to move away to their sleeping quarters. Freydis didn't linger on the beach. Not only had she arrived in Leifsbudir exhausted but she had been up since dawn, unpacking and putting the Greenlanders' rations and goods in order.

Hauk's next move was to approach Freydis in the morning. He arrived at the shed early in order to find out if her husband slept with her. Freydis's thrall woman answered his tap on the door and bid him wait outside while she wakened Freydis. Freydis came to the door wearing a cloak which she had thrown over a linen shift.

"What do you want?" She spoke crossly, displeased to have someone at her door so early in the morning.

"I came to ask you to send the thrall you call Ulfar to the shipbuilding cove. I'm going there myself and will put him to work in a way that suits you."

If Freydis was pleased by Hauk's words, she hid it well. She merely said, "Ulfar has chosen to sleep some distance away from the rest of us, but I can send someone to fetch him. Where is the cove?"

Hauk pointed toward the forest beyond the meadow. "It's not far. Tell him to follow the path through the woods." He looked boldly at the outline of breast he saw beneath the linen where the cloak had fallen away. "You may come too, if you wish. If you dress quickly, I'll take you there myself. You can see where I'll be building your ship as well as repairing the *Vinland*."

This brought the smile Hauk expected. He knew the ship was important to Freydis, though not in the way it would be to him.

Having gained the advantage, Hauk looked over Freydis's shoulder and asked if they were waking her husband.

"He's not here."

"Probably he's with one of our ambatts," Hauk said. "I know he made some arrangement with Helgi about using Mairi."

More than one of Hauk's conquests had been women whose husbands kept an ambatt in the house. Hauk watched Freydis closely, prepared to comfort her if it was required. Sooner or later, wives in Freydis's position needed someone like himself to provide attention unless their cunts were made of ice, in which case no amount of thawing would help.

Freydis showed no sign of being troubled, though her neck flushed an unbecoming red.

"If you wait here," she said, "I can dress quickly."

She went inside, leaving Hauk feeling pleased with himself. The sun had barely risen and he had already found a way to make his life in Leifsbudir diverting.

Before going to the ship cove, Freydis sent Louse Oddi
with a message for Ulfar. Then she and Groa crossed the
meadow with Hauk.

Freydis was reluctant to enter the forest. Though she
lived in a country without forests, she had heard tales
about the dangers they held. But she followed Hauk along
a path through the woods, hurrying to keep up while Groa
lagged behind. The trees on the east side were low, being
alder and stunted spruce. But the trees to the West grew
thickly and towered overhead. These trees were so close
to the path that their branches touched Freydis's body as
she passed. Freydis kept her head down lest she see
something move in the branches. Hidden folk were said to
live in trees, and there might be skraelings. Leif said there
were no skraelings in Leifsbudir, that they were much further South. But the two men from Karlsefni's expedition
who had come to Gardar claimed to have seen them here.
The men had told Freydis that skraelings moved about
and could appear at any time. Freydis didn't mention this
to Hauk; she already knew he was the kind of man who
was zealous in finding the weakest part of a woman. She
did ask him if the ship cove could be easily reached by
walking along the shore. Hauk replied that there was a
beach path but he preferred the short cut they were using.
Didn't she like it?

"I like it well enough," Freydis said, "but I prefer walking along the shore."

Finally they reached the ship cove. Although it had not
taken long to walk, to Freydis the distance seemed far.
The cove was at the end of an inlet crooked like a finger
into the land, which made it well protected. The woods
were at the head of the cove, the land on either side of
the inlet was grassy and open. The beach was already covered with wood chips. There was the smell of spruce in
the air.

The pram's keel was laid down, supported by sticks
and braces of wood.

"Today we'll fell logs for rollers and keel stumps and
haul the *Vinland* ashore for repair," Hauk said.

"How long will that take?"

"A few days. We need to make the *Vinland* seaworthy as soon as possible in order to fetch pine if we can find it for your ship mast. Keel wood I can get here. I intend to use spruce. There's also some tamarack which I can make use of. As for knee wood, it shouldn't be too difficult to find spruce knee wood in these parts. With luck your ship should be finished by Yule, except for the planking and oars. I'll make the steering oar during Winter."

"It appears I'll have to start weaving sailcloth if I'm to keep up with you."

"It'll take more than weaving to keep up with me."

Hauk put an arm around Freydis's waist to feel where it was.

Freydis moved away but not very far. She was waiting for Ulfar to arrive. If Ulfar's skill was as good as his reputation, Freydis wanted to make sure he was put to work on the ship, not wasted doing menial chores.

Hauk hadn't met Ulfar; the previous evening Ulfar had gone to his shelter soon after he had eaten in order to work on a manuscript. Hauk was intrigued to hear that Leif Eiriksson's thrall was a scribe from the Hebrides who was writing an account of the voyage. Hauk had known slaves before who were cleverer in some ways than their masters. It was a situation that made him wonder about the fairness of capturing slaves. Hauk didn't wonder much or brood about the injustice for long. Every man knew the Fates controlled a man's luck and that he was powerless to change it. All a thrall could do with misfortune was to let it run its course as Hauk had done himself in Greenland.

When Ulfar arrived in the ship cove, Hauk immediately saw that here was a man who refused to accept his misfortune, for he neither slouched nor cowered and had a determined set to his jaw. His eyes were wary and watchful in a way that suggested he was at all times prepared for the worst. In one quick motion Ulfar swung a leather tool bag from his shoulder to the ground. The fact that he carried tools impressed Hauk. The thrall must be skilled if

Leif allowed him to carry his own tools; thralls didn't usually possess such goods. It was fortunate for Hauk that
Leif had provided a woodworker with tools, since the
Icelanders were short on both counts. The tools were a
measure of Leif's wisdom; he knew a skilled worker must
be provided with the means to accomplish what he did
best.

"Just the man I want to see," Hauk said as if it had
been his idea and not Freydis's that he make use of Ulfar.
"Yesterday I went aboard the *Vinland* to assess the damage. Unless I'm mistaken, we need three new strakes.
While we're waiting for the others, we can find ourselves a
spruce that will serve our purpose."

Satisfied that Ulfar would start out working closely with
Hauk, Freydis told the shipbuilder she would return to the
houses.

"I'll walk you through the woods," Hauk said. More
than once he had glanced over his shoulder and seen the
furtive glances she had cast at the trees on their way to
the cove. It amused him to see how cautious folk from
northern islands were in the forest, how suspicious they
were of the trees.

"I prefer to go along the shore," Freydis said.

Hauk stood watching Freydis as she walked away, Groa
shuffling behind. He tried to imagine Freydis's legs. He
often entertained himself by wagering with other men
about women's legs. The breasts and arms he could see
beneath the shift and robe. He could also surmise the
width of a woman's hips by the way she moved. But
women's legs were too well hidden to see and ankles were
deceptive. Until he saw them, he couldn't judge their full
sweep and shapeliness or their length in relation to the
waist. And it was difficult to assess a woman's waist since
her robe was never belted but loose. Some women were
short waisted and long legged, while others were the
reverse. Hauk's preference was for a short waist, though
not too short, and long legs. He thought these proportions
most pleasing to the eye.

Hauk Ljome looked at a woman's body the way he looked at the woods. He couldn't look at a forest without seeing a long ship or a storfembøring or a skútur take shape. When he stood in a Norwegian forest, he saw a keelson in a young fast-growing oak. His eyes measured the worth of a tree trunk by counting how many strakes could be cut. He saw knees and ribs in the spreading broad-leafed branches of a crooked oak. He saw the old woman in the thickened base where the tree became root and estimated the pole size she could support.

The night after her first walk through the forest, Freydis dreamed she was being attacked by tree giants with long beards and limbs that twined around their prey. These giants were several times the height of the shed. Their fingers were so thin they could reach through smoke holes and creep beneath doors which they opened from inside. That was how one of them entered the shed while Freydis was sleeping. Its long arms reached through the open doorway and groped toward Freydis's bed. She held herself rigid so the hands wouldn't recognize her as a person but pass over her body as if it were a pile of bedding on the wooden bench. The hands were rough and scraped her skin as they explored her face, poking into her nose and trying to force open her lips. The fingers moved into her hair where they twisted and tugged. Freydis called for help but no sound left her lips, which were clamped shut to prevent the tree fingers from getting inside. The giant dragged her from the bed and across the floor to the meadow and the forest beyond. Now she was underground where the tangled tree roots became cages for captured folk. Freydis was shoved into a cage where finger roots explored every opening in her body until no part of her was undefiled. Her teeth were forced apart and worms and other foul creatures stuffed into her mouth. Freydis choked and gagged and finally screamed. It was the scream that woke her.

Had Thorvard been there he might have rescued her, but he was sleeping elsewhere. Groa was asleep on the shed floor, but she slept like the dead. Freydis got up and went to the small hearth where coals glowed in an ember box. Lifting the stone lid and the iron tongs, Freydis took out three or four coals and set them in the firepit. Then she added wood chips and bark. As the flames brightened, Freydis sat on a stool and pulled a robe over her shift to warm herself. She found comfort in watching the tree wood burn, knowing she could destroy tree giants by setting them on fire. From now on she would make sure a small fire burned throughout the night to keep the forest away.

This dream was like the one that had frightened Freydis as a child. After her mother had disappeared and Freydis was still living in Dyrnes, she dreamed frost giants with long beards and ice fingers came out of the sea and dragged her down into the cold darkness of Hel's Kingdom where she was shoved inside a sea cave beside a woman who might have been her mother. It was difficult to say since the woman had black limbs and white hair, and her eyes were green, whereas her mother's had been blue. The corpse kept lifting her arms to stroke Freydis's hair. She had no hands but stumps that bled yellow slime. This dream only came to her once or twice before Freydis imagined another mother for herself and cast her into the sky with a goat.

* * *

After her mother's death, Eirik the Red did not appear in Dyrnes for two years. By then Freydis was seven years old and living with Halla Eldgrimsdottir. Halla was a strong, sturdy woman, well past marriageable age but young enough to manage a dairy. When Halla was younger, her father had arranged a marriage for her before he died, but the man changed his mind when he saw that Halla's eyes were badly crossed. Halla lived on a small steading next to Bribrau Reistsdottir's farm. Because she had known Freydis since birth and liked the child, Halla regarded her as kin. After Illugi and Bribrau's deaths, Halla had been pleased to foster Freydis. Halla moved out of her small hut and into Bribrau's two-room house. Bribrau's parents,

Vigdis and Reist, accepted this arrangement; neither of them wanted to take Freydis in. Reist never recovered from Bribrau's drowning. Within a year of her death he fell down while going to the privy and never got up. The following year Vigdis's heart gave out. Dyrnes folk said Eirik the Red had waited until Reist and Vigdis died before coming to Dyrnes in order to avoid difficulties over claiming his daughter. Some folk said Eirik was more interested in reclaiming the land he had given Reist than he was in his daughter. At that time there was no one else in Greenland who could rightfully claim it. Others said Eirik was claiming the land on his daughter's behalf in order to discourage Bolli Illugisson's kin from thinking they might have it. Halla had refused to foster Bolli, saying the boy was too ill tempered for her to manage. Bolli went to live with his father's sister two steadings over from Bribrau's. Illugi's sister was married to a man named Rodrek, who used a whip to keep Bolli in place.

As she always did when a stranger came to the door, Freydis concealed herself behind one of the roof supports so that she could see the large, red-haired man before he saw her. She had never seen anyone fill the doorway the way Eirik did since visitors to Halla's hut, men especially, were few and far between. Eirik ignored Freydis's caution and snatched her up from behind the post. Freydis beat his chest with her fists. She didn't like having a coarse bushy face close to hers. Eirik laughed and set her down.

"A lively maid," he said. "And healthy too. In some ways she favours her mother, though her eyes are paler and her hair like mine."

The stranger sat down on the sleeping platform and began asking Halla questions about Freydis. After a while Halla said, "Go to the dairy and fetch a bowl of sour milk for your father." That was how Freydis learned her father wasn't Grettir Gormsson, as she had supposed, but this stranger.

When Eirik got up to leave, he patted Freydis's hair and said that they would be seeing more of each other.

Freydis took this as a threat rather than a promise. Her father's words told her things were bound to change. Freydis was too young to want this; she was content living with Halla, since it was an improvement on what she had known before. Halla's disposition never varied. She could be relied upon to do exactly what she said. Every morning without fail Halla got up and lit the fire, then went to milk the cows, returning later with bowls of milk for Freydis and herself to drink. Then they washed in cold water and dressed. After the two rooms were swept and the sleeping platform tidied, they went to the dairy hut and set to work, Halla straining and churning the milk, Freydis washing the livestock with dampened moss. Freydis talked to the cows and goats while she scrubbed them down. Halla had explained the importance of staying on the good side of animals if you expected them to give you milk. It wasn't necessary to praise pigs and sheep, since, unlike cows, they had nothing to withhold. After the livestock were clean Freydis could do as she pleased, which in Summer meant riding the fields with Bolli and his friends. They rode ponies that had gone wild and had to be chased down first. These were pack horses that had been set loose to graze.

When Freydis was nine, Eirik persuaded Halla to take over a farm above Brattahlid so that he might have his daughter close by. This was a small steading that had belonged to Orm Magnusson, who had been one of Eirik's tenant farmers before his death. The steading came with a herd of cows and goats, a dairy and a two-room house. Eirik told Halla that the farm was a reward for looking after his daughter. Eirik put Reist and Bribrau's land in the hands of tenant farmers with whom he was on good terms. He made it known that they would farm it until Freydis was old enough to take it over herself. Eirik knew Reist had left a son behind in Iceland but neither he nor anyone in Dyrnes expected him to challenge Freydis's right to the land.

Before Halla moved into the house in Brattahlid, she slaughtered a goat, and dipping juniper boughs into its blood, smeared the rocks and stone walls marking the boundary. In this way the old gods knew the steading belonged to her. She hung the boughs over the doorway of the house and dairy to keep Orm Magnusson away should he become a night walker and try to reclaim his farm.

In Brattahlid Halla's life continued much as before whereas Freydis's changed. She no longer helped with the dairying or ran with the boys. Instead she learned weaving from her step-mother, Thjodhild.

Though many folk in Brattahlid had known about the daughter Eirik had sired out of wedlock in Dyrnes, Thjodhild didn't learn of it until Freydis was brought to Brattahlid, or so it was assumed. Because Thjodhild was highly regarded, no one had told her about Freydis. Siring children on thralls was one thing but siring a child on the well-born wife of another man invited disgrace. Eirik's sons had known about Freydis for some time because they went about the countryside more than their mother and had heard the rumours. They might not have told Thjodhild about Eirik's daughter in order to keep matters calm between their parents. Since their mother had become a Christian, she and their father had more to quarrel about than before. Eirik seldom missed an opportunity to express his disapproval of the new religion which he said was mainly for weaklings and women. Thjodhild did not take kindly to these remarks and pointed out that Eirik's son Leif had espoused the way of Christ yet was no more a weakling than his father.

A month after Freydis and Halla moved to Orm Magnusson's steading, Freydis met the first of her half-brothers, Thorstein. He had ridden up to the fells with their father. Eirik the Red was rich enough to own horses; most Greenlanders went without. At nineteen, Thorstein was Eirik's youngest son. Overwhelmed by his beauty and shining youth, Freydis forgot to hide when she saw him. When Thorstein dismounted and came walking toward her, Freydis stared at him boldly. He had yellow curls, bright blue eyes and a small red beard. He wasn't as heavily built as his father; for that reason he was better made. He wore an embroidered headband with an eagle feather stuck in one side. The feather enchanted Freydis.

Thorstein came close to her and smiled. Unlike her father's, his teeth were white and his breath smelled sweet.

"Your brother will teach you to ride properly," Eirik said. He turned to Thorstein. "So far she has ridden nothing but wild ponies."

Thorstein asked if that would please her. Freydis told him it would.

"Then we'll get on well together."

They got on too well for sister and brother. Thorstein brought Freydis a small dark horse named Sterkur. He told her it was a gift from Eirik and hers to keep. Thorstein said that as long as he had nothing better to do he would ride with Freydis in the afternoons. He liked being in the company of so fair a maid. They had not ridden together for more than a month when one afternoon, Halla dressed Freydis's hair with ribbons and bid her put on the gift clothes her father had brought her. These were a linen shift and a scarlet robe trimmed in fur with a cloak to match. Halla said that instead of riding with Thorstein, Freydis would be meeting her step-mother, Thjodhild, as well as her other half-brothers, Thorvald and Leif.

Eirik and Thjodhild lived in a large house overlooking Eiriksfjord. The main sleeping hall was hung with coloured weavings and furnished with benches, stools and chests, many of them ornamented with carvings as were the posts and beams. In the centre of the room were four high seat pillars and between them two carved settles facing each other across the hearth. These posts and high seats were so well oiled and polished that they gleamed in the firelight. There were a number of roof holes above the hearth, which meant the room smelled fresh and not at all smoky. The sleeping platforms were piled with white furs. In some places, such as beneath the loom set against the wall, there were white furs on the floor. Elsewhere clean rushes had been strewn about. There was even a small indoor stream flowing through the house by way of a narrow channel dug close to one wall. The channel was both lined and covered with flat stones to keep the water clean. Seeing all this, Freydis thought her father must be a king. Halla had told her tales of kings living in Norway, describing such wealth as there was here. Halla said the kings and queens were tall and noble looking, by which she meant dressed in jewels and silks. Thjodhild was tall, though not so tall as Eirik, and full figured without being fat. She wore a linen shift and a purple robe held by two silver clasps. There was a gold ring on one finger.

"I see she's well made," Thjodhild told Eirik, then added, "and not intimidated by her betters."

Freydis continued her bold staring, since there were aspects of her father's wife that made her want to persist: the silver cross about her neck, the silver bracelets, the silver hair.

"She will have to learn to lower her eyes," Thjodhild remarked. "Some folk are put off by baleful staring."

"There will be time for acquiring manners when she's older," Eirik said. "Meanwhile I'm sure she would like to be shown about the place."

Thjodhild made no attempt to hold Freydis's hand or touch her as Eirik often did but led the way to each room before standing to one side while Freydis looked around. There were several sleeping compartments, two fire rooms for cooking, two storage rooms, a workroom and an indoor privy where the stream flowed outside.

"You can see we are so comfortably set up that during the worst of Winter we need not go outside at all," Thjodhild said. When Thjodhild and Freydis returned to the main hall, Leif, his wife, Jorunn, and babe were there. Thorvald, the next oldest, was there as well. He and Leif didn't look like brothers. Thorvald was brown haired and small, whereas Leif was tall and fair. Leif was friendly to Freydis from the start but Thorvald ignored her. The family sat around the hearth while they were brought delicacies: barley cakes and honey from Norway, neither of which Freydis had tasted before. After she had eaten, Freydis wandered around the room looking at the fine weavings, the iron lamps, the bronze jugs filled with dried flowers. She was waiting for Thorstein. When it was time to leave, a house thrall brought Freydis her cloak and she and her father returned to Halla's. Before they dismounted, Eirik asked Freydis if she would like to move into the large house and promised her a sleeping compartment of her own. Freydis told him she preferred to stay where she was. Then she asked the question that had been troubling her during the visit: where was Thorstein? Eirik replied that Thorstein had gone to the hot springs in Siglufjord. He had injured his shoulder in a fall the previous year and found the hot water healing. Eirik said that while Thorstein was away, he would take Freydis riding.

What her father meant by riding was taking her here and there to meet different folk. Every second afternoon, Eirik took Freydis to the house, where Thjodhild gave her a weaving lesson. Thjodhild began by showing her how to clean fleeces. Sometimes they carried the fleeces to the large outdoor stream and washed them there; more often they washed them in a wooden trough outside the house. Thjodhild showed Freydis how to comb the wool with iron combs. She showed her the various looms she used and how they were threaded. Thjodhild had three looms of different sizes: the largest was used to weave sailcloth and wall hangings; the middle one, robes and shifts; the smallest made cloths of various kinds. Thjodhild gave Freydis a spindle whorl carved out of cherry wood, which she said came from the land of the Franks where fruit wood grew. She also gave Freydis a set of ivory tablets. These small squares were threaded with coloured wool and used to weave borders and trims. Freydis was nimble fingered and quick to learn spinning and tablet weaving, especially since she was allowed to take the work home and practise. Freydis trimmed Halla's cloak and shift in tablet weaving. She trimmed the washing cloths and wadmal coverings they used against the cold. Halla grumbled that this was a waste of good wool. She said the trim on her clothes would discolour from splatters of milk and blood, but she was pleased nonetheless.

* * *

Freydis had been in Leifsbudir five days but she had yet to set up her loom. Before she could begin weaving sailcloth, she had to finish arranging the Greenlanders' accommodations. She arranged to have locks put on the doors of the shed and the storage hut. Leif had sliding bolts mounted on the inside of all the doors in Leifsbudir, but this wasn't enough to satisfy Freydis. With so many folk wandering freely here and there, she wanted to be sure her goods and provisions could be secured from the outside with a lock and key. She had the iron worker Nagli mount two locks she had brought with her from Gardar. Once this was done, Freydis put the keys on the wool string she wore around her neck. This was where she kept her other keys as well as a pair of scissors.

Now Freydis turned her attention to tables and shelves. With so much undressed wood piled here and there on the terrace there was no need to use stones. Fortunately there were others beside Ulfar who, given half a chance, worked tidily with an axe. Among them were Ozur, Ozur's son Thrand and Freydis herself. In Greenland Freydis used her axe mainly for cutting fish and meat. Now she began trying her axe with wood. Together with Ozur and Thrand, she shaped enough slab wood to make shelves for the hut as well as a table of sorts, one that would serve well enough for dairying. When the shelving was in place, Freydis set out the cheeses and butter she had brought from Gardar as well as leftover rations from the voyage. This was mainly deer meat, most of the dried fish having been cast into the bilge water and spoiled. Ozur made shelves for Freydis's shed so that she could store her goods above the mud floor where mice and voles would be less likely to find them. Freydis had left her marriage chest in Greenland. But she had brought a small chest of beaten copper her father had given her to hold her bronze ring, her glass beads, brooches and combs. Freydis also kept the iron belt Hafgrim had made her inside this chest.

Ozur and Thrand made a table and a bench for Freydis's shed. Once this furniture was in place and everything put away, the shed was far more pleasant than the hut Freydis had left behind in Greenland. To add to its comfort Freydis hung wadmal on the wall behind the sleeping bench as well as around the privy. These improvements added a measure of luxury she hadn't enjoyed since before her marriage. While she was arranging the shed, Freydis sometimes thought about her children. Although she missed them, she didn't regret leaving them behind since their being elsewhere meant there was less to distract her attention to what needed doing here.

When Freydis had finished organizing the outbuildings, she turned her attention to the Greenlanders' houses. The rooms in the end house had been mainly taken over by Thorvard and his men.

The rest of the crew occupied the middle house. Freydis didn't care where the Greenlanders slept, except for Thorvard. Although she had chosen to sleep without him in the shed, she wanted to know where he bedded down in case he was needed. Freydis sent Groa to sweep the house floors and tidy. In Gardar the old woman finished these chores smartly, but in Leifsbudir there were seven times the number of people and their gear. Groa took so long to clean up after them that after a time, Freydis would have to send Louse Oddi to help her out. She couldn't have her brother's houses looking as if they were being lived in by pigs.

In addition to overseeing cleaning chores, Freydis had livestock to attend to. Since the Greenlanders' arrival the cow and goats had been staked on the terrace and the sheep and the pigs confined to pens. While the sunny cool weather held, Freydis had Bolli take Kalf and Orn into an alder thicket to cut fence withies. This chore would require several days' work since Freydis wanted large paddocks built on the edge of the meadow behind the Greenlanders' end house where the animals would be easily seen. This area was beside the stream, which made watering the livestock convenient. One of the advantages of the stream was that it moved around stones in such a way that pools of shallow water formed here and there. Farther along was a larger pool where clothing and dairy pails could be scrubbed. This arrangement was far better than what Freydis had in Greenland where her hut was a long walk to the crag pool where Gardar folk fetched their water.

Since their arrival in Leifsbudir, Freydis and Thorvard had seen little of one another. Thorvard had been occupied taking the *Vinland* to the ship cove, a task that required most of a day: the ship had to be rowed around the cape and across several inlets before reaching the cove. Thorvard and his men also hunted the edges of the woods for small game with some success, returning with a number of hares and grouse. This food was a welcome change from the fish soup they had been eating since their arrival. Fortunately cod was in good supply here, during Summer at least. Freydis made stews from the game, simmering the meat with angelica stalks which grew alongside the stream. These meals were served in mid-morning and then again in late afternoon. They were cooked on the hearth of the end house. The men lined up with their bowls while Freydis spooned out a share. As for the thralls, they ate whatever was left, which was rarely enough.

The sixth day in Leifsbudir, Freydis went into the end house to prepare the meal and found Thorvard in bed with the ambatt Hauk had referred to as Mairi. They were in the compartment inside the door. There was no curtain in front of the compartment so that anyone could have watched the coupling had they been around. Instead Freydis shouted to Groa to fetch a pail of water; she had it in mind to throw cold water on the pair. But the old woman moved so slowly, Thorvard had finished before Groa returned with the pail half-full. Thorvard came into the main room, tying his breeches. He approached the hearth where Freydis sat on a stool, her back to the com-

partment, adding pieces of cod Gisli and Balki had caught
earlier that morning to a pot of water.

"Today I intend to hunt deeper into the woods,"
Thorvard said. "Perhaps I'll get lucky and come back with
a deer."

Freydis turned and saw the ambatt watching her from
the doorway. Freydis looked back at her husband.

"Am I expected to feed that girl? Or will she be returning to the Icelanders now that you've finished with her?"

"I've made an arrangement with Helgi Egilsson for her
to live with me."

"Then before you go hunting, you'd better come to the
shed and discuss the situation, that is if you want to prevent a divorce," Freydis said. "In the meantime you could
put her to work fetching water for washing up afterwards."

When Thorvard came into the shed, Freydis asked him
what he had traded away for the concubine.

"Walrus rope."

"In addition to what we already promised in exchange
for the ship?"

Thorvard knew he couldn't avoid telling Freydis what
he was giving Helgi. Better to get it over and done with
now. If Freydis objected to his taking an ambatt, she had
no one to blame but herself. "Helgi didn't sell me Mairi,"
Thorvard went on. "She's merely a loan."

"What else did you part with?"

"Ivory."

"Is that all you gave?"

"I'm letting the Icelanders use Flosi, Lodholt and Avang
for Winter hunting."

"They are three of our best hunters!"

"There was no point in giving them the worst,"
Thorvard said. "They won't be living with the Icelanders,
merely helping them on the ice when the sealing comes."
He looked closely at Freydis, trying to measure her anger
by the shape of her mouth. Her bottom lip was loose
which was a good sign. He went on. "It turns out the
Egilssons are upset by the extra men in our crew. As you
know, I was against bringing extra men along. By lending

them three of ours I smoothed out matters between us." When he had been talking to Helgi, Thorvard had found it useful to mention that he had opposed the idea and had left the matter entirely in the hands of his wife and Evyind Hromundsson.

"Those extra men were brought along not only for our protection but to help us procure cargo," Freydis said. "It seems to me that in your eagerness to have an ambatt, you bartered away advantages we can't afford to lose. As a result you've made us poorer."

"Hardly poorer. We have more men than the Icelanders and better hunters. We also have livestock. Taking all that into consideration, we have as many advantages on our side as the Icelanders have on theirs."

"You are a fool, Thorvard, if you think providing the Icelanders with extra cargo and hunters will make up for our lack of a shipbuilder," Freydis said, calmly enough, at least as far as Thorvard could see.

"We have Ulfar."

"No thrall is a match for a free man like Hauk Ljome," Freydis said. Now she didn't bother hiding her contempt. "There is something else you should consider. The Egilssons won't take kindly to you getting their thrall with child, since once she has been returned to them, they'll have another mouth to feed."

"I doubt one more mouth to feed will matter to the Icelanders," Thorvard said. "In any event not every woman is got with child as easily as you. Mairi's young. She may not conceive at all."

"How young?"

"Fifteen years."

"So you have stooped to lying with a maid."

"She is hardly a maid, Old Woman."

Freydis gave Thorvard one of her baleful stares. Then she switched tactics.

"Since you've betrayed me by making an arrangement with Helgi Egilsson behind my back, you owe me something in return," Freydis said.

Thorvard was a man who preferred to get along with everyone, including his wife, if it didn't inconvenience him too much. He asked Freydis what she thought she was owed.

"I want you to provide Mairi for my use during the day. Groa can't keep up with what needs to be done. Preparing two meals a day for a crew of hungry men has been taking up most of my time. Unless more help is provided, I don't see how I can cook meals, see to the dairying and live-stock and weave sailcloth for two ships. I could use anoth-er thrall to help me."

Thorvard was relieved that this was all Freydis wanted, that she hadn't come after him with the shuttle as she was inclined to do when her temper got loose. He was also relieved she hadn't threatened to go to Helgi Egilsson and insist Mairi be returned.

"What you suggest is a good arrangement," Thorvard said. "It would also suit me, since I expect to be away from Leifsbudir hunting from time to time." Thorvard thought it wise to warn Freydis against being over harsh with his ambatt, as she sometimes was with thralls. Mairi was as gentle and meek as a fawn. Thorvard didn't want her being beaten and kicked. He knew better than to threaten his wife, but he thought she might mistreat Mairi as a way of forcing her return to the Icelanders.

"Helgi doesn't beat his thralls," Thorvard told Freydis. "If we were to beat Mairi, he might demand her return."

"I think I'm in a better position than you to decide the best way to handle thralls," Freydis said. "Be assured I'll do nothing to make us look worse in the Icelanders' eyes. They look down at us enough as it is."

Thorvard didn't share Freydis's view but he let the mat-ter drop. His wife had accepted his ambatt better than he had expected. Better to leave her now while they had reached an agreement of sorts.

Freydis had the last word. "From now on," she said, "you would be wise to speak to me first before you make any more arrangements with the Icelanders. As long as we are husband and wife, we should consult each other before decisions regarding our livelihood are made."

After Thorvard went hunting, Freydis bid his concubine come into the shed. When Mairi was inside, Freydis bolted the door. The girl stood there, her head hung low. Mairi had long dark hair, badly tangled. The hair fell over her face in such disarray that it was difficult to see her eyes. Her tunic was torn and filthy, her skin patched with dirt.

"Remove your tunic," Freydis said.

Mairi didn't move.

"If you do as I say I won't hurt you," Freydis told her, thinking she might be afraid, "but you stink and need cleaning up. I won't have a thrall around me unless she can keep herself tidy and neat." Freydis regarded the fact that Thorvard hadn't insisted on cleanliness himself as an indication that he didn't expect much from Mairi.

Mairi drew off her tunic and stood grasping her elbows. Freydis stared at her nakedness. The girl was too thin and flat chested for beauty, scrawny and plain as a pole. There was a thicket of black hair between her legs, coarse as a man's. The girl's ungainly appearance gave Freydis some satisfaction. If Thorvard's ambatt had been exceptional, he might have trouble giving her up later on.

"Listen carefully," Freydis said. "You are to haul water into the compartment where my husband sleeps and bathe all over including your hair. I'll send Groa to comb and plait it. Afterwards you are to wash this dirty tunic and set it out to dry. I'll give you another tunic to wear instead."

Freydis fetched a mended tunic and gave it to the girl. Mairi put her dirty tunic back on and Freydis unbolted the door.

"When you finish cleaning yourself, you and Groa are to pick blueberries in the meadow. If we don't harvest them soon the Icelanders are bound to take them all."

After Mairi left Freydis began setting up her loom, leaning it against the south wall of the shed where she could work protected from the wind, while at the same time she could keep an eye on the meadow and the livestock. She

had decided to work outside as long as the weather permitted, to take advantage of the light. While she worked,
she weighed the advantages and disadvantages of
Thorvard's ambatt living under their roof. She thought
Thorvard's men might come to resent his taking a concubine when they had none themselves. Leif had warned
Freydis and Thorvard against bringing unmarried women
on the voyage; Leif had avoided bringing women here
himself, anticipating his crew would quarrel over their use.
If the Greenlanders began quarrelling over Mairi, Freydis
would lose no time in returning her to Helgi Egilsson. In
the meantime she would make full use of the girl around
the place. Another thrall would come in handy when it
came to dairying, cooking and cleaning chores. Freydis
told herself that she didn't care one way or the other if
Thorvard used a concubine. It wasn't uncommon for men
to lie with other women besides their wives; she herself
was the result of that fact. Had Mairi been a well-born
woman of accomplishment and beauty, Freydis might
have felt differently. As matters now stood, what she felt
mainly was relief, for by using Mairi Thorvard would forego
his right as a husband and would leave her alone. What
Freydis objected to was that Thorvard had traded away
more than the concubine was worth. By using Mairi herself, Freydis could make up for the poor bargain Thorvard
had arranged with Helgi. Freydis used a set of bronze
weights to measure rations of cheese and butter; she
thought arrangements between the Greenlanders and the
Icelanders should be measured like dairy goods. If any
favours were being given, they should be weighted in such
a way as to give the Greenlanders more.

These weights didn't apply to Freydis's marriage. From
the outset she had known that the marriage would be
unfairly weighted in favour of Thorvard Einarsson for by
then she had learned that her mother's brother hadn't
stayed in Iceland as expected, but had moved to Dyrnes
and claimed both Reist's and Bribrau's farms. As a result,
the weights between Thorvard and herself would never be
even. How different it might have been if she'd had her

mother and grandfather's land to use as dowry. She might have married a prosperous farmer in Dyrnes and settled there. Or she might have married her half-brother. If Thorstein had married her instead of Gudrid Thorbjornsdottir, Freydis wouldn't have cared one way or the other about keeping matters even between husband and wife. Or so she thought. She thought that given the chance, her passion for Thorstein would have overridden all else, that in their own way, they might have become King and Queen of Greenland.

WHAT FREYDIS HAD ENJOYED MOST about the move from Dyrnes to Brattahlid were the frequent rides with her half-brother Thorstein. Most days during Summer she and Thorstein rode out together. It was Thorstein's contention that they were doing their horses a favour since Sterkur and Svartur preferred being ridden together. Usually Freydis and Thorstein rode to other farmsteads or along the fjord. They picked berries in the upland pastures or waded in a stream. Thorstein was high spirited and did these things naturally, not in the manner of someone trying to please a young girl. Thorstein was agile and quick with his hands. One afternoon he wove Freydis a basket of shore grasses and filled it with shells he found on the beach. Another day when they were riding along a marsh, he cut hollow reeds of different lengths and bound them with sinew. He gave the reeds to Freydis, urging her to play a tune. When Freydis tried the reed pipes, Thorstein said she sounded like a rutting bull. He held his sides laughing and rolled on the ground. Afterwards he put his lips to the pipes and played her a tune as sweet as the song of the lark that came to Greenland in Summer.

One day when they had dismounted in an upland pasture, Thorstein began picking meadow rue and harebells, which he wove together into a wreath of flowers. He set the wreath on Freydis's head and stood back and waved his hand as if he were addressing an assembled crowd.

"Behold, the Queen of Greenland," he said and bowed. Freydis was well past eleven when this happened, a flat-chested clumsy girl who sometimes found herself overtaken by shyness, especially if she thought, as now, that someone had guessed her thoughts. She had the idea Thorstein knew she had begun to dream about becoming the kind of woman he would one day want for his wife.

When Freydis was twelve, she was taken to the big house to live. By then Thjodhild had come around to agreeing that if Eirik's daughter was to be skilled at weaving, she would have to spend more of each day working on an upright loom. Judging from the speed with which the girl had learned spinning and tablet weaving, given enough time she was bound to master the floor loom. Thjodhild was also of the opinion that there were many household skills the girl must learn. As matters now stood, Freydis knew only what her foster mother had taught her about dairying and was inclined to be wild. Though Eirik often gave in to his daughter, in this matter of household instruction he stood firmly behind wife.

The day Eirik rode up to the fells to fetch his daughter, he may have expected a show of temper. More than once he had seen Freydis stamp her foot or stalk off if something didn't please her. He may have been agreeably surprised when Freydis did neither but gathered her bundles and left Halla's steading without a backward glance. Freydis knew she would miss her foster mother, but she thought she stood a better chance with Thorstein if she was living with him under the same roof. And she wouldn't be so far from Halla that she couldn't visit her from time to time. Earlier Thorstein had told Freydis he had overheard his parents talk of moving her down to the big house. This had given Freydis time to consider what she thought she would like. By the time Eirik came to fetch her she had decided that all things considered, she would be better off living in her father's house.

The change took some getting used to. Thjodhild had many rules she expected Freydis to follow. Freydis must wash before and after meals. She must keep a small cloth on her lap at meal times in order to wipe her mouth and hands. Twice a day before she ate she must kneel and pray to the Christian god, asking him to bless the food before it passed her lips. Sometimes the priest ate with them. At such times he would keep them on their knees so long the food grew cold. Freydis's father refused to eat when Geirmund Gunnfard was present; Eirik said he wouldn't kneel for anyone, neither man nor god.

It was Thjodhild's contention that a woman must work as hard as her thralls, and she kept Freydis busy proving this. She must learn to cook soups and stews, how to roast meat and fish. She must learn to serve this food without spilling. After each meal Freydis must help the house thralls clear away the trenchers and cups so that she would know firsthand how each household task should be done. She must help take down the trestle tables and shake the linen cloths outside before folding them away in chests. She must not leave a room without permission, even to go to the privy.

It was Thjodhild's habit never to raise her voice or shout even at thralls. All the same she seldom held back from giving her opinion about this or that. Thjodhild told Freydis that it was her Christian duty to train her husband's daughter so that a suitable marriage could be arranged for her later on. In addition to householding, she would teach Freydis how to make tablecloths, blankets, robes, and the kind of hangings that decorated the walls of Eirik's house.

Three times during the first year Freydis ran away. The third time, Thorstein rode up to Halla's steading and fetched her back. Thorstein didn't return Freydis to the big house directly. Instead, he and Freydis rode to the meadow where two Summers earlier he had crowned her queen. After they dismounted, Thorstein told Freydis to sit beside him on the grass and listen to what he had to say. He told her he was leaving Greenland on the first ship to come up the fjord. It was his intention to travel to Norway. He was of a mind to see that part of the world before he settled down in Greenland. When he returned in a year or two, he expected to find that Freydis had become an accomplished young woman any man would be pleased to wed. Thorstein said this unaware of the passion he had inspired. His words set Freydis dreaming of living with him as his wife. They would build themselves a fine house and rear children who would ride out with them to the meadows and fields.

During the years she lived at the big house in Brattahlid, Freydis learned everything Thjodhild knew about weaving and dyeing. Her stepmother took her different places and showed her madder root and various mosses used for colour, mainly yellow and brown. She taught her to add cow piss to lichen to make it red. For purple and blue Thjodhild relied on dyes bought from traders. Freydis learned how to separate the inner wool from the outer wool, something Thjodhild preferred to do by hand. Because of its softness and fineness, the inner wool—Thjodhild called it hair—was used to weave shifts and household cloths. The outer wool was used for robes, tunics and cloaks, since it was tough and springy and, being oily, resisted cold.

Thjodhild often reminded Freydis that a good weaver must never be without her spindle. Freydis learned how to twirl the spindle so that it hung spinning away from her body, which allowed her to do two things at once. Like Thjodhild she could spin while minding various pots and cauldrons or walking about. As a result of spinning and weaving, Freydis's hands became strong, the skin softened with oil. At the same time, she grew more graceful and her figure filled out. Her hair was combed every day by one of Thjodhild's thralls until it gleamed. Freydis became so comely and well favoured that in the Winter of her fourteenth year, Eirik decided he would take her to the Althing the following Summer so that she would be seen by marriageable men. He also gave her a carved wooden chest he had bought from the Norwegian trader who had taken Thorstein away the previous Summer. Eirik said he had bought the chest especially for the purpose of giving it to Freydis so that she might have a place to store her marriage goods. The inside of the chest was fragrant with yew, which made Freydis want to store only her finest goods inside. Into the chest went Freydis's work: the first length of cloth she had woven on the floor loom, two grey blankets edged in blue and white, a red and blue striped wall hanging, a white tablecloth, a smaller embroidered cloth edged in white lace which her step-mother had bought from the Norwegians. Since ships couldn't be relied upon to come to Brattahlid yearly, Thjodhild kept a store of goods that were unavailable in Greenland. In addition, Freydis had a cloak, two shifts and three robes which Thjodhild had made.

On the first day of the Althing, Eirik bid Freydis dress in a new scarlet robe. Freydis was pleased about this, since it gave her a chance to show off her clothes. She took particular care with her hair, telling the thrall to plait coloured wool into it. The Althing was being held in the field below Eirik's house where tents and booths were set up. Eirik led Freydis to Einar Grimolfsson's booth, a stone-walled enclosure with an awning for a roof. There were furs on the floor. In the middle of the room was a wooden chest and around it two or three stools. Einar was a wealthy farmer from Gardar who had a son named Thorvard of marriageable age. The son was nowhere to be seen, but his mother and sisters made a point of looking Freydis over. Freydis's main interest in the women was seeing what clothes and jewellery they possessed. Einar's wife wore a silver amulet around her neck and a silver bracelet on each arm. One of the daughters wore bronze brooches on her robe. This was a married daughter named Inga. None of these women warmed to Freydis. This didn't trouble her at all, she had no intention of marrying Thorvard Einarsson, wherever he was.

Later that Summer Leif sailed from Brattahlid with thirty-four men to find lands to the West which the Icelander Bjarney Herjolfsson had seen years before when blown off course on his way to Greenland. Before Leif's departure Freydis had been caught up in the voyage preparations. Every day, she had ridden up to Halla's dairy to help make cheese and butter for Leif's provisions. Usually Halla gave Freydis the job of churning the butter while she made the cheese, draining the whey from the curds and pressing it into soapstone moulds. Freydis often rode Thorstein's horse, Svartur, to keep him exercised. She rode to the meadows to pick cranberries and blueberries which were dried by the hearth before being stored in sacks. She worked alongside Thjodhild, bundling strips of dried fish and meat. Freydis watched the ship depart with some satisfaction, pleased with the work she had done for Leif.

The following Summer Thorstein returned to Greenland. Freydis, who had been watching the fjord all along, was the first one in the family to see the Norwegian ship. While Thjodhild and Eirik and some others went down to the fjord, Freydis ran inside to bathe and put on the red kirtle that flattered her waist.

When Thorstein stepped ashore wearing bright green leggings and a purple leather hat, Freydis thought she had never seen a handsomer man. The old clumsiness returned; Freydis thought others could plainly see what she felt inside. She was so used to keeping her passion for her half-brother secret, she was unwilling to let it out until Thorstein knew about it himself. Thorstein didn't appear to notice her awkwardness; when he saw her standing beside the fjord he made a fuss over her, sweeping off his hat and bowing from the waist.

"Is this the sister I left behind?"

"The same."

"Hardly the same. I can see that you're no longer a maid but a woman."

Later he gave Freydis a string of pretty glass beads, which Freydis regarded as proof that he'd been thinking about her while he'd been gone.

Thorstein talked for two days without ceasing. He talked about the whirlpool the ship had narrowly escaped while crossing the Greenland Sea. He talked about the storm that had forced the crew ashore in Iceland for ship repair. He described the hot springs in Reykjavik which were so numerous folk used them to heat their homes. He

had seen a geyser that swelled like a greenish bubble
before flinging scalding water into the air. Thjodhild and
Eirik had seen these sights long ago when they lived in
Iceland, but Thorstein's telling was so vivid they said it
was as if they were seeing them over again. Thorstein
went on to describe the Hebrides and the dark-haired
beauty of the Celtic women living there. In Norway, the
women were beautiful too, but it was the kind of beauty
Thorstein was accustomed to so he didn't remark on it as
much. Thorstein said that whenever he met Norwegians
who hadn't travelled, they questioned him closely about
his home. They had heard peculiar tales about Greenland
and wanted to know if they were true. Did the
Greenlanders wear furs next to their bodies as skraelings
were said to do? Did the Greenlanders' skin take on the
green colour of the sea? Did the women conceive when
they drank the water?

When Thorstein had exhausted himself from talking
about his adventures, he and Freydis began riding along
their favourite paths again. Freydis was biding her time
until she could talk to Thorstein about her plans. She had
the idea that Thorstein had considered marrying her but
was waiting until she was old enough. She wanted to
assure him that she was well able to marry, since she was
now a woman in all respects. Although they laughed and
raced their horses as before, Freydis thought Thorstein
had changed. Since his return he was more restrained and
less carefree. She put this down to his reluctance to discuss his intentions with her. She began to look for the
chance to assure him that she was ready to marry.

One day when they were riding in a meadow, Freydis
dismounted and began picking meadow rue and harebells. Thorstein didn't help with this but after tethering the
horses, sat down on the grass and watched Freydis weave
a wreath. When she finished, Freydis reached up and
placed the wreath upon his head. "Behold the King of
Greenland!" she said and put her lips to his. They lay back
and tumbled in the grass, kissing and fondling. Freydis
would have continued in this, since it was what she had

wanted but Thorstein sat up, took the wreath from his head and tossed it aside.

"This never happened," he said. "Remember we are brother and sister."

"Half-sister."

"The fact remains we are close kin, too close for lying together or marrying. We must put such thoughts out of our minds. Our father would kill us if he knew about this."

Freydis had no intention of putting such thoughts out of her mind. When they had been tumbling about in the grass, Thorstein had been as eager as she, lifting her shift and placing his hand between her legs. As for their father, she doubted he would resort to killing either of them. Freydis thought she would be able to explain the situation to their father in such a way that he would allow Thorstein and her to marry. Freydis wasn't discouraged by Thorstein's reaction and thought of their tumble in the meadow as something that would lead to better things later on.

That Summer Eirik again took Freydis to the Althing. This time Thorvard Einarsson was waiting outside his father's booth. Right away Freydis recognized his ordinariness; he had none of Thorstein's beauty yet he was not ugly either. His manner was dull compared to Thorstein's colour and dash. Thorvard asked Freydis to walk with him to the fjord. When they reached the water, Thorvard looked across Eiriksfjord and said, "In Gardar I have a caged falcon. When we're finished here, I intend to go after more falcons. I've worked out a way of snaring them that seldom fails."

Freydis knew Thorvard was trying to impress her; falcons were highly valued as trading goods.

"Do you have a trader in mind?"

"Of course. Much as I like hawking, I wouldn't go to the trouble of capturing them unless it served a purpose. Falcons fetch a high price with the Norwegians who are said to trade them with the Moors."

After he had spoken, Thorvard waited as if he expected Freydis to speak of what she could provide. Freydis didn't mention the goods inside her marriage chest which she had put together with Thorstein in mind. In any case, she didn't think Thorvard Einarsson had enough goods to match her dowry which then included the Dyrnes land. Later, after he had taken her to meet the sons of other farmers, her father expressed the same view. "Some of these farmers have a long way to go," he said, "before they'll be rich enough to marry the daughter of Eirik the Red."

When Leif Eiriksson returned to Greenland from Vinland late the next Summer, he brought not only all of his crew but also eight shipwrecked Icelanders he had rescued from a reef in Lambeyarsund. Among the survivors were Thorir the Easterner and his new wife, Gudrid Thorbjornsdottir.

From the start Eirik made a fuss over Gudrid. Years earlier, before the settlement of Greenland, Gudrid's father had supported Eirik against his enemy Thorgest just before Eirik was exiled from Iceland. For this reason Eirik insisted Gudrid and Thorir sit on the high seat opposite himself and Thjodhild. He bade his sons extend the seats by piling chests and benches on either side so that all his children could sit with him above the hearth. Thorstein and Thorvald were eager to do this; neither of them wanted to miss a word of Leif's tales. Both of them planned to make the same journey as their brother someday. Freydis had it in mind to make the journey with Thorstein. Listening to Leif's tales convinced her that if Eirik disallowed their marriage in Greenland, she and Thorstein could move their thralls and horses to Vinland where no one would bother a brother and sister living together as man and wife.

The feasting and tale telling that followed Leif's return continued long after Summer was over and Winter began. Leif had brought back such a quantity of wine that night after night folk gathered in Eirik's house to celebrate the country that lay across the Western Sea. The hardiest of the merrymakers were folk who knew they would never see Vinland and depended on Leif and his tale tellers to transport them there.

Shortly after Yule the drink ran out and the tale telling came to an end. Folk were content to stay close by their own fires at night. It was well for them that they did, since a plague visited the house of Eirik the Red. Some folk said the illness might have been caused by the lack of sleep and hard drinking that followed the voyagers' return. Others were more outspoken and said the Icelandic survivors had brought the illness into Eirik's house. Whatever the reason, the plague came with a vengeance. It was a vomiting sickness accompanied by raging thirst; the afflicted men couldn't keep anything down, not even water. Thorir the Easterner fell ill first, and was soon followed by five of his crew. When Eirik the Red fell ill, Thjodhild sent his children away. Leif and Jorunn took their son and went across the fjord to stay with Jorunn's sister in Stokkanes. Thorvald was already visiting a widow in Vik. Thorstein stayed in Solarfjoll with one of Eirik's tenant farmers. Freydis returned to Halla. Thjodhild's instructions were that none of Eirik's children were to return until after she had sent word that the plague had passed. This took much longer than anyone thought. Eirik and Thorir were the first to die. The crew took longer. Being young they held on for as long as two months, eventually dying from lack of air. After each man died, a stake was driven into his chest at Thjodhild's insistence and he was placed outside in a storage shed which had been cleared to make room to store the corpses until the ground thawed. There the frozen corpses remained as fresh as if the men had newly died.

When the frost finally left the ground, the corpses were carried out, laid upon the ground and unwrapped. The stakes were removed so that the priest could pour holy water into the hole inside. Thjodhild had sent out word of Eirik's burial. She wanted folk in the area, especially Eirik's children, to see his final resting place. While Geirmund Gunnfard said a prayer over him, Eirik the Red was buried by himself some distance from the front of the church; the others were buried together about the same distance off to one side. Watching this from the hillside, Freydis thought her father must have agreed to his burial place in a delirium since when he was alive, he had little good to say about Christians, and in his right mind would have preferred to have been buried any place else but in the churchyard. After the burials, the hut where the corpses had been during Winter was burnt to the ground.

No one else died from the plague at that time, a fact that was attributed to Thjodhild's firm handling of the arrangements. The dead men's bedding and clothing were burnt. Gudrid also burnt her clothes in case she had been a carrier of the disease. After taking a sweat bath in the stone hut outside, she was given new clothes by Thjodhild. Only after all this had been done and the house thoroughly cleaned, aired and blessed would Thjodhild allow her sons and step-daughter to return.

That Summer none of the Eirikssons attended the Althing out of respect for Eirik, except Leif whose duty it was to go, since he was now gödi in his father's place.

Freydis spent most of the Summer riding. Sometimes she rode Svartur instead of Sterkur, since Thorstein seemed to have lost interest in riding together, being much taken up with helping his brother Thorvald provision his ship. Despite Eirik's death, Thorvald Eiriksson intended to sail to Vinland later that Summer. As before, Freydis helped Halla make extra cheeses and butter, then took these provisions down to the ship. In this way she saw more of Thorstein than she otherwise would. Thorstein had become distant with Freydis and was much in the company of Thorir the Easterner's widow, particularly after Thorvald had sailed.

From the outset Freydis didn't like Gudrid Thorbjorns-dottir and spurned her attempts to make friends. She thought Gudrid was someone who sought to please others so that she might be highly thought of by them. Freydis had no intention of becoming an admirer of Gudrid's, but she watched her nonetheless to see how she managed to get her way so easily with men. Gudrid had a habit of swaying her slender body like a flower in the wind so that men rushed to her side to keep her from falling. Freydis knew this was unlikely, since beneath her robe Gudrid possessed a pair of legs far sturdier than Freydis's own. Freydis had grown to like being the daughter in her father's house and thought Gudrid was trying to unseat her. Although Gudrid was six years older than Freydis and supposed to be mourning, she tended to be lively in her ways. Gudrid was dark haired and girlish. It didn't take much to make her laugh, which seemed to please Thorstein; he was more animated when Gudrid was around. He was quick to fetch her cloak or spindle as if she were helpless and unable to fetch either herself. He began accompanying Gudrid to his mother's church.

Thorstein gave Gudrid a silver bracelet in exchange for a silver cross. The exchange galled Freydis especially since she had recently given Thorstein a varicoloured headband she had woven. Thorstein treated the headband carelessly, hanging it from a post instead of putting it on. Thorstein didn't notice Freydis's bitter disappointment; he seldom spoke to her any more. It was Leif who noticed. One day after he had followed Freydis's baleful stare as she watched Gudrid laughing at some joke Thorstein had made, Leif came up to Freydis and said, "We must find you a husband at the next Althing. Otherwise you are apt to waste time looking in the wrong place for something you cannot have."

"It seems to me Gudrid Thorbjornsdottir is in the wrong place," Freydis replied. She was convinced that if it weren't for Gudrid, Thorstein would be hers.

Gudrid couldn't ride, so every day Thorstein took it upon himself to teach her. He gave Gudrid a brown horse named Bute that had once been Eirik's. He said he had chosen that particular horse because it matched Gudrid's hair which was the colour of chestnuts he had seen in Norway. After she overheard this remark, Freydis barbed Gudrid's leather whip with thistles, which caused Bute to throw Gudrid off though to no ill effect since Thorstein managed to catch her before she hit the ground. Another time Freydis knotted Gudrid's undergarments, soaked them in water and scorched them over the fire. These pranks had more to do with spite than anything else. The scorching was blamed on a house thrall who did the washing since the girl had been vindictive once before when she had been required to wash Gudrid's clothes.

Early one morning toward the end of the Summer, Freydis resorted to witchcraft of a sort. She crept to Gudrid's sleeping compartment with her scissors and cut off a lock of Gudrid's hair, intending to weave a spell that would turn Thorstein away from Gudrid. It was well known that a spell woven from hair could bring about a desired result. Before Freydis could get away, Thjodhild came upon her holding the hair. To avoid disturbing others, Thjodhild took Freydis by the arm and led her outside where she could plainly talk. When they were well away from the door, Thjodhild looked at Freydis who was in no way ashamed by what she had done and returned her step-mother's look with a defiant stare.

"I have done my best to teach you the womanly skills you need," Thjodhild said, "but I can do nothing about the black tricks you have been playing on our guest. You resist all attempts to make you kind hearted. I am returning you to Halla Eldgrimsdottir. You are to leave at once and empty handed. I will send your goods along later, including the loom I have set aside for your marriage. I know you have your mind set on having your half-brother and nothing but evil can come of that. If you stay away from Thorstein, what you have done to Gudrid will remain a secret between us. I know Thorstein would think less well of you if he knew of your tricks."

Freydis didn't regret trying to come between Gudrid and Thorstein; she had merely been following her father's advice. More than once he had advised her to do whatever she could to achieve what she wanted. What she wanted more than anything else was to marry Thorstein. As for Thjodhild, she had never liked Freydis. Ever since Eirik's death, her step-mother had been biding her time until an excuse could be found for sending her away.

Not long after Freydis left her step-mother's house, Thorstein Eiriksson married Gudrid Thorbjornsdottir in Thjodhild's church. Freydis didn't go to the wedding but she couldn't avoid hearing about it since the elaborate festivities were much talked about afterwards.

The next Summer Leif came to see Freydis. He told her Bribrau's brother had come from Iceland to claim his inheritance in Dyrnes. As a result Freydis's marriage settlement wouldn't be as large as he had thought. Leif said he would provide posts and beams for a dowry as well as a brass bowl edged in beaten gold if Freydis would marry Thorvard Einarsson. Einar had agreed to the marriage and said he would give up a large home field as well as a hut and three or four thralls. Freydis told Leif she would consider the offer.

A month later Freydis went to Gardar and married Thorvard. There had been no other offers and prospects of bettering her Luck were poor if, like Halla, she remained unwed. Although Freydis was fond of her foster mother, she had no wish to live like her. She thought Halla did not wish it either, since all along it had been understood between them that Freydis had been destined for a better fate.

The Summer following her marriage when Freydis was pregnant with Thorlak, she heard the news that Thorvald Eiriksson's crew had returned from Leifsbudir without him. Thorvald had been killed by a skraeling arrow somewhere in Vinland. Halla brought this news when she came to Gardar to midwife the birth. Halla also brought the news that Thorstein and Gudrid intended to sail to Vinland themselves the next Summer. Not only had Gudrid managed to steal the man Freydis wanted to marry, she had taken her dreams as well. This was the time when Freydis underwent an emptying-out, not only expelling the babe but discharging tender prospects she had nurtured earlier so that she might replace them with a harder core. After this she was careful to choose only those dreams that she thought she could bring about, even if it meant souring relations between Thorvard and herself. From the beginning Freydis's marriage to Thorvard lacked sweetness, but it wasn't entirely lacking in taste, being more like cheese than honey. During Winter when the humiliation and discomfort of living in a poor hut in Gardar preoccupied her thoughts, two things prevented Freydis from walking the frozen length of Einarsfjord all the way to the sea: one was the grudge she bore Gudrid, the other was the resolution to improve her Luck.

Two years went by before Freydis learned the outcome of Thorstein's expedition from Nagli Asgrimsson. By then Thorlak was walking and Freydis was again with child, this time with Signy.

At the bottom of Thorvard's home field, where the turfs were cut, was a small ore bog his sister coveted. Freydis wanted the ore bog used before Inga and Guttorm could look for ways to take it over. Ever since Freydis had married Thorvard, Guttorm and Inga seldom missed a chance to remark that they would help themselves to the ore if Thorvard and Freydis had no use for it. Freydis hired Nagli to make iron tools from the ore in exchange for food and a place to sleep. For several nights running, before he bedded down on the opposite side of the hearth from Freydis and Thorvard, Nagli would sit beside their fire and tell his tales. The story Nagli told first was *The Tale of Thorstein Eiriksson's Death*. This story had been told to Nagli by a kinsman on his mother's side, which made it second hand. Even so it was the truth or so Nagli claimed.

"According to Adalric who told me this story, Thorstein Eiriksson's attempt to reach Vinland was doomed from the start. Thorstein, his wife, Gudrid, and their crew put out to sea in Leif's ship. They were barely out of sight of land when the weather turned against them. Foul winds kept them shrouded in fog so that for days on end they never knew where they were. The bad weather continued until it was nearly Winter, which meant that when the fog lifted, Thorstein and his crew were forced to land up the coast at Lysufjord, since the time had passed when they could expect a safe crossing to Vinland. They had no choice but to put off the voyage for another year. I've never been as far as Lysufjord but Adalric, who was hunting up North, told me there aren't many folk living there."

Here Thorvard spoke up. "Adalric is right about that. I've passed Lysufjord many times on my way to Northsetur. Most of the land thereabouts is too poor to be farmed."

Nagli didn't like having a tale interrupted, since it interfered with remembering the story exactly as it had been told to him. Before Thorvard could say more about Lysufjord than was wanted, Nagli returned to the tale. "Thorstein found winter accommodations for his crew, but there were none for Gudrid and himself. As a result he and his wife faced the prospect of spending Winter in a tent aboard ship.

"Word of Thorstein's situation reached the ears of a farmer named Thorstein the Black who had a steading at the end of Lysufjord. One day Thorstein the Black rode to the ship to see Thorstein and Gudrid, who were sleeping when he arrived. Thorstein the Black decided to awaken them and shouted Thorstein Eiriksson's name.

"When Thorstein Eiriksson awoke and came out of the tent, Thorstein the Black invited Gudrid and him to spend the Winter at his farm. Noticing the silver cross hanging around Thorstein's neck, Thorstein the Black warned him that he was of a different faith. He said Christianity hadn't yet reached Lysufjord, and that he hoped that his not being Christian wouldn't prevent them from getting along, for he and his wife, Gunnhild, liked matters the way they were and had no wish to be converted by overzealous followers of Christ. He said his farm was off by itself and that he and Gunnhild had become dull and unsociable from having little to do with other folk. Thorstein the Black concluded by saying that if his invitation was accepted, he would return tomorrow with enough horses to carry Thorstein, his wife and their goods to his farm. Thorstein Eiriksson replied that he would consult Gudrid and went inside the tent. Gudrid said she would go along with whatever her husband decided. Thorstein Eiriksson therefore told Thorstein the Black that he and Gudrid would be pleased to move to his house. The next day Thorstein the Black returned with the horses as promised and your brother and Gudrid left the ship."

Now Thorvard began to snore; he liked tales which were short and fell asleep if they were overlong. Nagli didn't attempt to waken him but continued his tale, speaking to Freydis as if her husband wasn't there.

"Adalric said your brother and Gudrid had not lived with Thorstein the Black and Gunnhild longer than two months before disease broke out in Lysufjord, beginning with various members of the crew. Apparently this disease was much like the plague that killed your father as well as Gudrid's first husband, for it was accompanied by high fevers and raging thirsts. Gunnhild fell ill before your half-brother. She was a large woman, larger than many men. Even so the disease laid her low. Then Thorstein caught the disease and for a time, the two of them were ill side by side. Gunnhild died first. It was the custom in Lysufjord to use a corpse board. Although he had many thralls, it was a source of pride to Thorstein the Black that he fetch the corpse board himself. Adalric said that when Thorstein the Black went out to get the board, Gudrid bade him hurry back quickly, for she did not like being left in the room with a corpse even though her husband was still alive. While Thorstein the Black was outside, Gunnhild pushed herself up from the bed and began groping on the floor for her shoes. Just as she found them, her husband returned and Gunnhild fell back on the sleeping platform and died a second time. Adalric said Gunnhild was so heavy that the house beams creaked when she fell. Even so, her husband was big and powerful enough to get her corpse onto the board and out of the house without anyone's help.

"Three days later your brother expired. Gudrid was sitting on a stool beside his sleeping platform when he died. Noticing her grief Thorstein the Black got up from his place near the wall and picked up Gudrid. Then he sat opposite your dead brother, holding Gudrid in his lap to console her. He promised he would take her and her goods back to Eiriksfjord as soon as the weather improved.

"'I'll also bring my thralls,' he said, 'to provide you some comfort during our journey.'

"According to Adalric, no sooner had Thorstein the Black made this promise when your brother's corpse sat up and asked, 'Where is Gudrid?'

"Adalric said your brother repeated this question twice more but Gudrid refused to answer. Maybe she didn't know how to answer a corpse or perhaps she thought her husband would take her away with him if she did. The third time her husband spoke, Gudrid asked Thorstein the Black if she should speak. He advised her not to answer. Then he lifted her up and carried her near the platform where your brother lay. Thorstein the Black sat on a stool holding Gudrid on his knee.

"'What do you want, Thorstein?' he said.

"'I want to tell Gudrid her fate,' your brother replied. 'I want her to know that I am now in happy repose. I want to say to her also that she will marry an Icelander and that they will have a long life together. Their children will be of excellent stock and will prosper. She and her husband will leave Greenland and live in Iceland. There they will achieve a high reputation.'

"That was all your brother said before he fell back for the last time."

Freydis had sat through this tale in silence. Now she burst out, "Gudrid Thorbjornsdottir made a fool of Thorstein," she said. "By making him wear that foolish cross, she made him feeble minded. He deserved to marry someone better than a cowardly bitch who sat on another man's lap and asked his permission to speak to her husband. I wouldn't be surprised if Gudrid hadn't infected him with the plague as she did with her first husband and my father. The sooner she goes back to Iceland, the better it will be for everyone here."

"I doubt you've seen the last of Gudrid," Nagli said. "Thorstein the Black has brought her back to Brattahlid. I saw her there recently when I was repairing a cauldron chain for Thjodhild. I was also retained by an Icelandic trader named Thorfinn Karlsefni, who wanted me to make iron rivets for his ship. While I was there, I couldn't help but notice the attention this trader paid your brother's widow. It might be that he's the Icelander your brother spoke of before he died, and that in due course, he and Gudrid will marry."

Early one morning shortly after Nagli had left Gardar and Thorvard was away hunting in Vatnahverfi, Freydis took a broad axe, a length of strong rope and a sheepskin bag and walked over the hills to Eiriksfjord accompanied by her strongest thralls, Kalf and Orn, who then rowed her across the fjord to Brattahlid and walked with her up to Halla's farm. Although Freydis's horse was of no use to Halla, Freydis still kept him there. Thorvard's home field was needed to graze Freydis's cows, which was why she preferred to keep Sterkur in Halla's field, or so she told Halla.

Freydis ordered the thralls to blindfold Sterkur and tie him down. Then she lifted her broad axe and whacked it against the horse's neck. After the head was severed, the thralls put it into the sheepskin bag and carried it to the pram, leaving the horse meat for Halla. Halfway across the fjord, Freydis bade Kalf and Orn throw the bag over the side. Freydis was back in Gardar in time to put Thorlak to bed. She went to bed herself shortly thereafter and slept without dreams, convinced that she had rid herself of a passion that had given her more pain than pleasure.

I have been in Leifsbudir a month. Now that the memory of our perilous crossing has diminished, I am well pleased that Heaven's Lord—through Leif Eiriksson—directed me here. The land itself does not impress; though flat, it has the same rawness as Greenland as if Our Creator made it last and had no time left to make grassy knolls and fine white sand. But the place is satisfactory in other ways, being well supplied with timber and fish. Since our arrival here I have been dressing spruce wood for the Greenlanders' ship. Because the weather has been fair, we have managed to lay the keel. The mastfish, which Hauk Ljome calls the old woman, has been shaped. Hauk hunted around for a tree with a large enough root to support the mast. It took him two days to find the right tree, a large tamarack. Hauk says hunting for the tree was well worth the effort since finding the right wood is half the job. I have learned much from the Norwegian stemsmith. He uses a system of clamps and supporting sticks to good effect. He piles large rocks on the lower strakes after they have been caulked to force them tightly together. The caulking is twisted woollen thread soaked in tar. Nagli, the iron worker, knows how to make tar from peat. The thread is pressed into the grooves on the underside of the strakes.

*   *   *

Ulfar stopped writing; he didn't want to waste ink describing every detail of the ship. On the other hand he had never worked on a seagoing vessel from the beginning and wanted to record the steps.

Ulfar was writing inside the shelter which he had built with a combination of slab wood and driftwood above the beach to the West of the houses where the land rose in a long ridge running North to South. Ulfar had chosen to live apart from the houses. He was by nature hermetic, and after a day working with shipbuilders with whom he had otherwise little in common, craved solitude even more than food. Sometimes he didn't even bother eating the meals Freydis and the women prepared but roasted sea trout he caught that day. Trout were so plentiful in the bay they could be fished from the rocks. Helgi Egilsson had invited Ulfar to eat with the Icelanders whenever he chose. Ulfar had gone to the Icelanders' house once, but had no wish to return since the food hadn't been prepared the way he liked.

Ulfar's shelter looked like a box with an opening on one side and a smoke hole on the top. Inside he slept on spruce boughs which he preferred to a platform of wood. He had built himself a table and a bench to use while writing. Beneath this was a wooden box where he stored his writing materials and the vial of holy water.

Ulfar intended to show Geirmund his manuscript one day and tried to include matters that would interest the priest, such as his daily struggle for redemption.

*   *   *

I have had two meetings with a woman named Groa who is enthralled to Freydis and is Christian. We were able to pray together on the beach. The next time we met for prayer, Groa brought the thrall named Mairi who like us is Hebridian. Though little more than a girl, she is being used as a concubine by Freydis's husband. This distresses me much since I cannot help but regard her as unclean. I pray to Christ daily to help me overcome this shortcoming. Considering the

*sinfulness of my origin, it may be that Heaven's Lord
regards Mairi as cleaner than I. Groa never speaks of
herself but has told me something of Mairi.*

*Mairi is from the Isle of Mull, a short distance
across the water from Iona. She was a fisherman's
daughter. She was helping her father empty crab traps
when Vikings attacked. Her father was murdered when
he tried to prevent her abduction. Mairi was taken to
Bergen, where she was traded to Helgi Egilsson.
Though Groa didn't mention it, I have no doubt Mairi
was abused by Helgi's men and by Helgi himself. But I
must not dwell on the girl's abuse, for it only calls to
mind how I was abused myself. Instead, I will ask the
Lord to look kindly on her.*

*   *   *

Though Thorvard took Mairi into his bed each night, he
had little to do with her otherwise. Now that he had
become better acquainted with the forest, he and several
others went into the woods every day to hunt. Thorvard
was learning how to look for tracks and droppings on the
forest floor. Once he saw bear scat but couldn't find the
bear. He had better luck with caribou, finding the tracks of
several cows which he followed. Using axes and spears,
he and his men managed to bring down two female strays.
The cows were very like the deer he had hunted on
Hreinsey, though somewhat larger. There were signs that
wolves had killed the other cows. The presence of wolves
told Thorvard that there was a large caribou herd somewhere, probably migrating further South. Thorvard and his
men usually returned to Leifsbudir at the end of the day
with grouse and partridge shot with arrows, and hares
caught in snares.

Thorvard kept an eye out for skraelings. He had seen a
skraeling once when he had been sealing in Northsetur.
He had only seen the skraeling from a distance, as it was
paddling through the open water in a skin boat. Thorvard
and the other sealers had been too far away to give chase,
especially with so much open water between the pans of

ice, but they had seen well enough to know the creature was dressed in furs and had dark skin and hair. Thorvard had no idea what a skraeling who lived over here would look like, but he thought it likely the creature would be short and squat as trolls were said to be, with sharp teeth and bushy hair. Thorvard didn't know anyone who had seen a troll and was going mainly by what he had been told in tales from sailors who came to Greenland from forested lands. Leif had told Thorvard that there were no skraelings in Leifsbudir that he knew of. Even so, Thorvard and his men went into the forest armed with not only bows and arrows and spears but axes and knives of various kinds. Thorvard had heard from two of Thorfinn Karlsefni's men that they had encountered skraelings over here, though it wasn't clear where. Thorvard knew Thorfinn had run into skraelings in the place he named Hop, and Leif had often said he had seen skraeling signs further South. Before leaving Greenland, Thorvard would have liked to have taken the *Vinland* to Herjolfness and learned more about Thorfinn's experiences over here. Freydis had been against using the ship to visit the Icelander. She had pointed out that a journey to Herjolfness would delay the Greenlanders' sailing by many days. She'd been right about this, since their departure from Greenland had been delayed long enough as it was.

* * *

Hauk Ljome usually came to visit Freydis in mid-afternoon. At that time of day Freydis's husband was off hunting somewhere, and Hauk and his men were finished a long morning's work and in need of rest and diversion. The *Vinland* had long since been repaired and returned to the bay. The new pram was finished and now in use. The Greenlanders' ship was partly framed, which was to say the keel and stem posts were built and the first strakes laid and caulked. Before the mastfish could be placed, knee wood had to be found. This was naturally crooked wood, usually spruce. Together with two cross beams, the knees would keep the old woman, and therefore the mast, firmly in place. Knee wood was also required to support the planking which would be laid after the strakes and the ribbing were done. By searching widely for wood, Hauk was following Arnljot's advice, which was to let nature do the work. Arnljot maintained that the strength and suppleness of a ship lay in using wood in such a way that took advantage of its natural shape. By now the men Helgi had provided for Hauk's use had become able enough that they could be trusted to shape the upper strakes while Hauk was away searching for knee wood. Hauk thought that when Freydis heard he would be leaving Leifsbudir for a few days, she might be persuaded to let him under her shift. So far she had allowed him to stroke her arms and once, her breasts.

Freydis was where Hauk expected she would be, outside working at her loom on the south side of the shed. The fine weather had been holding so well that Freydis wove outside every day, dressed in nothing more than her shift and robe. Today when Hauk came to see her, Freydis was wearing a brown cloak against the breeze; a chill wind was blowing off the water and could be felt even here, in the lee of the shed. But the south side of the shed was warmer than anywhere else, being in sunlight all day. The sun now fell on Freydis's hair, burnishing it the colour of copper wire. Hauk put out his hand and stroked her hair, which felt soft against his roughened skin. She turned and smiled. What a comely woman she was, for a Greenland farmer.

"I'm here to talk to you about the sail," Hauk said.

"I can't think of a better reason," Freydis replied and laughed; the sail had become something of a joke between them.

Freydis put down the whalebone shuttle. "Come in," she said and went inside the shed.

Hauk stooped and entered.

Freydis sent her grey-whiskered thrall to fetch bowls of sour milk. They always began his visits with a drink of milk. The milk had become a luxury for Hauk, since the Icelanders had no dairy goods except for the few cheeses which were among the provisions they had brought with them from Greenland.

Hauk sat on a bench. Though he knew it well, he looked around the room at the woven hangings on the walls, the bedding folded on the sleeping platform, the clean rushes strewn on the floor, the amulet Freydis wore, the woven ribbons in her hair, blue to match her robe. He thought how pleasant and attractive a woman could make even the smallest room, how clean and tidy her person. He had no idea this tidiness included wearing an iron belt beneath her shift.

When Groa came back with the milk, Freydis set her to work scouring the sleeping bench. Hauk noticed that Freydis always found something for the old thrall to do that would keep her inside the shed while he was here. Freydis sat on a stool and picked up her spindle and wool. While he drank his milk, Hauk watched Freydis spin. He liked the graceful way she rolled the spindle against the curve of her hip then down her thigh to set it spinning.

"This past year I've spun so much wool I'm sure I must do it in my sleep," Freydis said. She set down the spindle, drained her bowl, then wiped the milk from her lips with a cloth she kept nearby. Since he had left Norway, Hauk had never seen a woman do this. The women on Skeggi Arnesson's farm had used the back of their hands to wipe their mouths, the Icelanders' concubines, the edge of their shifts.

"How many poor sheep have you turned into wadmal on your loom?" he said.

"Hundreds," Freydis said. "More than I can count. When will you be cutting the mast wood?" She had asked this before.

"After I've fetched knee wood."

"Tell me again how many lengths I'll need for the sail." He had told her this too.

"Sixteen."

Each length was an ell's width and sixteen ells long.

"That means I've a long way to go before the first sail is finished, since I've only two lengths woven so far. Now that the days are getting short, I'm slowing down. I find it difficult to weave in firelight. By nightfall my eyes are too sore to work."

"What you need is a diversion," Hauk said.

"Sometimes my work is diverting."

"Not diverting enough, surely." He reached for her hand and rubbed it with his own. The undersides of her fingers were firm and shiny from handling oily wool.

"I'm a married woman."

He laughed. If he were a scribe he could have written down what they would say next, it had been said so often.

"I'm a married man and it hasn't stopped me."

"Surely you know there are different rules for men and women."

Hauk looked around the room, pretending to search.

"Rules, what rules? There are no rules in Leifsbudir, except those we choose to bring from elsewhere."

He became serious and solemn.

"Tomorrow I'm leaving Leifsbudir," he said.

Freydis withdrew her hand and again picked up the spindle.

"Where are you going?"

"Southeast along the coast to look for knee wood."

"Will you be taking Ulfar?"

"I thought of leaving him here to supervise my men, since he's the most skilled worker I have. But he has a keen eye and will be useful to take. Moreover he's small which will be an advantage. Gnup, who's the same size, will be going. Ulf Broad Beard and Bolli are also going because of their size. Being so large, they can carry twice as much as other men."

"I'm pleased our men are of use to you." Freydis twirled the spindle in her hands.

"I'll be gone for some time," Hauk said.

"How long?"

"Three or four days."

"Is that all? My husband often goes away for months at a time."

"If I were your husband, I wouldn't leave you alone for so long."

She laughed. "That's because I'm another man's wife."

"Perhaps you could give me a kiss before I leave."

"Perhaps."

Freydis sent Groa to the stream for water. As soon as the old woman had gone outside, Hauk put his lips to Freydis's and kissed her long. He managed to get both hands inside her shift and stroke her breasts. Freydis's mouth softened in such a way that Hauk thought she might give in. Hauk was about to suggest they bolt the door and lie down when Freydis stood up and moved away. She straightened her shift and smoothed her hair.

"Be sure to call on me again when you get back," she said and went outside to resume weaving.

Reluctantly Hauk stood up and followed her out.

The visit had not gone much differently than those before. Sometimes the conversation varied. Freydis would ask Hauk about Ulfar. Or she would press Hauk to tell her what he had done that day in the way of shipwork. Unlike most women, Freydis never asked about Hauk's wife or other women. Nor did she disclose much about herself. Hauk thought Freydis's secrecy was partly sham, that she didn't have as much to hide as she pretended, that she knew too much knowing would make her dull. If there had been another wife in Leifsbudir half as comely as Freydis, Hauk might have tried his luck with her. But he would have returned from time to time to court Freydis since when it came to bedding a woman, he rarely acknowledged defeat.

Hauk had never taken a woman by force. Even his first conquest, the daughter of his mother's sister, had come to him of her own accord. Hauk didn't like to force a woman since it put him in an unfavourable light. He preferred to think he was providing a woman with what she wanted. In this regard he ran into difficulty with Freydis. She was a woman with an overabundance of pride and therefore not easily won by flattery. Moreover as their visits in the shed continued, she appeared to like joking and banter better than he. She would inevitably begin speaking to him in a lively and challenging manner and wouldn't easily give it up. Each time he suggested they show their liking for one another in a way that would satisfy them better—as he pointed out they were both young and healthy—Freydis would turn the conversation in such a way that Hauk soon found himself talking about something else. More than once Hauk had resolved to stop his visits with Freydis and for a time avoided the shed. But he was obsessed with what he couldn't have and after a short absence returned. At the same time he pushed himself and his workers hard in order to finish the ship. Hauk hadn't forgotten the smile on Freydis's lips that told him it was the ship she wanted more than anything else. Hauk had seen that smile on the faces of others wanting him to build them a ship. But those had been wealthy men eager to give Hauk what he wanted in return, usually silver, though sometimes a daughter or a concubine. Despite her pretensions Freydis was poor, which meant that before she took possession of the ship Hauk was building, she would have to give him what he wanted in return.

Hauk's situation hadn't gone unnoticed by the Icelanders. They remarked that after Hauk left Freydis's shed, he immediately put himself between Grelod's legs. He became the butt of sly jests. As esteemed as Hauk was, no Norseman was so highly respected that he escaped jokes made at his expense. It so happened that Surt, who was skilled at composing verses, had made up a small poem about Hauk. Surt was the dwarf twin of Svart and like him had a fierce squashed-looking face. Surt wouldn't risk saying the verse to Hauk himself; over the years he had received enough kicks and blows for reciting verses to folk who spurned them that he had learned to have someone else speak them abroad instead. Whenever he made up new verses or revised old ones, Surt would chant them softly to himself, yet not so softly that anyone standing beside him couldn't hear. In this way Vemund and Ulf picked up the poem about Hauk and Freydis. They began to chant the verses to Hauk after he returned from

Freydis, which made him sullen and ill at ease. The poem failed to show him as being rewarded for his efforts in the way he liked.

> The stallion gallops across dry waves,
> Pounding them flat beneath his hooves.
> He wears himself to the bone
> Trying to mount a Greenland milch cow.
>
> The cow is left in her pen
> While her thrall-rousing stud
> Follows deer scat with his hunters
> In the place of the standing spears.
>
> In her corner the spider Norn weaves
> A web to catch a steed of another's making.
> In his dream the sea stallion rides her.
> His tool is never idle.

The next day after Hauk had set out with four men to look for knee wood, Freydis asked Thorvard to come with her to the ship cove. When Freydis had gone there with Kalf and Orn, she had avoided the short cut through the forest, instead walking along the shore which took twice the time as through the woods. So far Freydis had been too busy to do this more than once. Over and above the cooking, dairying and cleaning chores, her days were given over to weaving lengths of sailcloth.

Since their arrival in Leifsbudir Freydis and Thorvard hadn't spoken much to each other. After the morning meal Thorvard and his men went hunting for most of the day, returning well past the midday meal so that their share had to be set aside. In the evening Thorvard went to bed early with Mairi and seldom came near Freydis's shed. Their lack of conversation didn't trouble Freydis; she and Thorvard never had much to say to each other. But she thought it prudent to exchange information about matters important to them both. This was the main reason she asked Thorvard to accompany her to the ship cove.

"How are you liking it here?" Freydis said conversationally as they were crossing the meadow.

"I like it well enough."

"I'm liking it too," Freydis said. "Though I miss our children."

"That's to be expected," Thorvard told her. "You've never left them before." He didn't miss his children himself, being used to leaving them behind.

"I enjoy living in a proper house," Freydis said. "It will be hard to go back to living in a hut."

Thorvard said nothing aloud but remarked to himself that even here Freydis couldn't forget the burning of Leif's posts and beams.

"And I like having Mairi."

This was a pleasant surprise, if she meant it.

"She does twice the work of Groa," Freydis went on, "and is quick to learn."

Freydis wanted Thorvard to know she bore him no grudge for taking a concubine. The ambatt was quiet and hard working. She now did the milking and washed the cow and goats. So far the animals weren't giving enough milk to make new cheeses, but there was sometimes enough to make butter which Mairi churned.

"As far as I'm concerned, she's more than satisfactory," Freydis said. When Thorvard didn't reply to this, Freydis went on, "She's with child. Or so I suspect."

Freydis knew this from the vomiting the girl now did every morning on the grass.

Thorvard didn't doubt the truth of Freydis's words. Women knew such things. But he was surprised by the news on account of Mairi's youth.

"It remains to be seen what Helgi Egilsson will think about her pregnancy," Freydis remarked. This was said not so much to have the last word but to remind Thorvard that when it came to considering the matter, he would do well to heed her words.

By now they had reached the short cut through the forest. With Thorvard at her side, Freydis didn't fear the

woods as much as before. Her husband was strong and
well armed. Freydis herself was carrying an axe.

Several Greenlanders were already in the cove when
Thorvard and Freydis arrived. They were the timber cutters
Thorvard had organized earlier to provide firewood for the
houses. Every morning after they had eaten, these men
set out to cut poles that were dragged back to the terrace
and stood on end in a circle to dry. Before beginning this
work, the woodcutters would invariably stop at the ship
cove to review the ship. In fact all the Greenlanders found
reasons to come to the ship cove at one time or another.
Admiring the ship had become one of their pleasures.
Every strake was inspected for an imperfection; every nail
and rivet that came from Nagli's forge was examined. The
stem posts were stroked and patted as if they were horses
being praised for their sleekness and strength.

For a time Thorvard and Freydis watched the
Icelanders Hauk had left working on the ship. These men
were busy cutting and shaping the upper strakes, except
for Vemund who had been given the task of cutting the
caribou hide Thorvard had provided. The deerskin, which
would be used to lash the ribs to the planking, was being
cut crosswise, which interested Thorvard since it was the
same way he cut walrus hide rope, to give it strength.

On the way back to the houses with Thorvard, Freydis
came across a large patch of late blueberries in the meadow that pickers had missed. When they reached the houses, Freydis put on her cloak, fetched a pail and returned
to the meadow. For her this was a diversion, since her
thralls usually did the berry picking. But as Hauk said, she
needed a diversion. Of course he had an entirely different
diversion in mind. Freydis smiled. Yesterday she had been
tempted to indulge Hauk's desire, not to mention her
own, which was why she had worn the iron belt in antici-
pation of his visit.

The meadow was so large and open that no one could
appear at Freydis's side without being seen a long way off.
The openness was an aspect of Leifsbudir Freydis liked.
Out here in the meadow she felt unburdened and light.

The lightness didn't come from the thinness of the air as it did in Greenland, for even on clear days like this, the air in Leifsbudir was heavy and moist so that voices were muffled. Moreover the breeze that blew constantly from the sea stole words from speakers' mouths and carried them off. Freydis thought Njord snatched the words so that folk might listen closely to the waves lapping on the beach and the cry of sea birds. Njord's voice reminded Freydis that she wasn't as far from Greenland as it might seem, that her children were just there, on the other side of the water, behind the wind.

Freydis knelt and began picking the smoky fruit. She put a handful into her mouth to taste. The berries were tart. Perhaps they should be left until after the frost had sweetened them. But no, if she left them, the Icelanders would pick them for sure; she had seen the ambatts the Icelanders called Grelod and Alof out here berrying from time to time. They were the same women who often came to the stream beside Freydis's shed to wash and fetch water. As she picked, Freydis thought that before the weather moved into Winter, she would send her thralls out here to harvest livestock fodder. Leif had said his Winter in Leifsbudir had been mild but Freydis thought it prudent to be prepared for the worst. Freydis's livestock were grazing in various pens not far from where she picked. The fencing had been built in such a way that it could be moved to a better grazing place. The sheep pen had already been shifted once after an area had become over-grazed. This arrangement meant the manure didn't have to be spread but could be left to improve next Summer's grazing.

From time to time Freydis glanced around to make sure she was alone. After she had filled the pail, Freydis spread her cloak on the ground, tucked her shift and robe behind her knees and sat down. How pleasant it was to see her livestock growing fatter each day, how satisfying to see the smoke curling from the roof holes; she could smell the smoke from here; how reassuring to see the firewood drying outside. This was no dream. There was the

Vinland newly repaired, anchored in front of the houses, and behind her in the cove a ship of her own in the making.

The next day when Freydis went out to the storage hut with Mairi to fetch provisions for the morning meal, she noticed one of the smaller cheeses was missing. The previous day there had been six cheeses on the shelf; now there were five. The theft perplexed Freydis. The door had been locked before she opened it and the key was hanging with the others on the braided cord around her neck. There was a smoke hole in the hut but it was too small to admit anything larger than mice and voles. If small animals had eaten the cheese there would have been tell-tale droppings scattered here and there. The cheese had vanished neatly without a trace. Freydis sent Mairi to fetch Nagli from the smithy.

After trying the lock several times Nagli told Freydis that as far as he could see there was nothing wrong with it.

"Then the thief must have stolen the cheese when the door was open," Freydis said.

"Or picked the lock and relocked it afterwards." Nagli took a small pick from his waist pouch and put it into the keyhole. He turned the pick this way and that until the lock sprang open.

"I've never seen that done before."

"That might be your answer. As you can see, anyone with a pick and enough patience could have opened your lock."

"I doubt it was just anyone," Freydis said. "I suspect one of the Icelandic thralls stole the cheese. Grelod and Alof are forever hanging around our place."

"If I were you I would forget the matter," Nagli said. "A case against the Icelanders would be hard to prove and making a false accusation will only cause trouble later on." Since Nagli had started working with Hauk and the shipbuilders, he had come to regard the Icelanders as likeable fellows. He was against anything coming between a Greenlander like himself and the Icelanders, especially something as trivial as a missing cheese.

Freydis was too clever to make an accusation. Once an accusation was made, it had to be taken to the Althing and there was no Althing here. In any case a small theft like a cheese would be thrown out by the lawspeaker of the Althing; he had more pressing matters to consider such as murder and the theft of cattle and land. For that reason folk had other ways of handling small thefts. They knew that to allow petty thieving to go unchecked was unwise since it opened the door to further crimes. Freydis didn't want to put herself on the bad side of the Icelanders or Hauk Ljome by mentioning the cheese, but neither did she intend to forget the theft.

Of all the buildings in Leifsbudir Freydis's storage hut was closest to the stream. In fact the end buildings she had taken from Finnbogi Egilsson were the most conveniently placed in Leifsbudir, since their location made fetching water an easy chore. The Icelanders had the furthest to go. The dwarf twins Svart and Surt hauled most of the Icelanders' water. They used the beach path, keeping a safe distance between themselves and the Greenlanders' house. Not so Grelod and Alof. Grelod was a thick-girthed woman whose broad flanks showed she often heaped more on her trencher than was her share. Alof was gorbellied and full-buttocked but shorter. Alof was too simple minded to be wily and followed Grelod's lead. Grelod was sly and cunning. She would taunt those Greenlanders who were working outside chopping firewood or mending their gear until the men became boisterous and raunchy. On their way to the river Grelod and Alof would often linger near the Greenlanders' houses, shouting coarsely at the men.

The afternoon after the cheese was stolen, Freydis put on her cloak and stuffed her shoes with wool, for the ground had grown cold, and went outside to weave. She had barely begun when Grelod and Alof went by on their way to the stream. "Without their wool, the Greenland sheep must suffer from the cold," Grelod said, "for they are much thinner than the Greenland women." Grelod was close enough for Freydis to hear this slur but well out of Freydis's reach.

Returning later carrying two buckets, Grelod passed closer by Freydis and chanted, "*When the warp is crooked, the weft is loose.*"

Freydis immediately let loose with the whalebone shuttle. Freydis knew from the sound of the clout that she had landed a strong blow. Grelod dropped one of the buckets but she didn't whimper or whinge. Alof went ahead but Grelod stopped, picked up the fallen bucket and glared at Freydis. Freydis made a move to strike her again but Grelod stepped out of her reach and spat.

That night Freydis's arm became too sore to use. When she pulled back her shift, she saw a bluish mark above the elbow of her right arm. The mark was swollen and painful to touch. It was in the same place where she had clouted Grelod. Freydis knew that Grelod had put a blast on her arm in retaliation for being struck.

Two days went by and still Freydis's arm was no better. She couldn't weave or spin. Even turning a key in a lock was painful. Freydis went out and found herself a smooth round stone. She covered the stone with cloth to make a witch doll's head. Then she drew Grelod's face, using a sharp stick dipped in charcoal. She fattened the body by stuffing it with moss. Because it hurt Freydis's arm to sew, the doll wasn't as well made as those she had made for Asny, but for the purpose she intended, it would do well enough. After the legs and arms were in place, Freydis jabbed a sharp needle into the doll's right arm. That night Freydis sat by the hearth until she was certain the Icelanders were asleep. Then she carried the doll across the terrace and hung it over the Icelanders' door. Freydis never once considered waking Groa and sending her to hang up the doll. It was well known by anyone who used a witch doll to settle a score that its power was weakened if anyone but the spell maker placed the doll. Greenland women often spoke about such matters around their hearths. Since women couldn't participate in the Althing they found other ways to check evil doing.

No one was about when Freydis hung the doll, which was fortunate since the moon was bright and she would have been plainly seen if someone had been outside. The next morning Freydis's arm had improved enough for her to resume weaving. But the weather had turned windy and sharp so that the loom had to be carried inside the shed. For this reason Freydis didn't see Grelod and Alof pass the shed on their way to fetch water. Nor did she hear the riddle Grelod chanted as she passed the shed, *"What hag stirs the privy hole by sticking needles in a doll?"*

* * *

By now Hauk Ljome was near the end of a half-day's journey by pram from the ship cove. With him were the men he had chosen: Gnup and Ulfar; Ulf and Bolli. Hauk needed the smaller men to cut the knee wood. Spruce crooks grew on the north side, at the top of ridges and cliffs where they were bent by wind and snow. These places were hard to reach, especially by anyone over middle size, for the cutters would have to wriggle through narrow openings and crawl on their hands and knees to places where the land dropped off. Ulf and Bolli would be doing the bull work, which now included rowing the pram. None of the others lifted an oar. As Ulfar was to write later, when he looked at Ulf and Bolli at the oars, it was difficult not to be overtaken by the sin of pride. He couldn't help thinking that since his years as a galley slave, he had come up in the world.

They were towing a second pram loaded with awnings, leather sleeping bags and several days' provisions. This second pram would hold the knee wood. In the meantime it would serve as a sleeping place. The men wouldn't be sleeping on the beach, but would anchor off shore and stretch out on the floor of the prams beneath the awnings. This was a precaution against attack. Should skraelings appear, it would be an easy matter for the woodcutters to row away.

The woodcutters anchored in front of a rocky beach beneath a ridge that rose sharply above the sea on the

north side of a bay. Along the ridge top was a stand of
bent spruce. Soon after their arrival, the men cut a path
up the back of the ridge to the top, which gave them clear-
ance to move up and down. The cutting took until the
evening of the first day. There were no signs of skraelings.
The only droppings in the wilderness were from animals of
various kinds. The men thought it unlikely they would
meet skraelings in a place like this, since the woods were
so thickly grown there was no place to put houses or tents
unless the land was cleared. There was no indication that
the forest had been touched except by lightning or wind.

On the second day the men began to harvest knee
wood. The work was arranged in the following way: the
men climbed the path to the top, all except Hauk who
remained on the beach, below the ridge. Gnup and Ulfar
crawled through the underbrush to the cliff edge and Hauk
pointed out the knee wood he wanted. After finding a tree
to hold on to, a cutter would chop the spruce Hauk wanted, being careful not to damage the crook where the tree
bent away from the wind. Once it was cut, the knee was
passed back to Ulf and Bolli, who trimmed off the branches and stacked the wood at the top of the path for carrying down later. By dividing the work in this manner, each
man was used in the way that suited him best. The men
seemed to know this, for there were no harsh words or
animosity, at least not at the outset. By the end of the second day there was a large pile of knee wood on the shore.

It so happened that Gnup was the sort of man who
drew attention to himself by making fun of others. Being
lively and quick, he often imitated a man behind his back
in such a way that others would laugh at the man's
expense. For some time he had been doing this with Bolli
Illugisson. Bolli had a habit of scratching his head and
dropping his jaw when perplexed and this made him
appear stupider than he was. On the second day when
they were extending the path along the top of the ridge,
Bolli, who was ahead of the others, came to a tangle of
growth that seemed to perplex him. He stopped to scratch
his head while deciding where he might best place his

axe. When Bolli turned abruptly and saw Gnup mocking him, he raised his axe over the shorter man's head.

"Lower your axe!" Hauk shouted. He was just behind Gnup. Surely the oaf knew Gnup was joking.

Bolli hesitated, though not for long. He lowered his axe and continued work.

That evening when they sat on the beach around the fire, Hauk told the men that with Luck tomorrow they could cut all the knee wood he wanted in the morning and be back in Leifsbudir by night.

Mid-morning of the next day there was a second pile of knee wood on the beach and it did seem the men would finish their work by noon. The men continued as before, with Gnup and Ulfar working near the cliff edge and Hauk remaining on the beach to point out the crooks he wanted cut. Now harvesting became more dangerous, since the cutters had to work at the end of the cliff where the soil was loose. Inevitably this was where the best crooks grew. Ulf and Bolli continued stripping branches and hauling wood down the ridge to the beach.

Hauk didn't know exactly when Bolli disappeared. He was occupied with instructing his cutters and didn't notice Bolli's absence. It was Ulf who remarked that Bolli hadn't carried down a load of knee wood for some time. "And I didn't meet him on the path," Ulf said. Hauk turned away from the cliff to ask Ulf to repeat what he had said. Ulf repeated his remark and Hauk told him to go in search of Bolli. When Hauk turned to the cliff again, Gnup had already lost his footing and was on his way down. Hauk heard the crack of bone when Gnup hit the rocks.

By the time Hauk and Ulf had leapt across the rocks and reached the body, Bolli had reappeared. Ulfar, who was at the far end of the ridge, took longer to come down. The corpse was put into a sleeping bag and loaded into the pram with the knee wood. Because they had to row against the current and were towing a heavy load, the men didn't reach the ship cove until evening. Gnup's corpse was buried the next day in a mound of earth at the end of the beach.

The Icelanders were mystified by the accident, since they had been told that Gnup Glamsson, whom they had taken on in Greenland, was a sure-footed man. When the incident was discussed around the Icelanders' hearth, Hauk spoke about seeing Bolli threaten Gnup with an axe their second day out. He remembered Bolli being absent from the beach at the time of the fall. Ulf said that although he had no liking for Bolli Illugisson, he didn't think Bolli could have pushed Gnup to his death and appear on the beach as soon as he had. Ulf said he had asked Bolli why he had disappeared for so long. Bolli had replied that he had been relieving himself in the woods. "I told him he must have had a bung up his arse," Ulf said.

In the end it was decided that Gnup's death was the kind of accident Norsemen had to expect if they wanted to do better than survive. They reminded themselves that even if they had never left where they had been born, they would have encountered dangers of one kind and another, since survival in northern lands depended on taking risks.

During the next month the men doubled their efforts on the ship. Hauk wanted the ship finished before it was covered with a Winter shed. Now there was rime on the grass in the mornings instead of dew. The frosty nights had turned the leaves alongside the stream red and orange. In the woods the tamarack was yellow. Tamarack didn't grow in Norway, for which reason Hauk enjoyed working with it. He found the tree harder than spruce, though not so hard as maple or oak but supple and strong. Hauk was pleased enough with the new wood that he used it to make cross beams for the ship. This worked so well that he cut down more of the fine-needled trees and used them to make ribs. Hauk thought that when he returned to Norway, his reputation would be much enhanced by his knowledge of foreign woods. In Norway shipwrights were so used to working with oak, they doubted solid vessels could be made from anything else. With the supply of oak wood dwindling, Norwegians would value a shipwright who knew how to work with different woods.

After a month's work all the strakes had been riveted together and caulked. The old woman was secure. The ribs were in place as were the knees and the cross beams. The Greenlanders and the Icelanders were impressed; the Greenlanders because it was their ship, the Icelanders because they had brought the shipbuilder to Leifsbudir. Hauk was more impressed than any of them. He had come to a strange country and, working with inexperienced men, had managed to build a ship in three months. The ship was far from being the finest he had made, but it was seaworthy all the same and would serve the Greenlanders well enough. Of course, there was still work to be done. The steering oar had to be carved, as well as toggles and barrels and rowing oars, but they could be worked on over Winter. Only one thing remained to be done before the snow came and that was to procure pine wood for the mast. Arnljot had often said that there was no substitute for pine. Pine was the only wood that was light yet strong enough to withstand heavy gales. When Hauk spoke to the Egilssons about going for mast wood, Finnbogi declined to go. Although *Sigurd's Steed* had long since been cleaned and caulked, Finnbogi had no intention of taking it out of its Winter shed to search for mast wood. "Use the *Vinland*. After all, it's the Greenlanders' ship you're building," Finnbogi said. "They owe you a favour for repairing Leif's ship."

Thorvard and Freydis agreed readily to let the *Vinland* go South before Winter. In fact Thorvard said he preferred to take Leif's ship, for he had in mind to hunt caribou somewhere along the way. He was sure that if they sailed a day or two South, he would find the main herd. As for Hauk, he knew Leif Eiriksson had spoken to Helgi about a place he called the Bay of Maples, which was a two-day sail from Leifsbudir. Leif had told Helgi pine and birch grew there as well as maple.

"Let's hope Leif hasn't misled us," Hauk said. "And we return from the expedition with the ship wood I need."

A MONTH AFTER GNUP'S DEATH, fourteen men made the journey to the Bay of Maples aboard Leif Eiriksson's ship. On the Icelanders' side were Hauk, Helgi, Ulf Broad Beard, Vemund, Olver, Jokul and Grimkel. Except for Helgi these men had worked as planksmen on the Greenlanders' ship. On the Greenlanders' side were Thorvard, Evyind, Teit, Hundi, Bodvar, Falgeir and Ulfar. Except for Ulfar, none of these men were experienced with wood. Though Bolli would have been useful for hauling logs, Thorvard decided against taking him. There was talk that Bolli might have pushed Gnup to his death from a cliff, though this rumour was quashed by Ulfar, who when questioned, claimed to have seen Gnup fall. Ulfar said the tree Gnup had been holding for support had broken; he had heard the crack himself. Despite this explanation Thorvard thought it prudent to leave Bolli in Leifsbudir. He didn't want someone with a reputation as a troublemaker to come between the Icelanders and himself. And Freydis said she wanted Bolli to stay behind. Since Thorvard and his men would be gone for some time, she found it useful to have an ally of Bolli's strength nearby. And she had something in mind for him to do.

The ship cleared the bay in front of the houses and set a westerly course until they passed the islands and rounded a cape. There they set a southerly course, sailing into water that looked like a fjord but was, as Lief had told them, an inland sea with Markland to the West. The men sailed close to the eastern shore to avoid the current flowing West. At first the land they sailed past was much like what they had left, which was to say rough meadows with low mountains here and there. In some places the shoreline was coarsely sanded while in others it was layered with rock. After a time they came to an inlet where a river emptied into the sea. The low mountains in the interior had now become a spine running North to South. The Markland shore had fallen away, which was an indication that open water lay in the West. Late afternoon the ship entered a river which was much the same as the one they had passed. Here the men dropped anchor and spent the night.

The next morning the men continued their journey. The wind remained brisk, and after the ship cleared the river mouth, the men were sailing at a lively pace. The further South the men went, the more attractive the land became. When they passed the openings to several fjords, Helgi said he found it difficult not to follow them to their ends, for the choicest land usually lay at the head of inlets and bays. By early afternoon the men had entered the Bay of Maples. Once they had passed the islands at the mouth of the fjord, the men saw that the hills on either side were thickly forested all the way down to the water's edge. The fjord shone dark green and deep as the fjords in Norway. Hauk pointed out the maples which had begun to appear in the woods. "The best time of year to harvest hardwood," he said, "is when maple leaves are as bright as kings' banners and can be plainly seen." None of the Greenlanders had seen maple leaves or king's banners. Even so, what Hauk said seemed to be true, for as the ship went deeper into the fjord, the colours brightened in a way the men found difficult to describe. Fed by the banquet of crimson and gold, their appetite for wonder increased.

At the end of the fjord close to the shore was a low flat island bearing a charcoal smudge which the men thought had probably been made by Leif Eiriksson's crew. The smudge was evidence of Leif's prudence, for by anchoring on an island he had put some distance between his ship and the woods, no doubt as a precaution against skrae-lings. Leif had told both Thorvard and Helgi that he hadn't met skraelings here but had seen their abandoned houses in the woods. He said there was no sign that the house owners raised sheep or cattle, which meant they were probably nomadic, following game from place to place.

The Norsemen kept Leif's words firmly in mind and after anchoring beside the island, bid four men remain on the ship while the other ten went ashore in the pram. The shore party's task was to locate the houses Leif had men-tioned to see if they had been recently used. Armed with axes and spears, the men made their way through the underbrush that went all the way to the large river flowing into the north side of the fjord. The men passed the stumps of trees Leif's men had felled fourteen years earli-er, now overgrown with bracken and moss. When they came to the forest, the men spread out in a line and went forward slowly. They had not gone far when Bodvar and Falgeir, who were nearest the river, came upon a clearing and shouted that they had found the abandoned houses. There were three houses altogether; in fact the dwellings appeared to have been more like tents than houses, being man-made depressions in the ground. The size of the holes and their depth suggested that the sides were walls that had been tented over to make booths. There was no sign that the booths had been recently used. A maple tree had taken root inside one of the depressions. "Unless I'm mistaken," Hauk said, "these holes haven't been used for a very long time. That tree is at least thirty years old." The abandoned tent holes were regarded as evidence that there were no skraelings close by. For this reason the Norsemen did not post watches and every man worked at felling and dressing timber. The men did not go so far as to sleep ashore but returned to the ship before nightfall and bedded down there. The fine clear weather continued for many days, which meant the men were able to harvest timber without interruption. They found misshapen trees

Hauk called mossur alongside the river. The mossur looked like the swollen elbows and knees of folk severely afflicted with joint ill. The Norwegians used these swellings to make cups and bowls. On the other side of the fjord from where they were anchored they found a large stand of pine. Besides harvesting wood at their disposal, the men did little else except sleep and eat.

After the men had been twenty days in the Bay of Maples, Thorvard had grown weary of eating dried rations and fish. He had worked hard felling timber and was eager to go after caribou while the clear weather held. He knew from the droppings he had seen near the river that caribou were close by. He therefore proposed that he take three others hunting. Hauk and Helgi agreed to this proposition. Although the leaves had begun to fall, the air remained pleasantly sunny. As long as the fine weather continued, they were loath to leave off cutting timber themselves but would welcome a feast of deer meat. Accordingly it was decided that Thorvard and the Greenlander Bodvar would go caribou hunting with the Icelanders Grimkel and Jokul. None of these men had much experience stalking game in forests. Grimkel and Jokul had the least but offered to go in order to bring the Icelanders their share of the meat. As for the Greenlanders, they excelled at sealing and whaling. The caribou they hunted in Greenland were on the treeless island of Hreinsey. But Thorvard was confident that after three months of hunting with Bodvar and others in the woods behind Leifsbudir, they could find their way around the forest. It was true Thorvard failed to take the Icelanders' inexperience into consideration. Had he done so, he might not have suggested the hunters separate in the woods. By encouraging the men to break into pairs he was following the same methods he used on Hreinsey. How was he to know there were skraelings close by? Later on he was convinced that the skraelings had been watching the woodcutters all along and had been biding their time in order to strike. What Grimkel and Jokul thought about the matter was never known, for soon after the hunters split up they disappeared. It was left to the Greenlanders to explain what had happened. Their explanation, which in later retellings became known as *The Tale of the Invisible Wretches*, did not satisfy the Icelanders listening, but without Jokul or Grimkel to prove otherwise, they had no choice but to let the explanation stand.

Thorvard and Bodvar returned from the hunt without caribou or weapons; they returned by water not on foot. It was night-time and the woodcutters were sitting around a fire on the island, waiting for the hunters to appear, when they heard splashing and seized their axes, which were close at hand. Then Thorvard and Bodvar appeared, swimming toward them. As soon as the hunters were hauled onto the rock, they were asked about the whereabouts of the others.

"They were taken by skraelings," Thorvard said, his chest heaving; like Bodvar, he was out of breath and shivering. "Douse the fire and board the ship. We are being followed by invisible wretches."

The fire was quickly put out and the men got aboard. Thorvard and Bodvar stripped off their clothes and got into sleeping bags. There was some roasted fish that had been left for the returning hunters but no one mentioned it. The night was moonless. With only starlight to lighten the darkness, the men were no more than blurred shapes to one another. The men waited patiently for the hunters' shivering to subside. When Thorvard and Bodvar had calmed themselves, Helgi urged them to explain what had happened, and slowly, haltingly, Thorvard began to speak.

"When we left here early this morning, we followed the river searching for a place caribou might cross. Eventually when the sun cleared the trees, we came to a glade where a stag and seven cows were grazing. Here we spread out, Jokul and Grimkel going behind the caribou in order to drive them toward the river, Bodvar and I staying close by the water to head them off. We took care to be quiet, waiting for the Icelanders to charge. For a long time we crouched by the water until we realized the caribou were moving not toward the river but further East. Rather than lose our chance we crept up behind a cow that was some distance behind the others and brought her down with a spear. The stag and the other cows got away. After the carcass was gutted, we left it and began searching the woods for Jokul and Grimkel. There was no sign of them anywhere and it had been a long while since they'd been seen. We stopped several times and made the rutting call but there was no reply, though we had agreed to use the call if we lost each other or needed help. We continued to search."

Here Bodvar took up the tale. "Now the shadows were getting longer and we heard wolves close by. We began to think Jokul and Grimkel had either returned to the ship or lost themselves. If they were lost, we needed more than ourselves to cover the ground. We decided to return to the ship. With this in mind we went to fetch the carcass, intending to tie it to poles for carrying out. To our amazement the cow was gone. In its stead was a leather belt which we recognized as Jokul's. There were signs of struggle, broken branches and flattened brushwood which had not been made by the cow, for she had dropped in her tracks and died cleanly and had been dragged not carried away. There were splatters of blood on leaves higher up that had nothing to do with gutting the carcass. We caught sight of Grimkel's shoe hanging on a branch. Putting all this together, it became clear to us that Jokul and Grimkel had met with foul play."

Bodvar paused, waiting for a listener to comment. When no one did, Thorvard took up the tale again. "Bodvar and I were about three bow shots from the river. Fortunately we covered this distance without being attacked. We lay back on the water and allowed the current to carry us along. It was too dark see anything move in the woods, but I was sure we were still being watched by invisible wretches who could see in the night. Whether they were skraelings or some other creatures, I couldn't say.

"The river was shallow and swift-moving, which meant we were carried quickly along. By the time we reached the

river mouth, it was pitch black, which allowed us to leave
our weapons on the shore and swim to your fire on the
island. In this way we were able to reach you without
being killed."

When Thorvard had finished the tale, he said that he
had heard it said that if you went too far into the forest
you were bound to meet trolls and invisible creatures of
various kinds. In that respect he was content to live in
Greenland, where there was nothing to prevent a man
from seeing clearly what and who was close at hand.

Hauk was well aware Thorvard and Bodvar were badly
shaken, but this in no way prevented him from speaking
his mind. "In all my years building ships in forests," he
said, "I've never once come across a troll in the woods. I
don't believe there are trolls and am suspicious of men
who use such imaginary creatures to explain their own
heinous crimes."

No one tried to defend Thorvard or Bodvar, though
some of the men thought the Norwegian had been overly
harsh with his words. Instead the men discussed their
departure; by now all of them were eager to get away.
They had harvested the timber they had come for and
more besides. No one could sleep; instead the men dozed
fitfully, weapons at their sides.

In the morning armed guards, Thorvard and Bodvar
among them, kept watch while the timber was loaded
onto the ship. The loading took most of the day. During
that time there was no sign of skraelings, which caused
the Icelanders to question the truth of Thorvard and
Bodvar's tale.

On the return journey the Greenlanders kept to the
stern where Evyind was steering; the Icelanders stayed in
the bow where they examined the Greenlanders' tale from
beginning to end. Olver said he thought it odd skraelings
would abduct two men in the very place where a caribou
had been killed. Vemund agreed. He said it was also odd
that the abductors had left behind a shoe and a belt. Ulf
Broad Beard said it was beyond belief that two men and a
cow could be stolen from under Thorvard and Bodvar's

noses, then added, "Perhaps that can be expected of folk who are slow witted at best."

"It's odd that both times I've taken Greenlanders woodcutting, it's been our crew who have lost their lives," Hauk said. "From now on we would be well advised to avoid going on expeditions with the Greenlanders, since it's our luck that has been diminished, not theirs."

"That was hardly the case at the outset," Helgi said. "Remember the Greenlanders' crossing was unluckier than ours." He was disturbed by the talk against the Greenlanders. From what he had seen of Thorvard Einarsson, he didn't think he was the kind of man who would murder two Icelanders, if that was what Hauk and the others were suggesting. He didn't think Hauk believed it either, but was disappointed to have lost two men who had worked with him on the ship. Like the others Hauk was probably upset by the uncertain explanation of what had happened to Jokul and Grimkel and found some satisfaction in grumbling about the Greenlanders. "There's no use blaming men for doing what they can to save their skins," Helgi said. "If I'd been in the woods, I would have done what the Greenlanders did." Helgi continued speaking in this way until the others came round to thinking that it wasn't the Greenlanders' fault Jokul and Grimkel had been carried off. Helgi knew it was important to keep relations between the Icelanders and the Greenlanders from becoming worse. He thought there might be a time when he would want Thorvard to give him the benefit of the doubt.

Hauk came around to Helgi's thinking, at least he thought he had. He didn't like to think of himself as a grudge bearer, not liking grudge bearers himself. "One thing can be said with certainty," he said. "Either Thorvard and Bodvar are clever liars or tellers of a fantastic tale." Before the *Vinland* was halfway to Leifsbudir, Hauk had gone up to Thorvard and said the same thing to his face. By the time the ship was once again anchored in front of the houses, the Greenlanders and Icelanders were mixing together on board.

As soon as they came ashore, Thorvard sought out Freydis and told her what had happened. He never once thought of telling his tale to Mairi; the girl seldom spoke to him, though he went out of his way to be kind. Freydis listened closely to what Thorvard said. She was impressed by several aspects of the tale, not the least of which was Thorvard's courage in going deep into the woods. Sometimes in Greenland, when after months away Thorvard returned with falcons, white bear fur, narwhal horns and tales of what had been required of him in Northsetur to procure these goods, Freydis was so impressed by her husband's resourcefulness in achieving what he did that she lost no time in getting him to bed. Freydis did not speak of her admiration now, since she thought Thorvard might interpret it as an invitation to lie together. Instead she said, "It seems skraelings aren't fierce after all, for they could have left Jokul and Grimkel dead and captured you as well."

"They might be dead."

"It seems to me if skraelings killed the Icelanders, they would have left them there. Why bother hauling corpses somewhere else?"

Thorvard admitted he had thought much the same thing. He said what was troubling him was that the Icelanders and Hauk regarded Bodvar and him with suspicion.

"What's the reason for that?"

"They find our explanation of what happened too fantastic to be believed. Hauk thinks we made up the tale to cover some crime or other."

Freydis laughed, amused by the idea of Thorvard making up a fanciful story. She had never once seen any sign of imagination in her husband and thought him incapable of inventing a tale; Thorvard's lies were unspoken, mainly what he chose to withhold.

"Hauk and the others are disappointed to lose two men," she said carelessly. "They'll get over it." Freydis was annoyed that Hauk had scoffed at the idea of there being invisible folk, especially since this country was as unknown to him as it was to her husband.

"I have it in mind to hold a Yule feast as a way of smoothing over relations," Thorvard said. "And to repay Helgi for giving us a feast when we first arrived. We could hold matches and games in the afternoon before the eating and drinking begin."

"What drinking? We have nothing but water and milk."

"Helgi told me a month ago that he was brewing honey and water for Yule. It should be ready by now."

"What else have they been hoarding for themselves?"

"I'm suggesting they supply the mead and we supply the food," Thorvard said. "You could roast two goats and one of your pigs."

"I didn't bring livestock to Leifsbudir to feed the Icelanders but to see us through Winter."

"You know as well as I do that there'll be food enough for Winter. After the feasting we can tell verses and tales."

"When do you propose this event take place?"

"As soon as possible. It's somewhat early for Yule but we should take advantage of the clear weather while it lasts. I suggest four or five days' time. That should allow us enough time to make preparations."

"Us?" Freydis said. "Since when did you prepare food for sixty-odd men?"

"There are more preparations than women's work."

Freydis's sourness was deceptive. The prospect of a Yule feast in fact pleased her. While Thorvard and the others had been in the Bay of Maples, she had been working steadily on the sail. Without Hauk's visits to distract her, she had managed to weave three more lengths. Moreover, with fewer mouths to feed, she had been able to send Groa and Mairi to scour the meadow for the last of the berries and dry them for Winter. Kalf and Orn had been sent off each day to collect wood chips for the fires and forage for the livestock. Bolli she had kept busy nearby building a turf wall that went from the end house, around the back of the storage hut and the shed. The wall would serve as a livestock enclosure and force Grelod and Alof to walk at some distance from the Greenlanders' houses when they went to the stream. The wall would also serve as protection against flooding should the stream overflow. At present this seemed unlikely; in fact the stream was low from lack of rain. But Freydis had seen enough flash floods in Gardar when the stream overflowed after heavy rains to want to take precautions. Working from early morning until dark, Bolli had finished the wall single-handedly. Freydis was pleased with this improvement and satisfied that the Greenlanders were well prepared for Winter. With one sail half done, she welcomed the opportunity to dress in her finest clothes.

As it turned out, the feast was delayed until Yule. Cold windy weather made it impossible to hold matches and games outdoors. Finally, the weather improved and it became clear and sunny enough for preparations to begin.

Early on the morning of the feast Freydis bid Kalf and Orn slaughter two goats and a pig, spit them and build three fires on the terrace for roasting the meat. Then she and Groa and Mairi stewed fish as well as hare and grouse. The stews were flavoured with seaweed, juniper berries and what remained of angelica stalks. When all this had been done, Freydis bade Mairi and Groa heat water so that she might bathe and wash her hair. After Freydis's hair had been brushed dry, Groa drew it back between two ivory combs. Freydis put on a clean linen shift embroidered in red and yellow, her blue robe, red kirtle and Thorstein's beads.

By then the men had marked off a small area of the terrace for the matches and games and set planks along the sides for spectators. Freydis sat at one end of the planks with Groa and Mairi, well away from the Icelandic thralls. She noticed that Mairi made no attempt to speak to the other ambatts. Freydis thought the girl withdrawn and quiet for her age. Occasionally she saw Mairi say something to Groa and once she saw her talking to Ulfar on the beach. Apart from that, the girl scarcely spoke and when she did, her words sounded so strange that Freydis could make no sense of what she said.

The air was cool and brisk; a light breeze was blowing off the water—Leifsbudir was never windless. The pleasantness of the weather meant the men were able to strip to the waist for the wrestling matches. At the beginning there were five pairs of wrestlers on each side. The idea was to disqualify everyone until they came down to the Greenlander and the Icelander who would wrestle each other in a final match. A man wrestled until he was defeated; the winner moved on to another match. So it was that Thorvard came up against Bolli to whom he lost. On the Icelanders' side, Hauk came up against Ulf Broad Beard and lost. This meant the Greenlanders were represented by Bolli; the Icelanders by Ulf. The match between the men went on for some time, both of them being uncommonly strong. Eventually Ulf was able to trick Bolli in such a way that he got him flat on his back and held him down. Ulf Broad Beard also won the log toss. Bolli came in second. Both wins put the Icelanders ahead. The Greenlanders won the ball game, for they had men like Thrand with younger legs who could easily outrun the Icelanders. This was a game where six men on each side had to kick a leather ball into a hole dug into the terrace, in order to score. After the field events were over, there was one last match before the games were finished. This was water wrestling and took place in the lake that was south of the houses, and west of the trees. This meant the Greenlanders and Icelanders had to cross the meadow, wrestlers and spectators alike. Five pairs on each side stripped and leapt into the shallow water where they tried to see who could be held under the water the longest. The lake was cold but the men did not expect to be in the water very long. Thorvard also took part in this event and again managed to win until he came up against Bolli who bent him double, sitting on his back so long that he had to be pulled off by others. Thorvard had some difficulty regaining his breath and, after he had spat water onto the grass, didn't re-enter the match, though he might have charged Bolli with foul play and been given another turn. Again the wrestling came down to Ulf and Bolli. After thrashing about in the water for some time, Ulf managed to straddle Bolli and force his head beneath the water. He kept Bolli's head submerged far longer than Bolli had held Thorvard under. Finally Bolli collapsed and Ulf dragged him from the lake and threw him onto the grass where Bolli gagged and coughed up water. As the Greenlanders and Icelanders were preparing to leave the lake, Bolli rolled his eyes and began to jab and punch the empty air as if he were wrestling trolls. The Icelanders were much amused by these carryings on. Ingald remarked that Bolli Illugisson seemed to have lost his wits.

Freydis did not see this event, having stayed behind with her thralls to make sure the meat was tended and the pots kept warm. There were also trenchers and bowls to lay out. Freydis had decided to use the hearth in the middle house for cooking. The middle house had a long room that would serve them well when the storytelling began. The Icelanders' house had the largest room of all, but there was no question of Freydis using that. The middle house also had the advantage of being roughly halfway between the end houses, though not quite, since it was closer to the Greenlanders' other house than the Icelanders'.

When the men returned from the lake, the feasting and drinking began. House doors were left open so that folk could visit freely back and forth. Freydis did not go so far as to unlock the storage hut. She had no intention of giving away any more of the Greenlanders' Winter provisions than she had already set out. While the wrestlers put on dry clothes and others dipped cups and horns into the mead barrel, Freydis went about telling folk about the eating arrangements. Because no one wanted to eat at an appointed time, Freydis decided against serving the food, preferring to let everyone help themselves. She dismissed the thralls, saying she would expect them to clean up early next day. Until then they could do what they wanted as long as they didn't steal the food that had been laid out with others in mind.

It was the shortest day of the year. Oil lamps and torches were lit inside and out. The Icelanders had carried the mead barrel onto the terrace in front of the middle house so that everyone could share the drink. The Norsemen wandered about without thought of whose side of the terrace they were on, helping themselves to food and drink. At first there was a good deal of laughter and banter, mostly about the matches and games. Many of the men ceased thinking of themselves as Icelanders or Greenlanders, and regarded their fellow drinkers as Norsemen like themselves. In fact it had been less than two score years since the Greenlanders' forebears had been Icelanders. As they talked and joked together, some of the farmers and sailors discovered they had more in common than they had thought.

Unfortunately some of the men did not eat enough before they started on the mead and were soon vomiting onto the grass. It could be said that the Egilssons were overgenerous with their mead, having made available a greater quantity of drink than was good for folk who seldom drank anything except water and milk. Freydis helped herself to a cup of mead and found it pleasant tasting. Then she cut herself a strip of goat meat which she chewed as she walked around. She made sure she was in plain view of Hauk should he be looking. Freydis knew she was better turned out than the other women. During the games she had noticed Helgi's ambatt was wearing a robe of red silk which Freydis thought was entirely out of place. The robe was cut far too low for cool weather and only made its wearer look scrawny and plain. Freydis noticed Finnbogi's concubine was wearing the same green robe she had worn earlier despite it being soiled with charcoal and grease. Moreover the shift fitted tightly since the ambatt was far gone with child.

Freydis had not walked about for long when Hauk approached her as she stood beside the hearth of the middle house. After the wrestling match he had put on a yellow silk tunic, an embroidered sash and a hat of brown leather. He was carrying a large drinking horn, which he

held to Freydis's mouth, afterwards using his sash to wipe
her lips.

"It's been too long since we spoke," he said, watching
her closely. Since his return from the Bay of Maples, he
had stayed away from the shed. He had been occupied
with building a snow shelter for the new ship. During this
work the absence of Jokul and Grimkel had again troubled him in such a way that he was inclined to shun the
Greenlanders, including Freydis. But now that the
Icelanders had surpassed the Greenlanders at wrestling
and his belly was warmed by the mead, Hauk's interest in
Freydis returned. His eyes took in the details of her hair
and dress. He inquired about what she had been doing
lately.

Freydis waved a hand toward the hearth where various
stews simmered, and where cheese and butter had been
laid out.

"I've been busy with this."

"How is the sail coming along?"

"It's over half-finished."

"Then it's time you invited me to the shed so that I can
see it."

"I'm not against you coming to the shed, though nothing is farthest from my mind tonight than sailcloth,"
Freydis said, knowing this was the kind of remark Hauk
was fond of making. Then she walked away to visit with
others.

During the early part of the evening Freydis made a
point of speaking to Greenlanders and Icelanders alike.
She spoke for a time with Helgi but avoided his brother.
She refused to give Finnbogi the satisfaction of turning
away from her. All the while she visited with others,
Freydis was aware that Hauk was never far from her side.

When the mead barrel was more empty than full and
the food nearly gone, Helgi sent the dwarf twins to
announce that the entertainment would begin since folk
had spread themselves in various places inside and out.
By the time the verse and tale telling were about to begin,
everyone in Leifsbudir was crowded into the middle

house. Men squatted on the floor, leaned against posts, sat hard against the walls. Some men sat like women on other men's laps. Hauk placed himself on the edge of the sleeping platform next to Freydis, sitting so close she could feel his thigh against her own. Like the others Asmund had drunk a large quantity of mead and had forgotten his shyness. He was easily persuaded to repeat the verses he had made earlier. When urged to recite a new verse, Asmund said he had only one verse to offer, a short poem that had come to him in a dream.

> Valhalla men are drinking elf dew
> Gathered from meadows and woods.
> Here warriors build wind horses;
> The Norns make gods of us all.

The men thought this verse more riddle than poem and urged Asmund to repeat it twice more before moving on to something else.

Helgi got to his feet and announced that Hauk would honour them with Norwegian tales. Hauk immediately protested he was no tale teller and that he preferred to remain where he was, since it wasn't often these days that he got to sit beside a beautiful woman. This of course brought so many shouts of encouragement and laughter that with elaborate reluctance, Hauk got to his feet. The Icelanders had already heard Hauk's stories, but the Greenlanders could hardly be denied hearing them. He would tell them a King Harald story. Like poor folk in Norway, Greenland farmers could never hear enough about kings and queens.

Hauk told the story about Queen Ragnhild who had mighty dreams. She once dreamed a huge tree bled over Norway. Her husband, King Hvaldan, could not dream at all unless he slept in a pigsty, which he eventually did. Then he dreamed locks of many-coloured hair grew out of his head and spread in all directions. Wise men interpreted Ragnhild and Hvaldan's dreams as foretelling Harald's birth. In this they were correct. Not long after these

dreams Queen Ragnhild gave birth to a son named Harald.
Harald grew strong and became a doughty man well suited
to being king. Soon after Harald reached manhood,
Hvaldan's sled went through rotten ice and he drowned.
Hvaldan was so well loved, though not by his wife, that his
corpse was cut into four pieces and buried in various
parts of Norway.

"King Harald was as well liked as his father, especially
after he became unbewitched," Hauk said. Then he went
on to tell the tale of how King Harald was bewitched by
the Finns into making an unsuitable marriage.

"King Harald was enjoying a Yule feast in Oppalandene
when a Finn by the name of Svase sent a messenger
requesting Harald to visit him on the other side of the
stream, where Svase had an encampment. As soon as the
king crossed the stream, he was met by Svase's beautiful
daughter Snaefrid who offered him a cup of mead. When
Snaefrid passed Harald the cup, her hand touched his and
it was as if a fire had passed from her to him. He knew
then he must have Svase's daughter. Soon after this
encounter Harald married Snaefrid. From then on he
loved her so witlessly that he neglected his kingdom in
order to be by her side. He got four sons on Snaefrid
before she died. Harald refused to allow Snaefrid to be
buried. Instead he had her laid out on a bed where he
watched over her day and night in the hope that she
would come back to life. Thus he sat for three Winters. All
that time Snaefrid's skin never faded but remained as rosy
as when she had lived. One day a man named Thorleif the
Wise came to Harald and told him his wife's body should
be raised so that her clothes could be changed. Snaefrid
had been lying in the same clothes all these years and
they had become dirty and grey. Finally the king agreed.
As soon as Snaefrid was raised from the bed, she disappeared and there arose a stench so foul that onlookers
had to cover their noses. In Snaefrid's place there crawled
worms, adders and frogs. At this the king recovered his
wits and ordered the foul mess burned. From that day on
he ruled his kingdom so sensibly that he won back the

respect of men. His subjects had never cared for Snaefrid and all along thought he ought to have left her with the Finns."

Apparently Finnbogi's ambatt found the story's ending too sad to bear, for she began to snivel so loudly that Finnbogi took her from the room. Freydis thought the tale silly. For a king who behaved so foolishly, Harald was lucky to have survived. The story was probably false and made up to pacify Harald's subjects, who no doubt resented the fact that he had gone outside his own country to find himself a wife. It seemed Hauk thought much the same thing, since he went on to say that it was obvious Kind Harald had learned the hard way that it was often the woman close at hand who provided the sturdiest pleasure, not the woman who was farthest away. While he spoke these words, Hauk looked at Freydis with such boldness that she decided to leave her place. She thought it imprudent to encourage Hauk's frank approach in front of others. She was also weary of sitting in a room stinking of sweaty bodies and vomited food. The room was strewn with platters of gnawed joints, bones and gristle. Freydis had not gone to the trouble of preparing large amounts of food and dressing herself in her finest clothes in order to spend the night in an overcrowded and untidy house. She had expected the Yule festivities to give her more pleasure than what she had enjoyed so far. When Freydis got up to leave, her string of glass beads broke. Several of the beads tumbled to the floor. Freydis stooped to pick them up, groping among the bones and empty cups on the floor. It was this delay that changed the outcome of the evening, or so it seemed to Freydis later on. After she had finished picking up the beads, Freydis stood up, swaying slightly from the suddenness of the movement and the effects of the drink. Then she made her way to the entrance, intending to leave. She paused beside the open door, waiting for Hauk to give some sign that he would come.

The evening's festivities had overtaken Freydis in such a way that she was of a mind to do something defiant and rash. Since arriving in Leifsbudir, she had spent her days weaving endless lengths of wadmal, overseeing thralls, putting up Winter food and preparing meals for a large crew of men. She was tired of looking after the welfare of others. During her apprenticeship with Thjodhild, her step-mother had told her many times that the mark of a well-born woman was her ability to set her own desires aside in order to provide for the requirements of others. Thjodhild acknowledged the fact that while men might indulge themselves from time to time, women must remain above self-indulgence. She said the laws recognized this difference between men and women. That was why the laws offered no protection for a woman if she chose to follow her carnal desires. This was only Thjodhild's thinking. Judging from some of the tales that Freydis had heard about other well-born women, not all folk shared her step-mother's stern opinion. In these tales more than one married woman had found pleasure beyond what her husband could provide. In any event, as Hauk had said, there were no laws in Leifsbudir save those which folk chose to carry with them. Freydis thought it a stroke of good fortune that her monthly bleeding was about to begin for it meant she could lie with Hauk without getting with child. If she intended to pleasure herself with him now was the time, which was why she had left the iron belt in its chest. Freydis knew Hauk wasn't a man to lose his wits over a woman. He would never sit up on his deathbed and tell his wife she would wed a man who would succeed where he had failed. Hauk wasn't a man for blind devotion. Freydis preferred him this way, since it meant she could take him or leave him afterwards.

Freydis continued to stand in the doorway, all the while keeping an eye on Hauk. She noticed that he had crossed the hearth and was now sitting between Grelod and Alof. This delayed Freydis's departure. If she left now, Hauk might forget her, since like the others he was somewhat drunk. If she went back to the hearth, she would have to sit opposite Grelod and Alof. This Freydis would not do, even for Hauk. While Freydis stood there waiting for the

Norwegian, Thorvard left his place beside Mairi and went to the hearth.

Because they were unaccustomed to strong drink, the Greenlanders were ill prepared for its effects and when drunk were apt to do things they regretted later on. This was the case with Thorvard. Because he was drunk, against his better judgement he had been persuaded by several Greenlanders to tell the *Tale of the Invisible Wretches* so that those Icelanders who had not gone on the expedition could learn what had happened in the Bay of Maples firsthand.

The Greenlanders were not the only folk whose judgement was impaired. The mead had affected some Icelanders in such a way that they became gloomy and morose. They revived past grudges and enmities and brooded over the shortcomings of the feast. They complained that the food they had eaten had not been as tasty or as well prepared as food they had enjoyed other places. The goat meat had been tough and the pig had been far too small so that the meat had run out before some of them had eaten their share. The amount of cheese that had been offered by the Greenlanders had been stingy and the butter was rancid. Moreover, some of the Icelanders resented the fact that a Greenlander had a concubine while most of the Icelanders had to go without. Listening to Thorvard's story, which most of them had heard from Hauk's point of view, the Icelanders were reminded that because of the way events had gone, the Greenlanders had seven more men in Leifsbudir than they, which was hardly fair since it had been their understanding that the Icelanders and Greenlanders would have thirty able-bodied men on each side over here.

Thorvard had reached that part of the tale where after killing the cow, he and Bodvar were searching for Jokul and Grimkel. It was here Vemund made the call of a rutting stag. He did this poorly yet well enough that folk knew what it was.

"Why didn't you go after the Icelanders instead of chasing your tails?" Ulf shouted.

"You were afraid of invisible folk!" Grelod yelled. "What kind of a man is afraid of invisible folk?"

Hauk stood up and, ignoring Thorvard who by now had stopped speaking, addressed the others. "It seems to me that since I've come to Leifsbudir," Hauk said, "I've been living among invisible people and been building an invisible ship with invisible trees. I've come to a place that doesn't exist!"

Thorvard lingered in front of the hearth, uncertain as to what to do next. Though drunk, he was not so far gone that he failed to notice the malice in the shouts and jests.

Without any forethought at all, Freydis went to the hearth and taking her husband by the hand, led him past the others. She had to shove aside her own thralls and Ulfar to get out the door. Outside the torches had burnt themselves to a dull glow, but the moon was high and bright enough to light a path to the shed without them stumbling over three or four drunken men who were lying on the terrace.

Groa wasn't in the shed, which meant Thorvard didn't have to carry her outside as he sometimes did at home when he and Freydis wanted to lie together; if it was warm enough in Gardar he also carried the two older children outside the hut, bringing them inside after he and Freydis were finished. Freydis and Thorvard entered the shed and bolted the door. Then they took off their clothes and lay down. The sleeping bench was so narrow that during the course of the night, they fell off several times. There was much merriment about this, which had more to do with satisfying desire than taking strong drink. This was the boisterous coupling Thorvard preferred and which he never had with Mairi. Thorvard didn't give Mairi a second thought except later in his dreams. This may have been why he awoke before Freydis.

Thorvard left the shed early. He couldn't remember where Mairi had been when he had left the middle house last night with Freydis. He seemed to remember she had been sitting beside him when he got up to tell his tale and thought that the Icelanders might have taken her back. It was the girl's gentleness that made him want to find her. He wanted to satisfy himself that she hadn't been roughly handled. Before he set about looking, Thorvard went to the stream and splashed water on his face. His eyes and forehead hurt so much he held them under water until the cold replaced the pain.

Freydis awoke as Thorvard was leaving but she continued to lie in bed. She was so well satisfied and content from the evening's coupling that she had no wish to spoil the morning by harrying reluctant thralls to clean up last night's mess. Her thralls had no doubt made the most of their Yule freedom and would be difficult to rouse. Freydis continued to lie abed, waiting until Groa came from wherever she was sleeping to light the fire to heat bathing water.

Soon after he went out, Thorvard reappeared. "You had better come quickly. Your step-brother is lying near the stream. He's been badly beaten."

Freydis got up, put on her shift and robe and went outside.

Bolli was lying on his back. His legs were spread far apart; one of his arms was placed in such a way that Freydis could see it was broken as was his nose. His entire face was puffed and welted. Freydis had never seen a man beaten as badly as this. Thralls had to be thrashed from time to time, but Freydis could think of no reason why Bolli should be so badly treated. Whatever sympathy she felt toward her step-brother was overshadowed by anger at those who had beaten him. While Freydis looked at his injuries, Bolli watched her through slitted eyes.

"Who beat you?" Freydis said.

"Icelanders." When he moved his lips, Freydis saw a row of bloodied holes.

Freydis herself fetched water from the stream and put it on to heat while Thorvard took his axe and made wooden splints. Then he and Freydis laid the broken arm across the largest board and tied sticks in place with strips of torn cloth. Thorvard woke Kalf and Orn. The three of them carried Bolli inside the end house and laid him on a sleeping bench.

"We'll have to take the matter up with the Egilssons," Freydis told Thorvard. "We can't let this beating go unchecked."

"I suggest we go later on after they've had a chance to sleep off the effects of the mead and are more likely to be in a good frame of mind," Thorvard said. Then he went off to look for Mairi.

As it turned out, there was no need to look for Mairi, since she and Groa were already on their way back to the houses, having spent the night in Ulfar's shelter. Ulfar did not return with them; he had no intention of cleaning up after drunken men. He had better things to do. He unrolled a vellum and picked up his quill.

*   *   *

Last night the Greenlanders and the Icelanders held a
drunken feast to mark the Yule. The heathens would
have been better off to have fallen on their knees and
prayed to Our Lord rather than indulged themselves
with loose women and drink. The drink aroused the
men's lust in such a way that there was fighting over a
concubine's use and a man they call Ingald was killed.
I provided my shelter for Groa and Mairi so that they
would be spared abuse. After I had hidden the
women, I returned to the middle house. Though the
drunkenness sickened me, I thought the women
would be safer if I was in plain view of the men, since
no one would have cause to seek me out. If drunken
Norsemen had come to my shelter while I was guard-
ing it outside, I would have been unable to protect the
women from harm, being a small man with no
weapons, only the tools I use with wood. Helping the
women has provided me with a measure of hope, for
by sheltering them I proved that in my own way I am
capable of bettering someone else's fate, if not my
own.

*   *   *

The Icelanders took up the matter of Bolli before the Greenlanders made a move themselves. The Egilsson brothers approached Thorvard when he was on the beach dressing wood for a snow shelter he and his men intended to build for the *Vinland*. At the time of the brothers' visit, Freydis was inside the middle house supervising the cleaning. By now the trenchers, cups and bowls had been taken outside and washed. The room had been swept and Groa and Mairi were doing the last of the tidying. Freydis therefore knew nothing of Thorvard's conversation with the Egilssons until he told her afterwards.

"Helgi and Finnbogi have just told me that late last night there was a fight between Bolli and some Icelanders over a woman," Thorvard said. He and Freydis were standing outside the middle house. "During the fight Bolli picked up Ingald Snorrisson and threw him against the lintel so hard Ingald bled through the ears. He died soon after. The Egilssons are demanding Bolli's exile. They say if we don't banish him ourselves, they'll split his head open with an axe."

"They speak like Althing judges who have heard only one side of a case," Freydis said. "We should find others who can tell us their version of what happened in order to arrive at the truth."

Thorvard said they would have to move quickly since the Egilssons had only given him until next morning to get rid of Bolli.

"I'm willing to talk to the others about what happened, but I've no doubt Bolli is guilty. I've told you before that your step-brother is a troublemaker."

"He's a troublemaker only when other folk mock him or treat him badly," Freydis said. "I'm going with you to talk to the others." Because Thorvard disliked Bolli, she didn't trust him to take Bolli's side.

As they went about talking to the Greenlanders, it became clear to Freydis and Thorvard that most of them had spent the night inside the room of the middle house and had been too mead soused and dull witted to have been aware that anything untoward was taking place.

"It seems likely the fight took place outside," Freydis said, "which would explain why no one seems to have seen or heard it."

Freydis and Thorvard were unable to find one Greenlander who admitted to witnessing the fight. All of them claimed to have drunk themselves into a deadened sleep.

Freydis remembered shoving aside Ulfar the night before as she and Thorvard were leaving the middle house. Reluctant as she was to trust his view, Freydis told Thorvard she thought they should ask Ulfar what he had seen. "He's far too pious to take strong drink and might have seen more than the others."

"It's worth a try," Thorvard said. "Unlike most thralls, Ulfar seems to honour the truth."

Freydis and Thorvard could see thin grey smoke coming from Ulfar's shelter so they knew he was there. Freydis had never visited the lean-to; she had far too much work to bother looking at what seemed to be nothing more than a wooden box. As she and Thorvard approached, they saw Ulfar through the opening that passed for a doorway. He was bent over one of his sheepskins which he had placed on some sort of table.

"It seems to me we are wasting our time coming here," Freydis said. "Anyone who scratches black marks on sheepskin with a bird's feather is hardly in command of his wits and cannot be trusted to say anything sensible."

Thorvard said they had come this far, they might as well hear what Ulfar had to say.

At first Ulfar was unwilling to say anything about the night before. Freydis put his reluctance to speak down to the gloomy aspect of his nature. When Thorvard spoke about the Egilssons' demand that Bolli be exiled, Ulfar said, "Banishment is too good for someone as evil as Bolli Illugisson."

"Such remarks are better not spoken around me," Freydis said. "As you know, Bolli is my step-brother." One day Leif's thrall would choke on his self-righteous judgements.

"We're here to talk about what happened last night," Thorvard said. "After my wife and I went to bed."

"If you expect me to speak freely, then your wife should step aside," Ulfar said.

Freydis had to remind herself why they had come to see Ulfar before she agreed to withdraw so that the two men could speak alone. While she waited, Freydis brooded over Ulfar's insolence. Like Grelod, Ulfar's impudence and scorn showed what happened to thralls who were given leeway to do what they wanted. Freydis thought if fate had made Ulfar a thrall owner like herself, he would have been as high handed as Olaf Digre in harrying folk to take up Christ.

Later when they were returning to the houses, Thorvard told Freydis Ulfar's version of what had happened.

"Ulfar says he left the middle house shortly after we did but returned again and stayed as long as the tale telling and verses went on, which they did for some time. When the men began making up lewd riddles, Ulfar got up and went outside where he came upon Ingald and Bolli fighting over an ambatt. Alof was holding on to Ingald while Bolli was trying to get her away. Bolli had Alof over his shoulder and was carrying her off when Ingald began calling him sheep mounter and other scurrilous names. Bolli dropped Alof, picked up Ingald and slammed him against the door lintel of the middle house. Ulfar said he heard Ingald's head smash. Alof started screaming which roused several Icelanders including Ulf Broad Beard. By now it was light enough to see Bolli carrying Alof across the terrace. The Icelanders jumped on Bolli, dragged him into the high grass near the stream and began to beat him. Ulfar said that as much as he disliked Bolli Illuggison, he found no pleasure in watching men fighting over a woman and he left." Thorvard concluded Ulfar's tale by saying that it was clear that Bolli was in the wrong. It was Thorvard's opinion that Bolli's worst enemy was himself. "The sooner we take him away, the better," Thorvard said, "since if we don't the Icelanders will come for him."

"Bolli's in no condition to be taken anywhere," Freydis replied, then added that in her opinion, the Icelanders had something to answer for. "After all it was they who provided the loose women and drink."

"The Icelanders can hardly be blamed for sharing their drink with us," Thorvard pointed out. "You would have been the first to begrudge them if they'd hoarded it for themselves. Either way, matters are too far gone now to waste time laying blame. The only way to set the matter straight between the Icelanders and ourselves is to outlaw Bolli. You had better see to the provisions. No matter how much I dislike the man, I would never send him away empty handed. I'll also need three days' provisions for those of us taking him away. We'll leave early tomorrow."

Bolli was given a sleeping bag, a three-month supply of dried fish and meat, a small cheese and a pouch of berries. He was also provided with an ember pot and a bundle of hunting weapons. Since it was early in the morning, no one saw Bolli and the others leave.

When Freydis got up later that morning, she immediately began to work on the sail in order to push all thought of Bolli out of her mind. She was troubled that he had been sent away, since she thought that considering everything, he had been misjudged. On the other hand, it was true that Bolli's worst enemy was himself. It was equally true that by bringing unmarried women to Leifsbudir, the Icelanders had been asking for trouble. They had also been short sighted in offering so much mead; it would have been far more prudent to have locked half of it away until later on.

The same day Bolli was taken away, Ingald Snorrisson's corpse was buried some distance behind the Icelanders' house. While the hole was being dug, it began to snow. The first snow came in flurries that melted soon after they touched the ground. Gradually the snow thickened, coming down so heavily that the Icelanders who were burying Ingald were shrouded in white.

It was still snowing the next day. By then a northeast wind had moved inland, and was piling snow into a ridge on the terrace; yet other places were nearly bare. Dressed in a cloak, leggings and wool-stuffed shoes, Freydis went to the meadow with Mairi to see how the livestock were getting on. The animals seemed well enough but Freydis thought if the wind continued to arrange the snow in the same pattern, the livestock would become difficult to tend. The meadow grass was bare enough to provide forage but if the ridge of snow running alongside the houses grew any higher, they would be prevented from milking the cow and goat and tending the pig and sheep. Soon after Freydis and Mairi returned to the houses, it stopped snowing. Now it began to rain. The rain continued for most of the night. By the next morning the snow had vanished, leaving behind low ridges of ice.

Thorvard and his men did not return for two more days, having laid up ashore to wait out the storm. They had taken Bolli more than a ten-day journey away on foot which meant they had a strenuous journey back, rowing against the current all the way.

The day after Thorvard's return, the Egilsson brothers came to the door of the end house just as Freydis, Thorvard and several others were sitting down to their midday meal. Thorvard invited them inside. To Freydis's annoyance, for milk was in short supply, he offered them each a bowl. This was declined. Thorvard asked the reason for the brothers' visit. Finnbogi began by saying that he was pleased Thorvard had gotten rid of Bolli Illugisson thereby preventing a second murder. He went on to say that there was a second matter that had to be settled if relations between the Icelanders and Greenlanders were to remain cordial. He said the Icelanders had discussed the matter of Ingald Snorrisson's death further. "It's our view," Finnbogi said, "that we ought to be compensated for his loss."

"Ingald was a valuable woodworker. We think it only fair that you give us a worker as skilled in return," Helgi said. Though he had gone out of his way to encourage good relations with the Greenlanders, Helgi was also cunning enough to try to wring concessions out of them.

"As you know, we've lost four men here," Finnbogi went on, "whereas you've lost only one. Moreover, you arrived with extra men, which means you can easily spare one for us."

"How can you make such a demand?" Freydis said. "You know there are no planksmen among us."

"There's Ulfar," Helgi said. "He's more skilled than any of our woodworkers with the exception of Hauk." Helgi knew this demand was a gamble but he thought it was worth a try. At the very least the Greenlanders would be reminded that they still owed the Icelanders a favour.

"I'm surprised at you, Helgi Egilsson," Freydis said. "You know Ulfar is my brother's thrall. I think Leif would be displeased to know that in addition to the use of his house, you expect the loan of a thrall he provided for me. You can be sure that if you persist in this matter, my brother will hear of it later on."

"Your brother strikes me as a man who's exceptionally fair minded," Helgi replied pleasantly. "He's therefore likely to understand that since his half-sister's husband has the use of one of our thralls, we can expect the use of one of his."

"Once again I'm surprised," Freydis said. "For despite your friendliness, you can be as iron nosed as your brother."

Thorvard spoke up. "In my view, Ulfar himself should be asked his preference. Since Leif thinks so highly of the woodworker that he promised him manumission, then we should respect Leif's judgement enough to consider Ulfar's wishes."

The Egilssons said they would be more than willing to hear what Ulfar had to say. Kalf was sent to fetch Ulfar from the middle house where he was eating. Now that the fishing had dropped off, Ulfar was taking his meals with the Greenlanders. Freydis was so put out at Thorvard and the Icelanders that she couldn't trust herself to speak without making matters worse, especially since Ulfar might again refuse to speak his mind with her there. She there-

fore withdrew to the sleeping compartment and waited to
see what would happen next.

When Ulfar arrived, Thorvard explained the situation in
a few words and told him it was up to him whether or not
he went over to the Icelanders.

Ulfar looked at the Egilssons. "I've no wish to take up
with you Icelanders, for you seem to me to be as heathen
as everyone else here. I was persuaded to come to
Leifsbudir by a Christian I respect in order to better my
prospects. If you require my skills to help you build your
ship next Summer, I won't hold them back, for I've
learned much from Hauk Ljome. Until then I have woodworking chores enough to keep me occupied here."

"I know you sleep by yourself in a lean-to beyond the
terrace. Where will you live if the weather turns bitter?
You'll freeze to death sleeping out there," Finnbogi said.

Listening from the compartment, Freydis thought it
unlikely these remarks were made out of concern for
Ulfar's well-being. She thought it more likely Finnbogi was
trying to cover his humiliation at being thwarted by someone else's thrall.

"I'm used to deprivations," Ulfar said. "If the weather
makes it impossible for me to stay by myself, I'll move my
gear into the middle house, for it's there I prefer to be."

"Remember, if these Greenlanders mistreat you,"
Finnbogi said, "you can always cross the terrace to us."

Freydis knew Finnbogi was a man who refused to take
no for an answer and would look for other ways to make
Ulfar his own. Helgi was little better, having shown himself
to be as arrogant as his brother. Surely Thorvard could
now see that whatever dealings they arranged with the
Egilssons would result in the Greenlanders getting the
worst of the bargain.

After the Icelanders had gone and the platters and
bowls had been cleared away, Freydis took Thorvard aside
and gave him the rough side of her tongue. She was angry
that her husband had risked their Luck by asking Ulfar's
opinion, that arrangements with the Egilssons had
depended on what a thrall would say. But she was angrier

at the brothers and, unable to take it out on them, berat-
ed her husband for the difficulties he had caused. "It
seems I've married someone who's all too eager to trade
away more for less."

"Say what you like," Thorvard said. "But I've no intention of giving up Mairi, especially after what the Egilssons
have put us through."

"I agree with that," Freydis said. "Mairi's as useful to me
as she is to you, especially since Groa's infirmities have
grown worse of late." The dampness of Leifsbudir had
affected the old woman's joints in such a way that she frequently dropped platters of food and slopped the milk
bucket. Freydis no longer trusted her to carry the food.
Some days Groa's hands were so clumsy Freydis bid Mairi
do her hair instead. The girl was nimble and quick. Despite
her pregnancy she did Groa's work as well as her own.

The day after the Egilssons' visit a second storm swept
through Leifsbudir during the night. This time the snow
did not drift but there was far more of it and the air was
bitter cold. In the morning the Greenlanders walked in
snow halfway to their knees. Using spades and buckets
they made a path between their houses. This chore took
them much longer than they thought it should. The
Greenlanders were well used to snow, but snow that was
light and dry, not heavy and wet. When the path was finished, the men cleared the enclosure between the end
house and the outbuildings. This was an easier chore,
since the snow had drifted outside the wall Bolli had built.
Although there was less snow in the meadow than around
the houses, Freydis decided to move the livestock to the
walled enclosure so that they could be tended without
walking far. Nagli and Ulfar moved their sleeping gear
inside, Nagli to the end house, Ulfar to the middle house.

These arrangements were made just in time, for two
days later a third storm swept through Leifsbudir. This was
the worst storm of all. There was five times the amount of
wind as before and ten times the amount of snow. The
combination of wind and snow meant that most of the
snow drifted over the houses. It became impossible to

work outside. During the early part of the storm when it was plain the animals would perish if left where they were, Freydis had her gear moved from the shed into the end house so that the shed could be used as a byre. Freydis had no intention of sharing a sleeping platform with her husband and Mairi. As a result Thorvard moved his gear into the main room where Evyind and Ozur slept with their sons, and Freydis and Groa took over the compartment at the end. Freydis was no better pleased with this arrangement than Thorvard since it meant her privacy was gone.

By the time the storm ended four days later, all intercourse between the Icelanders and Greenlanders had ceased. The houses at either end of the terrace had been entirely cut off from each other. In fact snow covered Leif's buildings so completely that, except for the smoke, anyone looking at the settlement from a distance wouldn't know it was there. Through arduous shovelling the Greenlanders maintained pathways between their own buildings. The walls on either side of the paths were high white cliffs, being well over the tallest men's heads. These pathways had to be cleaned out several times daily, since they continually drifted in. As well, the men had to take turns climbing onto the house tops and cleaning the roof holes which were frequently clogged, making the houses smokier than they liked. Earlier the Greenlanders had laid in a large quantity of firewood and stacked it against the walls. The wood cut down on sleeping space but the Greenlanders had more than they needed to begin with so that no one was forced to sleep on the floor.

The compartment where Freydis and Groa now slept was inside the door of the end house. Though it was smaller than the shed, it had benches on three sides. Freydis folded several lengths of sail and arranged them on the widest bench under her sleeping bag. She hung a length of wadmal over the doorway and another one in the corner in front of a privy bucket. She also hung wadmal on the walls, against the frost. Freydis's loom was set up in the large room beside the fire, beneath a smoke hole so that she could make the best use of the winter light.

Weak though it was, there was far more light in Winter in
Leifsbudir than in Gardar where by this time of the year,
darkness continued all day. Even so, the air inside the
house was often too smoky for weaving. Not only were the
roof holes choked with snow, but there was Nagli's forge
smoke to contend with. The iron worker had built a small
forge at the far end of the room where he made an assortment of rivets, hinges and hooks to pass the time.
Fortunately most of the men did cleaner work such as
mending weapons and tools. Some of the better carvers
made deer antler combs and spoons or whittled wooden
axe handles and gaming pieces to keep themselves occupied. These gaming pieces were often put to use as the
Greenlanders sat around the fire.

* * *

Even though the Greenlanders had more time on their
hands than they knew what to do with and there was constant going back and forth between their houses, they
never did open a tunnel through the snowbank to the
Icelanders' house. The Icelanders had no reason to come
to the stream, which was now frozen over. Like the
Greenlanders they drank melted snow. Occasionally a
Greenlander would make a passing remark about an
Icelander or about one of the concubines, but none of the
Greenlanders sought contact with the other side. Although
the Greenlanders had disliked Bolli Illugisson, some of
them thought his Winter banishment unnecessarily harsh
since any of them might have accidentally killed another
as a result of hard drinking. Others regarded Bolli's exile
as just, but thought the Icelanders high handed to have
demanded the use of Ulfar on top of that. Freydis encouraged these views. More than once she reminded the
Greenlanders that the Icelanders were occupying a place
that belonged to her brother. That being so, she had
expected the Icelanders to maintain close contact with
their hosts, out of consideration if not respect. She said
the Icelanders had failed to shovel a pathway through the
snow and kept themselves apart because they regarded

themselves as superior folk. Even as she spoke, Freydis knew she was playing false. The fact was she had no wish to see the Icelanders since there was the strong possibility that such contact would bring more trouble. She thought the Icelanders would make more demands upon her, especially for food. She thought that considering the ill will on either side, the Greenlanders and Icelanders were better off being separated into two camps for the Winter. As it was, the Greenlanders were foul tempered enough from being forced to remain inside.

A month past Yule three events occurred which Freydis thought were unlucky. The first was that the cow and the remaining goat dried up. The animals had been producing less milk each day, the result of bitter cold and poor fodder. Freydis bid Mairi keep a fire going in the shed and feed them double rations. Even so, their milk supply dwindled and finally stopped.

A further setback was the appearance of Helgi Egilsson's ambatt at the Greenlanders' door. Finna came through the snow one day accompanied by two Icelanders with shovels. They had avoided the worst of the drift by walking along the beach and shovelling through the snow until they came to the Greenlanders' house. Freydis knew these men only by sight. Thorvard knew them. He addressed them as Karl and Solvi and invited them inside to sit by the fire. The men refused to enter. Nor at first would Finna come inside. She said she was covered with too much snow, which was true enough. Even her eyebrows and hair were white. Although she had no wish to see the Icelanders at close quarters, Freydis thought their refusal to come inside was unfriendly. Later she was to comment on this unfriendliness to the Greenlanders many times. Finna stood in the doorway with her cloak wrapped tightly around her, the biting cold rushing inside.

"I've come for cow's milk," she said. "Olina has a new babe who's starving for want of milk."

So Finnbogi's ambatt survived childbirth only to find she had no milk in her teats.

"There's no cow's milk here," Freydis said.

"You have a cow."

"She's dry," Freydis said. "And the goat is no better."

Finna stared at Freydis as if staring could discern the truth. Freydis stared back thinking how pinched-looking Finna was; surely Helgi could have done better by way of a concubine.

"Do you have any cheese?" Freydis asked.

"No," Finna said. "It's been gone long since."

"I have some I'd be willing to exchange with you," Freydis said.

The proposition seemed to confuse Finna. She said nothing one way or the other but continued to regard Freydis with suspicion.

"The cheese can be softened with warm water," Freydis explained, "and fed to the child."

"I'll ask Olina," Finna said."If it's her wish, I'll return for the cheese."

"Suit yourself."

Finna asked Freydis what she wanted in exchange for the cheese.

"That can be decided later on. It seems to me the main thing is to make the child well." Freydis thought Finna foolish for refusing to accept the cheese especially since she had come all this way through the snow. Freydis wanted Finna to take it. She wanted the child to live. She bore it no grudge even if it was Finnbogi's. It also occurred to her that doing what she could to help the babe might prove useful, since the Icelanders could be reminded later on that she had helped them out.

"I've given softened cheese to my own children with good results," Freydis said. "If the babe takes the cheese, I'm sure we Greenlanders won't mind forgoing our cheese rations. All of us know the importance of good neighbours, especially in a place such as this."

As she spoke, Freydis watched Finna. She thought Helgi's ambatt was regarding her in a mistrustful way.

"I prefer to take nothing from you until I've spoken to the babe's mother," Finna said. "There's no point accepting food the babe will refuse."

"I'll give you a piece," Freydis said, "since you won't know one way or the other unless you try feeding it to the babe."

Finally Finna agreed. She was also persuaded to come close to the fire. Freydis put on her cloak and went to the storage hut to cut a large slice of cheese. When she returned, she wrapped the slice in a clean cloth and gave it to Finna.

That was the last Freydis saw of Finna. Finna never returned, which Freydis took to mean the child had refused the cheese.

The day after Finna's visit, Mairi went to the shed as usual to feed the stock. She returned soon after with the news that the cow was lying on her side and refused to get up. Freydis went out to the shed to see for herself. Both the cow's nose and udder were hot.

Nothing would do but Freydis had the cow carried into the house and laid beside the fire. Freydis was convinced that one of the Icelanders' ambatts, probably Olina, had put a curse on the cow for not being able to provide any milk. Freydis was determined to resist the spell by whatever means she could. Despite the grumblings of those who complained that the room was foul smelling enough, Freydis kept the cow inside the house. Once a cow of Halla's had been cursed for fouling a neighbour's water supply. Halla had turned back the curse by tying braided hair around each teat and laying a sharp knife beneath the tail. Freydis used several strands of her own hair to make the spell. Then she laid out her knife as Halla had done.

It took five days for Halla's measures to work. One morning Freydis awoke to find the cow standing by the hearth.

"At last my Luck has turned for the better," Freydis said.

In this she was mistaken. Several days after the cow recovered, Groa fell ill.

The old woman was carrying trenchers toward a tub of melted snow for washing up. She was shuffling along, one foot turned inward. Her breathing was noisy but that was nothing new. As she passed Freydis, who was weaving by the fire, one of the trenchers fell onto Freydis's foot.

Freydis's hand went out to cuff Groa for her clumsiness and struck empty air. Groa had fallen to the floor, the trenchers with her. She was clutching her breast and moaning. Freydis was used to seeing the old woman stop and catch her breath, but she had never heard her moan in this way.

"Lift her onto the bench," Freydis said to the others. There were several men in the room, including Ulfar.

Groa was placed on the bench and wrapped in a cloak. Mairi rolled up a fur rug and put it beneath Groa's head. The old woman lay there with her eyes closed and her mouth open. For a time the Greenlanders stood and watched her, but when it appeared she wasn't dying, they sat down and took out their game boards or got busy with whittling and carving tools. Mairi picked up the trenchers.

"I want a Christian burial," Groa said loud and clear. This close to death she had nothing to lose by speaking out.

Freydis gave no indication she had heard but continued weaving. She had never seen Groa make the Christ sign but assumed the old woman was a follower of Christ. Most thralls were. What fools they were to think their Christ cared whether they lived or died.

"Will you give me a Christian burial?" Groa shouted. Freydis stared at her. The old woman looked pop eyed and strange.

"If it means so much that it makes you shout, you may have it," Freydis said crossly. Why would anyone want to be buried in the name of a god who lacked the power to keep himself from being nailed to a tree? "Though it seems to me you're far from dead."

"Make no mistake, I'm dying," Groa said. "And I want my body blessed with holy water and my bones buried in Thjodhild's churchyard." She lifted her head and looked about. "Unless I'm mistaken there's someone here who can do as I ask."

"Doubtless there is," Freydis said, aware that Ulfar was still in the room waiting for Nagli to finish a hinge for a folding bench Ulfar had made. Freydis had not forgotten that the priest had given Ulfar the vial of water in front of

Leif. She thought it prudent to go along with Groa's request to avoid trouble with Leif later on. Freydis was also aware that Christians sometimes became spiteful revenants if their burial wasn't to their liking.

"Should you die, I promise to bury you as you've requested," Freydis said. "Now you'd better rest."

Before long Freydis regretted this promise.

Groa died the next night during another snowstorm. This presented the Greenlanders with the problem of what to do with the corpse. The body could not remain close to the fire without rotting. It could not be set outside because of the wolves which had begun to howl at night. It could not be boiled inside because of the stench nor outside because of the weather. There was no choice but to put the corpse in the storage hut until the weather improved. A stake was driven into Groa's chest so that later on, holy water could be poured inside. The body was tied in a sack and put with the provisions. Even though the corpse was covered and placed on planks above the food, Freydis did not like this arrangement. She took care never to enter the hut before or after daylight in case Groa turned out to be a night walker. Freydis always took some-one, usually Mairi, with her to the hut.

Later on that Winter the second pig died. Although the animal was too thin for good eating, Freydis used it to make a stew. While the Greenlanders sat around the fire sucking the bones for marrow, Thrand, who considered himself something of a joker, wiped the grease on his breeches and remarked that he never knew the joint of an old woman tasted so good.

Freydis chided Thrand for this unfortunate remark. "Our Winter has been unlucky enough without meeting up with a night walker," she said. "I'm sure I speak for the others when I say that none of us wants to be visited in our beds by the ghost of Groa's unburied corpse. Who knows what grudges the old woman may have taken to her death?"

I, GROA, TOOK THE CHEESE. I opened the lock on the shed door with a pick I found in the grass one morning and later discarded. I put the cheese in my bucket, carried it to the stream and hid it behind some rocks. I gave Mairi half the cheese and ate the rest whenever I went to fetch water, to keep down the hunger.

Now that I am dead, I am untroubled by hunger or pain. Aching belly, rankling joints, swollen feet, freezing shins are nothing to me.

I am without shape or substance. I drift about like smoke or mist. Between twilight and sunrise I move over the landscape unencumbered. So light are my movements that I leave behind no marks or prints of any kind. I float through walls. I pass through bone and flesh. I become air. After twenty-six years of enslavement, my body has finally separated from my self.

This was something I was unable to do in life, though not from want of trying. When Vegest Bjornsson kicked me about the ribs after I told him I could no longer work in harness unless I was better fed, I tried to will my self away from his farm beneath Hekla to my parents' croft in Seilebost. When Bjartmar's wife, Thorkatla, branded my arm with hot iron after I told her the shoes she wanted were on her daughter's feet, I struggled to put my self in the meadow at Horgabost beside the fairy stone. Eventually I learned to avoid such punishment by never speaking my mind. I said nothing to my masters unless

required. Nor did I speak to other thralls. I learned early
on that except for Ronan, thralls were not to be trusted.
Who can blame the wretched for using betrayal to better
their Luck?

I was measured in cow value. Vegest Bjornsson paid
Kollgrim four slaughter cows for my service. Bjartmar
Halfgrimsson paid Hilde, Vegest's widow, three cows capable of breeding, in milk, without defects. This was much
less than my sister Maeve's value. What she went for eventually I never knew since we were separated after Kollgrim
reached Iceland. My guess is that she might have gone for
as much as eight cows, perhaps even some silver. Unlike
me, Maeve was comely in appearance. Even before scars
lessened my value, I was regarded as defective, having
been born with a lame foot. And I had a short, wide body.
The top of my head seldom reached past a Norseman's
chest. For that reason, at the time of our capture I fared
better than Maeve, since even rapacious Vikings spurn
mounting a cripple when there is a beautiful maiden to lie
upon. When I refused to give up my name, Kollgrim called
me Groa. He traded me using that name, pointing out to
haggling buyers that I was wide hipped and strong enough
for field work.

The worst feature of Norsemen is their desire to own
whatever they come across, whether it be people, goods
or land. They are quick to fence in territory they think
should be theirs and will fight anyone who tries to wrest it
away. In this respect the women are as greedy as the men.
If someone takes what they have, they regard it as a
crime. They call it stealing. They think nothing of killing
someone who takes a sheep or cow and will cut off a
thrall's hand for taking the smallest trinket. Though I
helped myself to food whenever I was sure I would not be
caught, I never regarded it as stealing. Is a fox stealing
when he takes a freshly killed bird? Is a bird stealing when
he eats a berry plucked from a bucket? Long ago in
Seilebost, I heard my father say Stealth and Deceit were
wicked abominations. How was he to know that without
Freedom, Stealth and Deceit become allies?

Once I took a blue glass bead belonging to Thorkatla which I found when I was sweeping. I put it in my mouth. Later when I was hauling stones in the field I spat the bead onto my hand and held it toward the sun. Everything around me, the sky, the hills, the ice, was a bright shimmering blue. That afternoon I stopped work many times to look through the glass bead. I liked the way it transformed the country. Later I swallowed the bead. To look at me in my ragged tunic you could not have guessed I was carrying a cherished jewel inside. Eventually I passed the bead. It was found by a thrall named Bratt when he was manuring the field. Bratt returned the bead to Thorkatla. By that time it was too late for accusations and I kept my hand.

Now that I am unowned, I am free to go where I please. Sometimes I enter the Greenlanders' minds whose countries interest me more than the place they live. Soundlessly I enter their ears. I slip between their teeth as they mumble in their sleep. I float into their dreams. Some of the Greenlanders have terrible dreams, the result no doubt of their confinement and meagre rations. Though Freydis Eiriksdottir has plenty of food laid aside, she is stingy with meals. When the men complain, she tells them they could be stuck inside a snowbank a long time yet, that it is better to be safe than sorry.

The Greenlanders sleep poorly. Often they are awakened at night by wolves padding about on the roof tops, circling the smoke holes, howling over the frozen sea. Balki and Gisli are convinced that the loudest howl is Bolli Illugisson's. They say Bolli has returned to Leifsbudir as a werewolf. Nagli Asgrimsson tells the brothers a tale about a woman who was attacked by her werewolf husband as she tended their sheep. Nagli says that if Balki and Gisli want to become werewolves, they should go into the woods and find themselves a she-wolf who is pupping and put the afterbirth on their heads. The Greenlanders relieve their boredom by frightening each other in this way. They tell stories about headless men who wander through the dark, mothers who smother sleeping bairns, ghosts who push enemies into the fire.

Teit Evyindsson has a dream soul. Tonight I follow his soul when it leaves his body and becomes a squirrel tunnelling beneath the snow, looking for seeds. The trail of seeds leads to an ice cave inside which Teit sees two jewels winking in firelight. He thinks he has discovered treasure. Until he seizes one of the jewels and it becomes a troll's eye. Thrand Ozursson dreams he is being attacked by a red creature who is half-man, half-beast. The monster carries him far into a wilderness where even the trees are red.

Dreams mislead. They lead us away from well-known paths, taking us places we have never been: inside a wolf skin, an ice cave, a forest of bloodied trees. Some dreams beguile, leading us to islands of warm white sand, passing off fool's gold as riches. They pretend to lead us to Paradise only to leave us stranded without any way back. We dream our lives; we dream our deaths. Before I died I gave my dreams to Mairi: a pair of wool-lined shoes, a bowl of porridge, a round of bannock.

* * *

Two sisters sitting on the overturned boat eating oatcakes. Around them the golden sand of the Hebrides. To the South the nipple of Rybha Mac a Chnuic; to the North Loch Tarbet; straight ahead the Isle of Tarasaigh. Behind and above them, the mahair white with daisies and humming clover. In the middle of the meadow, the fairy stone. At their feet the croggan of bait for their father's evening fishing. One sister is tall and fair; the other squat and dark. The older sister is seventeen, old enough to wed a crofter's son from Taobh Tuath. Soon she will be doing her own baking and weaving. There will be no younger sister to help her. There are eight sisters altogether. Six of them are married and live on crofts round about. Maeve and I think our dreams are just beginning. How are we to know we have been dreaming all along, that we are about to be rudely wakened? After we finish our oatcakes, we lie in the sweet-smelling meadow beside the fairy stone, lis-

tening to the bees. We sleep. When I open my eyes, he, he
... No that was later.

We took our eyes off the water. Oh yes, we did. We dis-
obeyed our parents who told us repeatedly to keep close
watch on the water when we were near the sea. There had
never been a raid in Horgabost in our lifetime, but when
our mother was a child, she had kin abducted from
Hornish Strand and told us that if we should see an unfa-
miliar ship on the water, we were to run home quickly with
the warning. Better to abandon the croft and take to the
hills, since charred rubble could be rebuilt whereas no
amount of hard work could repair a young woman once
she had been manhandled by Vikings. Maeve and I
thought we knew better. We thought the fairy stone would
protect us. There was no fairy stone on Hornish Strand,
which was why folk there had been unlucky. That was
what we said to each other.

We lie in the fragrant meadow and make ourselves
drowsy by singing,

> *Bu tu marbhaich `a bhradain*
> *`s an eoin-bhain bhios air bearradh nan carn.*

All the while shadows creep up the rock face. Did I
dream this as I slept? I cannot remember. I think I awoke
just as Maeve was being carried away, screaming. Oh the
folly of hindsight. He was there, blond bearded, grinning,
flipping me onto my belly with his toe as if I was a worm
he had uncovered beneath a rock. Then he picked me up
and slung me over his shoulder, carrying me away like a
sack.

*   *   *

Freydis Eiriksdottir has nightmares: tree giants march
across the forest floor and drag her into the woods; she is
beneath the sea in Hel's dark kingdom, caged with a rotting corpse; she has lost her children and wanders aim-
lessly about the fells. When I slept near Freydis, I used to

wonder what demons drove her to thrash about and grind her teeth.

Sometimes Freydis has a dream that soothes her. She is inside her new house in Gardar with her children around her. She is showing a visitor around. I drift alongside as she points out the polished house beams and high seats, the carved chests and benches, the floor drains in the fire room and privy, the red and blue wall hangings, the fur rugs and pillows, the gleaming bronze bowl. How proud of all this she is. She urges her small daughters to offer me honey cakes and sweet wine and bids her son show me the toy ship his father has carved. When her son brings forth the ship, which looks like the new ship anchored in the fjord, she says he will be a merchant trader one day and take his mother to Norway. Freydis removes a jug of sweet-smelling flowers from the high seat and insists that I sit there beside her. She places a clean cloth on my lap. Oh, I am treated like a queen.

Once when we were sitting side by side on the high seat, I whispered in her ear, "It's me, Groa the Lame, who's dabbing my lips with your finest linen."

Freydis wakened with a scream. I frightened her, yes. Like the other Greenlanders she is riddled with mistrust and fear. She is poor enough to know her own freedom is far from safe. Were she not living on a distant, ill-favoured island, pirates would have ended her freedom long ago.

I pass through the Greenlanders' houses unaffected by the fetid air. I ignore the constant grumbling about lack of food and open space. The quarrels and blows mean nothing to me. Nor am I offended by those men who cannot trouble to use the bucket but empty their bowels on the floor at night so that others step in the mess and track it onto sleeping bags and clothing. When I was alive I cleaned up the smutch. Now such chores fall to Mairi.

I haunt Mairi's dreams more than the others. I am always careful not waken or startle her in any way. I whisper "Oidhche mhath leat" to give her hope. Mairi is young enough for hope. Awkward as a colt, she holds the promise of beauty. I do not know why the Icelanders let

Thorvard Einarsson have her. Nor does Mairi. Nothing about this man enters Mairi's dreams. She is better than I was at separating her body from her self. If an arm is twisted, she takes it off. If a leg is kicked, she puts it aside. Though Thorvard is gentle with her, Mairi never responds to his probings but lies beneath him unmoving. She has learned the power of withholding, that there are parts of her no one will ever own.

Ever since Mairi got with child, she has been dreaming of the bairn. Night after night she holds the bairn in her arms. She sings to him, croons over him while he sleeps, "Gael beag thu, gad beag thu." At such times I never linger too long inside Mairi's dreams lest the longing for my lost bairn intervenes. And I am sometimes distracted by Olina's bairn who was exposed before she was dead. On stormy nights the bairn howls into the wind, dragging her ragged clothes behind as she crawls from her stone grave under the snow, seeking redemption.

                            *   *   *

I was fourteen when I was abducted. My name was Moeid. I was the youngest of eight girls. My mother fed me extra helpings of porridge to make me grow. Moeid! Maeve! I hear her calling us across the fields. I see my father and my mother, my sisters and their husbands combing the meadow by the fairy stone. Calling. Calling. Looking for some sign of us along the shore. Kollgrim was clever. He hid his boat in the cove south of the traigh where it was rocky. In that way he left no tell-tale marks on the sand. The flattened grass showed our family where Maeve and I had lain, but where had we gone from there? Perhaps my mother thought we were taken by fairies. If that had happened, Maeve and I would be there yet. Fairies never give up those whom they lure inside their stones and mounds. They are fallen angels who God commanded to keep themselves and those they capture away from the living. Moeid! Maeve! I often wondered what it would have been like to have been taken by fairies. Would Maeve and I have suffered, watching our family search for us, sight unseen? The eternal damnation of Eve's hidden children whose faces she kept from Our Lord. No. No. Not for me the fallen angels.

By now my parents are long dead. Maybe some of my sisters, including Maeve. There is the slight chance Maeve was bought by someone who treated her kindly. In any event, sooner or later I expect to see my loved ones in Heaven, though in what shape or form they will be or in what manner we will greet each other I cannot say.

Kollgrim sold us separately. I was sold first to a farmer who had set up camp at the mouth of the Holsa River in Iceland. Vegest Bjornsson had a steading in the lava fields below Hekla. He had come down river to trade cows for thralls. Vegest already had a field thrall in chains, a boy much the same size and shape as myself. The boy and I were yoked together at our necks. In this way we walked the distance to Vegest's farm. Twenty days it took us, walking overland across cindered ground, fording icy streams, me dragging a step behind Ronan on account of my foot, until we reached Vegest's farm crouched below Hekla's brooding clouds. Ronan and I were there for eight years, working the fields like horses, eating from the same bowl, sleeping side by side in the byre. Often we heard Hekla rumbling. I was never sure if it was the volcano or thunder. The clouds in that part of Iceland were often driven by wind and rain. Occasionally the earth shook and shifted. Sometimes when the clouds lifted we saw glaciers glittering afar. On one occasion I thought I saw a flash of fire above the volcano. I told Ronan we had been cast into a Hell of fire and ice, but he said the fire was merely a lightning flash. Ronan liked Iceland no better than I. Neither of us was displeased when Vegest was exiled at the Althing for murdering his neighbour's son, Amundi. Amundi had ordered his thralls to dam up the river which provided Vegest's water supply. As a result of this murder Ronan and I were brought to Greenland.

Vegest took up land in Vatnahverfi. It was a poor steading, since by that time the best places in Greenland had been taken. Vegest and his family found it difficult to survive. Often Ronan and I bedded down in the byre with nothing in our bellies save whatever milk we squeezed from the dry teats of a cow. Less than a year after our move to Greenland, Vegest was killed in a duel with a neighbour named Hunraud. His wife sold Ronan and me to Bjartmar Halfgrimsson of Hofdi. She was trading up in cattle and wadmal in order to secure passage back to Iceland. Bjartmar was kinder than Vegest; it was Bjartmar's wife, Thorkatla, who was mean tempered. Bjartmar removed the chains binding Ronan and me, saying he thought we would work better with them off.

Ronan was of a mind for us to make a getaway. He said if it was to be done, it was now or never. We knew there was no way we could escape from Greenland, that the island was in all ways a prison but we decided that at the very least we could savour freedom, however fleeting it might be. Like me Ronan was Hebridian. He had been taken from the sands of Uig while mending his father's nets. Using the same stealth as Kollgrim, his captors rowed ashore earlier and hid in a cove. Ronan and I had much in common. Until we came to Greenland, we lay side by side like brother and sister.

*   *   *

A small meadow far back in the fells well beyond the lakes. The meadow is sunken—perhaps it was once a pond, since the grass here is much greener than the surrounding hills. A stream beside a stone hut. The hut is tightly made. Ronan and I have built many stone walls for Norsemen. We understand the language of stones, how to make them do our bidding. We have made two stone tables: one inside, one out; stone benches and stools. But for the bairn a willow basket lies waiting. Around us the slopes are bright with flowers: moss campion, mountain avens and heather. The sun streams through the thin Greenland air warming our nakedness. We have washed our tunics and laid them on the grass to dry. This is the way with Ronan and me; we have worked side by side for so long we do all our tasks together. Except ... Ronan strokes my belly with his hand. Then he lays his ear against my swollen skin and listens. He smiles. I smile. Oh, it is warm and clean and free in the meadow. We are light hearted and giddy with joy.

Every day we check our snares and traps. Sometimes we find nothing. Twice now we have found hares which we roasted over the fire. We scraped and cleaned the skins before using them to line the cradle. After the meat was gone, we boiled the bones in the firepot to make a broth. The firepot is small, since it was made to carry coals, but it is large enough for our cooking. Besides the firepot we have two cups, a knife and snares. We have snared six ptarmigan and cut them into small stewing pieces. There are blueberries and crowberries on the hills, but each day we must walk a little further to find them.

Ronan has the knife clean and ready. He wipes the sweat from my forehead with cool damp moss. I groan and pant. I think I am dying. Iron hands grip my back. They are ripping me apart. I am being torn in half. No, do not think about it. I did not know I remembered. Birthing is the pain a woman is most willing to forget.

At last Ronan holds up our daughter. He cuts the cord. He thumps her back. She cries. He lays her on my belly. She opens her eyes. They are blue as gentians. She is black haired like us but better shaped. Skin unblemished and white as snow. Ronan and I smile at each other. We smile and stroke each other's cheeks. We are delirious with pride. Ronan washes her carefully. He packs her in moss and lays her at my side. Then he washes me and puts the sinew harness between my legs. We call her Arneid. Arneid, we say again and again so she will know her name. Arneid and I sleep and suckle, suckle and sleep.

Now Ronan must go food gathering alone. Each day he is gone longer. He always returns with a hare or a bird. My milk is rich with his goodness. Arneid is content, Ronan is content. I am content. This is as close to Paradise as we expect to get.

It grows cold. The skins no longer keep Arneid warm. I hold her close and sit by the turf fire. I still cannot hunt with Ronan. Now he must walk such distances that were I to walk that far, my milk would run dry. The more work I do, the less milk there is for the bairn. I must rest. I sit by the fire with Arneid, waiting and singing,

Bu tu marbhaih `a bhradain
`s an `eoin-bhain bhios air bearradh nan carn.

Ronan expects to bring home a deer. He has sighted a small herd moving toward the lakes. He has made a spear of sharpened alder wood and hopes to wound a deer enough to bring it down. Ronan is gone most of the time. He returns with empty hands. My milk is poor. At night Arneid cries. One day Ronan returns carrying a sheep. It was easy to kill, he says. All he had to do was seize a stray by the leg and slit its throat. We make a sheepskin sleeping bag for Arneid and eat roast mutton. The juice enters my milk. Arneid suckles. So far we have been lucky. Ronan goes out again. Winter is coming and we will need more mutton and sheepskins.

The third time Ronan goes for sheep he does not return. I wait by the fire rocking Arneid, remembering the bed songs my mother sang me, "Gaol beag thu, gaol beag thu, gaol beag thu, horo." I wait and wait ... Ronan does not come. Must our dream end so quickly?

* * *

Thorkatla had a son named Kjaran by her first husband. Kjaran killed Ronan as he was slitting the sheep's throat. Ronan's corpse was thrown into a deep cleft between two rocks. I saw him there later, wedged part way down. He had fallen feet first; all I saw was the top of his head. Kjaran himself was killed several months later, ambushed when he was exchanging his mare for a neighbour's which was superior to his own.

I avoided capture by walking out. I thought prospects for Arneid would be better on the farm. By then my nipples were suckled raw. I walked ten days through deep snow to reach Hofdi.

That was the Winter heavy snow fell before the farmers in Vatnahverfi could harvest their hay. As a result dairy goods were scarce and famine was widespread. Arneid died early on in the Winter. I carried her thin cold body on my back for two days before I built her a stone grave. I blessed her myself.

After eight years with Bjartmar and Thorkatla, I was sold to Einar Asvaldsson in Gardar to pay off Bjartmar's debts. By that time Bjartmar owed Einar the use of his bull three times over as well as the loan of a grazing field. Bjartmar sold everything he owned except a hut and two cows in order to keep himself from debt thralldom. Shortly after this exchange Einar Asvaldsson arranged a marriage between his son Thorvard and Freydis Eiriksdottir. I was given to Freydis as part of the marriage agreement. By that time my joints were swollen and seized with pain. I was often short of breath. Freydis used me mainly for dairying and sent Kalf and Orn to the fields. She gave me shoes and a cloak and bade me wash every day, saying she would not have a dirty thrall working with her cows. For a woman who was newly married, Freydis was often sharp tongued and bad tempered. More than once I heard Thorvard's sisters say they found Freydis a hard woman to like. I neither liked nor disliked Freydis. After my years in thrall I held no opinions of any kind. If a voice was harsh and strident, I scarcely noticed. I could be prodded and shoved and never blink. I could be carried outside while I slept and laid upon the ground, and never trouble myself as to why. I had long since become used to being moved around to suit others.

* * *

Sometimes I visit the Icelanders' house. The Icelanders find Winter harder than the Greenlanders. They are badly overcrowded and provisions are low. They are constantly quarrelling over their women. They are tired of telling the same old stories and pick fights instead. At night they

writhe on their benches. They grope in the dark for hoarded bits of meat. They scratch where vermin have bit; they
sleep with their eyelids half-closed.

I do not know the Icelanders' women. When I was alive
they paid me scant mind. Occasionally one of them would
speak to me when we were fetching water, but I seldom
replied. Always I took the path of least resistance. I do not
enter these women's dreams. They are much the same as
Groa the Lame's. And there is something about these
women that troubles me. A pall, a cloud of doom hovers
over them. It seeps around the edges of their sleep like
fog or mist. Did I trail such clouds when I was living? Did I
carry the odour of defeat?

*   *   *

Eventually the blizzards pass and the snow wears down.
Freydis sends Kalf and Orn to search the beach for driftwood. She will not part with any of her hearth logs to
make my pyre. When they have collected enough wood,
they set it alight on the beach, put a cauldron of water to
boil and sever my limbs. My corpse is not so squat that it
will fit into the cauldron without cutting. Once the water
begins to boil, Freydis goes inside the house and shuts
the door, saying she has fulfilled her promise, that it is up
to Ulfar to collect my bones. I know he will do this, for he
is Christian as any priest. I drift above the fire, following
the smoke of my cooking flesh. I rise higher and higher.

Below the meadow, the terrace, the bay are white. The
frozen sea is motionless, hard as silver beneath the moon.
Stones whiten the shore like sleeping seals. Light glitters
from distant stars. The wind nudges me, gently at first.
Then picks me up and carries me far away, into the night.
I feel the presence of others, Maeve ... Ronan ... Arneid ...
is that you? Are we in Heaven? Is this Paradise? Ah, but I
am long past names and places.

LUCK

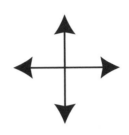

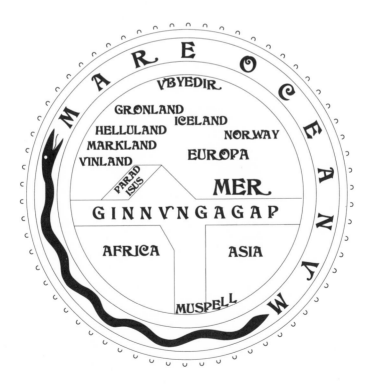

THREE MONTHS AFTER YULE the weather turned in such a way that winds brought more rain than snow to Leifsbudir. After the rain, the wind invariably turned frigid. The snow ridge was now worn down to islands of grey ice that lay on the terrace like piles of frozen fish. Sometimes a glitter storm silvered the stones and grass. The Greenlanders bickered, not about who would shovel snow but who would chop pathways through the ice and chip away the silver thaw that covered the firewood. Now the darkness was getting shorter and the wolves ceased coming at night. Even so, Winter had worn the Greenlanders down so far that some of them no longer got out of bed in the mornings but lay in their sleeping bags all day. This resulted in hard feelings, since it meant that time and again the same men went out in the rain and sleet to do the chores. Even Thorvard, known for his endurance and patience, became cast down.

Thorvard Einarsson was a man who could lie beneath a deerskin all day until a falcon swooped down to take a live vole from his trap. In the same way, he could outwait a ptarmigan approaching his snare. Men who hunted with Thorvard claimed he could, when it suited him, turn to stone. The wet Leifsbudir Winter did not suit Thorvard; he was used to the dry Winters of Gardar. Moreover, his wife was increasingly quick tempered and his ambatt disappointing. To take his mind off his troubles, Thorvard carved double-barbed gaffs of deer antler and a variety of

small arrow tips. He sharpened his sealing knives. He whittled a large number of wooden clubs and hafts for spears.
He made toys and skis for his children.

Earlier on, Thorvard had carved a calendar stick. Since
Yule more than ninety grooves had been cut. By this reckoning the seals should be arriving off shore any day now;
the pack ice had already moved down. Thorvard went outside first thing every morning and listened for seals.

Finally he awoke one morning and heard mewling
pups. These were babies crying for mothers who had left
them to go fishing. When Thorvard looked, he saw seals
stretched out on the ice as far as he could see. He lost no
time in going to the middle house and rousing his hunters.
He told them to dress quickly and take their gear onto the
ice; each hunter had a gaff, a club, a knife and a coil of
rope ready as well as wool-stuffed leggings and boots.
Thorvard sent Avang, Flosi and Lodholt to the Icelanders'
house to rouse them; there was no sign that the
Icelanders had heard the seals. It was important they get
out on the ice before a shifting wind took the pack ice
away.

Altogether ten Greenlanders struck out across the ice.
At first walking was easy, for the shore ice was smooth
and flat. After the Greenlanders had passed the first
island, they came across ridges where the ice had been
pushed up, then frozen. Occasionally a man slipped on
these hummocks, but for the most part the ice was solid
without a break.

The seals were twice the distance from the shore to
the second island, scattered on ice pans floating between
the shore ice and the polar pack. Now walking became
tricky. There were places where old ice had rafted onto
new, making jagged outcroppings and pinnacles that were
treacherous to cross since there was sometimes a crack or
a hole on the other side. Knowing one false step could
plunge them into ice water, the men slackened their pace.
As they neared the seals, Thorvard was elated to see that
the seals were not hoods, which they mainly hunted in
Greenland, but harps. This meant the killings would result

in a superior cargo, for the harps had white-furred pups much favoured by the Norwegians for making cloaks and boots. Thrand and Teit quickened their steps; it was their first time sealing. Thrand slipped between a crack and was hauled out by Thorvard before he disappeared beneath the ice.

Thorvard had killed coupling seals floating blissfully on the sea's surface. He had swum eye to eye with a humpback whale he later harpooned. Back in the days when Thorvard first went hunting, a sea cow mistook him for her young when Thorvard had fallen overboard. The cow slid her tusks around Thorvard's neck and carried him down to the sea bottom before letting him go. After he had been hauled from the water, Thorvard killed the cow with an axe.

Thorvard was an excellent sealer. When he was on the ice, he never altered his movements except when required but continued at a slow and steady pace. Thorvard had never been known to make a false step while sealing. The men readily followed him as he leapt with sure-footed ease across open water onto the ice pans bearing the seals.

The nursing pups were killed first. They were too young to escape and easily clubbed on the head. The females were more difficult to kill, being larger and more agile. Some took to the water at once where the males had been all along, but most of the females flapped among the white coats, either trying to protect them with their bodies or nudging them toward open water. The hunters went among the females with gaffs which worked better than spears, for if a female got away, she could be more easily hauled back. Before long the ice pans were splattered with blood and more than thirty seals, not counting pups, lay upon the ice. It had taken the hunters less time to slaughter the seals than had been required to walk to the killing ground.

"This is what I call a good morning's work," Thorvard said. "Now to haul these seals ashore." The men began to cut holes in the seals' necks for ropes; the carcasses would be dragged across the ice.

Oddmar looked at a seal herd that was farther out and said that he thought they should leave the slaughtered seals where they were and go after the others. Thorvard disagreed.

"It's better if we put food into our bellies first. Sealing is hard work and requires all our strength. Besides, those seals aren't as close as you think."

The other men agreed with Thorvard and soon were hauling seal carcasses toward the shore. Thorvard scanned the terrace expecting to see Icelanders setting out to hunt, but there was still no sign of movement. Thorvard thought this odd. Surely the Icelanders wouldn't pass up perfect sealing weather. The day was close to being windless. It was cold but not so bitter that they would have to concern themselves with frostbite. The sky was slightly overcast, which was preferred to brilliant light when sun glanced off the ice and blinded the eyes. When they reached shore, Thorvard saw the Icelanders were behind their house on the terrace, readying their gear. He saw Avang, Flosi and Lodholt inside the boat shed making wooden clubs. Apparently the Icelanders were so ill prepared that they had not thought of making clubs. The Icelanders had been much changed by Winter. They were thinner than they had been at Yule and slower to react. No doubt this was the result of poor rations, of not having been well enough prepared.

When Thorvard returned to his house, he saw that Freydis had made a large quantity of fish stew. The hunters did not trouble with washing but spooned up their food with bloodied hands which Thorvard thought was likely to displease Freydis. She was particular about such matters and had buckets of water set out for washing. Thorvard also chose to ignore the water. It was in small defiances like this that he sought to show Freydis that she couldn't always expect her way. When faced with a choice between pleasing his hunters or his wife, Thorvard invariably chose his hunters. He preferred not to do anything that would separate him from his fellows. It was Thorvard's opinion that Freydis didn't understand the easy give and take of men. Women seldom did. They didn't hunt and fish together; they had no knowledge of the special kinship of men. Working as she did at home, Freydis couldn't know how men bonded together to help each other out. How could any man explain to his wife that he found more contentment in the company of men than he did with her? This was especially true of a man who was married to a woman like Freydis who was often gripped by the furies of envy and rage. As Einar Asvaldsson's only son, Thorvard had felt smothered by his mother and sisters when he was a boy. This was why he eventually chose hunting over farming, since it meant he was away from women for long periods of time.

Soon after the hunters had eaten, they returned to the ice. This time the Icelanders went out. Thorvard set his pace to theirs. It was obvious from the slowness of their movements that the Icelanders were much weaker than the Greenlanders and would need their help once they got further out on the ice. So it was. Several of the Icelanders slipped into the water and had to be rescued; once Solvi went in as far as his neck and had to be taken back to the house for warming. Eventually the hunters reached the seals and began the slaughter. This time out the Greenlanders killed fewer seals. Often one of the Greenland hunters would allow an Icelander to do the killing so that he might keep the meat. The Icelanders might have considered this was being done to make up for past offences, but this was not the case. As far as Thorvard and the other Greenlanders were concerned, sealers always helped each other on the ice; in some situations a helping hand was all that lay between survival and death.

The next day both parties went out again. This time the Icelanders were much stronger from having eaten fresh meat. They were more vigorous and required less help which meant the Greenlanders were able to return with more seals than the day before. On the third day out

Thorvard thought the Icelanders were robust enough to enjoy a sealing match. Even with the loan of Avang, Flosi and Lodholt, the Icelanders had only eight men who could be regarded as hunters. Two more Greenlanders, Hrollaug and Bodman, went over to the Icelanders to make an even number on both sides. Each party marked their pile of seals with a gaff tied with coloured wool. At the end of the day's killing, each side counted their seals. Thorvard's side won handily which made up for the Greenlanders having lost to the Icelanders at Yule. As Thorvard expected, the match resulted in better relations between the Greenlanders and the Icelanders. By now there was a good deal of jesting and rivalry between the two parties. The Icelanders didn't seem to mind losing the match, probably because with the Greenlanders' help they had far more seals than they would have had otherwise. As for Thorvard he was pleased not only to have re-established relations with the Icelanders but also to have killed a large number of females before they whelped. Their foetuses could be made into pillows which were much sought after by the wives of Norwegian jarls, who used them as foot warmers. Thorvard had also heard that it was the fashion for high-born Norwegian women to walk about carrying seal pillows open at the ends so they might put their hands inside.

Ulfar did not help with the sealing. Nor did Thorvard expect it, knowing Ulfar's skills were better applied to making such things as bowls and cups. Throughout the Winter Ulfar had been turning out these items on a lathe in the far room of the middle house. While the Greenlanders were busy sealing, Ulfar had this room to himself, which meant he could take out his quill and ink and continue recording his view of events whenever he chose.

*   *   *

The seal hunt is now under way. I cannot go outside without seeing bloodied snow and ice. This sickens me, for it calls to mind the Culdean blood spilt on the

*white sands of Iona during my conception. Moreover,
when I see the skinned corpses, I remember the tale I
was told as a child about the fisherman's bairn who
was saved by a selkie. As far as I am concerned, the
Norsemen are killing selkies, which makes them no
better than wild savages who are said to eat each
other. I prefer to go hungry rather than eat seal people; as a result, I must fill my belly with water and
soup.*

*At last the worst of Winter is past. Fish will soon
return to the bay and I can once again live in my shelter. I continue to pray to Heaven's Lord for strength to
help me endure the coarseness of these farmers. They
are forever making vulgar jokes about their bodies
and the bodies of women. They appear to have little
else on their minds but lewdness and refuse to listen
to the stories of Our Lord which Geirmund bade me
tell them. I have tried many times to convert the
Greenlanders to Christ's teachings but have made little progress and have brought nothing but mockery
and crude jokes upon myself. For this reason I will be
better off in my shelter where I can meditate on Our
Lord in peace. When the weather improves, I will be
able to pray with Mairi. Mairi lost a true friend in Groa.
I know I can never show the same charity toward the
girl as Groa, but I shall do what I can to help her out.
With all of us confined to these buildings, there has
been no opportunity to pray together as we did last
Summer when Groa was alive. By praying with Mairi, I
hope to find within myself the power to forgive her for
being used by another woman's husband. When she
delivers the child she carries, she is bound to have
need of a Christian friend.*

*   *   *

Although contact between them had resumed, neither
the Greenlanders nor the Icelanders suggested sharing a
feast of seal meat. The hunters on both sides were weary
from being out on the ice all day and wanted nothing

more than a quick meal and a long sleep before resuming the hunt.

The hunters spent one more day sealing. Late on the last day the wind came from the South and turned the pack ice away. The Greenlanders and Icelanders managed to get safely ashore with their seals which they hauled to their houses for skinning and flensing. After the Greenlanders finished sculping and disembowelling the carcasses, they piled them on the ground outside the storage hut. By now the shelves inside the hut, including the plank where Groa had lain, were filled with seal carcasses. The air was still frosty enough both inside and outside the hut to keep the meat from spoiling.

The next day an incident occurred which the Greenlanders thought was as strange as any of the tales they had heard so far. To some extent the story was about Thorvard, but mainly it was about his wife. The incident, which happened in early morning, was so unusual that by nightfall of the same day the tale had taken hold of the Norsemen's minds. For several nights running, the Greenlanders sat around their hearths and told their version of what had taken place. These tellings varied in many small ways. Some men insisted Freydis had been wearing nothing except a shift under her cloak; others said she hadn't been wearing a shift or cloak but a tunic and breeches. Some claimed Thorvard hadn't gone outside for the purpose of relieving himself but had heard his wife cry out and had gone to her aid. This was the version Thorvard preferred. Although the tale tellers changed various details in the story, when it came to Freydis Eiriksdottir's bravery, none of them was able to diminish her courage in any way. The story, which later became known as *The Tale of Freydis and the Skraeling*, went something like this:

* * *

EARLY ON A LATE WINTER MORNING IN VINLAND, THORVARD
Einarsson came outside to relieve himself. Freydis
Eiriksdottir was also outside but Thorvard didn't see

her at first. He was around the corner of the house, pissing. As he was shaking himself off, he heard Freydis shouting. He looked up and saw his wife.

Freydis was backed up against the door of the storage hut, holding a pail. Coming toward her was a tall red creature carrying a spear. When the creature was near, he lifted the spear and pointed it at Freydis. She shouted again and reached inside the pail for her knife. The creature held his spear at her throat. Freydis dropped the pail, which went clattering to the ground. Then before her husband's eyes, she reached inside her shift, pulled out a breast and hit it three times with her hand. At this the creature lowered the spear and backed away.

Now Thorvard started shouting and came running toward his wife. The creature hoisted a seal carcass onto a shoulder and began running across the meadow. Thorvard went after it, then remembered he had no weapons. He turned back to fetch them.

Freydis was running about, her breast hanging out and shrieking, "Skraeling! Skraeling!"

"Cover yourself, Woman," Thorvard said. He went inside and shook the Greenlanders awake, Thrand Ozursson first since he had the fastest legs. While Thrand and the others were arming themselves, Thorvard picked up his spear and broad axe and started after the skraeling.

The skraeling had not gotten far, being slowed down by the weight of the seal. Thorvard thought that as long as the skraeling carried the meat, it might be possible to catch him. At least he could keep him in sight until Thrand and the others caught up. Thorvard put on a burst of speed. He knew from the shouts that the other Greenlanders were coming behind. The meadow was thickly grown with osiers and bog laurel in which snow had caught and deepened. This slowed down Thorvard's progress. It also slowed down the skraeling. When the runners reached mossy ground, their pace picked up only slightly, for here were

patches of slippery ice. Soon Thrand caught up with
Thorvard.

"Go after him as fast as you can," Thorvard said.
"As long as he keeps the meat, we can catch him!"

Thrand spurted on ahead, closing the distance
between himself and the skraeling.

The skraeling had yet to reach the woods. Without
turning he dropped the seal. By now Thrand was within
striking distance and threw his axe. The blow was not
enough to kill but it stunned the creature and he fell to
the ground. When Thorvard came up, he cleaved the
skraeling's neck with his broad axe, severing the head.
Soon the other Greenlanders had caught up. The men
looked at the corpse. No one touched the creature,
since by touching it, a man risked becoming the creature himself. The men stared at the corpse for a long
time without speaking.

At length Thorvard said, "So this is the kind of creature that carried away two Icelanders and forced
Bodvar and me to crawl through the woods on our bellies. I must say it's better made than I expected. I
always thought skrae-lings were small and ugly, but this
one is far from ugly and about our size."

*   *   *

The skraeling was as tall and well built as Thrand, though
thinner. Like the Norsemen the skraeling wore skin
breeches and a tunic. These were covered with something
red, as was his skin.

"I'm curious about his skin," Thorvard said. "It may be
that under the red covering it's similar in colour to ours."
Using his knife, he scraped some of the red covering from
the dead man's hand and sniffed it. "Unless I'm mistaken,
this covering is nothing more than coloured earth."

Except for Thorvard none of the others would touch
the corpse even with a knife, but hung about for a long
time at a safe distance before returning to the houses. All
day long well-armed Greenlanders and Icelanders crossed
the meadow in groups of four and five to look at the

corpse. There was a good deal of talk about what to do with it, whether to bury it or to cover it up. In the end it was decided to leave the corpse where it was, mainly because no one wanted to touch it. That night the Norsemen posted watches in their doorways and bid everyone sleep with weapons close by, but no more skraelings appeared at that time.

Whichever version of this tale was told, it was followed by a discussion about the manner in which Freydis had defended herself. Over and over she was asked by the men why she had bared her breast. It seemed an odd thing for a woman to do when she was cornered. When attacked, some women were known to use axes and clubs if they had them handy, or to kick and scratch. Most women wept and pleaded for their lives. Certainly the Norsemen had never heard of a cornered woman who matched Freydis for courage or, for that matter, bared her breast.

At first Thorvard was as admiring as the others about his wife's courage, but as the talk continued, he became somewhat churlish and peeved. He was troubled that other men were talking openly about his wife's breast. Freydis wasn't at all embarrassed. On the contrary she was well pleased with herself. "What did you expect me to do?" she said to Thorvard. "Stand there and be murdered?" During the course of the discussions, Nagli said that before leaving Greenland, he had heard one of Thorfinn Karlsefni's men say that he had seen a skraeling woman in Hop bare her breast during battle to avoid being attacked. "That's very interesting," Freydis said. "But I never heard that tale myself."

"Even so, you might have heard the story from someone and forgotten," Thorvard insisted. He preferred to believe that the baring of a woman's breast was some sort of battle custom. He didn't want any of his men thinking his wife was wanton or loose.

Freydis thought baring her breast must have had something to do with being the daughter of Eirik the Red. She thought there was a fierceness in her that came from him, a willingness to do something rash when it was required.

Freydis thought Thorvard would have preferred she not show her breast so that he could have saved her himself. But her father would have encouraged her to confront the skraeling. Although Eirik went along with the refinements Thjodhild had taught her, he had admired Freydis's grit and told her often to stand up for herself.

After this incident the Norsemen stayed close to their houses for several days in the event that skraelings might attack. They had no idea how many skraelings might be lurking in the woods. No one went into the forest to hunt, which chafed the men, for the weather was much improved from before, being bright and sunny and not too windy. After four or five days during which little happened, the men relaxed their vigil. It seemed pointless to stay inside fully armed when there was no enemy to fight. In the end it was decided that the skraeling had either been alone or with a small party that had been frightened. Gradually the fear of a skraeling attack ebbed away.

One morning Thorvard took some men into the woods to cut timber. When they walked past the place where the corpse had been, they saw it was empty. There were no bones or garments strewn about as there would have been had the corpse been eaten by wolves, only a patch of rust-coloured blood. Thorvard took this to mean that the skraeling had been carried away by one of its kind.

* * *

The Greenlanders killed a creature they call a skrae-
ling for taking a seal. I went to see the corpse before it
disappeared. It was a man covered with red earth. It is
clear from the encounter with the skraeling that this
country holds many folk we know not of and is
extremely large, for if the land was smaller, we would
have encountered more skraelings before now.
Moreover, judging from the harshness of the Winter,
we are very far North. It is therefore logical to con-
clude that we would have to travel much further South
in order to meet large numbers of skraelings or to
reach as warm a land as the Moors are said to enjoy.

I do not know where in the world we are.
According to the drawing Brother Ambrose showed
me of Solinus's world, if after leaving Greenland, we
had travelled far enough South and West, we would
have eventually reached Africa, since that country was
shown to be opposite Europe, separated from it by a
river flowing beneath the sea. I can say without doubt
that we are presently far from Africa, since Leifsbudir
has none of the characteristics of that country as
described by learned men. Solinus's drawing showed
Paradise as being between Africa and Asia, though off
to one side. Perhaps the storm we encountered during
our voyage here drove us to a country somewhere to
the North of Paradise.

                                *   *   *

The time came when Thorvard set about going after walrus which he needed for the hide in order to make more rope. He had brought some walrus hide rope with him but now had to supply enough for Helgi's ship, as well as rope for trade. Thorvard had already set aside enough rope to rig the Greenlanders' new ship and thought himself well positioned to uphold his part of the agreement. Helgi Egilsson had yet to fetch oak wood for his ship, let alone dress it. By the time Helgi got his wood, Thorvard expected to have slaughtered enough walrus not only to outfit the Icelanders' ship and provide the trade rope and ivory he had promised in exchange for Mairi, but to supply Freydis and himself with rope and ivory for the Norwegian trade.

As soon as the pack ice cleared the bay, Thorvard began rowing out to islands and skerries. He sighted a few walrus on ice pans that were drifting toward the Markland shore. From this it became obvious to Thorvard that the walrus herds were probably Southwest, along the Markland shore. This meant a ship would be required, since a pram was only convenient for hunting close by. The ship Thorvard had in mind wasn't the *Vinland* but the new one Hauk and his men had built. Thorvard expected to find walrus within a day or two's sailing of Leifsbudir and thought such an expedition would be a good way to break in the new ship without going far away.

On fine days Hauk and his men returned to the cove to finish off the mast and make what the Norwegian called final adjustments on the Greenlanders' ship. When he saw the shipbuilders going to work in the mornings, Thorvard followed them to the cove to see if he might hurry the work along. As far as he could see, only the rigging and sail remained to be done; Hauk had carved the steering oar and various fittings during the Winter and his men had carved the oars. When Thorvard asked when the ship would be ready, Hauk replied that many a ship faltered from being put to sea before it was ready and that he had no intention of making the same mistake.

During the Winter Freydis had finished weaving the sail lengths and sewn them together. When the ground was dry enough, the sail would be spread on the terrace and covered with a mixture of fat and boiled bark to make it watertight. Freydis had seen Thjodhild do this in Brattahlid, when her step-mother was making the *Vinland*'s sail. Thorvard was unwilling to wait until the ground dried and urged Freydis to do this chore inside the middle house, but Freydis said she preferred to do it outside.

"It's smelly work," she said. "Besides, until Hauk is finished the ship, there's no hurry. When he says our ship is ready, then I'll oil the sail inside."

Since work on the new ship had been resumed, Freydis had only been to the ship cove once to measure the mast length. Hauk had barely spoken to her. Nor had he come to the weaving shed, although Freydis was once again working there during the day. By now the livestock had been returned to the meadow, where they pawed the thin crust of snow that lay patchily here and there. The forage in the meadow was poor, since it was too early for the green shoots to appear, but it was better than the mixture of leaves and twigs which Freydis's thralls had managed to scrounge to help the animals through Winter. The weaving shed had been thoroughly cleaned and aired. Now wood smoke overcame the smell of manure. Freydis was using the shed mainly for daytime weaving: she had begun the second sail. At night she preferred to sleep in the compartment of the end house near the others in the event Groa night walked or the skraeling returned as a ghost.

Freydis's main reason for being in no hurry to oil the sail was that she was expecting Hauk to come to the shed as he had done before Yule and ask for it. She had no intention of handing over the sail, as Thorvard had done with the rope, before she was asked. She had worked hard on the sail and refused to have its worth diminished in any way. Freydis had long ago decided to overlook the careless way Hauk had treated her husband at Yule, since like the other men the Norwegian had been drunk. In his drunkenness he might have regarded her sudden departure from the Yule tale telling as a slight rather than an invitation. But even if that had been the case, why was Hauk now avoiding the shed? Didn't he know Thorvard was away all day in the pram? Freydis was confident that with Thorvard urging the Norwegian to finish the ship, sooner or later Hauk was bound to appear at her door.

As for Thorvard, it seemed to him the ship was ready and that the kind of tasks Hauk and his men were doing were so minor that it would be far better to see how the ship took to the water first, and make the necessary adjustments afterwards. When Thorvard put his view to the Norwegian, Hauk looked down his nose and said that a hunter could hardly be expected to know the finer details of shipbuilding and that he would tell Thorvard when the ship was ready and not before. This reply rankled Thorvard, since with each passing day the walrus were closer to returning North; like seals, sea cattle followed the pack ice, though more slowly, along the shore. Thorvard decided to try his luck with the Egilssons.

Crossing the terrace he saw the brothers on a bench on the south side of the house. By now the late Winter sun shone brightly enough for folk to warm themselves outside if they could find a place sheltered from the wind. Despite the fact that the Greenlanders had helped the Icelanders harvest seal meat, relations were not as cordial

as they had been before Yule. Neither of the Egilssons
asked Thorvard to sit. Thorvard did not expect to be
offered refreshment, since he knew the Icelanders had
less than the Greenlanders had to eat, but he did expect
to be offered a place to sit. Thorvard stood to one side
while Helgi asked him the purpose of the visit. Thorvard
told the brothers he wanted to use the new ship for a walrus hunting expedition. His wife had finished the sail and
he had handed over the rope for the rigging. In other
words, he and Freydis had kept their part of the bargain
and now wanted the Icelanders to keep theirs. Thorvard
said he wanted them to urge Hauk to put the ship to water
so that it could be tried. "Even as patient a man as myself
gets tired waiting."

Helgi told Thorvard that just that morning Hauk had
said it would be some time before the ship was ready. "In
any case, it's too soon for such an expedition," Helgi went
on. "You can see for yourself that the pack ice is still off
shore. As long as it's there, it's dangerous to put a ship to
water, since the wind can turn the ice against a ship at any
time."

Thorvard knew from experience that wherever there
was ice there was danger. He didn't need Helgi to tell him
this. It was true the pack ice was still close by. He could
see it as well as Helgi, not to mention the ice pans floating
in the bay here and there. But to a Greenlander, the water
around Leifsbudir seemed remarkably ice free for this
time of year.

"In Greenland we go walrus hunting when there is far
more ice on the water than we have here," Thorvard said.
He usually went to Northsetur aboard Arne Loftsson's ship
earlier than this. Sometimes Evyind had gone as well. "We
Greenlanders know how to work with ice. Were it otherwise, you Icelanders would have no rope or ivory for the
Frankish trade."

"That may be," Helgi said. "Every man has his own way
of earning his livelihood."

"In so doing, some of us risk more than others."

"Your risks aren't our concern," Helgi said. "As far as I'm concerned, we've kept our part of the bargain by building a ship."

During this conversation Finnbogi had been sitting with his legs straight out, his eyes closed to the sun. Now he became more alert, yawning and bending his knees before he spoke.

"Before you go off walrus hunting," he said, "you should consider the situation with regard to your wife."

"My wife leaves hunting matters to me," Thorvard said.

"I'm not talking about hunting, at least not the kind you mean. Haven't you heard?" Finnbogi said. "*When a man's back is turned, his wife's is pressed to the bed.*"

Finnbogi winked at Thorvard, then showed him his blackened tooth.

"Unless I'm mistaken you have slurred my wife," Thorvard said.

"*If the shoe fits, wear it,*" Finnbogi said. "As one man to another I'm telling you that, for reasons beyond my ken, there's someone among us who fancies your wife."

Thorvard rarely came across a man he disliked. When he did he was apt to regard it as a failing in himself. Now his dislike of Finnbogi came close to outright hate. Thorvard was not a hot-tempered man, but he was tempted to challenge Finnbogi to fight or take the slur back. What prevented Thorvard from making the challenge was the possibility that there was something behind Finnbogi's insinuation that had escaped his notice. If that was the case, he should find out what it was. Otherwise he risked being made a fool. Thorvard left the Egilssons and sought his wife.

Freydis was where he expected, in the weaving shed.

Thorvard went inside and said, "You'd better sit down. We have important matters to discuss."

For once Freydis did as her husband said. She laid down the shuttle and sat on one side of the hearth, Thorvard on the other.

Freydis looked at her husband. "It's clear you are severely agitated about something."

*"When a man's back is turned, his wife's is pressed to
the bed."*

"What's that supposed to mean?" Freydis said.

"Finnbogi Egilsson has told me that one of his men
fancies you."

"That's hardly surprising," Freydis said. "In a place
such as this where men are far from their women, they're
bound to fancy whatever woman is close at hand."

"Especially a woman who bares her breast."

"That remark is so foolish that it's better ignored. I
advise you to ignore Finnbogi's foolishness as well. His
remark is an untruthful slur."

"I'm unwilling to allow another man's slur against
my wife's reputation to pass without being avenged,"
Thorvard said.

"Since the remark was said against me, I should have
some say in the matter. My advice is to forget about
avenging the remark. By seeking retribution now, you
would give Finnbogi what he wants. It's clear he's trying to
stir up trouble between us. Everyone knows the weaker
the enemy, the easier he is to take advantage of."

"I've never cared much for Finnbogi Egilsson, but until
now I've never thought of him as an enemy."

"As far as I'm concerned, Finnbogi Egilsson has always
been an enemy," Freydis said. "By believing his false accusation, you're playing into his hands."

"That may be as you say, but I'm still faced with the
decision of whether or not to go walrus hunting, leaving
my wife on her own with a crew of Icelanders close by."

"You know better than anyone else how often I've
been left on my own," Freydis said. "I'm sure I can manage the Icelanders without you. The question is how did
you happen to be talking to Finnbogi Egilsson?"

"I went to their house to ask about using the new ship
for walrus hunting."

Freydis seldom passed up the chance to take offense.

"Once again you've spoken to the Egilssons without
me. You are a fool, Thorvard Einarsson, and deserve to be
cuckolded."

"I made no new arrangements with the Egilssons. I merely wanted them to urge Hauk to put our new ship to water so that I could take it walrus hunting."

"And what did they say?"

"Helgi said the ship isn't ready and even if it was he wouldn't let it be used for the expedition. He's against putting it into the water as long as there's pack ice off shore."

"Did you remind him that it isn't his ship to refuse? You should have told me you were going. I would have straightened Helgi out on the matter of who can speak for our ship. When it comes to dealing with people as high handed as the Egilssons, you need someone like me to stand up to them."

"I stood up to them," Thorvard said. "In any case it's over and done with. It's clear I'll have to take your brother's ship if I'm to go after walrus right away."

"Even if our new ship was in the water, it seems more sensible to take a ship that Evyind is used to handling rather than taking one that has yet to be tried," Freydis said. "There'll be plenty of time to get used to our new ship after the walrus have gone and Summer is here."

Soon after this Thorvard, Evyind and a crew of Greenlanders took the *Vinland* from its Winter shed. The keel was smeared with seal oil and the ship hauled on rollers to the water. While Evyind saw to raising the mast and the rigging, Thorvard set about deciding who should go on the expedition. Teit would have to go, of course, since Evyind kept his son close by. Besides Evyind and Teit, Thorvard chose ten others: the Gardar twins and two of their cousins, as well as Falgeir, Bodvar, Glam, Asmund, Hrollaug and Bodman, which left twenty Greenland men, including thralls, behind. After four days of preparations during which Freydis assembled provisions and the men readied their gear, the hunters were ready to leave.

Thorvard and his men left at daylight. With the brisk westerly winds, they expected to make good time even though they were towing two prams. While Greenlanders watched from shore, the *Vinland* sailed out of the bay.

Soon the hunters had rounded the cape and were out of
sight of Leifsbudir, heading Southwest, away from the pack
ice. Except for the ice pans floating here and there, the
water was as clear as the sky. The wind was brisk. By mid-
afternoon, the hunters had reached the place where the
water narrowed to Markland. Occasionally a walrus floated
past on an ice pan. The Greenlanders did not waste time
killing these passers-by; they were looking for a herd on
land. The sail was brought about so that the ship could
cross to the opposite shore. During the crossing the
hunters saw several walrus swimming. When they reached
Markland, they could hear bulls bellowing from the rocks.
By now it was too dark to hunt safely. The Greenlanders
dropped anchor and bedded down for the night.

In the morning the hunters awoke to see an expanse
of greyish brown where a large herd of sea cattle had
spread themselves on rocks. Evyind advised against taking
the *Vinland* closer in, since between ship and shore there
were bound to be rocks and shoals. The ship therefore
remained where it was. No one questioned this; their
minds were on the hunt. And they trusted Evyind's judgement; after all it had been largely due to the helmsman's
skill that they had survived the difficult crossing. The men
lost no time in piling their gear into the prams and rowing
ashore. Evyind stayed aboard the ship, but Teit went
ashore, eager to try his hand at walrus hunting.

There were more than a hundred walrus in the herd,
about twenty of which were bulls. The hunters knew that
once the slaughter began, the walrus would head for
water. Thorvard directed his men to row to either side of
the herd and after pulling the prams ashore, to approach
the walrus from the front. By killing the walrus nearest the
water, those behind would find it more difficult to escape
to the sea. This was dangerous work; when roused, bulls
became aggressive attackers. Many a hunter had been
gored when knocked off his feet by an angry bull. Two
men chose one walrus, staying with it until it was killed.
The walrus was clubbed senseless before a broad axe severed its head.

The men left the prams and waded into the water. The slaughter began. One by one the walrus were brought down by clubs and axes. Before the sun had risen even halfway in the sky, the hunters had killed more than sixty walrus. The rest had escaped into the water and swum away. The beach was strewn with bloodied carcasses and stranded pups which the Norsemen did not bother killing; at the time they were of little use. The walrus were skinned where they lay, their hides thrown into a pile. The heart and liver were cut out and eaten then and there; these organs were so large there was far more than the hunters could eat. By now the men's tunics were red splattered and greasy; the shallow water seethed with blubber and blood. After the walrus were flayed, their tusks were cut out. The ivory and hides were loaded onto the ship straight away. The blubber was left where it was; the Greenlanders already had a large supply of seal oil in Leifsbudir. Thorvard was unwilling to crowd the ship and prams with walrus blubber when space was better given over to ivory and hides. With the morning's killings, Thorvard reckoned he would be able to make enough rope to supply the Egilssons with the agreed amount. From now on any walrus slaughtered could be used for his own trade and those of his men. The Greenlanders were well pleased with themselves. They were so weary and body sore from the morning's exertions that after they reached the ship, they crawled into their sheepskin bags and went to sleep.

By afternoon the wind was still in their favour and the weather held clear. The anchor was hauled and the *Vinland* sailed further south along the Markland shore. The Greenlanders had not gone far when another herd of sea cattle was spotted on land. Again the anchor was dropped further out to avoid rocky shoals and the men went ashore. This herd was much smaller than the first one, being something more than half its size. The hunt did not go as well as the morning's, mainly because the shoreline was too steep to work on foot, which meant the men had to work from prams. Another drawback was that a light breeze had come up and the hunters were now downwind of the herd, which meant several bulls had caught their scent and swum away before the hunt had begun. Despite these setbacks, when the killing was over, the men had thirty walrus to show for their efforts. After the hides and ivory had been removed, the men hunted the walrus scattered on pans. For this kind of killing Thorvard used double-barbed gaffs which, after the walrus had been clubbed, hooked the carcass for towing ashore. In this way the hunters killed twelve more. Again the men ate what they wanted of the heart and liver and left the carcasses on shore. That night the hunters went to sleep knowing they had killed upwards of a hundred walrus without any of them receiving as much as a scratch.

During the night the wind changed their Luck. At first the wind change was imperceptible, rising so slowly that none of the men stirred from sleep. They were used to the rhythmic yaw of the ship, the scranch of its rigging. But as the wind increased, snapping the sail and straining the stays, Evyind got up and looked about. Then he woke Thorvard.

"The wind's from the Northeast," Evyind said, "which means we're in for foul weather."

Fortunately the moon was full and bright, which allowed the men a clear view of what was happening. They saw the ice pans had moved rapidly in from the North and were packing together around the ship.

"I'm of two minds," Evyind said, "whether to row the ship closer to shore or leave it where it is."

Thorvard walked around looking at the ice from all directions. By this time there was little open water. Thorvard thought that by choosing to anchor this far out, the decision had already been made.

"It seems to me we're locked in place," he said.

"There may be some leverage yet," Evyind said, "but I think we should stay where we are. Even if we could break the ice grip, I doubt we could get the ship closer to shore without the risk of hitting a rock and taking out the keel. We're better off waiting for the wind to shift and loosen the ice. In the meantime we should cut the prams loose. If the wind worsens, the prams will put extra strain on the bow."

The hides and ivory from the last hunt were still in one of the prams; the men had been too weary the night before to take them aboard. Thorvard wanted to transfer this cargo to the *Vinland*, but Evyind advised against it, saying the pram would stay closer to the ship with a load inside. This turned out to be Evyind's second mistake. He had not taken into account the way in which the current was shifting the ice. Thorvard cut the ropes and the prams moved slowly away. By now the others were awake; together they reefed the sail and lowered the mast. After this no man attempted to sleep, knowing the danger the ship was in. Instead they sat with their legs shoved into their sleeping bags, their backs against each other's, their cloaks bundled tight. The old ship no longer rocked but creaked and groaned as the pack ice tightened its grip. Whenever one of the men stood to look about, he saw that the ship was solidly locked in moonlit ice. Even the narrow channel cracks had closed.

"It may be we'll have to walk to shore," Thorvard remarked as much to himself as anyone else. Already the men knew they would have to abandon the *Vinland*; a ship trapped this tightly in pack ice couldn't be trusted to stay in one piece.

Toward dawn when the wind heightened, skirling and screeching, the ship began to shudder as the strakes gave way to the pressure of ice. Thorvard advised his men to take as much as they could carry among them, including the chests and oars.

The men moved as quickly as they could in the tearing wind, bundling up their sleeping bags and their provisions, trussing the walrus hides and ivory for hauling. They rolled up the sail and cut the rigging loose. They were undecided about whether or not to remove the mast pole. In the end they left it where it was. They put the chests on the ice for fetching later. After all this had been done, the men set out, backs to the wind, carrying their gear. Behind them the old ship made sharp, thwacking noises like an axe when it bites deep into wood. These were muffled by the ripping wind and by the men's cloaks which flapped against their ears. When the men finally stumbled ashore, they hunkered down in their sleeping bags among the rocks and pulled the sail over them. So far there was little rain to speak of, only splatters of sleet here and there.

The wind continued all that day and into the next without shifting. Through the thickly clouded sky, the men could see the blurred white ball of the sun. In that way they were able to mark the day's passing. Midway through the second afternoon, Thorvard took Bodvar, Hrollaug, Oddmar and Gisli and retrieved the goods from the ice. As they passed the *Vinland* on their way to the chests, the men saw that the old ship was now canted to one side, its bow stem tilted upwards, its strakes crumpled like a belt of splintered wood. But the keel stem held firm; it was the original wood hewn from Norway's forests back in the days when giant oaks were in good supply. Thorvard regretted not having taken the mast pole earlier. It was now too risky to go aboard.

Thorvard tried not think about what Leif or Freydis would say when they heard the bad news. He had been in enough difficult situations to know that thinking too far ahead, especially about something you were helpless to change, blunted your judgement of what was close at hand. What mattered now was getting his crew and their cargo ashore. He scanned the ice for the prams. There was no sign of the pram containing the hides and ivory from the second hunt. Apparently it had sunk under its own weight. The empty pram lay on the ice not far from the ship as lightly as a basket of woven grass. Thorvard beckoned the others to help him fetch the pram and the chests. When this had been done, the Greenlanders hauled the last of their gear to the Markland shore and arranged the pram and chests in a half-circle to break the wind.

During the next three days the gale continued unabated. The cloud cover thickened, blocking out the sun so that the hunters didn't know how close or how far they were from night. Without the sun Thorvard had to guess how many marks to cut on his calendar stick. So cold and stupefied were the men while they dozed that for them, time might have stopped altogether. Thorvard urged them to cut blubber and meat from the frozen carcasses. Twice the Greenlanders crawled out and killed whatever walrus pups they could find. Before cutting out the heart and liver, the men warmed their hands by holding them inside the carcass. They had brought an ember pot with them, but it was far too windy to light a fire.

Then the rains came. For three days the Greenlanders were pelted with freezing rain that slammed at them from all sides so that none of them could stay dry or warm. One way and another the rain found every slit in their clothing, every snick of uncovered skin. The heavy rains prevented Teit from feeding the embers with walrus blubber. As a result the embers went out. Though the men were disappointed by the loss of fire, no one chided Teit. Even if he had managed to fatten the fire, the rain would have eventually put it out. Fortunately Thorvard had a tinder box with him to use later on. The men took turns lying under the pram. Ten men scrunched together could lie beneath the boat with the sail spread over the top, which meant three men were left open to the rain. Exposed as they were, the men's hair and beards iced up as did their eyebrows and nostril hair. Their iced cloaks became stiff as tents, which made the men appear larger than they were so that when they moved about, they looked like a race of frost giants, those creatures of myth who inhabited the earth when the world was made.

Nine days after the men left Leifsbudir, the storm broke. On the tenth day Thorvard rose early. It had been his turn to spend the night outside the pram, which meant he'd hardly slept and was aware of the changing weather. The drop in the wind had also alerted Evyind and Falgeir who were outside the sheltering pram and sail. When Thorvard, Evyind and Falgeir stood up, their cloaks crackled from having been rained on, then frozen during the night. The rain had stopped. As their piss steamed in the frosty air, the men contemplated the eastern sky; it was dawn, the sun not yet fully risen. When they looked across the ice, the men saw the *Vinland* frozen fast. Both fore and aft stems were visible, held in the grip of ice. This was a good sign; despite heavy rains, the ice was far from being rotten and might be safely crossed.

Now that the storm had passed, the Greenlanders were faced with the decision of whether to remain on the rocky shore of Markland or to walk across the ice to Vinland. Bodman, Hrollaug and Glam wanted to remain where they were. They thought it would be foolish to risk crossing the ice. It was far more prudent to stay where they were until the pack ice moved North. The other hunters disagreed. They pointed out that the pack ice might not move for a long time yet. Why should they stay in an inhospitable place when it was far better on the opposite shore? Thorvard reminded the men that this was the season when white bears came south on the ice. With the number of walrus carcasses lying about, it was only a matter of time before a white bear looking for meat found his way to this shore. Although Thorvard had killed white bears in Northsetur, he had always used traps. Of all the animals Thorvard hunted, the white bear was the only one he feared.

"If a white bear finds us," he said, "it'll maim several of us before we can bring it down."

"That's a chance we'll have to take," Glam said. "I think we should stay where we are and continue hunting walrus. That way we can make up for the hides and ivory lost in the storm."

"Even if more walrus come this way after the ice opens up, we've only one pram," Falgeir said. "With thirteen of us and our gear crowded into the boat, we'd have to leave the extra hides and ivory behind."

"We can row across several times until everything is fetched," Glam said.

This prospect was immediately rejected for the oppo-site shore was far enough away as to require strenuous rowing. No one wanted to row across more than once, after the ice had cleared.

"Since walrus can't be hunted until the water opens up, I see no good reason for staying where we are," Thorvard said. "I think we're better off loading our ivory and gear onto the pram and hauling it across the ice. We can pull the hides on ropes." Thorvard looked at the opposite shore. "Without hauling gear of any kind, we can walk to the opposite shore in a day, two at the most. With cargo it'll probably take us three or four days to cross. Once we're on the other side, we can take our time returning to Leifsbudir, working our way along the shore as the ice opens up." Thorvard said no more for the time being. He was unwilling to force any of his men to go against his will, knowing the dangers they faced made them all equal on the ice. Each man had his say before the hunters agreed that the best course of action was to do as Thorvard advised.

The Greenlanders ate more walrus meat and made themselves ready. Thorvard said they should make four harnesses from the rigging they had brought ashore and attach them to the pram. In that way the boat could be pulled more easily across the ice. Hauling the pram would require enormous effort. There was no question of leaving the pram behind. Not one of the men was willing to abandon something of such value, for no Norseman liked being without a boat of some kind close at hand. While the harnesses were being made, the pram was carried to the ice, stowed with ivory and gear and covered with the sail. Much of the remaining gear went into the chests which were rigged for hauling. Holes were cut in the hides so they could be pulled by ropes. They and the ship oars would be hauled and carried by those who were neither pushing nor pulling the pram. Thorvard chose the strongest men to put on the harnesses: Falgeir, Hrollaug, Bodman and Glam. Evyind and Teit would push from behind. The four men were harnessed to the pram. Grunting with effort, they bent over and tried to pull the load over the uneven ice. After much shoving and straining, the pram reached a stretch of smoother ice where hauling was easier, though not for long. The ice again became uneven and the men slowed down. The haulers began stumbling from the exertion of trying to pull the pram over humps. They were replaced by four others including Thorvard. The replacements managed to pull the pram over several humps and onto smoother ice. This was no sooner crossed than the pram haulers reached a large ice ridge. Here the help of all the men was required to shove the pram over the top. After this the Norsemen stopped to rest.

"I don't think this will work," Evyind said. As the oldest man there, he hadn't been harnessed but together with Teit had continued to push from behind. "It's too hard on the pullers, not to mention the pram. It would be better if we unloaded half our gear and came back for it later, since if we continue as we are, we'll rip out the strakes."

Thorvard was reluctant to do this, for as the day progressed, the sun would weaken the ice to the point where it would be too risky to return for a second load. But he went along with the opinions of those who were in favour of what Evyind said. The chests were left on the ice as were the ship's oars. Some of the frozen walrus they had brought along for food was also set aside. Once again the harnessed men struck out. Now that the pram was half as heavy as it had been before, the men found the hauling much better, since the pram could be lifted over uneven ice with much greater ease. As the men went on, however, the number of ice ridges increased and there were fewer stretches of flat ice between. Earlier in the Winter during freeze-up when the ice had jammed together, its edges had been forced up at angles, then snowed on many times. As a result Thorvard and his men were now surrounded by a landscape of ridges and furrows. Huge ice boulders had been cast about everywhere.

At midday the men were still a long way from their destination. They had come far enough from Markland that there was no question of going back. The sun was high and strong. By the time the men stopped to eat, they were so warm they took off their cloaks. They cut strips from the bottom of their cloaks and tied them over their eyes as a precaution against snow blindness. Several of the men were already red eyed from the brilliance of sun on snow. The place where the Norsemen stopped to rest was pinnacled with sheets of upthrust ice. Thorvard, who was sitting beneath one of these on a snow bench, felt a drop of melted ice on his arm. The melting was an ominous sign. Thorvard urged the men to their feet. Again Falgeir, Hrollaug, Bodman and Glam took up harness. While they hauled the pram, Balki and Gisli scouted ahead, poking their gaffs into the snow, searching for openings in the ice. Because their eyes were partly bound, the pram haulers could not see as well as before and did not follow the path the scouts had marked with gaffs. Bodman and Hrollaug stepped into a hole and disappeared; the pram tilted slightly, dragged downward by their body weight. Fortunately Falgeir and Glam kept their feet. Cutting the harness, they lay on the ice and pulled on the ropes of the drowning men. After a struggle Bodman and Hrollaug, gasping and blue faced, were hauled onto the ice. They coughed up water and vomited the walrus they had eaten earlier. Then they were pulled to their feet and made to walk about while the other men righted the pram.

Once again the hunters were forced to consider the wisdom of hauling so many goods. It seemed if they continued in this way, they were unlikely to reach land as soon as they had hoped. Bodman and Hrollaug would die if they remained on the ice much longer; without body heat, their clothes would freeze. Thorvard was reluctant to leave the pram and walrus hides behind, since they had gone to so much trouble getting them. With the *Vinland* gone, it was essential that Thorvard arrive in Leifsbudir with enough rope to satisfy the Icelanders' demands; it was hard to say what the Egilssons might do with the new ship if he failed to give them what he had promised for Mairi. If the warm weather continued, the ice would break into pans and the current would move the pram out of their reach. Thorvard told the men that the best plan was to divide themselves into two groups: Evyind, Teit, Balki, Gisli and Glam would take Bodman and Hrollaug ashore, carrying the tinder box, hunting gear, sleeping bags, dried food and blubber; the remaining six would stay with the pram. The hunters readily agreed to this, since the alternative was worse for Bodman and Hrollaug. As soon as the gear was ready, the shore party set off, supporting the survivors. After a time they vanished behind the humps and ridges of ice. Thorvard and the others again set about pulling the pram, this time without the sail, which they decided was too heavy to haul. Thorvard would have liked to have kept the sail; he wanted some part of the *Vinland* to take back to Leif. He also liked the idea of using Thjodhild's red and grey sail for the Greenlanders' new ship; Freydis's sail could then be used for Helgi's ship. When Thorvard said as much to the men, Falgeir replied that it was far better to replace the sail than continue hauling it.

"Your wife can make another," Bodvar said.

Hogni and Oddmar agreed with this. Only Asmund sided with Thorvard.

"I think Leif Eiriksson would appreciate having his mother's sail," he said, "especially since we've lost his ship."

"A keepsake is a trinket compared to our lives," Hogni said. "Let's not waste more time arguing but leave the sail here and continue on."

This time the men did not use harnesses; instead, they tugged and pulled the boat toward the shore. Although safer this arrangement slowed their progress. Late in the day the men reached a plateau of hard thick ice and decided to bed down there. The men carried ice chunks onto the plateau and braced them against the pram to keep it level. Then they ate a meal of frozen walrus and snow. Afterwards they spread their sleeping bags on the ice close by the pram and slept. Thorvard posted himself as first watch to keep an eye on the weather. After dark had fallen, a wind rose from the South, bringing soft balmy air. Thorvard awoke Falgeir. He was beginning to get sleepy and thought it better if two of them watched the ice. Overhead small clouds drifted across the moon. All around them Thorvard and Falgeir heard the ice cracking and shifting as the wind pushed the ice pack from shore. At midnight a rift opened up beside the pram and a strip of dark water appeared. Immediately the others were awakened and told to put their sleeping bags onto the pram and keep it steady. The men stood around the pram, balancing it so that as the rift widened, the pram would not tip. Before long the water had widened enough to accept the pram. By then the ice pans on which the men stood were partly under water, wetting their feet. The men climbed into the pram, took off their boots and got into their sheepskin bags and went to sleep, satisfied they were as safe as they were likely to be. At dawn the men awoke to find themselves in a pool of water encircled by ice. The wind was still blowing strongly from the South, which meant the most prudent course of action was to wait until the water opened further and they could row ashore.

The men stayed in the pool of dark water for two more days. During this time the wind kept shifting. When it blew from the West, the pool narrowed as the ice pushed against the shore. When it blew from the South, the ice moved northward and the pool opened again. Each time the pool widened, it was larger than it had been before, which meant the situation was slowly improving. Once a grey seal appeared in the pool, but it disappeared before any of the men could kill it. This was no great loss since the men had enough walrus meat to keep them from hunger. Their main discomfort came from lying so long in their sleeping bags. By the sixth day the water had opened up enough so that the men were able to row between the pans of floating ice. In this way, they gradually closed the distance between themselves and the shore.

The hunters were far sighted from spending so much time scanning water and land; Thorvard and his men spotted their fellows long before they came ashore. Evyind's party had camped on a pebbled beach at the foot

of an embankment where the waterline was straight without any inlets or coves. As they drew closer, Thorvard saw
smoke curling upwards from a driftwood shelter on the
beach. Above the embankment the land was flat and
meadowed all the way to the woods. As soon as Thorvard
and his men landed, Evyind told them that Bodman and
Hrollaug were dead.

"Despite our urgings they lay down on the ice and
refused to get up. We had to carry them the rest of the
way. As a result they died sooner than they might have,
since it took us that much longer to get them ashore. We
buried the corpses together further along the beach
beneath a pile of stones."

"We took care to arrange the grave in the shape of a
ship," Evyind went on, "which was what Bodman and
Hrollaug would have preferred. Both men had been heard
saying many times that they were proud to sail on the
Vinland and would not have missed it for any price."

The Greenlanders decided to stay where they were
until the ice had completely cleared. There was a supply
of firewood handy and an abundance of game in the
woods. The return journey would be arduous and long.
Not only would the current be against them, but rowing an
overburdened pram would make progress slow.

The men camped beneath the embankment six more
days. Now that the danger was past, Thorvard and his men
mourned the loss of the Vinland. When the men looked
toward Markland, there was no sign of the ship; it had
gone under as the ice was breaking up. Thorvard often
walked along the beach to see if any of the chests and
oars abandoned on the ice had drifted in. He had already
observed where the current favoured the shore and each
day went to that stretch of beach. In this way he found
three oars, which he carried back to the campsite. Besides
the rigging they had cut loose, the oars were all that
remained of Leif's ship.

One evening as the men lay side by side in their sleeping bags, Asmund Gautsson offered this verse:

Made from forest kings,
Wind rouser and wave biter
Rode Njord's rolling meadows
Like a prize stallion.
Mares preferred him
Above all other steeds.

The day white crown threw
Down his winter robes
And galloped to the moving hills,
Wind charger became
Land seeker and star follower.
Braving serpent spume and troll spit,
He searched for the place
Where the elf candle glows.

Now he is shape changer and sea ghost.
When day quiet comes to the rolling fells,
The sea stallion will rise from his watery sleep.
Then brave land thralls who never rode him
Will honour his greatness in words.

A day or two after he offered this poem, Asmund recited another. In fact this was the new verse he had offered
at Yule, with a second verse added on.

In Valhalla men are drinking elf dew
Gathered from meadows and woods.
Here warriors build wind horses;
The Norns make gods of us all.

In Vinland battlefields are white.
Warriors set forth with spears and gaffs.
Walking on the snow roof of Hel's Hall,
They are greater than the tales
Told about them later on.

When the men heard this second verse, they thought
they understood the first verse in a way they had not before.
Even though the men were sober when they heard it this

time, they did not think of themselves as gods. They found more comfort in looking backwards to those men who had come through difficulties in the past than they did congratulating themselves for what they did by way of staying alive. Only a fool would become so satisfied with himself that he placed himself among the gods. Even Thor needed a magic hammer to trick giants who would otherwise eat him alive; Thor knew that once he became complacent and soft, he would cease to be a god. It may have been that gods did not see themselves as gods either, but neither Thorvard nor his hunters thought of that, except Asmund.

With so much time on his hands Thorvard brooded over another disappointment, which was his ambatt. Before taking on Mairi, Thorvard had never bedded any woman except his wife. He had thought himself poorer as a result, especially when Freydis refused to lie with him as she sometimes did. Moreover from talking to other men over the years, Thorvard had come to believe that a concubine was more exciting in bed than a wife, being freer and more open in that respect. His experience with Mairi had proved that the opposite was the case. Though Mairi offered no resistance when Thorvard took her to bed, neither did she show any interest in what he did. Thorvard had been gentle with Mairi, thinking she had been carelessly treated and abused. He thought his patient handling of her would improve her pleasure and consequently his. When Mairi was got with child, Thorvard thought the pregnancy would soften her in the way it did Freydis. In fact Mairi's condition had the opposite effect. Mairi became even more distant and unapproachable, which forced Thorvard to conclude that he had traded away more goods for the ambatt than she was worth to him. Helgi must have known the girl was a poor concubine and for that reason had been willing to profit by loaning her out. The fact was that Thorvard had risked his life and lost two men to provide cargo for men who were wealthier than he. Freydis had warned him that he would come out on the wrong end in his dealings with the Egilssons. It rankled Thorvard to admit that Freydis was right once again. He

knew that because she was so often right, he was inclined
to do the opposite of what she said.

Freydis was not an easy woman to live with. Not only
was she overfond of her way, she was impossible to
please in many respects. In the early days of their marriage, Thorvard would return from hunting with various
gifts to please his bride: a caged falcon, a white bear skin,
an ivory comb he had carved himself. Though he had
intended Freydis to keep the falcon for her own amuse-
ment, she lost no time in trading it for a roll of white linen.
Nor did she keep the polar bear skin which he had
brought especially for their bed. Instead she traded it for a
bronze ring then chided him afterwards for not having
done this himself. Surely he knew a wedded woman liked
having a ring, preferably of gold. As for the comb, that was
traded as soon as she found one she liked better. She
considered the comb he had made too poorly carved for
her use. Freydis had so often told Thorvard that if she
couldn't have superior goods, she preferred going without
that he no longer brought her gifts.

In the matter of the house which was a sore point
between them, if Freydis had been less particular, they
might have had a house in Gardar before now. The
Summer after the posts and beams had been burnt,
Thorvard found a driftwood log that, if properly cut, would
have provided enough support for a small house. Freydis
rejected the log. It was badly bent, she said, the wood pitted and scarred. She told Thorvard he mocked her by
thinking she would live in a house built with inferior wood.
She said she preferred to wait until they fetched straight
timbers from Vinland.

Early in their marriage Freydis had begun talking about
undertaking an expedition to Leifsbudir. She said Thorvard
had married into a family of voyagers and should take
advantage of the fact. Freydis seemed to think a voyage to
Leifsbudir would make the two of them rich in such a way
that they and their children could buy their Luck. This
Thorvard regarded as unlikely. He had been in so many
situations from which he had barely escaped with his life

that he was convinced Luck could be neither bought nor earned. And Thorvard thought Freydis was mistaken in thinking a rich house would make her content. He thought that once she had a house, she would find something else she wanted more.

Though living with Freydis had its drawbacks, Thorvard did not regret his marriage. He knew his wife had strengths he lacked. She was hard working, equal to running both a household and a farm. She was a shrewd trader of the goods he brought home from Northsetur, handling them in such a way that increased their worth. Another point in her favour was the fact that she had borne healthy children and was trim and tidy in her looks. When she put her mind to it, Freydis was lively in bed. Her ardour surprised him especially when they came together after being a long time apart. It made him think that perhaps Finnbogi's slur was based on fact. There was also the matter of Freydis's encounter with the skraeling, the bold way she had bared her breast. It seemed to Thorvard that the kind of woman who would show her breast in front of men would have no difficulty cuckolding her husband. But who would she lie with? Freydis showed a strong dislike toward the Icelanders. It seemed unlikely she would take one of them. But she was on friendly terms with Hauk who Thorvard knew from various remarks had left Norway as a result of bedding another man's wife. Hauk had gone out of his way to flatter Freydis at Yule; Thorvard had not been so drunk that he had failed to notice the attention Hauk had paid his wife. Of course it wasn't Hauk Freydis had lain with at Yule but himself, though afterwards Freydis had told him she wouldn't lie with him soon again, since she had no wish to be slowed down by a pregnancy. This remark made Thorvard think that Freydis had been right when she had said Finnbogi had slurred her reputation to stir up trouble and that there was no truth in his remark, since she would not want to be got with child by anyone.

No sooner would Thorvard convince himself that Freydis would never risk adultery than he would come around again to believing he had been cuckolded after all.

Then he would remind himself that any woman who would go to the trouble of procuring an iron belt was unlikely to lie with any man. Thorvard had been offended that Freydis would wear such a belt since he had never forced her to lie with him. Now it occurred to Thorvard that Freydis might have wanted a belt handy, not to keep him away, but to use as a precaution against living with a large number of able-bodied men who had left their women behind in Greenland. Freydis had not expressed this fear, but it might have been there all the same. Or it might not. Now that Summer was approaching and he was so long away, Freydis might not be wearing the belt. In a few months, they would be returning to Greenland which could mean she was now less concerned about being got with child than before. Freydis might at this moment be lying with a Greenlander. Thorvard couldn't guess who it might be; up to now he had trusted them all. He brooded over who among the Greenlanders might be bedding his wife. Ozur, perhaps? No, that was unlikely since Ozur slept with his son close by. As for Ivar, he had never married and showed no interest in women. Nagli was a possibility, though Thorvard had never noticed anything untoward going on between the ironworker and his wife. The other men were several years younger than Freydis which made Thorvard think it unlikely she would take one of them. Freydis guarded her reputation; if she cuckolded Thorvard, she would try to do it in such a way as to keep her reputation intact. As the days dragged on, Thorvard became increasingly disgruntled and downcast. Not only had he lost Leif's ship and two of his hunters, he no longer trusted his wife. Thorvard continued to torture himself about the truth of Finnbogi's slur until his only pleasure was counting off the grooves of his calendar stick. It was reassuring to know that the more days he counted off since his departure from Leifsbudir, the fewer remained before he could return to his wife.

HELGI EGILSSON BELIEVED IN PARADISE though not as a place you went to after you were dead. He didn't think Paradise was at the top of the World Tree or among the stars; he thought it was a place that could be found beneath The Tree, on Earth.

In the beginning there was no heaven or earth.
There was no land or sea. There were no flowers
or grass, only the black emptiness called
Ginnungagap.

So the scalds claimed.

Ice formed the North; Fire formed the South.
Heat rose and melted the ice so that the giant
Ymir came out. Then Audhumla, the cow,
emerged. Ymir fed on her milk. Audhumla licked
ice blocks with her tongue and Buri came out.
Buri fathered Bor who fathered the gods who
slew Ymir. From beneath Ymir's arm came the
first man and woman. From his blood came the
lakes and seas. His bones became mountain
ridges, his flesh the soil.

Helgi enjoyed hearing the old tales, the more fantastic, the better. When he told them himself, he was inclined to dress them up. He had giants emerging from Ymir's eyebrows and dwarves from his nail clippings. His eyeballs became the sun and moon. Although Helgi treated these tales lightly, one way and another they informed his thought. He had come to think of the world as being a place between two lands: Ubygdir was the roof; Muspell, the floor. Ubygdir was uninhabitable because of the cold, Muspell because of the heat. Between these two extremes was the disc of Earth surrounded by the Outer Ocean. Every sailor knew the disc was curved. How else to explain the way land came into view then disappeared? The sun and moon also curved, which explained why they came and went. The winds curved in the shape of the earth. The Outer Ocean, a place of tumult and chaos, was where winds were born. According to mariners Helgi had met in his travels, the Outer Ocean was as far as you could go. Helgi disbelieved this. The more he looked at the stars and travelled the seas, the more he thought the world never ended. He thought the Outer Ocean might not be at the end of the world at all but in the middle. He thought if he sailed southwest far enough, he would eventually come to Paradise.

Helgi wanted to do this. He wanted to travel as far as his imagination would go. To do this he needed to find Vinland. He had long believed Vinland and Paradise were one and the same. According to Leif Eiriksson, Vinland was a place of untold wealth. There were wine grapes and honey, fruits and nuts, cargo wood of every kind. These riches appealed to Helgi not only as trade goods but for the use he could make of them for himself. Helgi was a man of large appetites which he expected Paradise to satisfy. He liked wine, a woman's body, warmth and ease. Iceland was too close to Ubygdir for his taste.

As a young man raking the scythed grass in his father's home field in North Alftafjord, Helgi had often imagined warm places to keep his mind off the icy blasts that swept down from Vatnajokull. Winds from the glacier brought sudden snow squalls and sleet, which meant the hay had to be frequently turned. Despite these turnings, the cold and wet sometimes kept the hay in the fields so long it was never carried in but left outside all winter. Helgi's body was not built for such cold. He had always been tall and skinny; no wool covering or fur-lined cloak could keep his limbs warm enough for field work. He frequently suffered chilblains and frostbite. His father often accused him of laziness when he left off work to sit in hot stinking water up to his neck. There was a hot spring that pooled between the rocks above the byre. Living as he did on a glaciered island where fields were wrested from lava and ash and cold winds brought constantly shifting weather, Helgi Egilsson's idea of Paradise was a place of unchanging heat, a place where corn and wheat ripened without coaxing, where sweetmeats grew in abundance, where wild game and venison dropped at his feet. Helgi was a young man when an Icelandic trader first told him of Leif Eiriksson's voyage. The result of growing up with this tale was that Helgi believed that somewhere beyond the Outer Ocean was the legendary island of the blessed where honey flowed from hollow oak and water splashed lightly from a fountain.

Leifsbudir was a far cry from Paradise. As a place to live it was not much of an improvement on North Alftafjord; in some respects it was worse. Though Leifsbudir was far from glaciers, it lacked warm water of any kind. Nor were the meadows here any more lush than his father's fields, being crowded with alder and rock. Far from being blessed, the islands round about were mostly wind-blown and bare. Leifsbudir had only two advantages that Helgi could see: an abundance of firewood and proximity to Vinland.

* * *

Helgi had spent much of the Winter in Leifsbudir planning his escape. As he saw it, in addition to the weather, there were two obstacles which could prevent him from reaching Vinland: one was his brother Finnbogi and the other was a ship. During the tedium of Winter, Helgi had often spoken to Hauk and Ulf Broad Beard as well as several others about making the journey to Vinland. Although

Finnbogi never joined in these discussions, he frequently complained about finding such fanciful talk wearisome. He said he could enjoy a good tale as well as the next man, but that Leif Eiriksson's story about Vinland was so far-fetched as to be beyond believing. All the talk about white sand and grapes was the foolish talk of a dreamer. Anyone with sense knew that Leif had mistaken gooseberries for grapes, since he had never been to those lands where grapes grew or traded with the Franks and Moors. Moreover, even grey sand such as there was in Leifsbudir shone white when the sun hit it a certain way. Finnbogi pointed out that Thorfinn Karlsefni had stayed in Leifsbudir longer than Leif, yet he had never made such outrageous claims. In Finnbogi's opinion, Leif couldn't talk about Leifsbudir without dressing it up. It was Finnbogi's opinion that Leif spoke as if a scribe were taking down every word that passed his lips so that later on, ignorant folk would believe whatever he said.

In Greenland Helgi had spoken to Leif about Vinland on two occasions. It was clear to Helgi that Leif thought Leifsbudir was on the edge of Vinland. He told Helgi plainly that Vinland extended far south of here, though how far south he refused to say. Helgi thought Leif's reluctance to draw precise boundaries was deliberate so that his children might claim large areas of Vinland if they ever wished to come this way. Although Finnbogi was present during these discussions, he afterwards resisted any suggestion from Helgi that Vinland could be sought. Helgi's brother had made his way as a trader by being cautious and unyielding. He had no intention of taking what he regarded as unnecessary risks.

Helgi admired Leif Eiriksson more than he admired his brother. He admired Leif's courage and determination. He admired a man who could see more than what was in front of him, who thought about the dreams inside his head. It was no good to speak to Finnbogi about dreams. Finnbogi was one of those men who claimed he never dreamed, either awake or asleep. Last Summer during the crossing, when they had sailed here under the North star,

Helgi had often stood on the deck beside his brother. Once, looking up into the vast sky pierced with starlight, he asked Finnbogi if he had ever thought about there being other worlds up there. "If there are," Helgi had said, "perhaps other people are looking down at us. Maybe the sun is a giant star. Maybe each star up there has a world of its own." Finnbogi had replied that such thoughts were dangerous and misleading and got in the way of a man's judgement and common sense. Later during the voyage, Helgi discussed his ideas with Finna. Finna took such thoughts seriously and enjoyed imagining what sort of folk might live in star worlds should they exist. Finna said that when she was a girl, she had heard one of Christ's priests say that God's angels lived among the stars, that it wasn't cold and black as folk might think but warm and green.

"I've often imagined the stars being inhabited by folk who fly on wings like giant birds," Helgi said. He told Finna he could also imagine a world where people lived in the sea as mermen and seldom came to land.

Helgi and Finnbogi had always seen different worlds. Growing up in North Alftafjord, the brothers shared one thing in common: neither of them wanted to become a fisherman or a farmer. Together they conspired to leave North Alftafjord as soon as it could be arranged. Each brother in his own way believed that he would find something that suited him better elsewhere. It was lucky for Finnbogi and Helgi that they had four younger brothers who, when they were old enough, could one day help their father, Egil Bjornsson, thus releasing them from the farm. This release took some time. During the years when Finnbogi and Helgi worked the farm, Finnbogi married Ragna Skjoldolfsdottir from Heydales by whom he had two daughters. Despite this encumbrance Finnbogi managed to set aside a large quantity of trade goods. Whenever Egil had an especially prosperous harvest, he gave his older sons valuable goods. These were usually forged tools and weapons. Egil had an Irish thrall who was a skilled iron worker and made more goods than Egil could use.

Sometimes Egil gave his sons riding gear as a reward; he had large herds of cattle and horses and liked to keep his sons well equipped with bridles and whips. Helgi always traded these goods for something that struck his fancy more: a jug or two of wine, a leather hat, a copper weather-vane shaped like a whale; a trader always had something Helgi fancied. Finnbogi never gave anything up with ease; rather he hoarded his goods under lock and key. Even though Ragna urged him to make a trade that would give them a house of their own, for they lived with Ragna's kin, Finnbogi held out until he managed to buy a small ship that Halvard Onundsson's widow no longer wanted, for she preferred to have more farm goods instead. What could a widow with small daughters do with a ship? Finnbogi and Helgi used this ship, which was named *Fafnir's Foe*, to pick up trade in the Faroes and the Hebrides. In this way Finnbogi eventually got himself a larger ship, *Sigurd's Steed*, as well as a number of thralls, two of whom he left for Ragna's use and one of whom, Olina, he kept as his ambatt. Finnbogi managed to do all this without giving up his claim to his father's home field. Finnbogi wanted to keep this claim since he intended to return to the farm one day when he was rich enough to hire an overseer to handle the work.

Although Helgi had gone on these voyages with Finnbogi, he never managed to earn his half of the ship, since many things besides Finna caught his eye. He paid the Moors too much for a rich cargo of spices and silks only to undersell these goods later to the Danes and Swedes. Another time he bought a large quantity of Rhineland jugs, thinking to sell them in Greenland. By the time *Sigurd's Steed* reached Greenland, the pottery was in shards. As it turned out, the Greenlanders would not have given much for the jugs anyway, since they preferred more durable goods such as soapstone and iron. Although it was Finnbogi's contention that the Greenland trade was best served by bringing in timber, iron, linen, barley, salt, honey and a small amount of jewellery and silver, Finnbogi never advised his younger brother not to make these extravagant trades. Nor did he offer to share the goods he bought at a bargain so that Helgi could also make a profit by trading them at a higher price. Eventually Helgi concluded that Finnbogi did not want him to earn his half of *Sigurd's Steed*. By keeping full ownership of the ship for himself, Finnbogi always had the final say in where it went. Helgi knew he could talk until he was blue in the face and his brother would never agree to let him take *Sigurd's Steed* to fetch exotic goods from Vinland. Even so, the day after Thorvard Einarsson left Leifsbudir to hunt walrus and Helgi and Finnbogi were alone in the fire room, Helgi made another attempt at persuading his brother to lend him his ship. He said that as soon as the ice left the horizon, he intended to go after oak wood.

"Why must you go for oak wood? Why not fetch spruce from Markland or closer?" Finnbogi said. "That way your ship would be finished sooner."

"It seems to me that if an oak wood ship is good enough for you, it's good enough for me," Helgi said. He was relying on his brother's loyalty to kin to overcome his caution. Finnbogi had come to Helgi's rescue many times when he needed bailing out as a result of gambling losses. It was a point of honour with Finnbogi that a son of Egil Bjornsson pay his debts. Although Finnbogi could be scornful of Helgi's worth, when it came to facing others, Finnbogi would go far to protect the Egilssons' reputation.

"I can't always depend on your goodwill to get ahead," Helgi said. "I've waited a long time to have a ship of my own so that I can better my chances. You know as well as I do that I can never earn enough to buy one. Surely now that I'm this close to having an oak ship, you wouldn't deny me one."

At length Finnbogi said, "How long would you be gone?"

"No more than a month."

"How many men would you take?"

"Six not counting Hauk and myself."

"That leaves eighteen of us and thirty-three Greenlanders, not counting women."

Helgi pointed out that with the walrus hunters gone, the numbers were nearly even, since the Greenlanders were now down to twenty.

"My intention was to take *Sigurd's Steed*," Helgi said.

"I won't stand in the way of your getting oak wood," Finnbogi said. "But I refuse to lend you my ship. If you're determined to fetch wood from the South, you'll have to use the ship Hauk built the Greenlanders."

All along Helgi had known it would come to this, but he did not want to be blamed for taking the Greenlanders' ship. As he saw it, by refusing to lend *Sigurd's Steed*, Finnbogi was shouldering the blame. Taking the ship was bound to make matters harder between the Greenlanders and themselves. He said as much to his brother.

"Little I care about the Greenlanders. From the beginning they've shown themselves poor neighbours," Finnbogi replied.

"They might stir up trouble after we leave. You said yourself there would be eighteen of us and thirty-three of them."

"The numbers irk me only because Freydis Eiriksdottir went against our agreement and brought extra men. Freydis is a schemer and a troublemaker but she's canny enough not to do anything to spoil her chances of getting the ship. Though when she finds out you've taken it to fetch oak wood, the rest of us had better lie low. My advice is to keep your intentions between yourself and the crew. Some of our thralls can't be trusted not to pass along what they might hear. If Freydis gets wind of your plans, she might refuse to give up the sail."

"I intend to keep the voyage between ourselves and the crew," Helgi said.

"One last thing. In agreeing to this expedition, how do I know you won't go off on some half-witted search for Vinland instead?"

"You have my word," Helgi said truthfully, since he expected that Vinland and the place he would find oak wood would be one and the same.

The day after Helgi's conversation with his brother, a small whale grounded itself in front of the Greenlanders' houses. The Greenlanders hauled the whale ashore and cut it up. Freydis was in such good humour at the prospect of owning a ship at last that she offered half the whale meat to Helgi for the Icelanders' use. Helgi accepted the meat and sent the dwarf twins to claim the Icelanders' share and set it to boil. That night after they had eaten whale meat, several of the Icelanders doubled over with belly cramps and shit brown water. In the morning they were no better. Grumbling with discomfort, they sat in the main room around the hearth discussing the cause of their ailments. They had been in good health before eating the whale. To make matters worse, foul weather had returned. A northeast wind was battering Leifsbudir with snow and sleet. The weather did nothing to improve the Icelanders' tempers. After a Winter of being shut up in overcrowded quarters and dark fetid rooms, few of them could face more of the same without a souring of their dispositions. When the dwarf twins returned from fetching water, they came with the news—imparted by Orn and Kalf—that none of the Greenlanders suffered from having eaten whale meat.

"That's no surprise to me," Grelod said. "Freydis Eiriksdottir is the kind of woman who would keep the best meat for herself and give us the spoiled." To this Olina replied that you could expect no more from a woman who refused a cup of cow's milk to a newborn child. Although she was pregnant again, the loss of the babe weighed on Olina's mind and she found a kind of rough comfort in blaming Freydis. The woman, she said, was a witch, hanging a pin-stuck doll in their doorway, giving anyone who passed her house the evil eye. It was the witch doll that had made her babe sickly.

Helgi did not join in any of this talk but his brother did. Finnbogi's dislike of Freydis was such that he never missed an opportunity to call her down; like Olina he blamed Freydis for the death of the babe. But Finna had told Helgi she believed Freydis had been telling the truth

when she said the cow and goat were dry, pointing out
that there had been others in the room when Freydis
refused the request for milk who could have disagreed
with her and never did. If Freydis hadn't wanted to part
with milk, why would she have offered cheese? Finna said
she thought Olina should have given the babe the cheese,
as Freydis had suggested, rather than eating it herself.

Now the women's talk moved onto Thorvard's ambatt.
Grelod remarked that Freydis would no doubt expose
Mairi's child once it was born. She glanced sideways at
Hauk then patted her belly which held his child. "As a
Summer babe, this one should do well." Her words fell on
deaf ears. Hauk lay on top of his sleeping bag, eyes
closed, knees held to his chest. He had been one of those
whose whale meat had been tainted. Of the four women
present, two were without child. Alof had miscarried
before Yule and hadn't conceived again. Finna was barren.

Finna had been Helgi's ambatt for four years. He had
bought her from an Orkney Viking named Thorgeir
Andersson, who handed her over with welts on her arms
and legs. When Helgi inquired about these injuries,
Thorgeir said the reason he punished Finna was because
she would never submit to his needs without scratching
and gouging his skin. He was tired of the struggle and
wanted to get rid of her, despite the fact that she was so
good a cook she could make soup from stones. Helgi
hadn't bought Finna to bed her. He had another woman,
Vilgerd, at the time. He wasn't sure why he had bought
Finna. It wasn't because he and his brother needed a
cook. It may have been the welts; Helgi had always har-
boured a soft spot for mistreated thralls.

It was Vilgerd who made Helgi take a second look.
Without Thorgeir abusing her, Finna lost her sullen downcast look. She even smiled from time to time. She had
good teeth, better than Vilgerd's, and long brown hair that
shone when washed. Her body was small and well turned.
When she didn't scutter and cringe, she moved with a
swinging grace. Vilgerd took to showing Finna in a bad
light, which of course only made Helgi notice Finna more.

Vilgerd would stick out her foot when Finna was carrying soup, causing her to stumble in a way that Helgi had to steady her. Vilgerd complained about the soup, saying the new thrall must have spit in it, which meant Helgi felt called upon to praise it to the skies. Vilgerd said that underneath her shift Finna was ugly and misshapen, which caused Helgi to wonder what the truth of the matter was. One day when he and Finna were alone beneath the ship's awning, Helgi asked Finna if she would remove her clothes so that he might look at her scars. As a result of what followed, it became clear to Helgi that he would have to get rid of Vilgerd since he now wanted Finna in his bed. With the silver Vilgerd brought him—Vilgerd was strong and good looking and fetched a high price—Helgi bought Finna a red silk gown with silver clasps and shoes of soft-est reindeer. He also bought her a small rosewood chest with bronze hinges and a bronze lock. Inside the chest was a silver loop with a key attached. Finna went every-where with this key. Even when there was dirty work to be done, she wore the loop as a necklace with the key attached.

Helgi considered himself lucky that Finna had never conceived. He had no wish to be burdened by offspring. Once he had a ship of his own, he intended to travel the Western Ocean and wanted Finna by his side rather than minding children ashore. They had never discussed this. Finna was self-contained in her ways. She never prattled with the other thralls but went silently about her work. Sometimes the other women would comment on the way Finna kept herself apart but Finna continued on as if she had not heard. Finna's quiet disposition meant none of the men objected to taking her on the voyage south. Not so Grelod. Helgi was reluctant to include Grelod who, besides being pregnant, could be slack lipped and trouble-some when she chose. Hauk had insisted on taking Grelod. With Finna coming along, Helgi could not very well deny Hauk's wish. There was no question of Hauk staying behind since he was needed to choose ship wood.

The snow and sleet battered Leifsbudir for four more days. This was followed by several days of rain. Helgi used the foul weather to finalize voyage plans. One night after most of the Icelanders were asleep, he arranged for the seven men he intended to take south to meet him inside the fire room. This was the room where the women cooked during the day and Helgi and Finna slept at night. Sometimes Finnbogi and Olina slept here as well, but tonight they had chosen to sleep in the room at the back of the house. The fire room was away from the main part of the house and had its own door. The men Helgi assembled were Hauk, Ulf Broad Beard, Atli, Bjolf, Vemund, Bersi and Olver.

Helgi told his men he wanted to leave soon after the weather broke. "I want our gear and provisions ready to move at short notice," he said. "It will be impossible for us to do anything in the way of packing, but we can mend and sharpen our tools without arousing suspicion."

Helgi listed off the things they would need. It was his intention that they travel lightly in order to provide more space on the return voyage for goods they wanted to bring back from Vinland.

"My plan is that we carry our gear to the ship cove after darkness and row out of the bay that night," Helgi said. "I want to be under sail in early morning before the Greenlanders are up and about."

There was some discussion about when to put the ship to water.

"I advise against putting it in the water at night," Hauk said. "Especially since there are a good many rocks in the cove."

Ulf Broad Beard said that if the ship was put to water in daylight, the Greenlanders were sure to claim it.

"I've thought about that," Hauk said. "My suggestion is that we put it to water and take them sailing before we leave."

"Then we'll have to anchor close by here," Helgi said. "If we return the ship to the cove, the Greenlanders are bound to guess we're up to something."

"Then anchor here. That way we won't have so far to row or sail."

Not all the men were convinced that taking the ship from under the Greenlanders' noses was prudent. "If one of them should happen to come outside during the night, he might see us and rouse the others," Atli said.

"There's merit in what you say," Hauk said. "But there's less risk in anchoring the ship in the cove than there is in putting the ship to water at night."

"We can post a watch," Ulf said. "If a Greenlander appears, we can find some way of quietening him until morning."

In the end it was decided to launch the ship during the day and bring it around to the bay in plain view of the Greenlanders.

By now the ship was ready except for the rigging and sail. Freydis still had the sail. Helgi did not want to ask for the sail since he had put himself on Freydis's bad side earlier when he tried to get Ulfar to work for him.

"You're the one to fetch the sail," he said to Hauk. "If any man can have his way with Freydis, it's you."

"I've been thinking the same thing myself," Hauk said.

The next afternoon Hauk walked through the rain and sleet to Freydis's shed. He could see smoke seeping out of the roof hole before being swallowed by the wind. The terrace was soggy with melted ice which was all that was left of the Winter drifts. Hauk was uncertain as to how he would manage Freydis. Earlier he had thought that when the ship was finished, it would be an easy matter to get Freydis to bed, since he would withhold the ship until he got his way. Lately it had seemed to him that Freydis was deliberately withholding the sail, since he had expected her to deliver it to the ship cove long before now. Before Hauk left the Icelanders' house, Helgi had told him that if worse came to worst, his men would simply walk into Freydis's shed and take the sail. "But I prefer not to do it that way, since Freydis is shrewd enough to guess our intention to use her ship."

Hauk knocked lightly on the shed door.

He heard Freydis's voice.

"Who's there?"

"Your shipbuilder."

"Come in."

Hauk opened the door and went in, expecting to see Freydis working at her loom. What he saw instead was Freydis sitting, knees up in a wooden tub, having a bath. She was alone.

"Shut the door," Freydis said. "There's a cold draft."

Hauk did as he was bid without taking his eyes off her naked limbs.

"I've sent Mairi to fetch more water and wood," she told him. "I'm fed up with this storm and have it in mind to sit in this bath all day."

Freydis made no attempt to cover her shoulders or breasts which Hauk saw were pendulous with large brown teats.

"Why don't you sit down?" Freydis said matter-of-factly, as if she was used to passing the time of day sitting naked in a tub. She gestured to a stool on the far side of the room.

"I'd rather be at your side." Hauk knelt and kissed her on the neck and throat. He lifted the crooked hair and brushed the wet tips against his cheeks. Then he put a hand on her chin and brought her lips to his. Her mouth was softer than he had remembered and warm.

"Bolt the door," Freydis said.

No sooner had Hauk done this than Mairi knocked.

"Come back later," Freydis called out. "I'm busy now." She threw back her head and laughed.

Hauk knelt again and kissed her breasts. Freydis shivered, more from excitement than cold.

"You're freezing," he said and drew her up so that she might feel the stiffening between his legs.

Neither of them spoke again for some time. Hauk was pleased that Freydis was strongly built in the hips and legs for it meant she was able to lift him up and hold him while he thrust. Afterwards they lay side by side, spooned front to back on the narrow sleeping bench, the covers pulled over themselves.

When they finally spoke, it wasn't about the Yule feast or their avoidance of each other but about the ship.

"When can I have my ship?" Freydis said.

"As soon as we rig the sail."

"The sail needs oiling. With this rough weather I haven't been able to spread it on the ground outside."

"If the weather doesn't improve soon, we should do it inside one of the houses," Hauk suggested. As satisfying as their coupling had been, he had been infected by Helgi's belief that greater satisfactions lay in Vinland. "I'm eager to see the sail in place," he said.

The next day Hauk and Freydis had much the same conversation while they were lying on her bed. On the third day when he went to visit Freydis, afterwards returning to the Icelanders' house empty handed, Helgi asked him if he was having any luck with the sail.

"It's coming. It's coming," Hauk said. "Freydis is a hard woman to persuade."

In fact Hauk was enjoying himself so much he was in no hurry to return with the sail. With the foulness of the weather, there was no point in carrying the sail from one place to another until the storm had passed. Now that he had Freydis on her back, the sail was as good as his. Freydis had already questioned him closely about the oar holes and caulking. She wanted to know everything that had been done to the ship since it had been taken from its Winter shed. Hauk invented the same difficulties and setbacks he had used to prevent Thorvard and his walrus hunters from taking the ship. By continuing the deception, Hauk thought he could keep Freydis from guessing Helgi's plan to use the ship himself before handing it over to her.

After several more days of wretched weather, the wind shifted to the southwest and the sun appeared. A day or two later, cod were seen in the bay. Helgi sent the Icelanders out to fish. Fires were lit outside so the cod could be dried for the voyage. Finna cut thin strips of seal meat and wrapped them in leather bags. The only provisions the Icelanders would take on the voyage were dried fish and meat, for they intended to gather fresh food along the way. Hauk had the sail carried from the shed to the ship cove where it was spread on the ground and oiled twice. Freydis set Kalf and Orn to work applying the mixture of fat and bark; this was messy work, done on their knees. None of the shipbuilders spoke openly of their voyage south, since they worked side by side with Ulfar. Moreover, there were always Greenlanders hanging about the ship cove, getting in the way. The Greenlanders offered to fetch tools and hold braces and stays. Now that the ship was nearly finished, they wanted to say afterwards that they had lent a hand in building it. Hauk set these men to felling logs to use as rollers.

The sunny weather continued and the wind held to the southwest, which meant the pack ice moved steadily north. At last Helgi Egilsson awoke to see nothing but an expanse of empty blue beyond the bay. By now thirteen days had passed since the storm had ended. Helgi passed the word around that the ship would be launched that morning. The news spread quickly. Nagli heard it from Ulf Broad Beard when Ulf came for the anchor chain. Nagli lost no time in telling the other Greenlanders. Everyone in Leifsbudir, including the thralls, dropped what they were doing and made their way to the cove to watch the ship launch. There was no shortage of men to ease the ship onto the rollers and into the water; the danger lay in too many folk trying to help. A Greenlander by the name of Hundi slipped on the wet rollers and crushed his leg beneath the keel. Once the ship was in the water, the men clambered aboard to make the journey to Leifsbudir. There were more than forty Norsemen, excluding thralls and the injured Hundi, who were trying to get aboard. Helgi said he would allow no one but the planksmen on the ship until it had been safely tried and ordered the others to leave the ship. The planksmen rowed out of the cove, raised Freydis's sail and set out for Leifsbudir. The distance to the houses was much farther by water than by land; by the time the ship reached Leifsbudir, Greenlanders and Icelanders were lining the shore. All except Finnbogi and a small crew of men who were busy putting *Sigurd's Steed* to water.

"I can see we'll be spending the rest of the day sailing around the bay," Helgi remarked.

This was indeed the case. One group after another went sailing. Freydis herself went sailing twice. She told Helgi afterwards that she intended to slaughter her last goat for a feast that evening in order to honour the occasion. Freydis had the same carefree manner Helgi had noticed before the departure from Greenland and thought her light hearted enough not to become suspicious if he made an excuse. He told her his men were too weary from the day's efforts to enjoy a feast.

"We can feast later," Helgi said, "after your husband has returned and we've decided on a name."

"I've already decided on a name," Freydis said.

"Hauk's Horse," Helgi said slyly. He noticed Freydis reddened slightly.

"Greenland Trader," Freydis replied.

Helgi didn't tell her he had already decided on *Paradise Seeker.*

"I'm sure *Greenland Trader* will suit your purpose," Helgi said, "once you are back in Gardar."

At the end of the day the ship was anchored some distance out in the shallow bay. Because of the rocks, it had to be anchored closer to the Greenlanders' houses than the Icelanders' house.

That night Helgi, the two women and the crew carried their gear through the darkness to a pram, rowed out to the ship and climbed aboard. This was done with much caution and stealth. All that could be heard was the occasional creak of wood and dipping of oars. Once the crew had climbed the ladder, Helgi tied the pram to the ship for towing and went aboard. The ship oars were put into their holes and lowered into the sea. Soon the ship was moving through the darkness toward the cape, following the scythe-shaped moon shining on the water. When the ship cleared the cape, the anchor was dropped. The crew bedded down on the deck and slept. When dawn lightened the sky, Helgi roused the men to take up the oars. The anchor was hauled and the ship rowed out of the cove. They raised the sail and a brisk wind carried them across a much larger bay than the one they had left. They were sailing in open water before anyone in the houses had stirred enough to go outside. The Icelanders felt well pleased to have managed their departure from Leifsbudir so smoothly.

As they made their way south, Helgi kept a sharp eye out for the walrus hunters whom he wanted to avoid. The day before the Icelanders' passing, the Greenlanders had left their shore camp and rowed northward as far as a protected bay. Here in the lee of a promontory they had camped for the night. Early that morning at about the same time the Icelanders were clearing the headland, Thorvard, Falgeir and the Gardar twins had gone into the woods after game. They had yet to return. Evyind and the others were resting on the beach behind the headland which curved around the bay and blocked any view of the passing ship.

If the Icelanders had spotted the Greenlanders, they would have noticed the absence of the *Vinland*. They would have realized the Greenlanders had run into difficulties and were stranded without a ship. This would have put the Icelanders in a quandry: should they rescue the Greenlanders or sail on? If they chose the former, they would have been forced to forgo the latter. It was one thing to use the Greenlanders' new ship when they had a ship already. It would have been quite another to take the Greenlanders' ship when they had none at all.

Due to the lay of the land and Helgi's decision to sail well out from shore, none of this happened. It could be said afterwards that it might have been far better for those aboard *Paradise Seeker* if they had caught sight of the Greenlanders. While it is true that dreams can show the way to adventures, wise folk know Luck changes when dreams are pushed too far.

AST NIGHT I WITNESSED THE THEFT OF THE
Greenlanders' ship. I will now set down what I
saw in the proper order, since the Icelanders'
deception may have far-reaching conse-
quences later on. Ever since I returned to my
shelter to live, I have had difficulty with my sleep and
am often wakeful when others are abed. Last night as
I lay in my shelter, I heard faint noises on the water
and went outside to investigate. I saw a pram being
rowed alongside the new ship which was anchored in
the bay in front of the Greenlanders' houses. The
moon gave little light, being a quarter its size, but I
saw well enough to count eight people boarding the
ship. I was unable to see the anchor being hauled or
the oars put out, but I saw the ship moving forward
plainly enough. In the morning I told Nagli Asgrimsson
what I had seen. Nagli told Freydis Eiriksdottir. Before
long all the Greenlanders knew about the theft.

* * *

Ulfar had sat on a rock and watched the ship being rowed
away. Even after the ship had vanished behind the cape,
he remained on the rock, trying to decide what to do.
There was no point in going after the ship since no pram
would be able to catch up with it. At first Ulfar thought
Greenlanders had taken the ship, since *Sigurd's Steed* was
anchored on the other side of the bay in front of the

Icelanders' house. But why would Greenlanders steal their own ship? It occurred to him that whoever took the ship might return it in a day or two, but that thought was soon rejected. Anyone intending to return the ship would hardly take it under cover of dark. Without doubt the ship had been stolen, but by whom? Not knowing who had taken the ship made Ulfar reluctant to report what he had seen until daylight, when he could go among the Greenlanders and assess the situation.

Ulfar's overcaution came from a long way back. Despite Leif Eiriksson's trust in him, he was still a thrall which meant his word was worthless to many folk. Ignorant farmers were quick to dismiss thralls as liars and thieves. Moreover, there was his future to consider. Except for the discouragement of living with heathens, Ulfar was pleased he had come to Leifsbudir. He had learned much from Hauk about shipbuilding and had gained the Norwegian's respect. He had produced a large quantity of trade goods for the Greenlanders, thereby proving his worth. He did not want to do anything that would endanger his reputation or jeopardize the freedom he had been promised by Leif.

By the time the sun lightened the eastern sky, Ulfar had decided to tell Nagli what he had seen. Nagli was careful in all he did. Of all the men in Leifsbudir, Ulfar felt the most kinship with Nagli. Like him, the iron worker preferred to live alone, away from others, and was skilled in what he did. Nagli was also more worldly than the rest, having travelled around Greenland and lived in Iceland for several years. What counted against Nagli was his reluctance to espouse Christ's teachings. Nagli told Ulfar he would espouse Christianity if forced. Until then he preferred to go his own way. In this respect Nagli was like those Greenlanders who regarded Christianity as a Winter garment they would wear only when the weather turned bitter. As long as the cold was bearable, they went about dressed as they pleased.

Ulfar sat beside the forge and told Nagli what he had seen during the night. When he had finished his tale, the iron worker said, "We'll have to wake Freydis and tell her at once. It's clear the Icelanders have been up to something."

Ulfar said he thought Freydis might be aboard the ship. Mairi had told him about Hauk's visits to the weaving shed. Ulfar thought Freydis might have gone off with the Norwegian somewhere.

"Why would Freydis steal her own ship?" Nagli said. "I know Freydis Eiriksdottir. Let me tell you, she'll be even more surprised than we are by this turn of events."

"Even so, it would be wise to count the Greenlanders," Ulfar said, "to see if any are aboard the ship."

"Suit yourself," Nagli said. "I intend to tell Freydis what you saw."

This was what Ulfar preferred. He wanted Nagli to break the news to Freydis since he disliked reporting to her himself. Ulfar went through the rooms of both houses. Since everyone was asleep, it was an easy matter to count the men; none were missing except those who had gone hunting with Thorvard. As he was coming out of the middle house, Nagli beckoned Ulfar to join Freydis and himself. They were standing outside the end house. Freydis was barefoot and dishevelled, wearing a cloak thrown over her shift. She bade Ulfar repeat what he had seen, which he did. Ulfar thought Freydis accepted the news calmly. He had seen her red faced and fierce. When she was angry, she would scream at her thralls and shove them roughly aside. Now she seemed listless. Her face was white and her eyes distracted. She kept glancing at the empty place where the ship had been. After a time she told Nagli that since he was on better terms with the Icelanders than any of the Greenlanders, it was up to him to find out who among the Icelanders was missing and report back to her. Nagli said he would do this, but only after he had finished mending an iron pot that belonged to the Icelanders so that he could visit them on the pretext of returning it. "Then you'd better hurry," Freydis said. "When our men rouse themselves and notice the ship is missing, they'll want to be after the thieves."

Soon all of the Greenlanders knew about the missing ship. As Freydis predicted, several of them wanted to go over to the Icelanders' house at once. Freydis told the Greenlanders to meet in the large room of the middle house instead.

When they were assembled, Bragi expressed the opinion that the Greenlanders should take over *Sigurd's Steed* without delay. "If the Icelanders can steal from us," he said, "we can steal from them." Three or four others were in favour of Bragi's plan but Freydis argued against it, for the time being.

"For us to take over the Icelanders' ship we need more men. We have only twenty men, including thralls," she said. "If as Ulfar has said, there were eight of them, there are eighteen Icelanders left behind. To take over *Sigurd's Steed*, we need better odds than that."

"Not if we take over the ship at night as they did ours," Bragi said.

"It's not the taking over we must think of but holding it afterwards," Freydis said. "It's a good thing we smuggled extra men aboard in Greenland. Otherwise we would find ourselves in a weaker position than we are."

Sleita thought holes should be slashed in the Icelanders' prams. Uni was for confiscating the timber the Icelanders had brought back from the Bay of Maples.

"Until we know who took our ship and why, we'll do none of these things," Freydis said. "Nagli will be going over to the Icelanders shortly and will report back what he knows."

Not all the Greenlanders were satisfied to wait until then. Some of them went to the ship cove and scouted around. When they returned, they said the shipbuilders had removed all their gear from the cove, which made them think they had taken the ship. This was when Freydis realized that Hauk was part of the deception. Several Greenlanders posted themselves outside to watch the Icelanders' comings and goings. By the time Nagli had delivered the mended pot and spoken with the Icelanders, the Greenlanders had figured out who the thieves were

and were not at all surprised when Nagli returned and listed them off. Nagli finished his report by saying he didn't
think the matter was as serious as all that. "Helgi and the
others have gone for ship wood and will back as soon as
it's fetched." These words did nothing to pacify the
Greenlanders. A number of them insisted they should con-
fiscate Finnbogi's ship. It was Bragi's view that they should
hold on to Finnbogi's ship until their own was returned.

Once again Freydis reminded them of the odds. "To do
what you suggest we need more men than we have, since
the Icelanders won't give up their ship without a struggle.
Remember we fight to win, not to lose. I want Ozur to
come with me to the Icelanders' house. We'll tell you
afterwards what was said." Freydis knew the importance of
involving the Greenlanders closely in what was going on;
she would never leave Leifsbudir without their help.

Freydis and Ozur crossed the terrace. Although the
morning was clear and sunny, the Icelanders were
nowhere to be seen outside. Freydis knocked on the door
but no one answered. Ozur suggested they might have
gone fishing.

"I doubt all of them have gone. They're avoiding us,"
Freydis said. "If this house didn't belong to my brother, I'd
light a fire and smoke them out."

Late in the afternoon the Icelanders were seen rowing
in from their ship, Finnbogi among them. Freydis and Ozur
returned to the Icelanders' house to wait.

When Finnbogi reached the house, Freydis blocked the
doorway and said, "We've come to find out the whereabouts of our ship."

"My brother and a small group of men took the ship to
fetch oak wood," Finnbogi said.

"Why didn't he take your ship instead of ours?"

"He and Hauk wanted to try out the new ship to see
how it handled."

"We could have done that ourselves."

"Not as well as the men who built it," Finnbogi replied.
Arrogance came easily to him.

"When do you expect them to return?"

"A month from now."

"Listen carefully to what I say, Finnbogi Egilsson," Freydis said. "I made an agreement with you and your brother. My husband and I upheld our part of the bargain by providing the rope and sail. Not only that but I agreed to share Leifsbudir with you. In return your brother has stolen our ship. We Greenlanders will hold you to a month. If your brother keeps our ship any longer than that, we will find another way for you to uphold your part of our agreement. We Greenlanders refuse to tolerate a pack of thieves in our midst any longer than that."

Before Finnbogi could answer, Freydis turned and left with Ozur.

When this conversation was reported to the other Greenlanders, some of them were disappointed with the outcome. They thought Freydis had been too soft on the Icelanders.

"It's easy to be hot headed in matters," Freydis said. "What's needed here is a cooler head. I intend to do nothing about the Icelanders until my husband and his hunters return. It may be that by stealing our ship, the Icelanders have done us a favour, for by taking something that was rightly ours, they'll end up owing us more than they did before." What Freydis had in mind was a share of the oak wood Helgi brought back. "Now that Summer is here, we should redouble our efforts to set aside cargo for the journey home. For the time being we can forget about the Icelanders and their dirty tricks."

No one knew what it cost Freydis to say this. Since early that morning when she had been wakened by Nagli and told the news, it had taken all her will power to keep herself going. She felt the urge to go somewhere and lie down. She felt strangely weighted, as if she were hauling stones. The stones were tied to her ankles and wrists. Pulled tight across her breasts was a leather yoke with stones attached. These stones were so heavy Freydis could hardly breathe. There was a stone in her throat that made it impossible to eat. Without these weights keeping her down, Freydis thought she would fly across the terrace with a broad axe and cleave Finnbogi's skull. She would take a pram and row like Thor until she caught up with the thieves. She would pretend to woo Hauk and knock him into the sea.

That night Freydis went to bed and dreamed she was a Valkyrie flying over a battlefield of bloodied corpses, one of which was herself. While she was flying overhead, tree giants came and dragged her corpse into the forest. Freydis had this dream several nights running. One night the star goat appeared in the sky beside her as she was flying over the battlefield and scattered his blood. Freydis woke up soon after this, knowing what she should do. She must honour the gods in the old way, something she had neglected to do the previous Summer.

After bringing the Greenlanders safely to Leifsbudir, Thor would have expected the blood sacrifice of a goat. With so few goats, there had been none to spare for that purpose but Freydis could have made a sacrifice before roasting the goats for Yule. In that way she might have avoided certain difficulties such as the harsh Winter, Bolli's exile and the theft of the ship. And recently when she had offered to roast the remaining goat and share it with the Icelanders, making a blood sacrifice had been the last thing on her mind. Now Freydis told Kalf and Orn fetch the last goat for slaughter. She hung Thor's hammer around her neck, resolving never to take it off; neglecting to wear it in Leifsbudir had been another mistake. Freydis put on her flensing clothes and drew off the blood. She carried the bowl around the Greenlanders' houses, sprinkling goat blood here and there, unmindful of the Greenlanders who slept. She went outside and sprinkled the perimeter of the buildings. Then she dipped the spruce boughs Kalf and Orn had cut into the blood and hung them over the doorways, satisfied that she had done what she could. It was only prudent to do what you could to ensure the old gods were on your side, especially when you were threatened by difficulties, and major obstacles blocked your way. It was unlucky to look back later on and say you should have done this or that to better your prospects. The old gods were hardest on folk who sat around and complained and refused to take whatever needed doing in hand.

After the ritual was done, Freydis stripped off her bloodied clothes and bid Mairi fetch water for a bath. Freydis laughed as she sat in the tub of warm water but it wasn't a laugh of pleasure or mirth. It was the gloat of a woman defying the Fates. By casting events in a certain light, Freydis was able to persuade herself that in some matters she had gotten her way. How easy it had been to trick Hauk into her bed. Despite his courtly ways, it was Hauk's penis that ruled his head. He was no different from other men in that respect. How many baths had she taken in the afternoon while she had waited for him to arrive? She had known he would eventually come to the shed; sooner or later he would have to fetch the sail. Long before he had come, Freydis had decided to have her pleasure with Hauk. She had taken him coolly, or so she thought, though she now hated Hauk with a passion that even Finnbogi did not inspire. Helgi she merely disliked. Despite his good manners, she had known from the start that Helgi wasn't to be trusted any more than his brother. It was no surprise that he had taken her ship without asking. But Hauk was disappointing. He had been stealing from her at the same time he had been putting himself inside her; no matter how many times she reviewed that fact, Freydis couldn't find a way of looking at his duplicity that would erase the knowledge that she had been carelessly used. Like many folk, Freydis took care to nurture her suspicions and thought less of herself for having let down her guard.

Every afternoon Freydis took a long bath and went over these thoughts. This helped somewhat, since the bloody dreams stopped and the stones she was pulling were cut away. Freydis thought the improvement was the result of the blood sacrifice rather than the hardening of her will.

Oddly enough, Freydis found some satisfaction in the theft of the ship. It vindicated what she had been telling

Thorvard about the Egilssons all along. When Thorvard
returned from walrus hunting and discovered what had
happened, he would see how far the Egilssons would go
to please themselves. It was also convenient that Hauk
had left for it meant that the shipbuilder was no longer
around to remind Freydis that he had been in her bed.

When Thorvard returned to Leifsbudir and found out
Hauk had been pretending the ship was unfit for the
Greenlanders' use so that it could be used by the
Icelanders, he was bound to dislike Helgi and Hauk as
much as she. Thorvard was slow to anger, but once he
saw the unfairness of the situation, he would be prepared
to take matters in hand. Though Freydis had cautioned the
Greenlanders against attacking the Icelanders for now, she
would not allow the Icelanders' underhandedness go
unchecked. She was merely biding her time until she saw
a chance to turn the Icelanders' treachery back on themselves. She had no intention of remaining in Leifsbudir
another year. She wanted to return to her children and her
farm. Leifsbudir had much to offer, but to enjoy its advantages, ships were needed to go here and there to harvest
food, since there was no livestock and there were more
woods than grazing fields. Livestock could be brought
from Greenland and the land cleared of trees as farmers
were said to have done in Norway, but the presence of
skraelings over here was a major setback to anyone trying
to settle in these parts.

Now each day saw an improvement in the weather.
Spawning caplin appeared, casting themselves ashore in
great numbers, tumbling over one another on the beach.
Freydis had most of the caplin dried on outdoor racks for
taking back to Greenland; the rest was used to manure
the fields which were turning green. The caplin brought
whales. Two small whales ran aground in front of the
Greenlanders' houses. This meant there was no need to
hunt the humpbacks they saw breeching and blowing
beyond the bay. The grounded whales were of such a size
that they supplied more than enough meat and oil for the
Greenlanders' needs. Salmon came to the river to spawn.

The sheep were ready to be sheared. Now that they were grazing in the field, the eight yearlings had nearly doubled in size. Freydis did not trust Kalf and Orn to do this by themselves and went along to see it was properly done. After the shearing, Freydis bade the thralls wash the wool and spread it on the ground to dry. Now that she was back in the meadow, the cow was giving milk. Freydis drank half the milk and left the rest for Mairi to drink. She had heard the slur about her refusing to give milk for Olina's child and did not want to be blamed should Mairi deliver an unhealthy babe.

Mairi was now big with child. Despite her size she was still hard working. When Mairi washed the men's trenchers and cups, she set them in a wooden rack Ulfar had made. While they were drying, she cleaned the sleeping benches, carrying the bedding from one side to the other, sweeping the cleared platforms thoroughly end to end before setting the bedding to rights. Freydis regarded the girl's diligence as an indication that she preferred living with her to living with the Egilssons. All along, Freydis had intended to send Mairi back to the Icelanders before she and Thorvard returned to Greenland. She did not want Thorvard's ambatt living under her roof in Gardar. With the theft of the ship, Freydis was having second thoughts about this plan. She was against giving the Icelanders anything she found useful herself. There was no doubt about the girl's usefulness. Freydis also liked the fact that Thorvard's ambatt heated her bathing water, dressed her hair and washed her clothes.

Mairi seldom spoke. When addressed she would refuse to reply unless prodded or slapped. Even then she said little. When Freydis bade the girl do some task or other, Mairi gave no indication she had heard except to set about the work. This irked Freydis, particularly since the girl did not lack for words when she came upon Ulfar. Mairi and Ulfar spoke in the Hebridean tongue, which annoyed Freydis further, since she preferred at all times to know what was being said.

Ulfar had made Mairi a wooden bowl and cup for her use as well as a spoon. At meal times after the other men had left the house, Ulfar would linger inside to talk to the girl. At first Freydis was of a mind to stop this mingling. It seemed to her that since Summer had begun and the houses were open that she could not round a corner or come through a doorway without seeing the two thralls together. Lately Freydis had stopped interfering with these meetings since it occurred to her that they might have a useful result. Freydis thought the pair mismatched, that Ulfar was too old and sour faced for the girl, but Freydis had seen unlikely combinations before when thralls were married off to convenience an owner.

*　*　*

Heaven's Lord has heard my plea and softened my heart toward Mairi. By interceding in my prayers he has helped me cast aside the unworthy thoughts I once held toward her and I am now able to see that despite being used as a concubine, Mairi is far worthier of the Lord's attention than I.

Even so my sleeplessness continues. Each night when I retire to my shelter I wrestle with the decision of what I can do to help Mairi. It is my Christian duty to help her. The girl is about to give birth. Should she survive, I have no doubt she will again be used as a concubine. This is a situation I wish to prevent.

When Thorvard returns I will request his permission to marry her. By marrying me Mairi cannot be as easily used as a concubine. Thorvard has come to rely on my skill with wood and would be ill served by going against my will, especially since I am under the protection of Leif and have been promised manumission. Once I am free I can look forward to taking Mairi home to the Hebrides. The difficulty with this arrangement is that I can never lie with Mairi as man to wife since I lack desire in that regard. Whether I should undertake holy matrimony, therefore, is not my decision but God's. Although I have prayed constantly about this matter, I have yet to receive a sign from Him. It may be that Our Lord regards me as unworthy of marriage since I was conceived in sin. I therefore intend to write a full confession of my origin in the hope that Christ will forgive the dishonour of my birth and give me a sign as to how I should proceed.

My father, a Culdean monk, begat me on Eilean Nam Bara as the Danes were butchering the abbot and fifteen monks on the white sands of Iona. After my birth I suffered the humiliation of being brought up solely amongst women and cows. When I was taken across the water to Iona as a young boy, I was much abused by one of the monks, Brother Ofeig, who whipped and scourged me, then forced me to my knees where he used me foully. Later when I was abducted by Harek Eel Swallower, I was often used in the same brutal way. For eight years I endured this and other degradations and am much damaged as a result. It was not until Harek's ship blew off course and ran aground in Herjolfness, Greenland, that my Luck improved somewhat and Harek traded me to Leif Eiriksson in return for timber to repair his ship. It can be said that the only good thing to have come out of the wretched years I spent with Harek was that I became skilled at working wood. When we were not at sea, rowing Harek and his men places where they could rob and plunder innocent folk, we galley slaves were put to work in the woods near Molde in Norway making what Harek called trade goods, though they were hardly that, since what Harek could not obtain through barter, he took by force.

In addition to my origins I must confess to owning a melancholy nature, which causes many folk to avoid me. Moreover, I am sometimes overharsh in my judgements of others. It has occurred to me that with a better nature I might have won more converts to Christ and that I might have let Him down in that regard. Taking these weaknesses altogether, Christ's Lord may consider me unworthy of Mairi. If that is the case,

*I will abide by his Holy Will and give up all thought of
marrying her.*

* * *

Thorvard's absence was into the second month and there
was still no sign of his return. During this time, the barren-
ness of Leifsbudir was transformed by the welcome
colours of rebirth. Pink laurel, cloud berry and blueberry
bushes appeared as did starflowers, twinflowers, strawberries and wintergreen. Angelica flourished by the stream.
Alders and willows were leafing out. Small birds appeared.
Eider ducks came to the low green island which made it
convenient to row out and gather their eggs. The Greenlanders were used to eating birds' eggs raw but Freydis
liked to cook them with butter and milk. Salmon
appeared. They swam upstream in such numbers that the
Greenlanders waded into the water and caught them by
hand. The salmon were dried for the voyage home. Once
the spawning was over, and the days became long and
warm, Freydis would sometimes bathe in the stream. Not
far from the smithy below the grassy ridge was a sheltered
pool she liked to use. When Nagli was away from the
smithy, Freydis would bid Mairi stand watch while she
bathed. Afterwards Mairi would comb Freydis's hair. With
the warm weather, Freydis went about with her hair
unplaited, wearing her lightest shift. She took her loom to
the beach to weave. It was pleasant to stand in the warm
sun, a light breeze riffling her hair. The Greenlanders often
worked on the beach, where the breeze from the water
kept the insects down. Now that Summer was here, the
biting insects appeared in clouds, especially in the meadows and woods.

The beach was where the Greenlanders did most of
their woodwork, carving goods they intended to take
home. Already the men had made a large number of sea
chests, tables and stools. These goods were stored inside
a wooden shelter above the beach. Like Freydis the men
now wore looser clothing. Often they went about stripped
to the waist. When the men wanted to bathe, they swam

in the shallow river mouth. After the drudgery and depriva-
tion of Winter, Freydis regarded her surroundings with satisfaction. Not only was the weather agreeable but there
was more than enough food to go around. In fact there
was more food than could be harvested and taken back to
Greenland. The animals were frisky and healthy. It was a
relief to have made it through Winter without having to eat
all their livestock. Whatever Thorvard's kin might think,
Freydis had managed the year in Leifsbudir well. Knowing
it was her idea, they had scoffed about the wisdom of the
Vinland voyage, but then they often found cause to fault
Freydis for one thing or other.

Freydis seldom ignored their comments but countered
them vigorously with her own. When Thorvard's sisters
found it necessary to remind Freydis how little in the way
of goods she had brought to her marriage, Freydis listed
off the disadvantages of being married to their brother.
When Thorvard's mother took it upon herself to comment
on the sourness of Freydis's cheese, Freydis was quick to
say that the sourness was due to inferior grassland in
Gardar. If Thorvard's father chose to tell Freydis that
Thorlak was sissified and backward, Freydis retorted that
her son took after his grandfather Einar. No doubt when
she and Thorvard returned to Gardar with a ship of their
own, there would be more comments like this from
Thorvard's kin.

As far as Freydis was concerned, Leifsbudir had provided what she had come for: wood cargo and a ship that
would be theirs after Helgi Egilsson returned. Such was
the munificence and comfort of Summer that if Freydis set
the difficulties with the Icelanders aside, she was well
pleased with her situation, including her husband. This
was possible because Thorvard was no longer nearby to
remind her of his faults. Moreover, as his absence from
Leifsbudir lengthened, Freydis began to feel better dis-
posed toward him and often called to mind his strongest
points. Thorvard was a poor farmer and showed little
interest in either his home field or his children, but no one
could match him as a hunter. When it came to courage, it

could never be said that Thorvard avoided risk. During the worst of their stormy crossing, had he not crawled on his hands and knees to save her life? As for his manliness, though far from exciting, he was vigorous and long lasting in bed. The more time Freydis spent waiting for her husband, the sooner she wanted him back, not only because of the theft but because she knew she was with child by Hauk. Her breasts were sore and her belly queasy in the mornings. These tell-tale signs had only recently appeared but were so familiar there was no mistaking their cause. Freydis was disappointed by this turn of events but far from surprised; as Thorvard had said, she was easily got with child. As long as Thorvard returned within the month, there was no danger of him suspecting the child wasn't his. Fortunately she had conceived close enough to their departure for Greenland that the birth could be midwifed by Halla as the others had.

Freydis was near-sighted from close weaving and unable to see far in the distance. It was Hundi who sighted the hunters' pram since he had little to do but sit on the beach and cradle his injured leg. He saw the boat being rowed across the water toward Leifsbudir. The other Greenlanders were soon alerted and put down their tools to watch the hunters' approach. There were five men in the pram. Two of the men had their backs to the watchers so that it was difficult to say exactly who they were, but Thorvard, Evyind and Teit faced the shore and were soon recognized. The watchers began to remark about the unusualness of the hunters' approach. Why would the men arrive in a pram when they had left in a ship? And why were there only five men when thirteen had set out?

Freydis knew before Thorvard set foot on land that something terrible had happened to her brother's ship. At first she thought the *Vinland* might have run aground on some rocks and been abandoned until ship wood and builders could be fetched. That would explain why only five men were returning, since the other men would have remained with the ship. As the hunters neared the shore, Freydis saw that they looked very different from the men who had left. They were gaunt and their hair badly matted; their skin was burnt from sun and wind. The pram landed and the hunters came wearily ashore. The watchers waited, expecting the worst.

"The others are coming by foot," Thorvard said. "They'll be along later today. We took turns walking and rowing. We lost Bodman and Hrollaug. We also lost the ship. It was crushed by pack ice and went down." Having said this, Thorvard made his way to the river, where he pulled off his greasy clothes and fell into the shallow water. The other hunters did the same.

Freydis sent Kalf and Orn to the meadow to slaughter a sheep and set it to roast. Then she went into the weaving shed and lay down, a cold cloth on her forehead. After a time Thorvard came looking for her. By then he was wearing a clean tunic and breeches and had combed his hair. He sat down on the chest beside the sleeping benches and looked at his hands.

"I hear the Icelanders made off with our ship," he said.

"The situation couldn't be much worse," Freydis told him. "We are now much poorer than when we came. Not only will we have to give our new ship to my brother, we may be stranded here longer than we want while the Icelanders harvest oak wood."

"As long as there's a ship here of any kind, we won't be stranded," Thorvard said. "If worse comes to worst, we'll use *Sigurd's Steed*."

"I'm glad to hear you say that." Freydis sat up and took the cloth from her forehead. "Though I've been enjoying the Summer, being away from Greenland another year isn't something I want."

"How long since Helgi and the others left?"

"I make it fifteen days. Finnbogi said he expected Helgi to be gone a month. I told him we'd hold him to that. I said if his brother failed to return after that time we would find another way for him to uphold his part in our agreement. Some of our men wanted to take over *Sigurd's Steed* but I advised against it, since our numbers were too close to theirs to hold the ship."

"You handled matters wisely," Thorvard said. "For the time being we should leave things as they are and see what happens. It seems odd that if the Icelanders went for oak wood, they didn't pass us on the way."

That night the Greenlanders feasted on roast mutton and stewed salmon. The walrus hunters told the tale of the *Vinland*'s end. Asmund was persuaded to recite his new verses over and over again. Afterwards, Freydis took Thorvard to bed in the weaving shed.

Freydis did not hold the loss of the *Vinland* against Thorvard. It was clear from the telling of the tale that Evyind's judgement had been wrong. Now that Thorvard saw for himself how untrustworthy the Egilssons were, Freydis felt more closely bound to him. Moreover, he had returned with ten men, which meant there were now nearly twice as many Greenlanders as Icelanders in Leifsbudir. Despite the difficulties he had faced, Thorvard had brought back a valuable cargo of ivory and walrus hides. Each day Freydis reviewed Thorvard's assets and encouraged him to sleep at her side in the weaving shed.

The fine weather held, which meant the Greenlanders continued to work on the beach where a sea breeze made conditions pleasant. Thorvard and his hunters lay the walrus hide on the sand where they cut and braided it into rope. Nearby, Ulfar turned out more goods on his lathe. As soon as the cleaning and dairying were finished, Freydis went to the beach to weave wadmal, not with sailcloth in mind but for the Greenland trade. From now on, if Helgi wanted sailcloth, he would have to part with some of the oak wood he brought back. Taking everything into consideration it could be said that the Greenlanders made good use of the time they spent waiting for Helgi's return. They reminded themselves that even if their ship had not been stolen, it would remain anchored in the bay; it was too soon to make the crossing, since the Greenland fjords would still be blocked with ice. It therefore made sense to turn as much wood as possible into useful items; they would never have so much wood at their disposal again.

Not only did the fine weather improve the men's dispositions, but the varying food supply helped as well. Flounder appeared in the cove and were trapped in trenches. Lobsters were easily caught among the rocks. Strawberries began to ripen. As a result of this bounty and the fineness of the weather, many Greenlanders besides Freydis were prepared to overlook the absence of grapes so that they might believe they were enjoying the Vinland Leif had described. They lacked little in the way of comfort and couldn't imagine a life much better than this. It was true they had endured a hard Winter, whereas Leif's Winter here had been mild. It was also true they lacked wine as well as honey and nuts. On the other hand, the Summer was much hotter than Leif had mentioned it being, which lulled them into thinking they were living in his promised land.

After Helgi had been gone a month, Freydis told Thorvard she thought they should visit Finnbogi. At first Thorvard was against the visit, saying he preferred to give Helgi more time. He said Helgi and his men might have been delayed by foul weather, as he himself had been. Freydis argued that the main purpose in visiting Finnbogi was to warn him that if Helgi failed to return early enough for the Greenlanders to make a crossing this season, they would expect to use *Sigurd's Steed*. Since her last visit to the Icelanders, Freydis had not spoken to Finnbogi. She had seen little of the Icelanders except for the dwarf twins, who now hauled all of their water.

One evening Freydis and Thorvard went across the terrace in search of Finnbogi. Alof met them at the door and told them that Finnbogi was on the beach. By this she meant a beach to the east of the brothers' house. This beach was stonier than the one the Greenlanders enjoyed, but it had the advantage for the Icelanders of being out of the Greenlanders' sight. Freydis and Thorvard saw Finnbogi sitting with his ambatt on a driftwood log. Olina made no move to leave when Freydis and Thorvard approached. The Greenlanders were forced to visit standing up, which added to the unfriendliness of the situation.

Freydis began by reminding Finnbogi that a month had passed since his brother had gone to fetch wood in the Greenlanders' ship. To this Finnbogi replied that he was expecting his brother's arrival any day now.

"It had better be soon," Freydis told him. "My husband and I have decided that if our ship isn't returned at our convenience, we'll have no choice but to use yours."

Finnbogi laughed.

"You keep referring to my brother using your ship when in fact it hasn't been given to you yet."

"You must be joking," Freydis said. "You know as well as I do that the ship was built for us and not your brother. We Greenlanders know that your brother was holding out for a ship of oak."

"Maybe my brother changed his mind and decided to build his ship first. Maybe the ship isn't yours at all." Finnbogi looked at Thorvard. "I believe you still owe us ivory and rope for your concubine."

This angered Thorvard. He had no intention of handing the Icelanders any more goods except what was required for the second ship. "I can see by your foolish talk that you like to play games with honest folk. I advise you to be more sensible in what you say."

Finnbogi's ambatt began to laugh.

Freydis turned to Thorvard. "We might as well leave. It's clear we'll get nowhere talking to these thieves." Before she and Thorvard left, Freydis gave Finnbogi a warning, "Never let it be said, Finnbogi Egilsson, that you weren't given the opportunity to deal fairly with us."

The next afternoon when Freydis and Thorvard were working on the beach, Thrand and Teit came up to them and said that while they were searching for mussels among the rocks, they saw the Icelanders remove the sail and oars from *Sigurd's Steed* and carry them into the Icelanders' house.

"It appears someone besides ourselves is troubled by Helgi's absence," Thorvard remarked.

Despite Finnbogi's stiff-necked refusal to lend his ship, the Greenlanders continued to enjoy the Summer, though

not so much as they had before. Each day they scanned
the bay for some sign of their ship, only to see an empty
blue. In another month the Greenlanders would be
approaching that part of the Summer where it would be
almost a year since their departure from Einarsfjord. Now
the wild lilies were flowering and the laurel was fully
bloomed. The weather was so warm that the gooseberries
near the woods would soon be ready for harvesting and
the meadow was orange with ripe cloud berries. The
Greenlanders were especially pleased with the abundance
of cloud berries which grew sparsely in their country.
Cloud berries were known to grow in Norway, as well as in
the land of the Finns. The Finns found many uses for the
fruit, including the making of a powerful drink. There were
so many cloud berries in Leifsbudir that Freydis sent a
large number of Greenlanders to the meadow with buckets. She wanted to make sure the Greenlanders got what
they wanted before the Icelanders started to pick.
Apparently the Icelanders did their berry picking elsewhere for they could be seen carrying their buckets and
bowls along the shore to the east. Freydis and Mairi covered themselves with seal oil to prevent insects from biting and went out to pick with the rest. By now Mairi was so
large she couldn't stoop to pick but squatted on her
haunches. From the girl's shape and size Freydis judged
the babe was overdue. Several days earlier she had bade
Mairi sweep the compartment in the end house where
Freydis had slept all Winter. The sleeping benches were
scrubbed and covered with clean wadmal. A bucket of
water was set on the floor. The eiderdown pillows Freydis
had recently made for taking back to Greenland were laid
out along with clean cloths, moss and a sharpened knife.

One afternoon when Freydis and Mairi were berrying in
the meadow, water gushed from between the girl's legs.
Freydis and Mairi made their way back to the terrace
where Freydis urged the girl to walk about until the pains
grew strong. Freydis had followed this advice herself.
Though Halla had never borne children, it had been her
contention that birthing went more smoothly if a mother

walked out the early pain. While Freydis served the meal, Mairi walked back and forth in the small space between the storage hut and the shed. Freydis urged those Greenlanders who slept in the end house to bed down in the middle house if they expected to get any sleep. The men needed no urging to stay out of the way of the birthing; they knew such matters were better left in the hands of women. When the meal was finished and Louse Oddi and Kalf were set to tidying and cleaning, Freydis returned to Mairi. The girl was still walking, though more slowly. Freydis fetched a spindle and stood outside spinning where she could watch the girl. Every few paces Mairi stopped, wiped the sweat from her forehead and looked about. When she saw Freydis spinning, the girl put out her hand and asked to spin. The request surprised Freydis on two counts. The first was that the girl spoke without urging and the second was that she expected to spin; thralls were discouraged from spinning or weaving since those tasks were the work of the woman who ran the house. But this was hardly the time to rebuke the girl. Freydis gave Mairi the spindle without a word. The girl had an odd way of spinning, running the spindle the length of her outstretched arm, which she must have learned as a child. Freydis fetched another spindle and the two women spun until darkness fell. By that time a fire was burning inside the large room of the end house, and Mairi continued walking there.

Toward midnight the girl's pains were coming in rapid succession. Freydis sent her into the compartment. She removed Mairi's shift and helped the girl onto the bed. Freydis took up the knife and passed it three times over the swollen belly to cut the pain. Next she gave the thrall a drink brewed from some green leaves she had collected in the meadow. Halla had used these same leaves when Freydis was in childbirth to ease the pain. While Mairi drank the bitter liquid, Freydis knotted together three cloths so that when the spasms came, the girl could hold the knotted cloths between her teeth and bite.

Many times during the night Mairi bit this cloth. When the pains became monumental, she dropped the cloths and screamed. The girl became so pale and sickly looking that Freydis began to think she might die before giving birth. Her groans were so deep they seemed to be coming not from Mairi's throat but from somewhere deep inside. Mairi's body was speaking: it was saying it could do no more; the girl was too small, the child too large. Mairi lifted her head to one side and vomited on the floor. Freydis wiped her mouth with a cloth.

"I bore three children and here I am," Freydis said. But the girl was beyond encouragement or comprehension. Freydis thought of the dangers involved in birthing folk, how many women died, how many babes. People were born at enormous risk. It was Luck that delivered folk alive.

At dawn Mairi began to gasp and push and Freydis saw a white head tear the edges of the birth hole.

"I believe your efforts are about to be rewarded," Freydis said. She placed a clean sheepskin between the girl's legs and raised the pillows. Still the head did not come out; it appeared to be stuck. Freydis had never midwifed a birth, but she knew enough to reach in as Halla had done with Thorlak, and grab hold of the head. Several times Freydis's hands slid off the head before she could get the babe unstuck. On the fifth try she got hold of the chin and pulled it out. When the head appeared through the swollen lips, Freydis saw that it was encased in a caul.

"Push harder," Freydis said.

Mairi gave a grinding push and the shoulders emerged, followed quickly by the rest. Freydis caught the child in the sheepskin. It was bluish grey, like the half-frozen corpse of an old man Freydis had come upon once in Dyrnes, but the head was white, because of the caul.

"It appears you have a son who will be lucky," Freydis said, "for he has been born with a caul." When she removed the caul, Freydis saw a blue spot on the child's forehead but she had no idea what that might mean. She

cut the birth cord and held the child upside down, smack-
ing it on the backside as she had seen Halla do.

The babe screamed redly. Freydis wiped him clean,
wrapped him in the sheepskin and gave him to Mairi.
Freydis was pleased to be able to hand her a healthy
child. She was so well pleased that any resentments and
grudges she bore Mairi fell easily away. While the babe
tried to suckle, Freydis pushed her hand against Mairi's
belly until the afterbirth oozed out. Freydis threw the mess
into a bucket. She washed Mairi clean and packed moss
between her legs. Then she went to the weaving shed and
crawled into bed beside Thorvard.

"It appears you now have another son," she said.

Thorvard grunted; he was half-asleep. He had taken the
outcome for granted. Because his children's births had
been straightforward, he had never thought them remark-
able in any way. In this, he was like other men he knew.
Staying alive required such risks that folk were rarely
grateful for being birthed.

Within days Mairi was back on her feet and going about
her usual tasks, though now she was more slow than
quick. While she worked, she kept the babe strapped to
her back. Sometimes the girl sang to the babe as he suckled. She sang in the same tongue she used to speak to
Ulfar. Ulfar seemed much pleased with the babe. Freydis
often saw him fussing and smiling over the child which
gave Freydis reason to think he might have somehow
managed to be its sire. The babe did not resemble Ulfar in
the least, or Thorvard for that matter, being black haired
and pale like his mother.

Seven nights after the birth when Thorvard and Freydis
lay abed, Thorvard told Freydis that while he had been
making rope on the beach that morning, Ulfar approached
him with a request to have Mairi as wife.

"What did you tell him?"

"I told him I would think about it, that there was the
matter of the agreement I made with Helgi to consider
since in the first instance Mairi had belonged to him not
me."

"I hardly think that agreement counts for anything now. In my opinion, we should keep Mairi for now at least. I'm against giving the Egilssons anything that might be useful to us. There's also something to be gained by giving Ulfar what he wants. He's close to manumission. As a free man he could look after Mairi and the babe without cost to us. If we refuse Ulfar, then you'll have to support the child." Freydis patted her belly. "Unless I'm mistaken, we have another under way."

Thorvard accepted this news with the same matter-of-factness he had accepted the birth of Mairi's son.

Thorvard told Freydis that her points about Ulfar's marriage to Mairi were well made but he wanted to give the matter more thought. No one knew better than Freydis how long it took Thorvard to make a decision. She was shrewd enough to drop the matter and was pleased when several days later, Thorvard mentioned in passing that he had told Ulfar that as far as he was concerned, Ulfar might have Mairi to wed if he chose. Thorvard said Ulfar asked him to make a mark in ink on a piece of sheepskin as proof of good intent. According to Ulfar, by marking the vellum Thorvard was promising that when they returned to Greenland, Ulfar could have Mairi to wife.

Freydis wanted to know if Thorvard had made the mark.

"Why not? It seemed a small request."

"I distrust scratchings on sheepskin," Freydis said. "There might be something about the mark that can be used against you later on."

"I hardly think it matters one way or the other," Thorvard said. "We made no scratchings on sheepskin for the Icelanders and look at the mess we're in."

"Will you hold to that agreement once Helgi is back?"

"I've decided that considering the theft of our ship, even when it's returned, Mairi will be ours by compensation."

* * *

*I am now sleeping soundly at night for I made peace
with myself at last. I am not the same man. How foolish I was. Although Heaven's Lord gave us His Son as
a sign, such was the narrowness of my vision that it
did not occur to me that the sign Our Lord would send
me would be Mairi's child. After Mairi was safely delivered of a son, I was permitted to see him in her arms.
I had seen mothers and bairns before, but burdened
as I was by my own misfortunes I had refused to look
closely at them. My mother's sin had blinded me to
the virtues of women. When I saw Mairi with the bairn,
the bindings fell from my eyes and I saw in her the
purity and devotion of Our Holy Mother. This is not to
say I regarded her as some Popist goddess, but that I
was acknowledging the goodness of motherhood and
in so doing was at last able to forgive my poor mother
for birthing me. I confess that I wept when I thought
of her looking at me with the purity and devotion I
saw in Mairi's eyes. This was a great release for me. I
knew then that Our Lord had purged me so that I
might better serve Mairi and the bairn. I understood
that it was because I was free of carnal lust that I had
been chosen by Him to lead her from bondage by
marrying her.*

*Thorvard has given his consent to the marriage,
which can be sanctified by Geirmund when we return
to Greenland. My agreement with Thorvard is in writing. I took this precaution in the event that when Helgi
Egilsson returns, he will try to reclaim Mairi. Thorvard
assures me that if this should happen, he will not
trade her back, since the Icelanders have treated him
and Freydis poorly, stealing their ship and refusing to
lend them Sigurd's Steed. Mairi has named the bairn
Jon after her father. My greatest pleasure is to watch
her as she holds the child to her breast, for it is then
her face becomes radiant in a way that convinces me
that at last the Holy Mother has found favour in me.*

* * *

The Greenlanders continued to enjoy unusually warm weather; they had never known a Summer so warm. The fact that Summer could not go on much longer heightened their enjoyment, since it is the nature of folk to increase their grip on something pleasant when they know it will soon be taken away. Gradually the daylight shortened and the season of cloud berries and gooseberries passed. As the nights lengthened, blueberries and cranberries ripened, with low bush partridge berries close behind. Fireweed and goldenrod appeared near the woods. Salmon and flounder grew scarce but cod was still plentiful. A second month passed and there was still no sign of Helgi Egilsson and his crew.

The Greenlanders had finished readying their cargo. Many of their trade goods were stored inside the middle house, where it would be more convenient for loading a ship. The cargo included a large selection of trenchers, cups and bowls. There were carved chests and stools, trestle tables, posts and beams. As well, there was a large supply of spruce planking which had many uses at home. Greenlanders were always on the lookout for wood that could be used to make a sleeping bench or mend a pram. Ozur had woven a variety of baskets and wicker cages. Stored inside these items were coils of walrus rope, as well as the toys Thorvard had made. The cargo included tubs of whale and seal oil, bundles of sealskins and reindeer hides, a leather bag containing white seal foetuses from which Freydis planned to make foot and hand warmers. Another leather bag contained eiderdown for making pillows. There were rolls of tablet weaving which Freydis had made during Winter, as well as several lengths of cloth. There was a store of reindeer bone which had been carved into combs, spoons and gaming pieces, and two bags of walrus ivory. In addition to this there were vats of berries and bundles of dried cod and salmon.

Since all the maple and birch wood harvested earlier had been used to make trade goods, the Greenlanders grew restless as to what they should do next to add to the cargo, all the more so when the weather began to cool slightly and they were less inclined to spend time lying about on the beach. Now a discussion began as to whether or not they should build themselves prams. Though the Greenlanders lacked the knowledge to build a sea-going ship, they had always been able to make a pram of sorts. With an endless supply of wood and Ulfar's skill they could now build a superior boat. Evyind pointed out that if the return crossing was smooth, they could use these prams to tow cargo behind the ship and in that way take back more wood than they could otherwise. Freydis encouraged the building of the prams on the basis that the more goods they could take away from Leifsbudir the better, since it was doubtful they would come back this way. Once they arrived in Greenland, their ship would have to be given to Leif as recompense for the *Vinland*. Sometimes when she looked over the trade goods stored inside the middle house, Freydis was disappointed. The goods had been put together on the assumption that the Greenlanders would be returning home with two ships instead of one. It might be that some of this cargo would have to be left behind. Freydis brooded over the loss of the *Vinland*, not so much dreading what her brother might say—Leif would be quick to see that the loss of the old ship would result in him owning a newer one—but because she knew the prospects for becoming a shipown-er herself were dashed. She and Thorvard would never be able to take their goods to Norway but would have to trade them through someone else.

As the evenings lengthened, taking on the chill of the waning Summer, the Greenlanders gathered around their indoor fires at night and discussed how they would return to Greenland. Freydis pointed out that the time had passed when Helgi could expect to build himself a ship and sail it across the ocean this season.

"When he returns, he may expect to hold on to our ship until his is finished," she said. "In which case we'll be forced to remain here another year."

To a man the Greenlanders were against this idea; they saw the glaciered mountains of their country, the green steadings at their feet, the maidens and mothers beside the fjord awaiting their return. Again Bragi urged the Greenlanders to take over *Sigurd's Steed*.

Now Freydis encouraged this talk. She had come round to thinking that even if Helgi returned shortly with the *Greenland Trader*, she would prefer to make the crossing in *Sigurd's Steed*. Finnbogi's ship was much larger than the new one, which meant they could take more cargo.

"With our numbers nearly twice the Icelanders here, it shouldn't be too difficult to take over *Sigurd's Steed*."

"Unless Finnbogi refuses to hand it over," Thorvard said, "in which case the takeover might result in a fight. I for one don't want Icelanders' blood on my hands." He turned first to Evyind, then to Uni and Ivar, asking each in turn how much longer the Greenlanders could wait and still expect to make a safe crossing. The helmsmen agreed they had less than a month; after that came the season of storms.

"The days are getting shorter," Freydis reminded them. "We must make the crossing before the nights grow too long."

"I'm willing to give Helgi Egilsson some more time to return our ship," Thorvard said. "We hunters know the difficulties and setbacks men face when they travel in strange waters and appreciate it when those who are waiting for us take that into account."

"Has it occurred to you that Finnbogi himself might leave?" Freydis said. "That we might wake up one morning and find *Sigurd's Steed* gone?"

No one else admitted thinking this. Now that the idea had been expressed, the men agreed on the likeliness of it happening. Bragi said that it was fortunate Freydis bore the leadership qualities of her father for it convinced him that the Greenlanders' fate was in strong hands. Encouraged by this remark, Freydis went on to say that from now on, the Greenlanders should post a watch on the Icelanders day and night so that if they were seen doing anything suspicious, the Greenlanders would know about it right away.

The men posted to watch soon noticed how far the Icelanders went out of their way to avoid the Greenlanders. If the Greenlanders rowed to the place where the Icelanders were fishing, the Icelanders quickly moved off. If the Greenlanders were searching for shell-fish along the shore, the Icelanders would search some-where else.

While they waited for Helgi Egilsson to return, the Greenlanders went to the ship cove and cut spruce wood which they dressed for prams. When the pram building was under way, Thorvard announced he had a mind to go bear hunting, for he had seen bear scat here and there. Not only would bear provide good eating at this time of year, but black pelts were much sought after in Iceland. Moreover with the cooler evenings, the biting insects were falling off. Teit and Thrand were particularly eager to try their hands at bear hunting; they had never done it before. So it was that while the new boats were being built, Thorvard took a small party of hunters in a pram each day and rowed a short distance southeast to where the land was thickly wooded and bear more plentiful. Remembering what had happened in the Bay of Maples, Thorvard preferred hunting in from the shore so that he was never far from his boat. It was in the southeast direc-tion that some tale tellers said Thorvald Eiriksson had been buried after he had been killed by a skraeling arrow. Thorvard did not entirely believe this version of the tale, since he had also been told that Thorvald's grave was in Markland. He thought both tales should probably be equally disbelieved, since neither of them had been told by men who had been with Thorvald when he died. Even so, both tales spoke of meeting skraelings.

It could be said that the bear hunt hastened the Greenlanders' departure from Leifsbudir since it brought another encounter with skraelings. This encounter, which came to be known as *The Tale of Thrand Ozursson's Abduction*, proved that the skraelings knew the woods near Leifsbudir very well. Although the skraelings appeared to be more peaceful than warlike, their presence increased the dangers, since the Greenlanders, not being peaceful themselves, were far from convinced they were safe from attack.

* * *

The Tale of Thrand Ozursson's Abduction

ONE DAY IN LATE SUMMER, THORVARD EINARSSON TOOK SOME men and went bear hunting near Leifsbudir. He had seen bear scat earlier and thought to take some pelts back to Greenland for trade. Thorvard and six men took their axes and spears and rowed southeast. Among their number were two young men, Thrand Ozursson and Teit Evyindsson, who were new to bear hunting.

The first day out the men killed two bears easily, wounding the bears with an axe while they were feeding, then spearing them in the chests. The next day the men killed three more bears and brought back a live black cub. It was Thorvard's intention to capture a white cub in Greenland later on so that he would have a cub of each colour to trade. The third day the hunters killed a sixth bear. Each day the men went out, they rowed further south and walked more deeply into the woods, though not so deeply that they were far from shore. On the fourth day, the hunters picked up the trail of a very large bear and, forgetting their caution, followed it longer than they had before. By the time the bear was treed, the men were deeper in the woods than they liked. It was Thrand's turn to throw the axe to wound the bear. This he did. For the next while, the hunters were occupied with killing the bear and did not see Thrand disappear. The abduction was done with such stealth and cunning, the skraelings might not have been seen at all had Thorvard not looked up just as Thrand was being carried away. Thorvard knew by their red skins who the captors were. Exhorting his hunters to follow, he immediately gave chase.

The skraelings easily outran the hunters and soon disappeared from sight. The Greenlanders followed their trail until they came to a stream. The hunters saw that the woods on the opposite side had been broken in several places to confuse them as to which trail they should take. "It's clear to me that we would be foolish to go any further today," Thorvard said. "It's obvious the skraelings know these woods. They may also be better armed, since we have brought only axes and spears." The men returned to Leifsbudir before dark.

The next day the men resumed their search, carrying bows and arrows. They spent all day in the woods but found no trace of Thrand. Their third day out, they rowed far to the South, thinking the skraelings might have camped by the sea. There was no sign of Thrand, and the searchers returned to Leifsbudir empty-handed. The search for Thrand Ozursson was never resumed.

* * *

Whenever this tale was retold, some of the Greenlanders, Thorvard among them, expressed the view that the skraelings must have been watching the bear hunt from the beginning, waiting until such time as they could carry off someone. Thorvard said he thought the skraelings recognized Thrand as the one who had thrown the axe which had stunned the skraeling seal thief and led to his death.

"It's my opinion that the skraelings may have abducted Thrand to replace the one we killed, for had they wanted to kill Thrand they could have done so on the spot. Or they could have taken me, since I did the killing. Instead they took Thrand, who is the same size and age as the seal thief."

Not all of the Greenlanders shared this view. Thrand's father, Ozur, said his son had probably been taken for the purpose of thralldom. He said he hoped the skraelings treated thralls better than the Greenlanders did. Though she remained silent, Freydis couldn't help thinking that Thrand might have brought misfortune upon himself dur-

ing Winter when he made the foolish remark about eating
Groa's corpse.

Now that the weather was cooler, Freydis no longer
bathed in the stream but took her bath inside the shed.
One morning, after Freydis had gotten out of the bath and
was drying herself, a twig fell into the tub from the alder
roof. The twig was small, no larger than a bone needle or
a sliver of wood. The twig bobbed in the tub. Freydis
leaned over and splashed the water with her hand so she
could watch the twig bounce on the waves. The twig
reminded Freydis of a ship in the expanse of water they
had to cross in order to return to Greenland.

Considering the endless stretch of sea and the
unknowableness of the world, Freydis's dreams rested on
a twig even smaller than this. Men like her father and Leif
had gone upon the sea knowing survival was precarious
and dependent on risks. Freydis knew there was no other
choice now but to put the twig in the water and hope the
gods would carry it to Greenland. She was unwilling to
stay here any longer without her children since her intention in coming to Leifsbudir was meant to better their
position and she could hardly do that with a sea between
them. Freydis held the twig under but as soon as she
removed her hand, it bounced up again. She did it again
and laughed at the twig's refusal to sink. Death wasn't so
easy after all. This had not been her mother's view, but
then her mother had been weak minded enough to go
looking for death. Of all the things a woman could do with
her life, Freydis thought this was the most foolhardy since
death found everyone soon enough without being met
halfway.

That night Freydis's bloody dream returned. Again she
was a Valkyrie flying over the fields of the slain with a
broad axe. Whenever she saw one of the slain move, or
crawl toward the water, she would swoop down and cleave
his head. In the water was *Sigurd's Steed*. There were
Greenlanders on the ship, even Bolli was there. They were
waving at Freydis, encouraging her to come aboard, but
Freydis had to clean up the mess on the shore; she

couldn't board the ship until all the slain were tidied. Freydis had this dream well before morning. She awoke and sat up, waiting for the dream to fade. When it did, she lay down and went back to sleep. By morning she had forgotten the dream.

But she had made a decision that the time to return to Greenland was now. Her children were waiting for her and she was pregnant; she refused to stay in Leifsbudir one day longer than it took to ready the ship. If Finnbogi wouldn't give up the ship today, the Greenlanders would seize it. By staying here any longer, both sides would lose this Summer's crossing. There was no point in everyone missing out. She would go to see Finnbogi now without her husband; Thorvard might tell Finnbogi the Greenlanders would wait a little longer for Helgi's return, which would be a mistake. The *Greenland Trader* had been gone two and a half months which meant the Icelanders were long overdue. Why should the Greenlanders continue to wait?

Thorvard was still asleep. It was easy for Freydis to slip away without him knowing. She got out of bed and put on her clothes, but not her shoes. They were too far under the bench to reach without disturbing Thorvard. Freydis took her husband's cloak, wrapped it about her and went outside. A heavy dew lay on the grass, wetting her feet. She walked over to the brothers' house, to the door. Someone had gone outside earlier and left the door ajar: she pushed it open and stood in the entrance a while without saying a word.

Finnbogi was lying at the innermost end of the hall. He was awake. "What do you want here, Freydis?"

"I want you to get up and come outside with me," she replied. "I want to talk to you."

To her surprise—she had expected him to refuse—Finnbogi got up. When he appeared, Finnbogi indicated the log bench beside the house, but Freydis pointed to the beach where she and Thorvard had met with him earlier. Finnbogi made no objection and they walked to the beach and sat on the driftwood log.

"How are you getting on these days?" Freydis said. She was determined to get off on the right foot by speaking politely.

"I've enjoyed the Summer. Everything considered, it's a good country," Finnbogi said jovially. "But I dislike the ill feeling that exists between us. When you get right down to it, there's no reason for it."

Freydis was so amazed by Finnbogi's response that she was tempted to take his words at face value. She was about to say, "I can certainly tell you the reason," but she checked herself and said, "You are quite right, and I feel the same as you do." It occurred to her that Finnbogi was playing the same polite game as she. It also occurred to her that she and Finnbogi could sit on this log all morning saying polite things to each other without anything being resolved and that this was exactly what Finnbogi intended. Although Freydis was willing to exchange polite greetings, she was unwilling to give up more time to pleasantries than this, since after the Greenlanders took over the ship, it would take a day or two to make it ready for departure.

"As you've probably guessed, the reason I came to see you is because I want you to exchange ships with us so that we can return to Greenland this season," Freydis said.

Finnbogi turned to her and said, "I'll agree to that, if it will make you happy."

Freydis was confused by this pretence of politeness but resolved to continue.

"Very well," she said. "Then perhaps you would be good enough to fetch the sail and oars, for we have it in mind to leave for Greenland as soon as we're ready."

"Of course," Finnbogi said, "anything you say."

Freydis stood up. "I'll send some of my men over to get them."

Finnbogi stood up as well.

Just then an Icelander walked past carrying a bucket of fish. It had been he who had left the door open when he had risen early to jig for cod; while they had been talking he had been rowing his pram ashore.

"Ho, Gudlaug," Finnbogi said to him. "When you go inside, fetch the sail and oars, will you? This woman wants to take our ship to Greenland."

At this Gudlaug wrinkled up his brow and looked perplexed. "What's this? Some sort of joke?" He had been with Finnbogi for years and knew the Icelander would never give up his ship.

"Indeed it is." Finnbogi laughed. "But as you know, Greenlanders are so gullible they'll fall for anything."

"How dare you trifle with the fate of others!" Freydis screamed. She rushed at Finnbogi and beat him with her fists. Finnbogi took several blows before Gudlaug managed to pull her away and throw her onto the stony beach.

Finnbogi looked down at her. "You are a virago and a battle axe, Freydis Eiriksdottir, but you don't frighten me." He kicked her in the belly. "Now get away from here and quickly for the sight of you makes me retch."

Freydis gave no outward sign that her belly was hurting. She knew that any sign of weakness on her part would be met with scorn.

Before Finnbogi could turn away, she got to her feet and said, "I came here to give you a chance to make things fair between us. Since you've chosen to mock and abuse me, you can expect the worst to happen. I doubt my husband will put up with your dirty tricks much longer."

"It's well known that your husband is a weakling," Finnbogi said. "I doubt he'll be any match for me."

This was said to Freydis's back, since by then she had started walking to the Greenlanders' houses.

By the time she reached the shed, Freydis was trembling more from anger than from cold. She got into bed with Thorvard who was now awake. He asked her why her feet were cold. Weeping and snuffling, Freydis told Thorvard her side of the story, emphasizing that not only had she been abused but she had been insulted. She told him Finnbogi had kicked her in the belly and might have harmed the babe. Freydis wanted to incite all of Thorvard's righteous anger. She also wanted to prevent him from asking why she had not wakened him so they could have talked to Finnbogi together rather than approaching him on her own. Freydis aroused Thorvard's anger so well that there was no need to threaten him with divorce if he refused to avenge Finnbogi's wrongdoing.

Thorvard knew as well as Freydis how intolerable matters were and that something would have to be done. He was unwilling to wait any longer for the return of the Greenlanders' ship. This time it wasn't a question of Freydis's overstepping herself by being high-handed, which Thorvard had seen happen too often before. There was far more at stake than avenging Freydis's humiliation.

Considering everything that had taken place between the Icelanders and Greenlanders in Leifsbudir, Freydis had been within her rights to request the use of *Sigurd's Steed*. The fact that Finnbogi had shown nothing but scorn toward Freydis's proposition clearly proved he had no intention of relinquishing the ship and would continue to hold the fate of the Greenlanders in his hands. That Finnbogi could be so craven and narrow in his thinking disgusted Thorvard. As a hunter, he was used to men helping one another, even when it meant great risk to themselves. It was true that Thorvard had been slower than Freydis to see the lengths to which Finnbogi was prepared to go to get his way, but now that he saw them, Thorvard decided to remedy the situation at once. He knew from the grumbling and discontent of his men that they were more than ready to take over the ship. He also knew there would be bloodshed, since the Icelanders would fight hard to keep themselves on the winning side. Thorvard would do his best to capture rather than kill the Icelanders; except for Finnbogi, he regarded the Icelanders as not much different from himself.

Thorvard got up, dressed quickly and picked up his broad axe. Then he roused the Greenlanders in the end house and bid them arm themselves with axes and knives.

"There's dirty work in store for us if we're to take over the ship and it's best dealt with now and quietly," he told each in turn.

The Greenlanders in the middle house were roused in the same way, which was to say with stealth so as to have surprise on their side. As Thorvard rightly guessed from the careless way Finnbogi had treated Freydis, he would not be expecting the Greenlanders to attack. He had probably gone back to bed. This in fact was the case.

Thorvard had twenty-two men in all. Ozur preferred to remain behind with the injured Hundi and the thralls. Nagli refused to take sides and remained in the smithy. The thralls were considered unreliable fighters since they lacked good reasons to fight. The Greenlanders were able to sneak up on the Icelanders' house and catch all eighteen Icelanders by surprise. When the Greenlanders burst through the doorway, they seized a number of men who were still sleeping in the main room. The plan was to drag the men outside and bind their feet and hands so they would not interfere with the Greenlanders' plan to take the sail and oars. Finnbogi was not among them. Because he was sleeping with Olina in the small room at the end of the passageway, he managed to get up and arm himself without being seen. While the Greenlanders were either harrying the Icelanders inside the middle room or chasing down those Icelanders who had escaped outside, Finnbogi and his ambatt were able to make their way along the passageway and out the door.

Now that she had incited her husband and the others to battle, Freydis wanted to see for herself that the Icelanders were on the losing side. She picked up a wood axe and went outside. As an afterthought she went back into the shed and picked up a loom weight. Several days ago her loom had been taken apart and its frame strapped together for the voyage home. The weights were piled on the floor beside the frame wood, not far from the door. Freydis went outside again and crossed the terrace to the Icelanders' side. As she was approaching the house, Finnbogi and Olina came through the doorway. Catching

sight of Freydis they ducked around the eastern side of
the house and headed for the beach. Freydis knew they
would try to reach the ship.

"Stop them!" she shouted. She thought of hurling the
loom weight at Finnbogi, but he was too far away for the
stone to reach its mark. She shouted again. Several
Greenlanders, including Thorvard, were already on the
beach chasing down three Icelanders who were also heading for the ship. Thorvard and Glam broke away from the
chase and went after Finnbogi. Both the Greenlanders
were swifter moving than the Icelander and soon caught
up to him and cleaved his skull. At this a wail went up
from Olina. She turned, and seeing Freydis on the terrace,
ran past Finnbogi's killers toward her. Unmindful of being
poorly armed—she was carrying a stick of firewood—Olina
charged Freydis. Freydis lifted her axe and prepared to
strike, but Olina's fury won out. She brought the firewood
against the side of Freydis's head before Freydis could use
her axe. Freydis was momentarily stunned by the blow,
though not so stunned that she lost her feet. With a yell
she lifted her axe and brought it down on Olina's skull.
Olina fell to the ground, her head split open. Freydis
looked at Olina's corpse with a mixture of wonder and satisfaction.

She had never seen a human skull split in two and
marvelled at the blood welling up like a spring. The blood
continued to bubble and leak in such a way that Freydis
was transfixed. In an instant Olina seemed to have
become part of the earth; her robe was a clump of rough
grass, her head a hewn rock, blooming with crimson flowers. Soon a tree would spring up from the cleft. Freydis
was amazed by the finality of what she had done and
exhilarated by the power of the axe. She wiped the axe on
her robe and looked around for something else to do. She
saw Bodvar and Falgeir chasing two Icelanders across the
meadow. She saw Falgeir swing his axe and throw it at the
Icelanders. It caught one of them between the shoulders
and he fell on his face. Behind Freydis two Greenlanders,
Gisli and Balki, came out of the Icelanders' house, carry-

ing the mast. Freydis turned to watch the men and caught sight of Alof, cowering behind a pile of firewood outside the door. Before Alof could run away, Freydis threw the loom weight and stunned her. Alof fell to one side. Freydis went over and cleaved her skull.

Thorvard came up to Freydis and grabbed her by the arm.

"Enough is enough," he said. Freydis looked at him strangely. Her head was tilted forward so that her hair fell loosely around it. She looked out, pale eyed and unseeing, as if her sight was locked onto something far away. Thorvard was alarmed by the emptiness of her stare.

He who had killed animals by the hundreds thought his wife might go on killing unless stopped. He took the axe away from her.

"We have the sail and oars," he said. "Some Icelanders are still on the loose but as soon as they've been caught and bound, we'll begin readying the ship for our departure. Go back to the shed and bolt the door."

"What about the mess?" Freydis said. "Shouldn't I be clearing it away?"

Freydis could see herself flying above a battlefield of bloodied corpses, picking up the slain and carrying them off, tidying up the dead.

The last question disturbed Thorvard enough that he took Freydis to the shed himself. He opened the door, shoved her inside and told her to bolt the door.

Freydis did as she was told. Then she lay down. She was no sooner in bed than she remembered Thorvard had taken her axe. She took the small knife she always kept handy and placed it on the bed along with several loom weights. She wanted to be ready should any of the Icelanders come banging on her door.

None of the Icelanders made it as far as the weaving shed. Thrasi was killed as he left the house. Halldor was dragged from beneath an overturned pram and killed. Aesrod was killed before he got very far—it was he Freydis had seen being killed—but Aevar got halfway across the meadow before he was caught.

The Icelanders Gudlaug, Hrapp and Eystein started swimming and were halfway to the ship when the Greenlanders caught up with them in a pram. All three men resisted being hauled into the boat. They were hit over the head, and drowned. As a result of all this scattering, rounding up the Icelanders proved more difficult and bloodier than Thorvard had intended. Karl and Solvi indicated they would rather fight to the death than be bound, which meant they had to be killed. During the melee they had managed to arm themselves with axes and spears. The two Icelanders fought strongly and held out for some time. They killed Oddmar and wounded Bragi in the arm before being brought down.

When the slaughter was over, five Icelanders were held captive along with three thralls. These were Mani and the dwarf twins, Svart and Surt. The captives were bound hand and foot and carried inside the Icelanders' house; Hogni and Avang were set to guard. Then Thorvard and several others gathered up the dead and rowed them along the shore where they piled up stones to make their graves. Thorvard took the trouble to do this, knowing Leif would be displeased to have slain corpses buried nearby. Finnbogi and Olina were buried first. When the last stone was put on their grave, Ivar remarked that the Greenlanders were well rid of the pair. No one disagreed. Karl and Solvi, the two Icelanders who had fought to the bitter end, however, were praised for their courage and bravery before they were covered. The Greenlander, Oddmar received the most praise, for he had in all ways proved stalwart and loyal.

It was midday when the Greenlanders finished their grisly work. Well before that Freydis had gotten up and unbolted the shed door. For a time she had watched the men gathering up the dead. Then she went looking for her thralls who were inside the end house behind the bolted door. Freydis banged on the door until it was opened by Ulfar. Freydis saw that he was holding a knife and an axe but she didn't berate him for this. The other thralls had hidden themselves beneath the bedding. Mairi was inside the sleeping compartment with the babe. Freydis urged the thralls to come out of hiding. "We have food to prepare," she said. "The men will be hungry after all the efforts they are making on our behalf."

By the time Thorvard and his men returned to the houses, Freydis had a large pot of stewed fish ready. The men fell to eating without washing or changing their clothes. Blood was blood; whether it was animal or human it all looked the same. That was Thorvard's view. He waved away the bowl of water Freydis held out for his use. Freydis set the bowl on a chest and again washed her hands. She had washed them several times since the murders. No sooner would she finish washing than she forgot she had.

It took the Greenlanders the rest of the day to row their trade goods to the ship. Evyind saw to the stowing. He was particular about where things were put since he wanted the ship to be well balanced. The largest of the ballast stones were taken from beneath the deck and thrown overboard to make way for house beams and planks. Groa's bones were stored below deck as well. After the floorboards were put back, the chests were brought aboard as well as the barrels. Although *Sigurd's Steed* was roughly the size of the *Vinland*, there was more room in its hold. The Greenlanders were taking no livestock back except the cow and she would be tethered to the mast. This meant walrus rope and ivory, including the trade goods once intended for the Egilssons, could be stored in the hold, as well as various wooden and wicker goods. It must be said that Thorvard left behind enough rope to outfit Helgi's ship as he had promised. At Thorvard's insistence, Freydis left the four lengths of sailcloth she had woven, as well as the remaining sheep, save the one she intended to roast. She thought that considering what had happened, she was giving the Icelanders more than they deserved.

Freydis had the sheep slaughtered. She knew the Greenlanders would welcome roast mutton before their departure. She was going to some lengths to prepare an

evening feast, seething cod in angelica broth with juniper
berries, stewing dried salmon with seaweed, adding
crushed blueberries to sour milk. In addition to preparing
this feast, she had set aside food rations in small amounts
to avoid opening bundles and barrels on the voyage.
Freydis did much of the food preparation herself, having
sent Mairi to collect cow fodder in the meadow. Freydis
sent Kalf and Orn to the Icelanders' house with dried fish
and water for the captives. The thralls were well pleased
with this chore since it meant that for a short time at least,
they had the upper rather than the lower hand.

Freydis arranged for Nagli to remove the iron locks
from the doors for use in her new house in Gardar. Then
she went round gathering up hooks and lamps. She had
no intention of leaving behind the metal goods she had
brought with her. Remembering that Nagli had kept himself apart from the capture of *Sigurd's Steed*, Freydis
thought it prudent to warn him that there was a price to
be paid for detachment.

"By choosing to occupy the middle ground, you let others do the bloodiest work," Freydis told him. "If we hadn't
overtaken the ship, you'd be stuck here with the
Icelanders for another year. You'd be wise to side with us
from now on."

When Mairi returned with the forage, she and Freydis
set to work cleaning out the houses and outbuildings. By
now the men had begun to haul their gear aboard ship
which made cleaning easier. Mairi carried the rushes outside while Freydis swept the iron tailings and wood shav-
ings into the corner, thinking they could be shovelled outside later. As it turned out, this shovelling was never done.
Freydis was interrupted by Thorvard who wanted her to
come aboard to oversee the placement of her goods. He
did not want to be pestered when Freydis came to him
afterwards, saying she was unable to find this or that.

In the evening the Greenlanders lit a fire on the beach
and ate their feast there. The sea was so calm that for the
first time since their arrival in Leifsbudir, it seemed as if
the wind had deserted the place. Evyind remarked that if

the wind didn't pick up in the next day or two, they would be rowing back to Greenland.

The Greenlanders made short work of the food Freydis had prepared. During the meal Freydis spoke kindly to Ozur when he expressed a reluctance to leave. More than once during their conversation, Ozur said that while he doubted the skraelings would release Thrand, or that he would escape, if either happened he wanted to be here to welcome Thrand back. Freydis thought both outcomes unlikely and reminded Ozur that he had a wife and children in Greenland who would be much affected if he failed to return. One difficulty must be weighed against the other. "Either way it will be hard," Freydis said.

Ozur seemed to find Freydis's words helpful and later that evening joined the other Greenlanders aboard the ship. The Greenlanders had decided earlier to bed down on *Sigurd's Steed*, since all their sleeping gear was there. Ulfar had made his bed against the bow much in the same place as he had on the *Vinland*. The difference was that this time Mairi and the bairn were beside him.

Before bedding down for the night, Thorvard sent the Gardar twins to relieve Sleita and Alf who had replaced Hogni and Avang as guards. So far none of the Icelanders had caused any trouble; they sat about in the gloomy depths of their house, talking and dozing. As for the Greenlanders aboard the ship, they were so weary they fell asleep before it was fully dark. Except for Bragi, who moaned whenever he rolled onto his wounded arm, the ship was quiet enough for sleep.

Toward dawn, Freydis was awakened by a scrabbling against the bow of the ship. She got up and looked over the side. Below her standing in one of the Icelanders' prams was Bolli Illugisson. He was dressed in furs and had deer horns tied to his head. His beard and hair were dishevelled, his nose badly bent. Freydis thought he must have been watching the Greenlanders' departure for some time and had chosen this moment to come aboard.

"Throw down the ladder so I can climb up." Bolli spoke through missing teeth.

"You can't climb up. We're overloaded," Freydis said. "The last thing we need is a berserk aboard." For the most part, she had forgotten her step-brother and had no wish to be reminded of him now.

The scrabbling continued.

Freydis looked over the side again. "I told you, there's no room. Now get away from here."

Freydis spoke in a vehement whisper. Even so she heard various movements and rustlings behind her and knew that others had been awakened by the exchange. Freydis looked around the ship and saw Ulfar. He was standing near the mast, staring at her. The closeness of his presence and his unblinking stare unnerved her in such a way that she was struck with fear. It occurred to her that when this man was freed by her brother, he might turn against her in a way that could do serious harm. Freydis had no clear idea how he could do this, but the fear took hold nonetheless. She decided then and there that she would take steps to block anything he or any of the others might do by way of harm. She resolved that before the day was out, she would speak to the Greenlanders about the importance of keeping quiet about the killings. Though the Icelanders had brought the killings on themselves through their own deceit and betrayal, there might be folk in Greenland, especially those newly come from Iceland, who would suspect foul play when they saw the Greenlanders return in the Icelanders' ship.

Freydis awakened Thorvard. She told him that Bolli was trying to get on the ship and that she had turned him away. She said there would be no end of difficulties if he came aboard, for he appeared half-crazed. Twice Thorvard looked over the side of the boat and back at Freydis.

"You're mistaken," he said, "there's no one trying to get aboard." Freydis looked over the side again. Thorvard was right: there was no Bolli. Freydis knew then that what she had seen was her step-brother's hug. In this way she learned that Bolli Illugisson was dead.

Soon after this Evyind awoke and remarked that a wind was coming from the Southwest and that if they wanted to make the most of it, they had better finish loading. The Greenlanders agreed to put off eating until later in order to save time. In any case, none of them was ravenous, having eaten so well the night before. The Greenlanders went ashore to round up the rest of the cargo. The cow still had to be brought aboard as well as the wicker cage containing the black bear cub. The two prams loaded with timber needed to be harnessed for towing behind the ship. Thorvard took some men and went to check on the captives, since he wanted to be sure they were still securely bound.

While the men finished loading, Freydis made one last walk through the buildings to see if anything had been left behind. She did this without regret, despite the fact that the buildings in Leifsbudir had provided her with more space than the hut where she lived in Gardar. She could do this because she was certain she would soon be living in a house far grander than anything Leif had built over here. Of course Leif had never intended these houses to serve as anything but temporary quarters. In the end Freydis thought so little of the houses that she did not bother sweeping up the refuse piled here and there. She left without finding the cloak pin she had dropped after the killings, or the spindle whorl Mairi had misplaced. Nor did she see the glass bead that had fallen onto the floor during the Yule feast and rolled away. Freydis did not linger over the winding stream, the pool where she had bathed or the shed where she had lain with Hauk. She looked at the broad sweep of meadows and thought that compared to Greenland's pastures, they lacked freshness. She looked at the hills and thought them too low for beauty. She looked at the sea and thought it too open to wind and weather. She much preferred the inland fjords of Greenland. In this Freydis was much like those folk who, when they are about to move elsewhere, must find fault with the place they are leaving behind.

The Greenlanders' plan of departure was this: when everyone was aboard, one of the Icelanders would be freed so that after the ship had left, the free Icelander could untie the other captives. Except for the sheep, the Greenlanders left no other food. Late morning, when all of the Greenlanders were aboard the ship save Thorvard and three others, Skum's foot bindings were untied and he was led to the beach. Then his hands were freed. This allowed Thorvard and his men time to get back to the ship before Skum could manage to free anyone else and come in pursuit. Not one of the Icelanders appeared to watch *Sigurd's Steed* leave the bay.

Before the rowers aboard *Sigurd's Steed* picked up their oars, Freydis stood on the bow platform and demanded silence so that the men could hear what she had to say. None of the Greenlanders were surprised by this command. They knew that all along it had been Freydis who had been in charge of the expedition. Some of the Greenlanders had failed to see this at the outset and had been troubled when they realized the extent of Freydis's reach. Now even those men saw that Freydis had inherited many of her father's strongest traits. Were it otherwise, the Greenlanders would not be sailing away from Leifsbudir with a rich cargo a year after their departure from Greenland, leaving unluckier men behind. It was also true that Freydis was clever in all that she did and seldom spoke without having a plan in mind. The men were therefore willing to listen to whatever she had to say.

Freydis had not forgotten there were others besides Ulfar aboard who in some circumstances might regard themselves as Christian. She remembered the men whom the priest had prime signed before the *Vinland*'s departure. Since coming to Leifsbudir she had never once seen any of the men speak outwardly about Christ; only Ulfar wore Christ's amulet around his neck. She therefore thought she was well positioned to remind the men that for the return voyage, they would be better off throwing in their lot with the old gods, since the words the priest had spoken to Christ before their departure from Greenland had not helped them avoid a storm.

"Let us call upon the old gods to help us make a safe crossing and avoid the foul weather we had before." Freydis paused when she heard voices shouting praise to Thor. Then she went on, "I want to warn you that there is apt to be more than foul weather against us. There may be more treachery ahead." Freydis looked carefully around the ship until she located Nagli. Then looking him in the eye, she continued, "It's important to keep what happened in Leifsbudir among ourselves. When folk in Greenland see us arriving in the Icelanders' ship, it will be all too easy for them to misunderstand what we were up against." Next Freydis looked for Asmund. When she found him, she gave him a baleful stare, "There will be no verses about how we came by this ship," she warned him. "They could make it difficult for us later on."

Freydis again waited for her words to take hold. "I say to you," she was shouting now, "that if we get back to Greenland safely, anyone who breathes a word of what happened yesterday will have to answer to me. Our story will be that the Icelanders stayed on here, which is true. We don't need to say that some of those who stayed are corpses. Don't forget some of our own folk are no longer alive."

It was cunning of Freydis to end her speech here. She knew that when Evyind gave the order to take up the oars and the ship was being rowed away, that the men would begin talking about those Greenlanders who had been left behind. As Freydis rightly predicted, once reminded, the men made much of the fact that though they had started out with thirty-five men, only twenty-five, excluding thralls, were left and two of them were wounded. It seemed to the Greenlanders that this loss of men made up for the Icelanders who had been killed in Leifsbudir. Not only did the Icelanders have eight men, including thralls, in Leifsbudir, they could expect more to return any day now. If it occurred to any of the Greenlanders that Helgi and his men might not return, they did not say so. All along they had wanted to believe that Helgi and the others had delayed their arrival because they were gathering a rich cargo of wood which they would bring back to Leifsbudir before Winter set in. When Helgi returned, the Icelanders would have a total of sixteen men, which was closer to the number of Greenlanders now aboard. In juggling these numbers, the Greenlanders were quite willing to overlook the fact that they had not included four male thralls in their count.

It suited their purpose to look at the numbers in a way that would make them appear fair minded in their own eyes. Now that they had accomplished what they set out to do a year ago, none of the Greenlanders wanted to sail away from Leifsbudir believing they had in any way acted dishonourably. What they preferred to believe was that they had acquitted themselves well in difficult circumstances and had done nothing that would in any way tarnish their reputation.

*   *   *

As luck would have it, the Greenlanders' return voyage was favoured by a southwest wind, which meant they made good progress early on. Evyind sailed *Sigurd's Steed* well out to sea yet not so far out that the ship had to fight the northern current flowing south. On the other hand, he wanted to keep the land on the port side in view without sailing too close. Until he was more familiar with how *Sigurd's Steed* took the water, he preferred to steer wide of offshore skerries and shoals, especially since they were towing prams which slowed them down. On the second day, the Greenlanders were sailing past the Wonder Strands of Markland which Leif had spoken of. The Greenlanders were too far at sea to see the paleness of the sand, since the beaches were adjacent to a keel-shaped headland Evyind sought to avoid.

For three more days the Greenlanders sailed off the coast of Markland, the land becoming bleaker and less forested the further north they went. Freydis had reached that part of her pregnancy when she felt sluggish and faint. It seemed this pregnancy was worse than the others had been. Freydis congratulated herself for having been prudent enough to avoid pregnancy until this Summer, since making the most of Leifsbudir had depended on her feeling well. Wrapping herself in furs, she leaned back against the bales of dried food and wadmal and slept. The bad dreams had left, but sometimes she awoke to see blood on her hands. When this happened she would direct her thoughts to the pleasanter aspects of the year. She reviewed the advantages of the voyage, leaving out the stormy crossing and the massacre. She would revise events in such a way that before long she was able to convince herself that all things considered, the time spent in Leifsbudir had been well worth the risks.

The seventh day out the Greenlanders saw the glaciers of Helluland. Because the weather held fair and the air was clear, they saw every land form that rose above the horizon, but they were too far away to see much of the low slab rock which made up the shoreline. The water was largely free of ice, which gave the voyagers an advantage, for directly ahead were large bays and sounds where most of the year ice collected. During the next three days the Greenlanders sailed past these bays on the northern leg of their journey. On the tenth day they came to a long narrow cape that stuck far out from the mainland. Here the ship turned east and headed for open sea. For the next few days the Greenlanders would be out of sight of land, which increased the danger, for if the weather clouded over not only would Evyind be prevented from using the sun and stars, but they would be vulnerable to drift ice.

Now an incident occurred involving Bragi. Since the Greenlanders had left Leifsbudir, Bragi's wound had failed to heal. His health, which had been steadily declining, took a sudden turn for the worse. He began to suffer chills and fevers that made him alternately shiver and sweat. Afterwards sweat stood out on his brow like rain. He blathered incessantly as if he had lost his mind. This greatly disturbed the Greenlanders, Freydis particularly, for much of his feverish rambling concerned the killings in

Leifsbudir, which she preferred to forget. Moreover these
ravings, for so they became, were such that no one could
sleep. Alarmed by this turn of events, Freydis called upon
the crew to amputate Bragi's arm and end his pain.

The wound was in the forearm beneath the elbow. By
now the infection was spreading toward the shoulder.
Nagli said he knew a man in Vik who had suffered a similar wound and had survived an amputation. Nagli himself
had survived the loss of a thumb. Ivar replied that he had
seen three amputations in his time and they had all resulted in death. "Even so it might be worth a try," Ivar said,
"for the poor man is so far gone that he is just as likely to
die if we do nothing." After more discussion it was decided that Nagli would cut off the arm above the elbow and
Ivar would tie up the wound with reindeer sinew. As the
arm was being severed, Bragi lost consciousness and
never revived. Due to the putrefaction that would follow,
there was no question of taking his corpse back to Greenland; it was tied into his sleeping bag and lowered into the
sea. It occurred to Freydis that this measure would save
the Greenlanders a good deal of trouble later on, for it
meant there would be no need to explain to anyone who
might ask how Bragi had come by his wound.

Bragi's burial took place thirteen days after the
Greenlanders left Leifsbudir. On the fifteenth day the
Greenlanders saw the glaciers of their country glittering in
the distance. Soon after this the black cliffs of Bjarney
were sighted to starboard. This close to home, the voyagers became more wakeful and alert. There was a good
deal of joking and self-congratulation. To have made the
crossing in a ship which was heavily loaded and towing
two prams was no mean feat. It was something the
Greenlanders could rightly be proud of. Now that they had
survived to tell about it, they knew that one day they
would look back on this year as being the most momentous in their lives. Only now did Freydis allow herself to
imagine her children running down the field toward the
ship. She saw them opening the bundles she had prepared, exclaiming over the toys, the spoons and cups, the

fine ribbons and various things she and Thorvard had made.

At Bjarney the drift ice began to thicken. The further south the Greenlanders went, the more the ice crowded in and slowed them down. Evyind said he doubted they could make Brattahlid this year. With this much ice in the water, the end of Eiriksfjord would be blocked solid by now. It would be far better to go up Einarsfjord and make for Gardar. All along, Freydis and Thorvard had been of two minds about disembarking at Brattahlid. On the one hand, they were eager to get rid of *Sigurd's Steed* by passing it over to Leif in exchange for the *Vinland*. On the other hand, they had no wish to carry their goods overland to Gardar from Eiriksfjord. They advised Evyind to take the safer route to Gardar. It was lucky for the travellers that this far north the sky remained light enough to allow them to continue sailing during the night without colliding with an iceberg. In this way they kept an open path through the water and avoided being closed in, which might have happened if the ship had been anchored. After they passed Hreinsey where the ice was thicker, they reefed the sail and took up oars. From now on the ship would be rowed. The rowing slowed down progress further but no one complained, since at least they were able to continue without being stopped by the ice. The twenty-second morning after their departure from Leifsbudir, the Greenlanders were halfway down Einarsfjord. Ahead was the sloping plain of Gardar.

For some time Gardar folk had been watching *Sigurd's Steed*. They had recognized the ship as being the one the Icelanders had left on a year ago and were curious as to why there were now so many Greenlanders aboard. As soon as the ship was close enough, prams were put out from shore and questions and greetings shouted across. The crew met these inquiries with questions and shouts of their own.

There were folk in Gardar who much later would remark how the voyagers from Leifsbudir had evaded questions that day. These folk claimed to remember thinking that at the time of the ship's arrival the crew were evasive and avoided making honest replies. For most this was unlikely to have been the case. The arrival of the Greenlanders was so joyous an occasion that few people had time for suspicion. After the greetings and reunions were over, the cargo was divided among the crew. This was followed by a good deal of gift-giving and feasting in Gardar before those who lived in Vatnahverfi and various other places went off to their farms. During the two-day festivities the voyagers were questioned several times about the whereabouts of the Icelanders, especially by those folk who had become acquainted with the Egilssons and their crew when they had overwintered in Greenland. Each time they were asked, the Greenlanders stuck to the story that the Icelanders had gone for oak wood and would be returning to Greenland the following year. This story was repeated so often that many of the tale tellers became convinced of its truth. Gardar folk were less inquisitive about the Greenlanders who failed to return; they were accustomed to the deaths of kin resulting from mishaps of various kinds.

Everyone was eager to hear the tales and verses of the travellers' adventures across the sea, and heard them over and over again. Some folk complained that the tale telling would have been much improved if it had been enlivened with drink. Freydis had been shrewd enough not to store any of the berries they had brought from Leifsbudir in water for she did not want the crew members' mouths loosened by strong drink. Besides, without honey to sweeten it, the result was bound to be sour and a waste of good fruit. Remembering the stories of the orgies which had followed Leif Eiriksson's return, many folk in Gardar thought Freydis was tight fisted not to have brought home barrels of drink. No one blamed Thorvard for this. Everyone knew that when it came to matters of wealth and trade, it was Freydis Eiriksdottir who wore the breeches. Folk persisted in blaming Freydis for the lack of drink even though she made no effort to hoard the berries for herself but apportioned them out among the crew along with their share of other food stuffs. Freydis went to some lengths to ensure the crew was well rewarded with goods.

Even so, some were dissatisfied. Bodvar, Falgeir, Glam, Hogni and Sleita especially grumbled about their share of the goods, saying they had expected far more for their efforts than what they received. Freydis might have haggled with these men and denied them more if the departure from Leifsbudir had been less bloody. As it was, she handed over more of her own goods than she wanted in order to keep these men satisfied.

Freydis's children had fared well. Asny was now speaking clearly and Signy and Thorlak were in good health. Halla, however, moved more slowly: her joint ill now made walking hard. In spite of this Halla had several large cheeses in the dairy and six calves grazing in the home field. Earlier in the year Guttorm had approached Halla about allowing some of his cows to graze in Thorvard's field. Halla's reply had been that if Guttorm provided Winter fodder for Freydis's cows, he could make use of the field. Apparently Guttorm disliked this arrangement. He took his cows across the fjord to graze and never brought up the matter again. One day Halla caught Guttorm on the wrong side of the wall cutting turfs. She soon put a stop to this by staring him down. Halla's crossed eyes came in handy when folk mistook her gaze for the evil eye. Taking everything into account, it could be said that Freydis's farm—for so most folk thought of it since Thorvard did so little farm work—had in no way suffered during her absence.

After the settlements and festivities were over, Freydis struck an agreement with Flosi, Lodholt and Avang that if they stayed with her for the next two months and built her a house, she would make sure they were well looked after. She pointed out that since they lived on the other side of Eiriksfjord, they would have to wait in Gardar until the ice was safe enough to walk across. That being the case, the men might just as well make good use of their time while they waited. Freydis also persuaded Ulfar to help build the house. She told him that he would be risking Mairi's life

and that of the babe's if he attempted to cross the ice
before it had frozen thick. She told Ulfar that building a
house was fair recompense for his being given Mairi. Ulfar
agreed to work on the house, though not without first
arranging separate quarters for Mairi and himself in one of
the huts Einar agreed to lend Freydis to house the extra
men. Freydis was pleased that the ice conditions were
working in her favour, for the delay in reaching Brattahlid
meant she would have a house of her own before the
worst of the Winter arrived.

Although it saved him work, Thorvard saw the unstable
ice conditions in Eiriksfjord as working to his disadvantage
since it meant he would not be able to hand *Sigurd's
Steed* over to Leif until next Summer. The ship would have
to be shore hauled and covered with spruce wood he had
intended for trade to overwinter it in Gardar. Thorvard did
not enjoy the prospect of building the Winter shed or having the ship nearby where it would remind him that its
owner was buried under a pile of stones some place else.

Shortly before Yule Freydis, Thorvard and five others
walked overland and crossed Eiriksfjord with a large quantity of goods. By then the ice was solid and smooth
enough for them to use sleds. Freydis and Thorvard had a
sled packed with ivory, mossur and various wooden items
as well as a black bear skin for Leif and a white foetus
muff for Jorunn. On top of these goods were three oars
from the *Vinland*. Thorvard pulled this sled while Freydis,
who was six months pregnant, walked alongside. Flosi,
Lodholt, Avang and Ulfar pulled five more sleds. In Flosi
and Lodholt's case, between the two of them, they pulled
three sleds. They were hauling heavy beams and planks
which slowed them down. Mairi, carrying the babe, walked
beside Ulfar. Freydis and Thorvard were ahead. When they
stopped to wait for the others, Freydis rubbed her hands
together and stamped her feet from the cold. "I don't see
why we can't go ahead by ourselves and let the others
come later," she complained. To this Thorvard replied that
he had gained all year from the efforts of these men and
he had no intention of leaving them now for at times the

sleds needed to be helped over hollows and bumps. He went on to say he was sure the men would not begrudge Freydis going on ahead, since in her condition she could hardly help.

So it was that Freydis Eiriksdottir reached her half-brother's house first and was able to tell him her version of what had happened in Leifsbudir before any of the others came along. Because she was so thickly bundled in wool, no one who glanced at the figure hurrying across the fjord recognized Freydis and she was able to take Leif and Jorunn by surprise. She knocked lightly on their door and without waiting for it to open, entered and threw back her cloak. Freydis was pleased when she saw the expressions of amazement on their faces. She saw that their delight in her return was in no way false. Leif and his wife were sitting by the fire when Freydis entered. Both went to her immediately and gave her an embrace.

"You're a welcome sight," Leif said. "When you didn't appear before freeze-up, I feared that like our brothers, you met with an unlucky fate. Then Nagli Asgrimsson came by not long ago and told us of your return."

"What did he say?" Freydis said.

"He was in a hurry to get to his brother's farm and didn't speak with us long. He merely said you'd arrived safely in Gardar and were well."

"You know me. I'm not so easily gotten rid of," Freydis said.

"Indeed, that's so." Leif laughed. He had no way of knowing that the truth of her words had carried Freydis further than he would have liked. He embraced her again. "It's good to see you." He looked at his wife. "I must say Jorunn and I are in need of cheering up for we have been cast down lately." Leif went on to say that Thjodhild had died in early Summer and had been buried close to her beloved church. "As you know, my mother was the kind of woman others miss when she has gone. I suppose that considering the discomfort she suffered toward the end, it's a blessing she was released."

Freydis also thought it a blessing but in a different way: it was a relief to her that Thjodhild was no longer around to interfere. Jorunn made the sign of the cross and said, "We take comfort from that, and from Geirmund's words that Thjodhild is now with Christ."

The piety rankled Freydis and made her ill at ease. She felt in some way shabby and underdressed despite the fact that she was wearing her blue robe and a clean linen snood. It took more than a robe and snood for Freydis to forget the carefree Summer in Leifsbudir where she had often gone without a robe and left her hair uncovered. The mention of the priest reminded Freydis that Geirmund Gunnfard came and went freely in this house and might soon appear. She did not want him around when she was telling her brother what had happened in Leifsbudir. She was suspicious of the priest and thought his presence would throw her off. Quickly Freydis gave her version of what had happened during the year. When she reached the part where the pack ice claimed the *Vinland*, she stopped so that Leif might speak. Leif took the news better than she had hoped.

"The old ship served longer than most and went places where others had never been," Leif said. "It's fitting that it rest in Vinland."

"Now you will have the *Greenland Trader*," Freydis said grandly. "When the Icelanders return with the ship built for us, you'll have it as recompense for the use of yours." Then she told him about the exchange the Greenlanders had made with the Icelanders. "The Icelanders won't be back until next year. Last Summer Helgi Egilsson took the *Greenland Trader* south in order to fetch oak wood for his new ship, which delayed the Icelanders' return." There was enough truth in this for Freydis to make the lie convincing. She made it seem as if Helgi had already returned to Leifsbudir. "The Icelanders agreed to lend us *Sigurd's Steed* for our return. As you know, we had originally intended to return with both your ship and ours. We therefore returned with more goods than we could have brought back in the *Greenland Trader* which was somewhat smaller than *Sigurd's Steed*. I suppose the Icelanders lent us their ship to repay us for their use of Leifsbudir. Though Helgi and the others wished to continue in Leifsbudir for a while, there was no reason for us to stay on. I was especially eager to return to my children." Freydis stroked her belly. "Moreover as you can see, I'm again with child and prefer to give birth here, especially since this pregnancy is turning out to be more difficult than the others."

Next Freydis brought up the matter of her foster mother. "Halla has decided to stay on with me in Gardar rather than return to her steading in the fells. She has said that you may either sell her cattle or keep them yourself, for at this point in her life she has no wish to look after them." When Halla had broached this matter with her, Freydis had considered bringing some of Halla's livestock to Gardar to increase her own herd. She had decided against this for two reasons: one was Thorvard's home field was already overgrazed, and the other was that she thought she could put the disposition of Halla's stock in such a way that it would seem Leif was being given further recompense for the loss of the *Vinland*.

Before this matter could be discussed, Thorvard and the others arrived. They were greeted warmly and encouraged to sit by the fire. Jorunn bade her servants bring soup and cheese. While the guests were eating, news of their arrival reached other ears. Folk came to Leif Eiriksson's in such numbers that soon there was a throng assembled in the hall. Freydis and Thorvard were urged to sit on the high seat with Leif and Jorunn. Benches were brought for Flosi and the others so that they might also sit up high. Then the tales began about their adventures beginning with the Bay of Maples. The men described the abundant forests and the varieties of trees growing there. There was a hush as they spoke of the red skraelings who lived in the forests and could make themselves invisible like hidden folk. Some men wept openly when Thorvard presented Leif with the ship oars and described the end of the *Vinland*. Asmund had returned to his farm long since.

In his stead Thorvard recited the poem about the loss of the ship. During the recitation Thorfinn Karlsefni appeared; he and Gudrid had moved from Herjolfness to Brattahlid earlier in the year. The Icelander was invited to sit on the high seat. Fortunately for Freydis, Gudrid had stayed behind in their house, being too close to childbirth to go about. Even without Gudrid her husband's presence spoiled the occasion for Freydis, since she was again reminded that despite the risks she and Thorvard had taken, they would not be taking their cargo to Norway themselves but would be forced to trade their goods with Thorfinn Karlsefni instead.

Ulfar did not stay for the tale telling; he and Mairi slipped away to talk to the priest about marrying. Much later when they returned to the main hall, the couple found the crowd dispersed. Leif and his wife had gone to bed as had Freydis and Thorvard. Ulfar made a bed by the hearth for Mairi and the bairn and another for himself. He wanted to be where Leif could see him plainly in the morning.

Leif woke him up with a nudge in the back. He looked down at Ulfar and said, "It's time we had a talk. Unless I'm mistaken, you are about to give me my freedom ale."

Ulfar rolled onto his back, opened his eyes and grinned up at Leif.

"If like Our Master, you can turn water into wine, then ale you shall have," he joked.

"It seems you have returned with a lighter heart than when you left."

"True," Ulfar said. "For I've returned with a woman I intend to wed."

Leif looked at Mairi and the babe. "I can see by these two that you've done much to increase your Luck. Now you must tell me about the young woman at your side."

Ulfar produced the vellum on which Thorvard had made his mark and explained how he had come to know Mairi, and that he wanted to make her his wife.

Freydis and Thorvard were awakened by this exchange and got up quickly. Thorvard wanted to tell Leif about the trade he had made with the Egilssons himself. Freydis was eager to return to Gardar that morning since the longer she and Thorvard stayed with Leif, the more likely they were to be questioned closely. When Leif asked them if they had been pleased with Ulfar's service, they replied they were well satisfied with the work he had done on their behalf. Thorvard was especially generous in his praise and said he and Freydis would not have been half so well off without the services provided by the thrall. Freydis kept her eyes on Ulfar while these words were being said, willing him to keep silent about what had gone on in Leifsbudir. The meeting passed without him mentioning the killings.

As she and Thorvard were about to leave, Freydis urged Leif to cross the fjord to visit them in Gardar.

"Now that we have a new house, we can entertain you in the manner you deserve."

Leif promised he would come over as soon after Yule as he could manage. There were three or four men in the district he had to visit in order to discuss various settlements that been decided by the Althing. He told Freydis that when these matters were finished, he would cross the ice and visit their house. With this promise in mind, Freydis and Thorvard returned to Gardar.

Now that she had so many fine goods around her, Freydis Eiriksdottir became exceedingly house proud. Her new house, which Ulfar and the others had built at the top of Thorvard's home field, was the largest in Gardar. In addition to the spacious main hall there was a fire room, a privy, a storage compartment and two smaller rooms. Both the fire room and the privy were so positioned that a trickle of water which had been diverted from the small stream feeding the crag pool flowed through a trench in the floor. Freydis had taken the woven hangings from her wedding chest and hung them about the house. There were woven coverings and furs as well as eiderdown pillows on the sleeping platforms. Beneath the high seats Ulfar had made were sealskin floor rugs. The carved pillars and beams glowed in the firelight from being rubbed with seal oil. Wooden chests and stools were plentiful through-out the house. On one of the chests was the brass bowl edged in beaten gold. It was true there was a dearth of sil-ver and glassware, but Freydis thought to acquire some next Summer when a ship arrived for trade, since by then Thorvard expected to have a live white bear as well as the black one to exchange for luxury goods. As for provisions there was so much food it had to be stored under lock and key in the hut that had once served as their house. Freydis was well pleased with her new living arrange-ments. She was a long way from knowing her Luck had run out.

After Yule the weather turned bitter. The cows were brought from the field and sealed in the byre. Even so many of them failed to survive the Winter. Freydis lost six, including the cow she had taken to Leifsbudir which can-celled out the number of calves she had gained earlier. One morning in Midwinter Halla failed to get up from her bed; her heart had stopped during the night. Her corpse was stored in a hut until the ground thawed. Halla's death was a blow to Freydis. Her foster mother had been some-one who had stood by her no matter what she did. Ever since that morning when Bribrau had disappeared into the sea, Freydis had relied on Halla to help her out. Halla had understood Freydis better than anyone else. For that rea-son alone, she could never be replaced.

The people in Gardar suffered much that Winter. One storm after another prevented men from getting out to hunt and fish. Birds and hares close by Gardar were scarce. The result of the food shortage was that many folk were forced to eat livestock. One day Inga sent Guttorm to ask Freydis for provisions to carry them over for a while. Freydis turned Guttorm away at the door, since by then it had come out that while Freydis and Thorvard had been in Leifsbudir, Guttorm had not only tried to graze his cattle in their home field and steal their few remaining turfs, but his children had been especially cruel to Freydis's chil-dren, once stripping Thorlak naked and tying him to a rock. Guttorm's children had also caught Signy and sheared her hair. Besides, Inga and Guttorm's herd was so large it would scarcely suffer if they ate a few more cows.

The bitter weather meant that some Greenlanders who had been on the voyage were forced to burn the house wood they had brought from Leifsbudir. This happened to Ozur whose family did not have enough fuel to get them through the Winter. Ozur burnt some planking but he put off burning his posts and beams. Instead he came all the way from Vatnahverfi to Gardar to ask Freydis for fuel. Freydis gave him some whale oil, but it was such a meagre amount that he grumbled, saying that he had not expected her to have so short a memory especially since he had stood by her through the difficulties in Leifsbudir and had lost a son on Thorvard's account. He went on to say that his memory was long in a way Freydis wouldn't like, and that if things got worse he might be required to use it against her. Thorvard came home before these grumblings were through and gave Ozur enough seal oil to last the Winter. After Ozur had gone, Thorvard rebuked Freydis, saying her miserliness was bound to make them unlucky if it didn't stop. Although Freydis replied sharply, she heeded Thorvard's advice and became more open handed after that. By then it was too late since folk who face hardship are quick to judge those who in the first instance are reluctant to help.

Meanwhile in Brattahlid rumours of the massacre had reached Leif's ears. After returning to Brattahlid, Avang had put a quantity of cloud berries into a barrel of water. To this his father had added a vat of honey he had been hoarding from the previous Summer when he had traded away some of his wife's cheese. Some time later when the mead was considered ready, Avang, his tongue loosened by drink, told a small gathering about the killings. He was much upset by what had gone on in Leifsbudir and welcomed the release that came with telling. Flosi and Lodholt, who were also drinking mead, spoke up as well. The traitors—as Freydis was to call them later—were aware that murder occasionally rose from dispute, but they had never seen a massacre, and needed to tell about what had gone on in Leifsbudir, especially since they had taken part. None of these men had killed an Icelander, but they were among those who had chased them down. Flosi, Lodholt and Avang claimed to have liked some of the men who had been killed, having worked with them on the ice. Although the listeners of the grisly tale had been sworn to secrecy before Avang and the others spoke, one of them, Skuli Grimolfsson, went to Leif afterwards and told him what he had heard. Leif would have preferred to disbelieve Skuli out of loyalty to Freydis but as gödi, he could hardly dismiss what Skuli had said. He therefore challenged Avang, Flosi and Lodholt to either verify or deny Skuli's charge. Now that they were sober, the men were reluctant to speak and fidgeted and mumbled in a peculiar way. This only roused Leif's suspicions further and he pressed them harder to tell the truth. Eventually they gave him a full account of the murders and how the Greenlanders took possession of the Icelanders' ship.

Soon after this Leif sent word that Freydis was to come to Brattahlid and give a truthful account of what had happened in Leifsbudir. Since she had deceived him earlier, Freydis preferred to avoid meeting Leif, all the more so since she was feeling poorly with the impending birth. When Freydis refused to heed Leif's summons, he went to Gardar himself. He declined her offer of refreshment and refused to look around her house. Instead he told her about Avang, Flosi and Lodholt's account.

"They're deceiving you with lies," Freydis said. "I told you before what happened."

"But you told me the Icelanders loaned you the ship, whereas Avang and the others say you took it over."

"They're confused about the facts."

"Do you deny there were killings?"

"There were struggles of one kind and another," Freydis said. "I can't remember them all," which was the truth; she couldn't recall the killings exactly. She remembered there had been corpses in Leifsbudir, lying here and there, but by now she was uncertain about the details of their deaths.

Leif continued to question Freydis but she provided only vague replies. Eventually he gave up and returned home without her confession. He thought Freydis guilty all the same and was disappointed she had made enemies of the Icelanders. Leif had been born in Iceland and brought to Greenland as a boy. He was ashamed that the Icelanders had been mistreated by the Greenlanders, since he regarded Icelanders as kin. When Guttorm Glamsson heard the news, he went to Brattahlid and urged Leif to bring the matter of the killings to the next Althing so that Freydis and Thorvard would be punished in a way that suited the majority of folk. Leif refused. "I have no wish to punish my sister, but I prophesy her descendants won't come to much."

In late Winter Freydis began birthing earlier than she had claimed she was due. An old crone by the name of Asgerd Hoskuldsdottir was brought from Skjalgsbudir to midwife since neither Thorvard's mother nor his sisters wanted the task. During a difficult labour Asgerd dragged forth a child with a massive head and a freakish face. She wrapped it in a shroud and buried it outside among the rocks. Afterwards Asgerd made it known that Freydis had given birth to a wretch with a misshapen head. One wag, harking back to the tale of Freydis baring her breast in Leifsbudir, said Freydis must have mated with a skraeling to produce such a child. Most folk had little sympathy for the outcome of Freydis's pregnancy, saying the result showed what happened to a woman bent on overreaching herself. There may have been folk who thought Freydis had been unfairly judged, but they were seldom heard, since harsher voices overrode theirs.

By the time Summer came to Greenland and the fjords opened up, rumours of the killings in Leifsbudir had spread far and wide. As a result Freydis and Thorvard were shunned, Freydis especially. Mothers held up Freydis as an example of what would happen to their daughters if they wore breeches and behaved like men. Einar disowned Freydis's children as being his kin.

Because Freydis was weakened by the difficult birth, it had fallen to Thorvard to trade their goods with Thorfinn Karlsefni who was returning to Iceland with his wife and children. Thorvard came away with far less for the cargo than if Freydis had been handling matters, for Gudrid's husband was a shrewd trader well used to getting his way. Later it was said that the cargo Thorfinn Karlsefni put together before his departure was so abundant that no ship left Greenland waters more richly laden.

Sigurd's Steed remained in its shed. Leif said he had no wish to do anything with it until he knew for certain whether or not the Icelanders would return. He still held out hope that Helgi Egilsson might one day arrive with the ship that would replace the *Vinland*.

The second Winter after the Greenlanders' return from Leifsbudir, Thorvard Einarsson drowned in Northsetur when hunters failed to rescue him from a huge white bear that forced him under water and held him there. Now Freydis was alone with her children and thralls. This blow was as severe as the loss of Halla, since as a result of the shunning, Thorvard and Freydis had come to rely more heavily on one another.

The following Summer a Norwegian ship bound for the Hebrides on its way to Bergen had aboard not only Ulfar, Mairi and her son but Teit Evyindsson and his younger brother Hallvard, who were also seeking a better life elsewhere. Before leaving Brattahlid, Ulfar gave Geirmund Gunnfard several vellums which he said were an account of the year he had spent in Leifsbudir.

"After I leave, I want you to read my manuscript to Leif so that he will know my view of the truth," Ulfar said. "Since my life is about to begin some place else, it's fitting that I should leave these particular vellums in Greenland."

Three years after the departure of Thorfinn Karlsefni, Leif Eiriksson traded *Sigurd's Steed* and the Egilssons' ivory to the Icelander Ingolf Hafnisson in exchange for silver and embroidered goods which he gave to his mother's church. He also obtained enough wood to build the priest a house in Brattahlid and furnished it as richly as his own.

He made sure he gained nothing for himself in the trade. He had no wish to profit by the treachery of those who had besmirched the place to which he had once proudly lent his name. His oldest son, Thorkel, had begun to speak of making the westward journey. Leif did not want Thorkel or any of his sons to take up his claim in Vinland since, except for himself, the place had brought his family nothing but grief.

Few of the Greenlanders who had been to Leifsbudir spoke of what had happened there. Those who did often contradicted each other as to precisely what had occurred. As is often the case with violent crimes, no one could be exactly sure what had gone on though many claimed to know the truth. As a result there were many versions of the story. After much retelling these versions became entwined in such a way that even those who had been in Leifsbudir during the massacre were unable to separate fiction from fact. It was safe to say, however, that the many tellings of the story affected the Greenlanders in such a way that even if a ship had been available to travel to Leifsbudir, none of the crew would have been willing to go. Talk of Vinland subsided. Folk seldom told tales of Vinland, for many were convinced that the place held more evil than Luck. Gradually the details of the final voyage faded until Vinland became little more than a mythical country hovering on the outermost reaches of the Greenlanders' minds.

As for the manuscript Ulfar had written, for many years it remained in the possession of Geirmund Gunnfard. After Leif Eiriksson's death the priest carried the manuscript with him to Iceland. Shortly thereafter a fire swept through the monastery at Thingeyvar and destroyed much of the manuscript, reducing it to a handful of fragments that later became known as the *Ulfar Vellums*, the last of which is recorded here.

* * *

About the massacre I have little to say, since I myself did not see it. In any case braver men than I have given a full account of the murders. As for the crimes of Freydis and Thorvard, whatever I know was told me second-hand. Though I never liked Freydis or her husband and thought the Greenlanders overwild and uncouth, it is my opinion that the Icelanders were no better than the Greenlanders and brought many of their difficulties upon themselves. There was deception and trickery on both sides. As far as I was concerned, when it came to evil doing, there was little to choose between. Both sides showed an excess of Heathenness for want of a priest. I sought to bring the message of Heaven's Lord to the attention of Leifsbudir folk, but most of them turned a deaf ear to my words. I was no priest and had no talent in that regard.

Our Lord gave me other skills which I hope to employ one day. I pray that soon He will bless my wife, step-son and myself with a safe journey to the Hebrides. Once Mairi and Jon have been delivered to her kin in Mull, I intend to return to Iona and take up my work as a scribe. It is my fervent desire to spend my last years working on the illuminated vellums of the Holy Book. If my skills with a brush improve, perhaps I will one day be chosen to paint the eye of an Evangelist or an Angel's hair.

DURING THE FIRST TWO DAYS of Helgi Egilsson's voyage *Paradise Seeker* had sailed south, passing the Bay of Maples and the crab-shaped promontory Leif Eiriksson had described to Helgi. Helgi had taken care to keep the land on his port side in view; he needed to see where the land ran out, since it was at the land's end that he must set a southwesterly course. Leif had told him the Outer Ocean lay to the East and advised him that for the time being he should remain within the sheltered waters of what appeared to be an inland sea. The travellers anchored at the land's end, and in the morning set out again. Sailing with a southeast wind, by Midday the Icelanders caught sight of giant rocks rising out of the water directly ahead. This was the nesting place of sea birds that had been passing them for some time. Leif had mentioned the rocks as a good place to harvest sea birds. There were so many birds, mainly murres and terns, that the men had smelled their presence early, the ship being downwind from the guano-streaked rocks. At first the Icelanders thought they were approaching three rocks, but as they came closer, they saw that the sea had bored a passageway through one of them so that what appeared to be three rocks was in fact two. These rocks were so steeply cliffed that it was impossible to land any-where. In any case the birds were plentiful enough on the lower reaches of the cliffs that they were easily killed without climbing. After filling their pram with sea birds the Icelanders continued their southwesterly course.

The sun was setting when the men came upon a small green island that, compared to the rock-bound coast they had left behind, seemed closer to what they were seeking. Even from the ship they could see lush meadowland between groves of trees. The meadows were brilliantly coloured with flowers of many kinds. As they looked, they saw a black bear come onto a beach. The bear nosed for a time in bushes then disappeared. The ship's anchor was dropped and the armed men rowed cautiously ashore. As Helgi said, there might well be skraelings in such a well-favoured place. Carrying axes and spears, the men explored the small island. They saw the bear again but it was too far away for them to kill. They also saw a fox. Fortunately there was no trace of skraelings. Bjolf and Atli wanted to spend the night on the beach but Helgi was against this. He wanted to get an early start in the morning. "There is also the risk that if you sleep in so pleasant a place," he said, "you might mistake it for Vinland and never want to leave." Bjolf and Atli regarded Helgi's advice as well spoken and after eating a meal of boiled sea birds cooked on the beach, agreed to spend the night on the ship.

Next morning *Paradise Seeker* had no sooner been under sail than the men passed a group of islands which taken together resembled a squid, for the islands looked like long narrow tentacles curling into the sea. The men made no attempt to go ashore. None of the islands was as well favoured as the one they had left. From here, the Icelanders set a more southerly course which took them to the bottom of the inland sea. They knew from the way clouds lay on the horizon that a landfall was ahead. Late afternoon this land came into view. It was a low, thickly treed place with beaches of reddish sand. The sand ran so far out that it was too shallow for the ship to anchor close in. The Icelanders sailed first south then north along the shore looking for an anchorage. At one point they saw a wide flat bay bronzed by the late afternoon sun, but even at high tide the bay was partially blocked by sand shoals and could not be entered by ship. After some discussion Helgi took Atli, Bjolf and Ulf Broad Beard and rowed ashore, for already Helgi could see this land was better than the green island they had seen yesterday and he was eager to explore. While Atli and Bjolf rowed through water purpled with jellyfish, Helgi scanned the shoreline for signs of life. There appeared to be none.

They reached shore and hauled the pram onto the beach. The men picked up their weapons and set out. The beach was impressive. Not only was the sand fine and reddish, it was bordered by flowering trees. Beside the beach was a meadow resplendent with flowers, beyond that thick woods.

"We'll begin with the meadow," Helgi said. The men waded into the knee-high grass. They had not gone halfway across the meadow when they came to a stand of corn growing in the red earth. The corn was about halfway to their knees.

"This crop has been recently sown in ploughed earth," he said. He did not recognize the corn for what it was, having never seen it before, but there was enough farmer in him to know when a crop had been planted by hand. From the way the corn grew in rows, it was clear to him and his companions that the corn wasn't growing wild but was being tended by men. This alarmed the Icelanders, for they were standing in the middle of an open field where they could be easily surrounded. They knew if skraelings attacked, they would soon be outnumbered. Quickly the Icelanders left the meadow. As soon as they reached the shore, they rowed back to the ship.

"There are skraelings in this place," Helgi said to those who had remained aboard.

"There are also oaks," Hauk replied. He had seen the mighty trees towering above the others and could tell from their shape what they were. "There also seems to be a good many ash and elm. It may be that this is Vinland and that there are grapes in those woods."

"Some might regard this as Vinland. For me the real Vinland is some distance yet," Helgi said. Now that he had come this far, Helgi was greedy to find a land that surpassed this one and was empty of skraelings. His idea of Paradise was a place without difficulties or obstacles of any kind. "I've no doubt we'll find a rich supply of timber there as well."

The sun was nearing the horizon. The Icelanders knew they had to find a safe anchorage before nightfall. Helgi sailed east, following the land until it came to a cape. Rounding the cape, he turned south and soon found an anchorage that suited him, for the land on the starboard side was too low and swampy to be of much use to anyone, including skraelings. After eating the last of the sea birds, the Icelanders bedded down on deck and spent a peaceful night.

The morning brought another fine day. The Icelanders could scarcely believe their Luck: since leaving Leifsbudir, they had enjoyed nothing but fine sailing weather. Now Helgi set an easterly course. By Midday he was rewarded by reaching an open-ended fjord that was wide at both ends and narrow in the middle. At the end of the fjord was the open sea Leif had called an ocean. The men anchored on the south side of the fjord.

On the sixth morning, the Icelanders entered the Outer Ocean. Here the waves were higher and the winds brisker than they had been on the inland sea. As it turned out this worked in their favour. They made better time with sea winds. Sometimes the wind carried *Paradise Seeker* along so fast the ship skimmed the wave tops without dropping into the furrows. Hauk was especially pleased and frequently reminded the others how much could be done with inferior wood. He said it was all a matter of the stem-smith balancing the various ship parts so that they worked as one. "Even with a large cargo, this ship can make a safe ocean crossing," he said. He looked at Helgi and grinned. "It may be that when we get back to Leifsbudir, you won't want to give it up."

Helgi said nothing. He was sure the oaken ship the Norwegian would build him upon their return to Leifsbudir would surpass all others, including *Sigurd's Steed*.

Well before nightfall the Icelanders came to a large bay where an island marked its mouth. Here they anchored for the night. Though the anchorage was safe and the evening mild, the Icelanders were in such high excitement they scarcely slept. The travellers could have sailed all night but thinking they must surely be close to Vinland, they did not want to give up any of its wondrous sights to the dark.

The anchor was hauled as soon as it was light and the ship rowed clear of the harbour. Here the Icelanders picked up a southeasterly wind which carried them swiftly south. It was late morning when they came to a large bay filled with hundreds of islands. Many of the islands were heavily treed with maple and oak, while others were little more than skerries.

The islands were so numerous and close together that the water around them was calmer than the open sea, except for those spaces between islands where ocean breezes rushed in. The erratic course slowed progress somewhat but the Icelanders were untroubled by this, for the archipelago had an understated beauty that appealed to them. When they came out on the other side of the islands, they caught sight of a wide sandy beach. No sooner had they sighted this beach than another one came into view. These were soon followed by others. These beaches were pure white and glittered with specks of gold. In some places the forest came down to the beach; in others the beach gave way to sand dunes and meadows of bright flowers. Some of the beaches had a river flowing into the sea at one end. Behind one such beach, the voyagers caught sight of a small lake shining in the sun. The Icelanders marvelled at the beauty of the land. As far as they could see, this green and white shoreline stretched ahead of them without end.

"Now we must find ourselves a place to stay," Helgi said. "As far as I'm concerned, we've reached the place Leif called Vinland."

The Icelanders hung over the side, exclaiming about the way the land curved neatly around a beach, how a shallow river mouth spread itself over sand, how a meadow rolled invitingly toward the woods. Each beach was so well favoured in its particular way that it seemed impossible for the Icelanders to choose among them. They came to a long narrow island within wading distance of the shore. It was one island of many, but the others were much further out and had no beaches, whereas this crescent-shaped island had two beaches that ran its length on either side. Moreover, the beach on the west side of the island curved around a small cove that was suitable for anchoring the ship. The island was small enough that it could be easily walked around in half a day yet large enough to provide much of what the Norsemen wanted, which was to say an abundance of trees and flowers. A further advantage of the island was that it was situated close by a river mouth. This was a small river that wound its way out of a forest and emptied into sand-ribbed shallows. On one side of the river was a forest; on the other a low, marshy stretch of land.

Helgi anchored *Paradise Seeker* in the cove on the west side of the island. Then he, Bjolf, Atli and Ulf Broad Beard got into the pram. When they were ashore, they picked up their weapons and went to explore. They walked along the beach to the promontory at the end before crossing a hilly meadow, which was in fact partly sand dunes. Coming down from the sand dunes, they walked the length of the east side beach. As they went along, they were much affected by the peacefulness of the place: the soughing trees, the falling waves, the droning bees, the scent of rose bushes and wild pea blossoms. "If there are any skraelings in this place," Helgi remarked, "they are certainly well hidden." In fact until now, the island had been untouched by men. When Helgi was satisfied that this was the case, he climbed a grassy knoll on his way to the island's other side and found a lagoon, a smooth rocky bowl of fresh spring water lying at the base of a large pine tree. The lagoon was about five body lengths across and no more than half a man deep. A small stream trickled from the pool, coursing through ferns and moss until it spilled onto the beach in such a way that the waterfall leapt upwards into a fountain. The men were so delighted with the lagoon that they flung themselves down beside it and drank the sweet and cool water.

Helgi was convinced that this was the land he had dreamed of these Winters past. He returned to the ship full of jubilation. But he was not yet so entranced that he had lost his caution. Before he would allow the women to go ashore, he wanted the mainland searched. He divided the men into two groups. Those who had been on board the ship were to explore the island further while he took Hauk and the others to scout the mainland. The mainland search party waded to the river mouth, leaving the pram for the others. Even with his untrained eye, Helgi saw so many kinds of trees that it was all he could do to keep himself from shouting.

"I've never seen such variety and abundance, not even in Norway," Hauk said. For a long while the men stood on the edge of the forest and gazed at the trees. Not only were there wild plum and pear trees, there were flowering trees of other kinds. As well there were oak, elm, ash, yew, maple and pine. Twisted around the trunks and hanging from the branches of these larger trees were grapevines. So numerous were these vines that they reached across the spaces separating the trees. Huge clusters of grapes hung from arbours. This sight was so wondrous that the men stood slack jawed with awe. They looked up into the vine-hung forest while around them thrushes sang and jays cawed over the fruit. What amazed them most about the place was that it seemed to be far deeper in Summer than the islands they had passed just a short while ago.

"It appears we have come upon a place with a climate that is very different from the rest we've seen," Helgi said.

"Such places are said to exist in the world," Hauk replied. "Though I've never been told exactly where they are."

A roe buck came out of the bushes, looked at the men, then leapt away. The sight of the deer broke Helgi's trance and he reminded the others about the need to explore. The men walked the edge of the forest along the shore and the river without coming across any signs of skraelings. The undergrowth grew so densely everywhere that it was obvious no one had come this way since they themselves had to use axes to cut paths. Upriver they came across a stand of hickory trees. Nearby was a grove of butternut. The butternuts were so numerous on the ground that the men could not walk without cracking the shells. The nuts looked as if they had been lying there for some time which confirmed the absence of skraelings, since the nuts would have been harvested had there been anyone living close by. The men retraced their steps and forded the river. Above the marshy area thick with rushes and sedge was a drier plateau. Here the men came across wheat which to them looked much like barley. The men paid close attention to the wheat. Unlike the corn Helgi had seen earlier, the wheat grew among grass clumps in such a way that it was clearly self-sown.

"There's no doubt this is Vinland the Good," he said, "for it's perfect and untouched in every way. Not only does it lack skraelings, but it has grapes and self-sown wheat. I've no doubt that in the morning we'll find sweet dew upon the grass." With this he let out a joyous whoop that the women heard aboard the ship.

Finna and Grelod lost no time in leaving *Paradise Seeker*. Wearing nothing but their shifts, the women went to the island to bathe in the lagoon. The men threw off their clothes and flung themselves into the sun-stroked shallow water that was heated as warm as a bath. When they tired of splashing about, the men lay on their backs and sunned themselves like seals. Eventually they put on their clothes and began carrying gear ashore. They built a cooking hearth of stones on the beach and filled their barrels at the waterfall. Helgi intended to use the barrels for making wine. The grapes were not yet fully ripened, but their sourness could be tempered with honey. Helgi and

Hauk, Vemund and Bersi waded across the river mouth to cut grapevines so that the wine could be started without delay. As for the others, they went in search of whatever food they might like to have. It was the nature of Vinland that no sooner did someone express a desire for a certain kind of food than the wish was granted. Olver said he had a hankering for fresh eel and straight away found eels in a pool a short distance upstream. Grelod expressed a craving for plums and was soon shown the tree where this fruit grew. Finna went with her, for she wished to make wheat cakes in the new oven. Before the day was out, Ulf Broad Beard had smoked a beehive from a hollow oak and returned with combs of dripping honey. The grape harvesters speared the roe buck in the heart when it reappeared.

That evening the Icelanders ate roast venison, fried eel and wheat cakes sweetened with honey. All of them claimed they had never eaten so fine a meal. After they had filled their bellies, they sat on the beach watching the sun drop behind the islands to the West. Finally the travellers unrolled their sleeping bags on the warm sand. Before going to sleep, they smeared their bodies with seal oil: their arms and legs were red and sore from the unaccustomed sun.

As he watched the sun slipping away, Helgi told Finna that it pleased him that Vinland had a night that was more or less equal to the day. After so much sun Helgi welcomed the cooling dark. It was true Norsemen were used to sleeping where light never left the Summer sky, but he preferred a place where darkness fell part of the time for when the darkness left in the morning, the world looked fresh and new.

The next morning while dew glistened on the grass, the men built a shelter from poles and rushes near the waterfall. That side of the island grew hot in the late afternoon and the Icelanders wanted a shady place to rest without having to leave the beach. Finna and Grelod wove sitting mats from sedge grass. These mats so pleased the men that during the next few days, the women made mats for sleeping as well. The men found their sheepskin bags too warm for their liking and preferred to lay their heads on fragrant grass. The men smelled better themselves from having spent so much time bathing. They now wore loin cloths which they had made by cutting up Ulf Broad Beard's winter cloak. The women discarded their winter robes. They cut their shifts so that the cloth fell above their elbows and knees.

Soon the Vinlanders—as now they called themselves—became so tanned they no longer needed to smear their bodies with seal oil to protect themselves from the sun. The women had taken to wearing fragrant beach pea and roses in their hair and shell ankle bracelets which rustled pleasantly when they walked. Together these things made them more attractive than they had been before. Even Grelod, who was thick waisted and swollen, moved with alluring grace. Vinland affected Grelod in another way. She became less abrasive and loud. Nothing seemed to annoy or upset her. Like Finna she seemed to be floating through a languid sea.

Vinland the Good continued to offer up exotic foods of one kind and another. There were sun-dried grapes, raspberries and blackberries, cherries, plums and pears, turtle doves and pheasants. Even fish and game the Vinlanders were used to eating tasted better here. Lobsters were so plentiful they crawled from the cold sea into the warmer shallows where they were easily caught. As for mussels, there were so many of these among the rocks, they could be fetched without a pram. In fact the pram was seldom used, since the Vinlanders preferred to walk or swim ashore. They spent so much time in the water that Helgi said he wouldn't be surprised one day to see them growing fins.

When they were out of the water, the Vinlanders lay about or walked around the island. They never tired of strolling through meadows starred with flowers, many of which they had never seen before. During the midday heat especially, they enjoyed lying among violets and ferns in mossy hollows shaded by elm and pine. Later in the day when it was cooler they walked along the beach on the east side of the island, enjoying the lavender-scented air. If they were hungry they forded the river mouth and foraged for food.

Occasionally Helgi or Hauk might say something about cutting ship wood but that was as far as it went. So entranced were they by Vinland that they preferred to lie around and talk about an oaken ship rather than do anything toward building it. After a Winter of cold and wet, being shut inside a dark, foul smelling house, the men were of a mind to linger in open sunlight as long as they could. The men seldom thought about Leifsbudir or Iceland. The longer they tarried in Vinland, the farther away these places appeared to be.

It no longer seemed important that the men get together trade goods or lay up provisions for Winter or build another ship. Who needed another ship when they had everything here they wanted and more besides? Now that they had found the earthly pleasures of Paradise, the Vinlanders could not easily give them up. This was especially true after they began to drink the second batch of wine which was sweeter than the first, having been made with riper grapes. The drink made them so drowsy and torpid that they preferred to avoid hard work. The men proclaimed the wine the best they had tasted. By now the Vinlanders were so accustomed to wine, it no longer made them vomit their food. The grapes were plentiful enough that they could drink wine throughout the day without running short. The combination of wine and warm sun cast the men into a languid swoon during which they did little but lay about.

The women also drank. Finna preferred her drink sweetened with extra honey. The honey dissolved inside her mouth, slid down her throat, warming her belly like liquid sun. The honeyed wine and the seductiveness of the place made her indifferent to her chores so that on some evenings she told the men no nut and wheat cakes would be served. She couldn't be bothered grinding grain when there was other food that was easily plucked from trees. No one complained about the absent cakes. With such abundance and variety of food, the Vinlanders didn't mind having one less thing to eat.

Occasionally when Helgi and Hauk lay side by side in the shallows, one of them would glance at the forest and remark that soon they should start felling trees. These remarks never went anywhere, for the men's attention would be caught by something marvellous to behold: a yellow bird flitting among the trees, a blue-grey heron fishing in the stream, an eagle soaring in the sky. There were some days when the eagle was too far away for the men to see.

Not only did the wine blur the landscape, but Vinland itself altered the men's vision in such a way that made them near-sighted with regard to time. In their minds yesterday, today and tomorrow merged as one. Time was endless and benign. Even Helgi, who had navigated *Paradise Seeker* with great care and caution, lost track of time. One morning he picked up a stick, intending to make another mark on the sand. Before the twin sirens of warmth and wine had taken hold, Helgi had made several marks above the tide line to indicate the passage of days. He had made some twenty-odd marks before he lost interest in making more. Now Helgi frowned and squinted over the marks, hardly realizing what they were for or why he had made them. Then he remembered and began to count how many days had lapsed since he had added to the marks. The pleasures of the island had altered his mind in such a way that he had difficulty staying long with one thought. It might have been twenty or twenty score; it might have been thirty. He didn't know. After a while Helgi threw away the stick. It hardly mattered whether or not he made a mark. Since each day was as satisfying as the last, who cared how many had passed? Nor did Helgi give much thought to where he was in the Outer Ocean or where the island was in relation to other places. He no longer cared if he proved the world was ongoing, or how close to the edge he might be on the disc. He knew he was closer to Muspell and was satisfied with that.

Every day the Vinlanders awoke to the same blue sky,
the same warm sun, the same light breeze, the same gold-
en sea, the same glittering sand. Nothing about the place
had changed since their arrival. No matter how much food
they ate or drank, there was always more. They had
reached a place of perpetual Summer.

Before coming to Vinland, Finna had never longed for
another lover. Even if she had been free to do so, Helgi's
gentle and steadfast attention was such that she had been
indifferent to finding satisfaction elsewhere. Now the combination of sweetened wine and waking slumber made her
crave others besides Helgi to pleasure her. Her hunger
was heightened by the fact that Vinland had affected Helgi
in the opposite way. His interest in lying with her had gradually diminished. In the case of Hauk and Ulf Broad Beard,
their appetite for women increased.

Vinland had been kind to Finna. The sun had
enhanced the tautness of her body, the neatness of bone
and flesh, the tawny skin fitted over elbow and shoulder,
the balance of her small breasts, each one centred with a
golden star. Beneath her breasts the skin swept through
the smooth hollow between her hips to an oasis the men
could not see: to them the oasis was a mirage shimmering
ahead of them in the midday heat. Here layer upon layer
was fed by an underground stream that kept the hidden
flesh moist. As the men lay on the beach, their eyes following Finna's movements, they imagined entering the
secret cave between her legs, leaving their bull sign on its
walls. Finna knew this, knew which men looked at her
with thirsty eyes as if they had been wandering over water-
less sands for many days.

One night after Helgi had fallen asleep beside Finna on
the beach, she slipped into the shadow of a sand dune
with Hauk Ljome and was entered several different ways
before the night was out. The next night, Finna lay with Ulf
Broad Beard both in and out of water. So pleasured was
she by these encounters that she began to slip away with
these men during the day when Helgi could see them if he
cared to look. Once Helgi might have used an axe against

a lover of Finna's but that had been long ago, when he thought it important to protect what he considered his. Now ownership meant nothing to him. Helgi was so enthralled by the idea of Paradise that the thought of dividing land into territory, or folk into freemen and slaves had become distasteful to him. He began to notice Finna going into the dunes with Hauk and Ulf but was not bothered by this. Surely Paradise meant that everyone was entitled to seek pleasure in any way they chose as long as others were unharmed. Helgi did not view this indifference to what others did as a weakness but as a blessing. Anyone fortunate enough to reach Paradise knew that it was foolish to want what others had, since Paradise itself meant either satisfying your needs or becoming needless. Vinland the Good had disarmed Helgi of desire and greed.

Not all the Icelanders found Vinland suited them so well. The wine and the swooning supernaturalness of the place had a peculiar effect on Olver. He had visions of sea monsters rising out of the water. A giant sea elephant with tusks as long as oars rose out of the waves and gored him. A whale with a huge mouth swallowed him whole. A fire-breathing serpent coiled around the ship and burned it. Olver had these visions both day and night. When he was so afflicted, he cowered shaking or ran about pointing at the vision and screaming for help until one of the others, usually Ulf, subdued him.

Bersi also had visions, but of a different kind. He claimed he heard women's voices calling from upriver. The voices were coaxing and as soft as whispers. Bersi often saw one of these beautiful creatures floating on the water. He said she had silver wings and green hair drifting around her head like sea grass.

One midday when the sun was hottest and the Vinlanders were lying about in the shadows of dunes and other shady places, Bersi waded into the water and swam upriver, as the others later thought, following the voices of the women. No one saw him leave. It was late afternoon before his absence was remarked. Even then no one was inclined to look for him, since it was assumed he might have crossed the river mouth to pluck fruit or nuts, then lain down as others had before and slept somewhere. Early in the evening, Atli and Vemund left the island and swam ashore to look for Bersi. Not finding him on either side of the river, they waded upstream, returning some time later towing Bersi face down. He was already dead when they found him snagged on the branch of an over-hanging tree.

The drowning brought the Vinlanders face to face with the implacable nature of Paradise. Since Vinland the Good seemed perfect in every way, they were alarmed by the realization that it could be a place of death, for they had come to believe that here time was at a standstill. Bersi's death was perplexing in another way, for he was found in shallow water. Helgi thought Bersi might have hit his head on a rock and turned the corpse over, looking for a bruise. There was none. The thought that an unseen, insidious presence might have caused Bersi's death flitted through the Vinlanders' minds but did not stay with them long enough for anyone to give it voice. The Vinlanders dis-cussed what should be done with the dead man. Hauk was for burying him at sea but the others were against this. They were uncomfortable with the thought of swim-ming in the same water with their shipmate's corpse. Helgi said he thought Bersi would like to be buried on the beach. The others agreed. So it was that the corpse was rowed in the pram some distance along the shore and placed inside a mound of beach stones. The mound was in sight of the island yet far enough away that even if the wind shifted, the Vinlanders would be spared the smell of rotting flesh.

Although Bersi's death weighed heavily upon the Vinlanders, it in no way diminished their thirst for wine. The strong drink soothed the loss and made their melan-choly mild enough to bear. When they spoke of Bersi, they comforted one another by reminding themselves that Bersi had toiled hard in a land of bitter cold and deserved a pleasant rest. It was far better that he die in the blissful warmth of Vinland the Good than be cast into the icy depths of Hel.

Several days later—judging from an empty wine barrel, it could have been as few as five—the Vinlanders awoke one morning to find that both Olver and the pram were gone. After a night's sleep the Vinlanders were more sober than they were later in the day so that when they noticed Olver's absence, they immediately set out to search for him. There was no sign of the pram anywhere along the shore which meant Olver must have taken the pram seaward. The men swam to *Paradise Seeker*, and for the first time since their arrival in Vinland, hauled anchor. Because there was no wind they had to row among the islands. They searched all morning before concluding that either the pram had been taken far away by a current or whirlpool, or that it had sunk. Vemund said Olver must have thought he was rowing out to fight one of the monsters that plagued him, for his weapons were gone.

The others agreed that this was likely the case. Hauk offered the opinion that strong drink sometimes cursed a man so that he could no longer think clearly and that this might have been the situation with both Olver and Bersi. Hauk added that not every man was so affected. Like the others he was unwilling to believe that there was anything in Vinland that would impair his mind. The men rowed the ship back to the island and anchored there. For much of the day they avoided the wine barrels. They were temporarily sobered by the possibility that the wine drinking had resulted in the loss of two men. Instead the men sought the lagoon's cooling water, searching, perhaps, for their former selves. While they were bathing Hauk remembered why they had come to Vinland and persuaded Helgi to go upriver into the forest and mark oak wood for cutting.

Such was the nature of the place that Hauk and Helgi were easily diverted by the pleasures at hand. While they were marking the trees, they became distracted by the number of butternuts in a grove nearby and fell to harvesting them instead of wood. That night they ate a meal of roast pheasant stuffed with nuts. Afterwards they sat on the beach near the waterfall and looked toward the setting sun, hoping to see some sign of Olver and the pram. But even with the evening's feasting, the Vinlanders became restless and dissatisfied once it grew dark, for neither cakes nor water could slake their thirst. Without wine or sun to warm them, they no longer knew how to lull their senses into a limbo of peaceful contentment.

The Vinlanders began to grumble about the place, saying it wasn't Paradise after all and that if they stayed, troubles were bound to increase. Atli said that it would be better for them all if they got to work first thing in the morning harvesting wood as they had originally intended. Hauk agreed, saying the wood would need to be dressed into planks on shore before it was taken to the ship by pram. He pointed out that before they began felling plank wood they would have to build a pram to replace the one Olver had taken. For some time the men contemplated the work of making another pram. Then Vemund remarked that Vinland might be the only place enjoying perfect weather. "It might be Summer here all year long while the place we came from might be heading for Winter. If that is the case, we might have difficulty returning to Leifsbudir early enough to make a safe crossing as we'd planned."

At the mention of Leifsbudir the memory of the sod house inside which the Icelanders had spent a wretched Winter again took shape in Helgi's mind. He saw a harsh, bleak place where trees were crippled by incessant wind and men ate little else but dried meat and fish. He saw a place where poor folk had to constantly struggle in order to keep themselves alive, where cold penetrated a man's bones so deeply that no matter how long he sat by a fire, he never grew warm.

Finally Helgi said, "Since we have been fortunate enough to find the Island of the Blessed why should we return to Leifsbudir at all? Are we not enjoying what most people seek? Why not stay here where life is sweet and we have everything we need? After all, what is Luck but the fulfillment of dreams?" Then he helped himself to a cup of wine.

At first the Vinlanders were surprised that Helgi would speak thus, for he was the adventurer among them and had often spoken of journeying to other lands. But after they had taken more wine themselves the Vinlanders began to nod in agreement. Now that the idea of staying, which had been in their heads all along, had been voiced, they were grateful and relieved. None of them looked forward to the prospect of returning to a Winter place.

Even so, a residue of discomfort lingered. The discomfort came from agreements and promises made to folk in the now distant past.

"What about the others?" Vemund said; he meant the brothers and sisters he had known in Breiduvik, Iceland.

Helgi thought he meant Finnbogi and the rest of the Icelandic crew.

"They have a ship of their own and can manage well enough," he said. "There are many Norsemen, my brother included, who wouldn't care for this place. They prefer the colder regions. I say let them have those places. We will keep Vinland the Good for ourselves."

The men dipped their cups into the wine barrel and drank to Vinland the Good. Soon any misgivings they had about remaining in Paradise slipped away. The Vinlanders had passed the moment when a sober reckoning of their situation might have been made. They scarcely noticed that the wind which had brought them here had never returned. They lost all interest in seeing themselves as others might. They lay in the sun, their lips stained the colour of overripe plums. They stopped washing their hair and combing their beards. They no longer bathed or kept themselves clean. The Vinlanders lost their fresh tangy smell. Instead they took on the musty odour of decaying fruit. Despite their ruination, the Vinlanders continued to believe that if they put their minds to it, they could return to Leifsbudir whenever they chose. From time to time they would say that when they were ready, they would cut ship wood and take it North. Each time woodcutting was men-

tioned, some excuse or other was found for putting it off.
They told themselves they would build a ship of oak later
on when they felt more inclined. The Vinlanders still
believed that if they wanted to sail north, they could find a
wind that would take them away. There was some truth in
this, for if they had cared to venture beyond the islands to
the sea, they would have felt the everlasting pull of the
wind.

AS FOR THE EIGHT MEN ABANDONED IN LEIFSBUDIR, they had perished shortly after the Greenlanders' departure in *Sigurd's Steed*. Ejolf had been the first to die. Ten days after the killings, he suffocated when a partridge bone stuck in his throat. Well before Yule, the seven who were left set out in a pram. They had given up waiting for Helgi Egilsson and his crew and were unwilling to stay in Leifsbudir any longer, since it had proved to be so unlucky a place. They thought it was a matter of time before skraelings appeared and either killed them or carried them off. The survivors knew they would meet dangers at sea, but they did not think they could be worse than what would happen if they remained in Leifsbudir. The sheep Freydis had left had long since been eaten and there was no more food except what could be hunted and fished day by day. By heading south the men hoped to stay far enough ahead of Winter to keep themselves alive. Using a makeshift sail, they managed to travel much the same route as *Paradise Seeker* before finding their death. Partway to Vinland they were caught in a hurricane. It was then Surt sang his final verse. This was no riddle slyly murmured under his breath lest his owners take offence. This was a bold proclamation that challenged The Shouter himself:

> *Once we rode a noble steed*
> *Across the water charm,*
> *That was long ago when we sailed*
> *Beneath the fair wheel.*

Now we ride in a pram
Rigged with bloodied spider cloth.
We drift beneath the helmet of darkness
Carrying the bones of our dead.

When evil folk go a-viking,
They leave little behind worth saving.
We had nothing to gain by staying.
Hope became our star guide.

Now squall blast has gripped us.
He is taking us eel home.
Soon I will be singing to the All Wise:
Verses of lost dreams and Luck.

* * *

IN THE YEARS following the last and fateful voyage to
Vinland, Christians became far more numerous in
Greenland. Not long after Thorvard Einarsson's death
they took over Freydis's house in Gardar saying they wanted to build a church in its place; by then Einar had
reclaimed the field. The Christians offered poor recompense and when Freydis refused to move, smoked her
out. Freydis managed to drag the loom and the wedding
chest outside. After this she lived with her children in the
fells above Gardar where the land was too poor for farming. Freydis built a stone hut up there close by the place
where she grazed her sheep yet well away from the hovel
where Hordis had lived and died.

Freydis kept her family alive by trading wadmal.
Though folk tried to beat her down, they eventually paid
Freydis's price, since they knew her cloth was superior to
most. Otherwise Freydis was avoided. A few people in
Gardar considered Freydis Eiriksdottir a mad woman. Most
held the view that she was not mad at all, though she was
certainly a nuisance. She was forever haranguing them
about neglecting the old gods and claimed Christ had
made fools of them all. Sometimes a householder who

had refused to buy her cloth would open her door and see a witch doll hanging there.

Although Freydis scorned wearing a snood, she continued to be neat and tidy about her person. In this and in other ways she attracted the attention of a widower by the name of Magnus Ingolfsson, an old farmer who had a small steading below and somewhat to the west of Freydis's hut. Freydis married Magnus and moved herself and her children into his two-room house, leaving her thrall, Gorm, in the hut to tend her sheep. Kalf, Orn and Louse Oddi had been traded away years before. Magnus's house was much smaller than the one the Christians had taken from Freydis; on the other hand, it was far better than the hut she had been living in for the past several years. Once again Freydis took out the coloured woven hangings, the brass bowl and the lace-edged tablecloth and arranged them here and there. Freydis was pleased with Magnus's house since it was set apart from Gardar and was of middle size. After her children left and Magnus died in his sleep, the size of the house suited Freydis even better for it was spacious enough to satisfy her whims yet small enough to heat with having to burn the benches and tables. Freydis continued to graze sheep and trade wadmal. She never became Christian and never repented for what happened in Leifsbudir.

Freydis Eiriksdottir outlived Thorvard's three sisters as well as several women who had been born well after her. Eventually Freydis was found in the fells with a broken neck, the result of a fall down a cliff; since Gorm's death she had been herding the sheep herself. By then Freydis was an old woman of fifty-six. Her children had left Gardar long since so there were no kin to bury her. The shepherds who found her piled stones over her corpse to make a grave.

As for Freydis's children, it appeared Leif Eiriksson's prophecy about them was true. When she was fifteen, Signy went off to Siglufjord and became the ambatt of a wealthy farmer who had a barren wife. She bore him several children and died birthing the sixth. Asny did not fare much better. She married a poor farmer from Gamli who, after siring four children on her, divorced her for someone else. Freydis had never shown her daughters the iron belt. Before they were old enough to lie with men, Freydis had the belt melted down to make a large hook to hang over the fire. She thought the iron better used as a result, since it was the idea of the belt she had liked, not the belt itself. The belt had never prevented her from doing what suited her, if she wanted it badly enough.

When Thorlak was sixteen, he hired himself aboard *Wave Rider*, a Norwegian ship which for the most part worked the fish trade, though occasionally its owner raided the Hebrides to pick up thralls. Though he preferred farming to sailing, Thorlak could never get enough goods together to buy a plot of land and for more years than he cared to count, lived a hand-to-mouth existence aboard *Wave Rider* as it plied its way between Bergen and Oban. On its last run the ship ran aground on some rocks near Mull. Thorlak was rescued along with several others by some fishermen who took them to Oban. They were dumped in a storage hut belonging to a wealthy fish merchant who lived with his wife and five children in a fine house nearby. Later the merchant's foster son, a young man with a blue spot on his forehead, was bidden by his mother to carry sleeping bags and a pot of hot soup to the hut. These were set on the floor beside the shivering men. The young man did not speak to the survivors or show any interest in their plight. He seemed to think he had nothing in common with the men, least of all the Greenlander who looked more sullen and downtrodden than the rest.

Shortly after this event Thorlak began hiring himself out to crofters on the island as a stone picker. In this way he managed to keep himself alive a few more years.

* * *

HELGI EGILSSON OUTLIVED the other Vinlanders. By how much no one, including Helgi, ever knew. It might have been a year, it might have been an age. In Vinland the Good one day was so like another that Helgi scarcely noticed when one day left off and another began. Each morning he filled his wineskin and went to the edge of the island where he lay on the smooth hard rocks beneath a hot coppery sun, watching the green sea water flood crevices and hollows. Day after day Helgi came to the cliff edge, sometimes with Finna, sometimes without. He had long since wearied of lying on a beach mat or in the warm shallows. He much preferred watching the shifting power of the sea. As a boy in North Alftafjord, Helgi had often spent Summer in much the same way. He had no clear memory of this now. Most of Helgi's memories were like faint stirrings of a mouse or some other small creature scuttling through grass. Helgi had no idea where Finna was. Like him she came and went with no knowledge of the other's whereabouts. Finna might lie by his side a whole day before Helgi noticed her. It was the noticing that made it seem as if she had just appeared. She could be absent for days without being missed.

So it had been for those Vinlanders who had disappeared. For all Helgi knew, the lost Vinlanders could have been gone for a year before he remarked their absence. Helgi did not trouble himself about these disappearances. He simply took what was. What wasn't there no longer concerned him. Apart from the Vinlanders' disappearances, Vinland the Good seemed unchanged: butterflies still fluttered over flowers, birds sang without ceasing, trees and bushes of all kinds blossomed. If a berry was plucked or an apple eaten, others soon appeared. Vinland the Good was a season of the mind as much as a place.

It was a season of excess and overripeness. Because Helgi and Finna were drugged on warmth and wine, they did not notice the decay, though sometimes when the other one slept close by, there would be a rough awakening. Helgi might notice the pouched skin beneath Finna's eyes or the sagging of her breasts. When this happened Helgi was surprised. His sight was now so altered he usually saw a young woman with smooth skin and a firm body. Or Finna might tease Helgi, calling him her ancient greybearded loon. She might remind him that soon his stained teeth would fall out of his head. Such brutal assessments were rare, since Helgi and Finna seldom saw each other as they were. Nor did they often sleep side by side. Helgi assumed Finna had gone off with Ulf Broad Beard or Bjolf. He did not remember that those men had been gone for some time.

Ulf and Bjolf had stayed far longer than some of the others. After Bersi and Olver had gone, Hauk Ljome disappeared. The Norwegian imagined a giant ash tree growing in the forest. Though no one else could see the tree, Hauk insisted it was there, towering above the others. He said that it was none other than the World Tree, Yggdrasill, and that there were three virgins sitting beneath. Their names were Being, Necessity and Fate. Hauk said he would go there and have each of them in turn. Unlike Helgi, who thought the Norns had already given him the fate he wanted, Hauk wanted the women themselves. Since Vinland the Good was a place where every wish was granted, no one was inclined to prevent Hauk from leaving. After he left, Grelod lay down in the ferns and never got up. Long before this the babe had slipped from her womb while she was bathing and swum away. The soil where Grelod died was so soft and deep that she sank into it and disappeared. Moss and violets soon took hold. The remaining Vinlanders sometimes walked on Grelod's grave without knowing what it was.

Ulf and Bjolf had also been infected by the old tales. They raved ceaselessly about gods that Helgi had long ago forgotten. Ulf said that Vinland the Good was Asgard, the realm of the gods. He claimed that when the sun was high, he could see it glancing off the golden roof of Gimli further along the coast where deserving men went after death. Ulf and Bjolf meant to go to Gimli. They were eager to be fussed over by the Valkyries who were sure to tend their needs. One day Ulf and Bjolf swam out to the ship in order to sail it to Asgard. They thought to impress the gods by arriving from the sea. By then the ship's lower strakes were wormy from having sat so long in warm water. It was clear from the amount of water inside the ship that it was close to sinking. Ulf and Bjolf set out to reach Asgard by walking along the shore and were never seen again.

Sometime later, Helgi awoke and saw that the ship had sunk, only its bow stem and mast could be seen above the water. Helgi accepted the loss of the ship with only mild curiosity. He had forgotten that Ulf had once told him the ship was worm-eaten and after it disappeared wondered why it had gone down.

Once, Helgi and Finna grew fish tails and swam underwater. As they swam around the cove, they saw the sunken ship. The sun's rays pierced the blue-green water in such a way that they clearly saw the outline of the keel and the mast which had tipped into the water. Barnacles covered the strakes and sea grasses rose up on either side. Helgi regarded this sight with the same disinterest he regarded everything else. Later he and Finna swam seaward among the islands where the water was cold. They saw something white glowing on the sea bottom. When Helgi dived down to pick it up, he saw what looked like a human skull but he in no way connected it with Olver. Once Helgi and Finna grew eagle wings and flew above the forest, but this did not provide as much pleasure for Helgi as staying on the island. The woods and meadows far below that held no interest for him. He had long ago lost the mariner's vision.

Atli and Vemund had been convinced there were skraelings in the woods. They had grown bored with the peacefulness of Vinland and were thirsty for blood. They claimed the skraelings were wizards and could easily change themselves into trees by painting their bodies green and putting bird feathers in their hair. This disguise only worked in sunlight. For this reason the skraelings must be killed at night-time when they were no longer disguised. For several nights Atli and Vemund took their spears and axes into the woods, stalking demons until sunrise. This continued until the moment each hunter mistook the other for a skraeling and they killed each other.

Helgi had his own demons. Sometimes these demons screeched so loudly inside his head that he covered his ears and stumbled about on the beach. One afternoon when Helgi lay on the rocks dozing, he looked up and saw the water dancing like a witch's oils and writhing with sea snakes. The snakes coiled toward him between flames of green and red, their tongues hissing and sizzling against the sea. Another time Helgi saw a monster with teeth like knives rise out of the waves, a giant eyeball in the middle of his forehead. Those nights when sleep eluded him, Helgi watched stars fall from the sky. One night a star fell on his head and exploded into splinters of light.

Now the hidden folk made the wine. It was no longer necessary for Helgi to cut the grapes. The hidden folk wove garlands of fragrant flowers for him to wear about his neck. They also plucked fruit and nuts, laying them here and there on fresh leaves, which meant there was no need for Helgi to leave the island unless he swam or flew. Once when he and Finna were bathing in the lagoon, a white horse came out of the woods to drink. It had a twisted horn on its head like a narwhal's. The horse was a mild, gentle creature whose presence pleased Finna especially. She seemed to think the horse had something to do with the silver key she still wore around her neck. Some time after this, Helgi saw Finna ride away on the creature's back, his white mane flowing across her breasts. It was the last time Helgi saw Finna or the horse. But he often saw elvish folk flying through the woods, trailing their wings behind them like silver mist, singing in high sweet voices that invited him to follow. By then he had grown so weak he could not easily move from place to place much less follow elves. In any case he had no wish to follow them since he was content to remain where and what he was. What more could a man ask than to be purged of ambition, envy, hate, greed and fear? Helgi did not fear death; he would welcome it whenever it came. He could think of no better place to begin a long and dreamless sleep than on the edge of the world where land met water and North met South.

Sometimes Helgi chose not to drink the wine left by hidden folk. At such times his memory returned and his vision cleared. He would remember that long ago when he lived in the land of ice and snow he had thought that the greatest journey a man could make was outside himself so that he might see unknown lands and wondrous sights. Now Helgi knew a different truth. He knew that of all the worlds he might discover the journey that gave a man the most satisfaction was the journey into himself since it was here that he was most likely to find contentment. How strange it was for a man to travel far and wide in search of dreams and Luck only to discover that his island of the blessed had been inside him all along and that after he died, his bones would be nothing but fool's gold shining beneath the stars.